Acclaim for Anthony Riches

'A masterclass in military historical fiction and demonstrates how the trauma of war affected the ordinary Roman soldier.'
Sunday Express

'Riches highlights the chaos and fragility of an empire without an emperor . . . dense, complicated and rewarding.'
The Times

'A damn fine read . . . fast-paced, action-packed.'
Ben Kane

'Stands head and shoulders above a crowded field . . . real, live characters act out their battles on the northern borders with an accuracy of detail and depth of raw emotion that is a rare combination.'
Manda Scott

'Riches has captured how soldiers speak and act to a tee and he is very descriptive when it comes to the fighting. It is a novel full of power, lust, envy, violence and vanity. The very things that made Rome great and the very things that would lead to its downfall. If you like historical novels, read this book.'
NavyNet

'This is fast-paced and gripping "read-through-the-night" fiction, with marvellous characters and occasional moments of dark humour. Some authors are better historians than they are storytellers. Anthony Riches is brilliant at both.'
Conn Iggulden

The Scorpion's Strike

Empire: Volume Ten

ANTHONY RICHES

HODDER

First published in Great Britain in 2019 by Hodder & Stoughton
An Hachette UK company

This paperback edition published in 2019

1

Copyright © Anthony Riches 2019

The right of Anthony Riches to be identified as the
Author of the Work has been asserted by him in accordance
with the Copyright, Designs and Patents Act 1988.

A CIP catalogue record for this title is
available from the British Library

Paperback ISBN 978 1 473 62870 0

Typeset in Plantin Light by Palimpsest Book Production Limited,
Falkirk, Stirlingshire

Printed and bound in Great Britain by Clays Ltd, Elcograf S.p.A.

Hodder & Stoughton policy is to use papers that are natural, renewable
and recyclable products and made from wood grown in sustainable forests.
The logging and manufacturing processes are expected to conform to the
environmental regulations of the country of origin.

For Helen, as always . . .
. . . and for Vicki Kidney, for going above and beyond

ACKNOWLEDGEMENTS

To say that this was a challenging book would be putting it mildly. Eighteen months spent ripping through the three novels in the *Centurions* series left me somewhat lacking in momentum. It's a pretty good exposition of the Batavian revolt once the reader absorbs the new characters and historical events that set the story up, and if you've not read it yet, I encourage you to do so, as I'm quite proud of the way that the story of Marius, Aquillius, Hramn, Alcaeus and Egilhard ended up. The fact that the end result in the form of this book you're hopefully about to read is as good a book as I've written – if only from the writer's perspective, and you can be the ultimate judge of that bold statement – does nothing to alter the fact that it was longer coming than we all wanted. I suppose it was almost inevitable, given post-trilogy ennui combined with a day job that I enjoy enormously and which puts me to the test on a daily basis.

Which means that my fervent thanks have to go to the people I work with at Hodder & Stoughton for their patience in the face of not one but two major delivery delays. This year's box of delights at Christmas is going to have to be something special as some small compensation for their having been mucked about so egregiously. Never before have I been quite so conscious of and grateful for the patience displayed by my editor Carolyn, and thanks must also go to several others (Madeleine, Kerry, Rosie and Alice) who variously oil the machinery that turns out the finished product, gets it in front of reviewers and puts me in front of audiences to waffle on about my characters' imaginary lives. Thank you.

Special thanks also to Sharona, who seems to know more about the *Empire* series than I do (and given I never want to read the books again once they're completed, that's a really good thing). Her brilliant copy editing was as ably assisted as ever by Viv, David and John, my beta readers.

My agent Robin is the reason why I get to put my stories in front of you, and so I remain eternally grateful to him for conjuring up the opportunity.

The biggest thanks, however, go to my wife Helen who, through thick and thin, has always been there to encourage, cajole and occasionally stroke a book out of me and to help celebrate the small victory of those two delightful words (when they're genuinely earned) – *the end*. I literally couldn't do it without you.

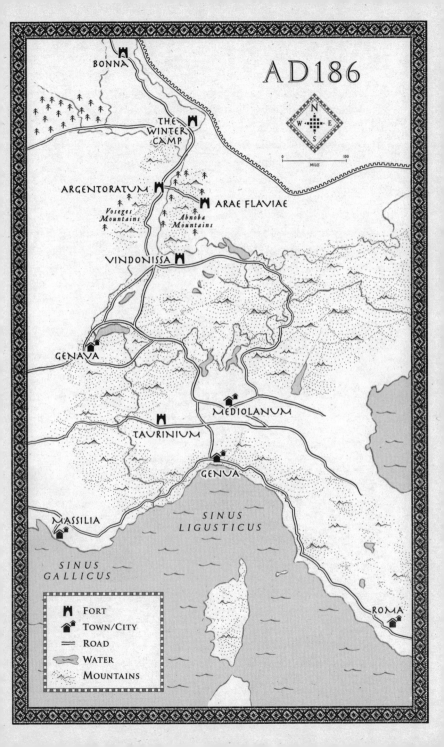

Prologue

'Tribune!'

The leading rider gestured down the road along which the search party was trotting their horses, drawing his comrades' attention to a finger of smoke kissing the horizon and waiting while the two officers rode forward to follow his pointing finger. The more senior of them, a strong-jawed man in his early thirties clad in the customary gilded armour and long purple-edged white cloak of a praetorian officer, leaned forward in his saddle and grimaced.

'Shit! That is most definitely not what I wanted to see. Of course, it isn't necessarily Maternus.'

The older man, a centurion with more years of service than he was willing to admit, shook his head in disagreement.

'That's Maternus, alright, Tribune. Why else do you think we were sent to fetch him back, other than the fear that he'd order his men to do something rash?'

The senior officer nodded grimly.

'In which case, we need to bring the fool to heel before he does something truly stupid and risks undermining the emperor's negotiations.'

As they drew nearer to the source of the smoke, it became increasingly evident that they were approaching a settlement. A wooden wall encompassed the usual cluster of roughly-built dwellings, which were carefully positioned for the best possible defence on a raised piece of ground adjacent to a small river, and surrounded by fields of recently turned earth on all sides. The village within the circular wall was already a ruin, dozens of houses consumed by the fires that had been set among them an hour before – but it was only when the detachment rode through the shattered gates that the full truth of what had happened to its inhabitants became clear. The tribune raised a hand to bring the column to a halt as he stared disbelievingly at the scene of devastation.

'Gods below. What the *fuck* have you fools done?'

The soldiers scattered among the smouldering remains of what had once been a bustling community turned to look at the newcomers with tired, fatigue-smudged eyes, their faces twisted in disdain as their senior officer shook his head with an expression of growing incredulity. Engaged in the usual post-battle rituals that had become commonplace during the course of a long and bitter war against the German tribes, they were busy carving grisly trophies from the corpses of the dead or digging in the ruins of the buildings for hidden wealth; they looked up briefly before turning back to their tasks. The tribune's eyes narrowed at their engrossment in the massacre's aftermath, opening his mouth to bark an order and then pausing as the distant screams and entreaties of mass rape reached his ears in the ruined village's silence. Dismounting with an expression of growing fury, he strode forward into the settlement's wreckage with a look of disbelief on his face.

'Where's your fucking centurion? Where's Maternus?' Looking about him, the incredulous officer set eyes on a man holding a heavy wooden staff bound with brass at both ends who was looking at him with an expression close to contempt. '*You!* Chosen man! Where's your officer? And show some fucking respect before I have your back scourged until your spine's on display and leave you to die with blood filling your boots!'

Straightening his posture fractionally, the man in question pointed to the far end of the village, where the despoilment of the captured womenfolk was so obviously taking place.

Nodding grimly, the officer turned back to his party and

signalled to the trumpeter, whose horse was alongside that of his grizzled first spear, ignoring both men's nervous expressions.

'Sound the recall! Blow it so loud you split the stones!'

A peal of mournful notes echoed across the ruined buildings and scattered corpses, and in their aftermath the tribune bellowed an order at the soldiers scattered throughout the village's ruins.

'Get into a fucking formation, you cock-sucking bastards! You can at least pretend to be the men you're supposed to be in the short time you have left!'

His senior centurion dismounted and walked across to join him, speaking quietly as the men of the century he had been despatched to retrieve wearily gathered into an approximation of a military formation.

'Tribune, if I might advise you?'

'Advise me of what, Centurion?'

The older man cast a meaningful glance at the men who were the object of his superior's ire.

'These soldiers, Tribune, are exhausted. Literally worn out. We've been fighting the Quadi for over two years and yet there's no sign of them giving up. We've beaten them in every battle that we've fought against them, but where a civilised enemy would have sued for peace, all they did was melt away into this infernal wasteland and harry us from the shadows. This century alone has lost twenty-five men, and less than half of that in any sort of straight fight.'

The younger man shook his head.

'We've all lost friends to their raiding, Centurion. That's no excuse for this sort of wanton disobedience. This sort of insub-ordination can only—'

'Tribune! Good of you to join us!'

A well-built officer was walking up the village's main street, pulling on his cross-crested helmet as he approached, his face creased into a wry grin at the sight of his superior's evident ire. While he seemed at first glance to be as fatigued as his men, his eyes were bright and calculating, clearly taking the measure of the situation before him as he approached the newcomers. Shrugging off the hand that his first spear had placed on his arm, the senior officer strode out to meet him, his fists clenched with uncontrollable anger.

'Centurion Maternus, what the *fuck* do you think you're doing here?'

The two men stood toe to toe, but if the tribune's expectation that his well-practised show of swaggering authority was going to cow his errant centurion into a show of contrition, he was disappointed.

'What do I think I'm doing, Tribune? I think I'm following the orders of our beloved emperor Marcus Aurelius. He ordered us to pursue and pacify the Quadi, and I'm following those orders faithfully and diligently. I've just pacified the shit out of this nest of vipers, pacified it so well that there'll never be any risk of my men being stabbed in the back in the night by one of its so-called *warriors*, or taking an arrow from some anonymous archer raised here.' He paused for a moment before speaking again, almost spitting out the words. 'Orders. Fulfilled.'

His superior shook his head in wonderment.

'You fool! Marcus Aurelius is *dead*! As you well know! His son is emperor now, and Commodus has ordered us to hold position and await the completion of a peace treaty that will see us home before Saturnalia. Which means that this' – he gestured furiously about him at the carnage the centurion's men had inflicted on the village – 'is nothing less than the most egregious of provocations! It's no wonder the prefect ordered me to bring you back, rather than leave you to your own devices! This *flagrant* disobedience of the emperor's orders can only have one result!'

The other man grinned lopsidedly.

'And what result might that be? My being reduced to the ranks? Whipped? Scourged? Made an example of, to discourage anyone else who might harbour thoughts of revenge on the bastards who've killed so many good guardsmen without ever giving them a chance to defend themselves?'

The first spear leaned close to his superior and whispered something intended solely for the tribune's ear, but his only reward was a barked laugh.

'What? Perhaps I might like to be merciful on this occasion and let this ride? Are you *serious*, First Spear?' He spread his arms in amazement, shaking his head. 'The fool has disobeyed an order from the emperor himself, and led his men here to commit an act of mass murder, robbery and rape that has every chance of ruining the peace discussions that are being conducted even now. And who will be the man singled out for punishment by Commodus if that happens, and he fails in his efforts to get himself out of this war-without-end and back to Rome? *Me!*' He turned back to face Maternus, his anger uncontrolled in its vehemence. '*I* will be the man to bear the weight of his rage, Centurion, not *you*, so you can consider your punishment my revenge for the anger that's likely to be visited on me before long.'

The first spear attempted to speak again, looking about him uneasily at the hardening faces of the soldiers gathered around them, only to find himself cut off by the renegade centurion's acerbic response.

'Threatening your career, are we, Tribune? Is *that* the problem here? Not the murder of innocent civilians, but the fact that we're pissing on your dreams of climbing the slippery ladder to the rank of prefect?' Maternus turned and waved a hand at the men behind him, a contorted mask of anger replacing his previous saturnine expression. 'Our mistake, Tribune, and our grovelling apologies. We made the fatal error of thinking that this was a war we were fighting. Time after time we found the bodies of our friends and comrades in the dawn, lying where they had been killed in the night by silent, gutless killers like these' – he waved his hand at the scattered corpses of the villagers – 'and we naturally assumed that we were caught in a fight to the death; dirty, bloody and without mercy. But now I can see that we're really only here to make sure that *you*, Tribune, have a good war, and achieve *your* ambitions. So when the emperor's pathetic excuse for an heir decides that he'd rather be in Rome than following his father's path, betraying the loyalty of the thousands of men who died for the empire in this wasteland, obviously we should have smiled and forgiven the bastards who tortured and killed our brothers. All in the cause of you becoming the emperor's next *lapdog*!'

The tribune whipped out his dagger, spitting fury as he looked down its blade at his subordinate.

'That's your death warrant, right there! I'll leave your corpse for the crows for that insubordination!'

He lunged at his centurion, his intention to kill him obvious, only to find his knife hand caught in a firm grip. Raising his other hand to free the weapon, he found it similarly captured. The two men stared at each other across the intimate space between them, and while Maternus made no immediate attempt to take the weapon, neither did he allow the tribune to move from the position in which he was caught. Shaking his head in bemusement, he held his superior's hands an arm's length away and lowered his voice in a belated attempt at conciliation.

'We can still put this fire out, Tribune. If you'll just put the blade away, we can—'

'*Never!*' The senior officer shook his head and spat an order at his own senior centurion. 'Get this man's hands off me, First Spear!'

Reaching for his sword, the older man froze as he found himself looking at the points of a dozen spears, the intentions of the men holding them as obvious as shouted threats.

'That's a wise choice, Julius. If that blade clears its scabbard, you'll find out what it feels like to be on the receiving end of a volley of *pila*.' Maternus looked into his superior's eyes, his gaze calm in contrast to the tribune's straining efforts and furious expression. 'This is your last chance. Do you really want to die here?'

The tribune's defiance was incandescent, his face contorted by fury and his efforts to break his centurion's grip.

'Your career, Maternus, is *over*! From this moment, you can never be anything more than a fugitive, harried by Rome's hunting dogs, with a price on your head that will draw civilised men and barbarians alike to hunt you down, like flies are drawn to shit!' He spat in the centurion's face. 'I spit on you! Rome spits on you! And you will die – all of you that have taken part in this act of disobedience, for which death is the only just punishment – like the animals you are!'

Maternus stared at him in silence for a moment, the saliva running down his face.

'Very well. If that choice is already made, I see little choice but to follow it through to the end.'

His biceps flexed, cords in his forearms standing out as he forced the tribune's knife hand down and round, then inexorably turned the blade's point upwards until it was inches from his superior's throat. Shuddering with the effort of resisting the stronger man's steady but irresistible force, the tribune stared white-faced at his subordinate as the hopelessness of his position hit him.

'Don't do this! My family . . .'

The other man smiled, testing his strength with an upward heave of the knife that the tribune barely controlled.

'Your family will be mortified that you died after the war's end, shamefully killed as a last resort by a man whose loyalty to Rome you rewarded with threats of death and infamy that drove him to the crime?' He pushed the blade upwards again, smiling as the point shuddered another inch closer to the tribune's throat. 'Your family will wonder what possessed you to provoke men for whom death has lost all fear?' He pushed again, and the blade's point slipped another inch closer. 'Your family, Tribune, will know only this . . .' He grunted with sudden explosive effort, ramming the dagger's blade up into the other man's jaw, pushing it home until only the handle protruded from his head. 'They will know that you were found dead on the blade of your own dagger. Forever shamed.'

The dying tribune staggered backward, choking convulsively as blood ran down his throat and then, as his eyes rolled back, slumped back onto his senior centurion.

'You've . . . *killed* him? You've killed a fucking tribune!'

Maternus smiled tiredly at the first spear's amazement, drawing his sword and raising a questioning eyebrow.

'He really left me no choice, you can see that. But you tried to prevent it, and the men behind you are no more guilty of any crime than we are. I have no desire to spill the innocent blood of fellow guardsmen.'

The other man shook his head stubbornly.

'If I go back to the prefect with the story that I wasn't able to stop you, he'll have me scourged until I've bled to death. There are better ways for a man to die.'

'I understand.' The renegade officer shook his head sadly, then stamped forwards and put the tip of his gladius through his superior's throat, dropping him choking and gurgling into the dust as his blood spread in a dark pool underneath his writhing body. He stared expressionlessly down at the dying man as he wiped and sheathed the sword. 'May you find your ancestors waiting with a jug of wine when you cross the river. I'll make sure you have a coin for the ferryman.'

'What about the rest of them?'

He turned to find his chosen man at his shoulder.

'The rest of them? They're just as much the victims of this war as we are.' He strode out in front of the remaining horsemen, raising his bloody hands for them to see. 'You are free to leave, brothers, and all I ask in return is that you take a message back to the praetorian prefect for me! Tell him that the blood on my hands is as much his fault as mine! Had he sent a better man to bring us back into the fold, then all might have been well; instead, his puppet tribune has rendered me, and as many of my men as will follow me, as outcasts! We know that we are under threat of execution from this moment on. But let him know that I am placing Commodus under exactly the same threat! When the time is right, when my plans have come to maturity, I will have revenge on behalf of every man who has died to no purpose in this war he's so eager to abandon!' He gestured to the southern horizon, his voice dropping in volume to an amused, conversational tone. 'On your way, brothers, and watch out for those treacherous German bastards. I need you to return to the cohorts safely and to spread the word as widely as you can. Rome has not heard the last of Maternus.'

He waited until the last of the horsemen was away through the settlement's broken gate, the two dead men's bodies tied across the saddles of their mounts, then turned to his chosen man.

'Get the men ready to march, we need to move on. We'll head west, away from the army, and stick to the woods. The roads will be thigh deep in cavalry within a day or two, all looking to collect on the reward that prick of a prefect will put on my head for killing his favourite bum boy. And I'm not ready to have my head paraded in front of the Guard just yet. After all, we've spent the last two years taking lessons in how to avoid the Roman army at the hands of the best in the business; now it's time to put all that learning into practice, I'd say, and see how long we can stay alive. Who knows, we might even make half-decent bandits?'

I

'You'll be happy to get back to some proper soldiering, will you, Tribune? Now that you've finished creeping round the swamps and forests at the end of the world kidnapping women, that is?' Gaius Rutilius Scaurus frowned at his senior centurion's jest for a moment without speaking, but far from being intimidated by the disapproval of his superior, Julius shook his head and chuckled.

'Yes, I know. There aren't any swamps and forests in Germania – that's all just an invention of men who've never been there to make it sound more outlandish, and to imply that its people are so lacking in civilised values that Romans should feel good about enslaving them.'

The muscular first spear turned and looked at the small party that was waiting on the transit barracks' parade ground, eager for the order that would dismiss them back to their various centuries after their long ride south from the empire's northern frontier to the gates of Rome.

'Let's have a look then, shall we, and see what you brought me back from the barbarian north? The men we lost died with honour, I presume? Qadir, you seem to have brought back somewhat less men than you took with you.'

A tall, rangy easterner in the scaled armour and crested helmet of a centurion stepped forward and saluted, his eyes seemingly fixed on the horizon.

'Four of my men died on the Germans' blades, First Spear, and not all of them quickly.'

The Hamian's usual soft voice was edged with something harder at the reminder of a loss whose scars were not yet fully healed. Centurion of the cohort's Hamian archers, he had watched his closest friend die by his own hand as a means of avoiding the inevitable revenge of their enemy for the deaths he had inflicted upon them, and had yet to reconcile himself to his comrade's absence. 'I could not have asked any more of them than to die in the favour of the goddess they worshipped every single day of the years we knew each other. And I am proud to have called each of them my comrade and my friend.'

Julius nodded his head in recognition of the archers' sacrifice.

'Thank you, Centurion. I share your pain at those losses and your pride in the way your men chose to meet their ends. I will sacrifice with you to ask for peace for their spirits. Dubnus?'

Another officer took a pace forwards, snapping to attention with a heavy axe resting on one shoulder. Heavily muscled, and just as impressively bearded as his superior, he turned an unblinking gaze on the senior centurion.

'Three of my brother warriors died, two of them overrun by the Bructeri horde and the third when a wound in his foot turned rotten and infected his blood. We were fortunate that the naval medicus treating him had the milk of the poppy to ease his passage across the river to the underworld.' Dubnus frowned at the memory of his soldier's painful, tortured death. 'But he died with his axe in his hand, his brothers around him to give him strength in his passing, and the blood of many men painted across his armour. You would have approved of the way each of them took their leave of this life.'

The hulking first spear inclined his head in respect.

'There was always going to be a price to pay, given the paths you were walking.' He raised an eyebrow at the big centurion. 'Although I see you still display the same gods' charmed life as ever. Are you still blowing that horn every night?'

'Yes, I am.' Centurion of his pioneer century, and one of the few men on the parade ground who could match Julius for both height and breadth, the Briton looked down his nose at his superior in a way that he knew was guaranteed to irritate the older man. 'And if I hadn't blown it as loudly as I could a few weeks ago, then most of us wouldn't be here.'

Julius shrugged.

'That's a story I suspect will have grown in the telling. But it still sounds like a bull having a noisy shit, right? You'd better go and practice some more, and take your muscle sisters with you. You too, Qadir, your archers will be keen to get back to their boyfriends.' Ignoring their mutual disgruntlement, he moved on down the line as the pioneers and bowmen fell out and headed for their respective barracks, their centurions nodding at each other in mutual respect as they parted. 'And I see you didn't manage to shake off any of the less disciplined members of the cohort either, Tribune.' He paused in front of a pair of soldiers whose stares remained steadfastly locked on the barrack behind him. 'Sanga, every bit as shifty as you were before, if not even more so, and Saratos, looking even more like a butcher's guard dog than usual. You two can both bugger off back to the Fourth Century, where I happen to know your centurion is waiting excitedly at the thought of hearing all your thrilling stories. Either that, or he wants to slap you both around just enough to show how much he's missed you. I'll let you work out which is the most likely. Dismissed.'

The two soldiers saluted and turned away. Sanga nudged his Dacian companion, urging him towards the gate and the city's myriad possibilities, but Julius's parting comment left them in no doubt as to what was expected of them.

'You're to report to Otho *immediately*, you pair of halfwits. He's expecting you to resume your duties as watch officers, and should you disappoint that expectation, he's under firm instructions to communicate just how let down he feels, and in his usual direct style. Don't say you weren't warned!'

He grinned as the two men changed direction and walked somewhat less eagerly towards the Fourth Century's barrack, then turned back to stare at the remaining men of the party that had gone to Germania at the imperial chamberlain's orders, addressing his regard to a pair of soldiers, one old enough to be the other's grandfather. They were standing alongside a pair of barbarians, one of whom, the tribune's German slave Arminius, was simply tall and powerful, while the other was a head taller than the first spear. A captive Briton who had long since become part of Scaurus's familia, his body was slabbed with the muscle needed to heft the beaked warhammer that he held casually, its iron head heavy enough to make the simple act of lifting it from the ground a strain for any of his comrades. Stopping in front of the younger of the two Tungrians, he shook his head in apparent disgust as the other soldier, a veteran old enough to have retired years before, looked back at him with his usual calculating expression.

'And here, despite the hopes and expectations of every gambling man in his cohort, is Morban, back among us without so much as a scratch.' He looked the standard bearer up and down before speaking again. 'And looking just as unsavoury as ever, with half a dozen punishable offences in the state of your uniform and equipment alone that I can see with one glance. On your way, statue waver, and get yourself smartened up before I'm forced to have you dragged in front of your centurion for judgement and a beating. And play nicely with your comrades; there are soldiers under my command who've not felt the gentle caress of your fingers on their purses for so long that they've almost forgotten the meaning of fear.' He flicked a glance at the young soldier standing next to the veteran, half a head taller than the last time he had seen him, and smiled despite himself at the almost comical mask of seriousness on the boy's face. 'And you can take this young bullock with you. I wouldn't have recognised the boy if he'd not been standing next to you. Have you dipped your spear in blood yet, Lupus?'

Morban answered for his grandson, an indignant tone in his voice.

'My grandson was true to his blood, when the time came. He did his duty, and killed his first man, First Spear.'

Julius nodded appreciatively, but any further comment was forestalled by the German Arminius, leaning towards him and speaking quietly but firmly.

'I see the seeds of greatness in the boy, and the priestess confirmed as much. He'll do more than just soldier for you; you can be assured of that.'

Julius raised an eyebrow at the interjection, tapping the German on his chest with the tip of his twisted vine stick.

'Whereas all I see is that the tribune still hasn't taught you the difference between intelligence and insubordination, eh, Arminius? You're dismissed, all three of you . . .' He shot a glance at the impassive giant of a man standing alongside them. 'And take that monster Lugos with you. I want to have words with your officers without having to tolerate a running commentary from either you, slave, or you, standard bearer. The boy can tell me about his exploits in the dark German forests soon enough, but for now the grown-ups have more important matters to be discussing.'

He waited until the four men were out of earshot before turning back to Scaurus and the centurions standing beside him.

'Word travels faster than horses when there's bad news to be told, and we heard most of the story of your trip north months ago. How you managed to get your hands on the woman the imperial chamberlain sent you to capture, and then lost her back to the tribe you stole her from as the price of your lives.'

Scaurus shrugged.

'I've always found it wise, First Spear, to take all news from far off places, be it good or bad, with a grain of salt, just in case it turns out to have been amended to suit the teller's bias. And who was it that told you all that? Nobody outside the imperial palace would have had access to that sort of information.' Scaurus looked at Julius questioningly, but the big centurion simply returned the stare in silence, knowing that his superior already knew the answer to his question well enough. 'Cleander?'

'One of his freedmen. He came down the hill a few days ago and told me that you'd be back in the city inside a week, and that

I was to ready both cohorts to march. Your friend the chamberlain has plans for us, it seems.'

The youngest of the three remaining centurions standing alongside Scaurus shook his head angrily, putting his hands on his hips and staring over the transit barracks' low walls at the bulk of the Aventine Hill rising behind them.

'The man has no pity! How can he expect us to march so soon after returning from such an arduous journey, with everything that's happened?'

Scaurus laughed softly.

'No pity? Of course he has no pity. He's the imperial chamberlain, Vibius Varus, he has the weight of the empire bearing down on him and few enough resources to hand when Rome's neighbours decide to test the limits of imperial strength. And in our cohorts, as he knows all too well, he has the perfect means to put out whatever fire it is that's been lit under his backside this time. Fifteen hundred of the best troops in the empire led by men whose instant, unquestioning obedience is guaranteed by the simple threat that hangs over every one of us, and those we hold dearest.'

The taller of his comrades nodded, his lean face set in grim lines at his superior's words and his knuckles white on the grips of his two blades, one a long cavalry sword, the other an eagle-pommelled gladius, the weapons that were his customary armament and had long since earned him the sobriquet of 'Two Knives' among the men of the Tungrian cohorts.

'This is unforgivable. I should just—'

'Take your son and vanish?' The tribune shook his head with a gentle smile. 'That wouldn't do anything to lessen Cleander's hold over us, would it, Marcus? Once a traitor, always a traitor, that would be his only response. We're bent over the table for him whether you're with us or not, aren't we, forever condemned for having sheltered you from the emperor's "justice" after your family's murder? A choice, I would remind you – before you consider jumping back into that bath of despond you were wallowing in not so long ago – that we all chose freely. And beside that, it's clear to me that you wouldn't last a month, not with Cleander's agents hunting you and with a small child to care for. At least this way your son is safe, under the wing of the very man who would have us all put to death in an instant if he thought we were anything other than totally loyal to him and him alone. No, for the time being at least, the best way to respond to Cleander's need to make us jump to his command is to have our boots in the air before he asks.'

He gestured at the hill.

'Go and see your son, Marcus. You'll have a short enough time with him without standing round here bemoaning a fate we can't avoid. And since I noted well enough the fact that you used the term "us" a moment ago, Centurion Varus, let us all be clear that you are hereby freed from your service to the Tungrian cohorts. Let's hope that your cousin the navarchus found the time to send your father the letter he promised, telling him what a hero you proved yourself while you were away.'

Varus grinned, shaking his head in amusement.

'My father? He'll greet me back in his usual manner, I have no doubt of that. I'll get a good stern talking-to once the women have finished weeping at my safe return, and then whenever his friends come to dinner, I'll be paraded forth as the hero of the day, with clandestine service to the empire in both the east and the north which, of course, can never be detailed and will therefore soon assume mythical status.'

'So it's back to being fawned over by a succession of simpering maidens and eager matrons then, is it? I can only shake my head in pity at your sacrifice, you young b—'

'Thank you, Julius.'

Waiting until he was satisfied that his senior centurion had fallen silent, Scaurus turned back to Varus, the son of a senator whose presence in his auxiliary cohorts' ranks he had never regarded as anything other than a temporary expedient.

'Go and make a start on re-establishing your relationship with your father. And I think it's for the best if we agree that your days marching with the Tungrians have reached their natural conclusion. With this experience under your belt, I'd imagine that you'd make an excellent legion tribune, and if your father has half as much sense as I suspect, then he'll pull in a favour or two and get you onto some legatus's staff as quick as he can. Some time spent out of the imperial eye would probably be well advised, given that you've deliberately chosen to associate yourself with men who can hardly be said to enjoy the emperor's favour.' He swivelled to address Marcus, waving a dismissive hand. 'And, you, Centurion, have a child who needs a father. Away with the pair of you, and leave Julius and I to consider what we need to have our men ready for, whatever it is that Cleander wants to throw at us next.'

The two men headed for the gate, and after a moment spent contemplating their backs, Julius turned to his superior and the remaining officer with a questioning look.

'He went away a broken man, more or less. I more than half expected you to come back without him, and I was ready to pronounce his death as a small mercy for such a tortured spirit. And yet there he is, looking more like the old Marcus than anything I ever expected to see again. What happened to work that change in him?'

'What happened?' Scaurus shook his head. 'I have very little idea.' He touched his side with a grimace. 'As the result of my own carelessness I was wounded in the act of abducting the priestess, and I spent most of the next few days clinging onto my life with very little understanding of what was happening around me. It was a succession of hills and rivers for the most part, and the most abominable water-logged pathway that seemed to go on forever. I didn't wake properly for days, by which time the whole thing was over, more or less, and our colleague had been transformed into the man you saw just now. Not quite the Marcus Valerius Aquila of old, but most definitely not the morose and almost completely taciturn individual we took north. He seems to have found . . . well . . . *peace*, I suppose.'

The last of the centurions – an older man with a face lined by experience, but still bright of eye and erect in his posture – shook his head.

'I know what happened, even if I cannot understand it. The witch we were sent to kidnap put him to sleep with a wave of her hand, it seemed, then woke him with a snap of her fingers. And when he woke . . .' He shrugged. 'You can see as well as I can that he's a different man.'

Julius stared at his old adversary for a moment, pursing his lips at the older man's lack of respect for his rank.

'As untroubled as ever, aren't you, Cotta? Did you kill any kings while you were across the Rhenus, anyone you can add to your tally? I doubt one emperor's enough for a practised killer like you.'

The veteran officer smiled back at him thinly.

'Untroubled? Or no more troubled than I was before? After all, we regicides have a hard time sleeping at night, burdened as we are by our crimes. But Germania was a walk in the park compared to some of the fun and games this one's put us through.'

He tipped his head at Scaurus, who smiled in his turn.

'It's never me that puts you through it, Centurion Cotta, and it's not even the apparent culprit Cleander either. You do it to yourself, as you know all too well . . .' He raised a hand to point at Marcus as the young centurion disappeared through the barracks' gate. 'You do it to stay close to the young man you trained from boyhood until he was too good with a sword to learn anything more from you, don't you?'

The older man shrugged.

'Everyone needs someone to look after. And besides, I promised his father, when he knew that his time was limited, that I would do whatever I could to protect him. Before the emperor had his family liquidated.'

Julius nodded.

'You're one man in a cohort of men who're dedicated to keeping the young fool alive, Cotta, and if he's anything close to his old self, I'm sure we'll all be busy again soon enough doing just that.' He turned to Scaurus. 'Do you know where we'll be marching to, Tribune?'

'Where? No. But when? Soon, from the sound of it. So I suggest you talk me through our readiness to march before I go and give this dirty skin a damned good sweat. Because I'm fairly sure I'll be standing in front of the imperial chamberlain before the sun sets tomorrow, and it would be as well to know what I need to demand of him.'

'How much longer must I tolerate this nonsense, Chamberlain? I swear that raddled old fool is deliberately stringing the ceremony out as a means of making some ill-considered point.'

The imperial chamberlain inclined his head respectfully, channelling every possible hint of submissive respect into his posture as he responded to the man who controlled the fate of a hundred million citizens of Rome by decree, and his own immediate future in a rather more intimate and sometimes disturbing manner.

'It won't be long now, Caesar. The Brothers of the Field have a sacred duty to make a sacrifice at all of the most holy shrines along the boundaries of the old city before nightfall, which means that they must surely—'

Commodus spat out his response in a vicious half-whisper whose sibilant violence was audible throughout the shrine's cramped confines, and whose last few words were barked out loudly enough to leave nobody present in any doubt as to their ruler's state of agitation.

'Which means, Chamberlain, that they must surely perform their rituals a good deal faster, if they are not to find their sacred duty impeded by the fact that *they will have become the sacrifices*!'

Those men among the eight toga-clad priests who still retained their hearing cast nervous glances at their imperious ninth member, whose ill-tempered observations as to their short-term futures were, as the chamberlain knew, a more than justified cause for concern as to their immediate safety. Called to their duties unexpectedly only the previous evening – and somewhat confused given that their usual annual rite of entreating the goddess Dea Dia to bless the empire's harvest had already been carried out months before – the priestly college had been aghast at Cleander's patient explanation of the likely unhappiness that would result were they, all men of high rank and great fortune, to decline such an august invitation to intercede with the gods on their emperor's behalf. Nudged by the men on either side of his place at the altar, the chief priest, abruptly transformed from his former air of omnipotent patrician superiority to one of sweating, pale-faced terror, gabbled through the remaining lines of the ancient and arcane rite at a breakneck pace that would have outraged his fellow priests, had they not felt the same cold-eyed threat playing across their ranks. With the words said, the sacrifice of a fine ram hastily made and equally-swiftly declared auspicious, with barely a glance at the animal's exposed organs, much less a proper examination, the blessings of all present were bestowed upon the emperor along with heartfelt wishes of long life and great strength, after which the Arval Brothers waited nervously for their master to express the degree of his satisfaction with their performance of the holy ritual. And, at length, after playing a long, heavy-eyed stare across his sweating colleagues, and to the obvious relief of all present, Commodus finally chose to relent.

'May the gods look down on you with favour, my brothers! Once again you have showed them just how much we men of the city worship them! Even those among us who have sprung from their loins . . .'

He cast a sly glance towards the room to the right of the altar, grinning as he saw their eyes follow his with fresh expressions of incompletely-masked fear.

'On this occasion, it seems, I will not have cause to open the sacred chamber and fetch out Mars's shield and spear, neither to defend Rome from those who might be encouraged by any hint of impiety on our part or indeed to punish any man unwise enough to mistake overly-long ritual for zealous worship. The gods, my fellow brothers of the fields, are no fonder of religious over-indulgence than I am. And who better to know that than I?'

The priests nodded and smiled – blankly for the most part, as each man sought to conceal whatever emotion he felt – as the man with absolute power of life and death over them all invited them to ponder the question of his lineage with an expression of the utmost seriousness. Standing behind the emperor, Cleander stared at each of them in turn, his famed attention to the smallest of details evidently focused on the city's richest men who had in reality been invited to join the ancient brotherhood for reasons that were obvious to all concerned. Commodus sighed wistfully, turning away from the room in which the holy weapons were stored, raising his hands for all assembled to see.

'You do not appreciate the sacrifice I make simply by passing up the chance to wield a spear in Mars's holy name. You may add my forbearance to your list, and shout it at the people as you progress around the old walls proclaiming that I, as Jupiter's son, have their favour. I, in the meanwhile, will go about my never-ending task of enlightening my people as to the godly nature of my presence among them.'

The priests nodded and muttered expressions of respect and devotion for their young ruler, clearly relieved by the prospect of being allowed to go out into the city and live at least one more day, exchanging surreptitious glances at their apparent reprieve. But as the emperor gathered himself to leave, his praetorians opening the temple's door onto a sunlit morning and the noise of the crowd that had gathered behind their shields to await his reappearance, his chamberlain coughed meaningfully.

'Ah yes.' Commodus turned back to face the men of the brother-hood with a half-smile. 'It seems that I almost forgot the most important matter I had intended to discuss with you. As men of substance, I find myself in need of assistance in dealing with a threat that might yet present a risk to the empire itself. Certainly those of you with estates in Gaul might already be aware of this brigand who goes by the name of Maternus?'

One of the senators stepped forward a pace and bowed.

'I have heard the name, Caesar. An upstart deserter who attracts fellow brigands and other assorted renegades to join him in ever greater numbers, and whose depredations in the name of some yet-to-be-defined *vindicta* grow ever bolder and rapacious.'

'That's the man.' Cleander nodded his agreement. 'I was discussing him this morning with the emperor, whose firm view is that something must be done to put this rebel in his place before real damage is done. The loss of a city or a fortress might make the people of the province question the value of our rule. Caesar's patience with the feeble efforts of the governors in question has reached the limits of his undeniably generous patience.'

Commodus nodded firmly.

'I would go to Gaul myself and teach this Maternus the last lesson he'd ever need, if it weren't for the needs of the city and my people. But others must go in my place, it seems.'

Cleander inclined his head in agreement.

'The city needs you too much for your absence to be tenable, Caesar. But we must send soldiers. At least a legion's strength.'

The senators looked at Cleander with fresh understanding, their previous relief dissipating as they realised the purpose behind his statement. The boldest among them stepped forward with a look of distaste. A man whose wartime reputation under the previous emperor had been that of a fearless and outspoken commander, his apparent predilection for frankness had led Cleander to predict on more than one occasion that his brutal honesty would almost certainly result in his premature death.

'And legions cost money, as I am sure you were about to point out to us.'

'Yes, indeed I was! And how perceptive of you, Senator.' The chamberlain beamed beatifically at the patrician's poorly-masked disgust. 'I'll have to keep an eye on you, that's evident! Yes, gentlemen, legions cost money. A lot of money. And all the legions we have are tied up keeping the empire's frontiers safe against the myriad peoples who would very much like to get inside them.

However, our military advisers are clear in their opinion that a full legion's power will be required when faced with several thousand desperate men who know that their capture can only mean their death. And so a legion must be raised.'

'How much?'

The chamberlain's smile widened.

'Straight to the point, eh? Such directness.' He shot a glance at his secretary, who inscribed whatever command it was that had passed between them into his tablet. 'And how much? A lot, Senator, a great deal of gold. For a start, all of the five thousand men in question will have to be paid, at the rate of three hundred denarii for each year of their service: so twelve gold aureii for each of them over the year will be required to deal with this problem. Add in another eight aureii to feed and equip them for that year, not to mention provide them with weapons and equipment. And then there are the hobnails to be taking into consideration.'

'Hobnails?'

Cleander turned to one of the less militarily-experienced priests, looking pointedly at his exquisitely-made leather shoes before commenting.

'Indeed, hobnails. Unlike you and me, the empire's soldiers possess only one pair of boots apiece, and these must be protected from the wear and tear of their arduous life. Legionaries on the march are the most prodigious consumers of hobnails, it seems. Apparently they prevent the leather soles of all those expensive boots from wearing too thin for use. But they must be replaced on a routine basis as they seem to wear out – or indeed in cases of careless maintenance, fall out – which means the empire has to manufacture and supply hundreds of thousands of the things to a legion on campaign. And these are the details that I grapple with every day, the demands on the treasury that have to be met. There'll be no change to be had from a sum of twenty aureii per man, I'm told.'

'And you'll need another five in gold per man to cover the expected exigencies of such a campaign?'

The patrician's acerbic tone would have made Cleander wince for the man's breathtaking lack of any instinct for self-preservation, had decades of palace service not trained the expression of any emotion out of him.

'I find it hard to argue with your well-found estimate, Senator! Although with legion cavalry to equip and feed as well, I'd say that even your proposed contingency might yet not be enough.'

The senator shrugged.

'I understand the nature of what you're asking for. So twenty-five aureii a man, and five thousand men, give or take, means that you're looking for one hundred and twenty-five thousand in gold. Three million denarii.'

Three million, one hundred and twenty five thousand, in point of fact. Let's call it four million, for the sake of safety.'

'And to make our *donations* a nice round five hundred thousand apiece?'

The chamberlain nodded equably.

'Indeed. And I congratulate you on your prompt voluntary offer of the funds required to put such a force into the field. My secretary will provide you with details of how to remit the donation. A praetorian escort will be sent to each of your houses to ensure that no loss occurs in transit to the treasury.' He extended an arm to usher the emperor out into the sunlight. 'Caesar? Your many-fold duties call.'

Commodus stepped out into the sunlight, raising a hand to acknowledge the cheers of the crowd waiting docile behind the deep ranks of the praetorian cohort that had been deployed to ensure his visit to the temple was uninterrupted.

'Four *million* denarii? Does a legion really cost that much to raise?'

His chamberlain smiled knowingly, gesturing to the praetorian prefect to bring the emperor's litter forward.

'My military experts tell me that the sum might well be a good deal less, Caesar, but I have always believed that a prudent servant of the state should ensure that there is no eventuality that he cannot afford to overcome. And besides, I recall you telling me how much you were hoping that your birthday celebrations would surpass last year's extravaganza; a good deal of gold will have to flow from the treasury to the gladiatorial schools if we are to be ready in time for the great day.'

Commodus nodded eagerly.

'Quite so, Chamberlain, quite so! And you're convinced that you can achieve such a spectacle and deal with this man Maternus at the same time?'

The older man simply smiled again.

'Ah, here's your litter. Away to your busy day, Caesar, and leave me to worry about the details of seeing off the empire's enemies. Prefect Aebutianus?'

The praetorian commander stepped forward and called out an order, prompting his men to a hurried repositioning to either side of the litter, forming a ring of hard-faced guardsmen to clear the emperor's path back to the palace and the day's entertainments.

'It went well, Chamberlain?'

Cleander regarded the prefect for a moment before replying, considering, as he always did, everything he knew about the man to whom he was speaking before venturing an opinion.

'It went tolerably well, thank you, Prefect.' The man was his own appointee, albeit one that he kept a close watch on given the power of his position, and he realised he would probably hear the story from his own men in the temple soon enough. 'Caesar managed to communicate to the Arval Brotherhood that brevity is most definitely a fine attribute when it comes to subjecting a bored emperor to religious ritual, and they repaid his kindness by hurrying through the order of the rite swiftly enough that he wasn't overcome by the urge to take the sacred spear to them. And the members of that most ancient and respected order have agreed to a generous funding of the army that will be required to deal with this new Gallic bandit. All in all, a successful morning from my perspective.'

'So we're raising another legion?'

Cleander shook his head in amusement.

'No, we're not raising another legion. The Eighth Augustan will cope perfectly well with this bandit and his fellow criminals from their fortress at Argentoratum, I'd have thought. But I will make a show of sending some reinforcements from the capital, just to give the Arval Brothers the impression that their money is being spent well.'

'Reinforcements? What reinforce . . .'

The other man's eyes narrowed as he realised what Cleander was hinting at.

'Yes. A cohort or two of your praetorians will make for a noble sight as they march out from the city, and it's about time they saw some action, wouldn't you agree? Not to mention the fact that this man Maternus is one of your own, which would make it both right and fitting for it to be the Guard that brings him back to Rome for punishment. And besides, I need some good loyal men to accompany the other military force I plan to send west. They're incomparable in battle, it seems, but their leadership is suspect, to say the least.'

The prefect shook his head.

'You mean the auxiliaries who've been camped in the transit barracks on the Via Ostiensis for the last six months, I presume?'

'I do.'

'If the stories I hear as to their exploits are to be believed, then they're not just suspect, they're dangerous. Why you haven't had their tribune dismissed, or simply put to death, is beyond—'

'Yes, I know. Well beyond you. But the thing is, my dear Aebutianus, when one's house seems likely to be overrun by rats, the last thing a wise man would do is kill his best dog. I send those men at the empire's enemies, and by one means or another, they always succeed in dealing with whatever threat faces Rome. In addition to that, it has to be admitted that they have performed certain services to the city – and to myself – that I view with a measure of sentimentality.' He raised a jaundiced eyebrow at the praetorian commander. 'And before you start smirking at the thought I might be capable of such an emotion, I'll point out that even you, resplendent in your finery, would not occupy that position of grandeur were it not for their actions in unseating your predecessor. But, as with any fierce dog, there's always the risk that they might bite the hand that feeds. So choose the men you'll send west alongside them carefully, and let's see if we can't dilute that risk a little, shall we?'

'Your father will be furious with you, you do realise that, don't you, Gaius?'

Varus smiled wanly at Marcus's question, raising a hand in salute to the guards as they passed through the Aventine gate.

'Furious? I expect he'll be a little exercised, but—'

'He'll be incandescent. He'll already know what happened in Germania, of course, because your cousin will have written to your uncle with the news. And while absconding from Rome to go and play at soldiers – because that's the way he'll put it to you – is one thing, interfering with matters of state is entirely another.'

Varus shrugged.

'There's no proof that we acted in anything other than the empire's best interests.'

His comrade shook his head.

'Proof? Who cares about *proof*? There was no *proof* when the last praetorian prefect had my family murdered, just a need for gold and a convenient target in my father and uncle as two of the richest men in the city. Not to mention our estate on the Via Appia, which he promptly took for his own. Cleander won't hesitate to have you and your family liquidated, if he discovers the truth of what happened to his spy in Germania. Don't misunderstand me, Gaius, I wouldn't change any of what we did, but there's a reckoning hanging over us both now. As it is, it's hard to see what's motivated Cleander to keep us alive as long as he has. Of course we've been useful, but how long that will last is anyone's guess. The best thing for you to do is to go home, accept whatever punishment your father hands you and keep your head down. Let's hope that this will all be forgotten soon enough, for you at least.'

Varus nodded glumly.

'Perhaps. Although what I'm going to do with myself is a bit of a mystery to me.'

'Well, for one thing, you can keep an eye on Annia and the children, when he sends us away again.' The two men paused, having reached the gate of the house where Julius's woman and the three children she cared for lived. 'Why not come inside for something to eat and to wash the road from your feet?'

Varus nodded.

'It'll delay the moment of truth a little longer.'

The gatekeeper was one of Cotta's former soldiers, left behind to care for Marcus's familia when the veteran centurion had re-enlisted to accompany the Tungrians to the east the year before. He answered their knock by pulling the gate open swiftly, a knife in his hand, while the gleam of an infantry sword's blade in the wall's shadow indicated that he was not alone. Both men bowed respectfully at the sight of Marcus, admitting the two officers and bolting the gate behind them.

'Apologies, Centurion, but there's been more than one stranger hanging around of late, so we decided not to take any risks.'

Nodding his understanding, the young officer led his friend into the cool of the atrium, raising an eyebrow as another of Cotta's veteran soldiers padded silently towards them with a finger to his lips.

'The children are asleep, sir, and the mistress treats us hard if they get wakened before it's time.'

Shaking his head, Marcus waved the man away with a quiet chuckle.

'Let's get the kitchen fire going and warm up some water, shall we? Once our feet are clean we'll feel a good deal more like civilised men, and rather less like—'

'The rough-arsed soldiers you are?' Varus took a step backwards as a naked woman came out of the kitchen to confront them, a bloody knife in one hand and both arms slathered in gore to the elbow. 'Julius sent a man to warn me that you would be home today, so I'm in the process of butchering a nice fat pig. And you two men have arrived at just the right time to help me hang him up for skinning.' Varus and Marcus exchanged surprised glances, but Annia obviously wasn't in the mood for any reluctance in the matter. 'Come on, get your armour off and strip to your skin, there's no point ruining perfectly good clothing. Once blood's into the weave it'll never come out, no matter what I do, and I'm not throwing away tunics that cost enough money to feed a family of ten for a week.' The two men looked at each other in shared confusion, and the de facto lady of the house gestured with her knife in what was an unconscious but nevertheless disquieting action. 'Get on with it! I've seen it all before, trust me, and I've seen longer and thicker than either of you two have got to show off, so you're perfectly safe!'

Bemusedly doing as they were told, both men removed their heavy armour and tunics while she tapped an impatient foot.

'You can leave your boots on, a bit of blood isn't going to do them any harm.'

Leading them out into the villa's back garden, she gestured to another woman, who had taken shelter from the sun in the shadow of the closely-planted trees that protected the house's privacy from the buildings clustered around it. A dead pig was lying close to the house's wall beneath a heavy iron hook embedded in the brickwork, a large pail full of its blood testament to Annia's thrift and no-nonsense attitude.

'Off your backside, Calistra, your man will be back soon, and we need that animal ready to roast!'

Varus frowned as the younger woman returned to her task. 'That's . . . ?'

'Dubnus's woman, the one he rescued from the gladiator school. She doesn't look half bad now that she's cleaned up and put some weight on.'

Marcus bowed to both women.

'Ladies, my thanks for the care you've evidently been taking of the children.'

Annia snorted her amusement.

'And what were we supposed to do while you were away, waft around the markets buying silk and making eyes at gladiators like the rich women?' She gestured to the wall hook with a look of impatience. 'Now get those muscles working and hang that fat little bugger up for me so that I can get his skin off and his guts dropped out. Once you've done that, you can take that blood inside and cover it to keep the flies off, then go and wash yourselves and entertain the children while we do the hard work. I've already tied the beast's back legs together, so all I need is for you two fine specimens of manhood to get him up on the hook. And you can stop goggling at poor Calistra; she's been through enough without having to put up with your lechery.'

The two men struggled to heave the dead pig's carcass onto the iron hook, as its blood-slicked skin kept slipping through their grasping fingers; only after several failed attempts did they manage to catch the thick twine that bound its ankles over the hook's point. Annia looked at the gently swaying beast with satisfaction, jerking a thumb back at the house.

'Good. Now off with you. You can send a pair of Cotta's idiots out to get the fire pit ready, and we'll get this beast roasting. Go and remind your son who his father is, eh?' Marcus nodded and turned away, only to stop as his friend's wife tapped him lightly on the arm with the flat of her knife blade. 'And Marcus, be warned. I've bonded with little Felix like a mother. If you do him the slightest harm, it won't be Commodus or Cleander that you have to worry about. And wash your feet before you go back inside!'

Nodding his understanding, he led Varus back into the house, where the two men used water already warmed over the cooking fire to wash away the blood and clean themselves, dressing in fresh tunics just as the first sounds of the children waking were heard.

'You'll be needing this, sir.' The oldest of the guards, clearly a family man himself, handed Marcus a terracotta feeding bottle that had been left to warm in the sun. 'The older two will still be digesting their lunch, but that baby cuts up rough if he's not fed after a sleep.'

Relieving the gate guards to go about Annia's bidding, they took the infants into the front garden, where Marcus sat in the shade of a cypress and fed the baby Felix while Julius's daughter Victoria sat talking to a rag doll and his own son Appius stared at him fixedly. Knowing what a daunting prospect his lean, scarred face must be, he waited quietly, smiling at the child until the boy felt sufficiently emboldened to speak.

'Are you my daddy?'

'Yes, Appius. I'm Marcus, and I'm your father.'

The child fell silent again for a moment, clearly considering his next words.

'Annia isn't my mummy.'

'No, Annia is a very dear friend who has been looking after you while I was away.'

'My mummy died.'

Marcus held his breath, waiting to see if the boy had anything more to say, unconsciously flicking a glance down at the baby whose birth had killed his wife, but Appius fell silent again, regarding his father unblinkingly.

'Yes, she did. And I've been away more than I should have. But I'm here now, and I won't go away without you again, not if I can avoid it.'

Again the child thought before answering.

'Do you promise?'

Suddenly it was Marcus's turn to fall silent, knowing that he couldn't lie to the boy.

'I promise not to leave you alone again.'

'Don't promise what you can't deliver, *Centurion*.' He turned to find Annia behind him, washed clean of the blood and dressed in a man's tunic. 'I left Cotta's men putting the pig to roast, with warnings as to what will happen to them if they make a mess of it. We'll have all their families to dinner tonight, as a way of thanking them for their protection while you've been away.' She shook her head at him fondly. 'Marcus, Julius loves you like a brother and so do I, especially after all you've been through, and I know you meant well when you tell your son that you won't leave him behind again. But how likely is it that Cleander will allow you to stay in the city, when he knows you must harbour thoughts of revenge on the emperor for all the pain he's heaped on you?'

She took Felix from his arms, putting the infant over her shoulder and rubbing gently at his back. Marcus held his hands out to Appius, who, after another moment's thought, got to his feet and walked close enough to his father to be hugged close to the young soldier's chest.

'I understand all that. But I've left Appius here twice in the last twelve months. The first time I left him his life was threatened along with that of your daughter, and he was only spared at the cost of another man's life. And the second time, I left him parentless at a time when he needed me more than ever, even if I was too numb with grief to realise it. I won't take those risks with him a third time.'

A rap on the gate snatched them back to the realities of the present, and Marcus put the boy down, reaching for the gladius propped up against the garden wall. Holding it in his left hand behind the door's wooden shield, he opened the gate a fraction. In the street outside, a praetorian guardsman was waiting impatiently, and the young Roman handed the forbidden weapon behind him to Annia before opening the gate wider.

'Centurion Marcus Tribulus Corvus?'

'Yes.'

'I carry a message from the imperial chamberlain, Centurion. You and Tribune Gaius Rutilius Scaurus are to report to his office in the Palatine tomorrow morning, at the third hour. No reply is required.'

He saluted and turned away, and Marcus stared bleakly after him.

'No reply is required.' Annia rested the sword against the garden wall and closed the gate, shooting the heavy bolts that secured it. 'He's reeling you back in, isn't he? Another task, another impossibility to be achieved, and this time my Julius will have to go too. I'll be left here with—'

'No.'

She frowned up at him in bemusement.

'You don't say no to Cleander, and you know that just as well as I do. If he tells you to march, you'll march, because you have no choice in the matter. And neither do we.'

2

'Rutilius Scaurus, welcome back to Rome at long last.' Cleander looked up from his desk at the tribune and his companion. 'And the man who goes by the name of Marcus Tribulus Corvus. It's kind of you both to spare me some time so soon after your return from Germania, and especially after so long away. Longer than I'd expected, in fact.' He gestured to the man waiting in silence to one side of his expansive wooden desk. 'You've already met Gaius Vibius Varus, of course, so no introductions will be necessary.'

Scaurus nodded to Varus, and Marcus smiled briefly at their friend's unexpected presence but, knowing the chamberlain's ability to unearth the best-hidden secrets, neither showed any sign of surprise at his presence at the focal point of Rome's power.

'I invited young Varus here after becoming aware of the unexpected role he seems to have played in your mission across the Rhenus into barbarian Germania. A mission which, to judge from your rather sparsely worded dispatch from Colonia Agrippina, seems to have ended in failure.'

All three men waited in silence as Cleander put down his stylus and stood, advancing round the desk in an impressive display of fearlessness given the presence of at least one man who would happily have beaten him to death given the opportunity, and who was only held back from that satisfaction by the obvious consequences of such an act for those he loved.

'So, gentlemen, shall we review exactly what it was that you *did* manage to achieve in the course of performing what, on the face of it at least, seemed a fairly simple task?'

Scaurus shook his head slightly, a smile of genuine amusement on his hawk-like features.

'Your simple task, Chamberlain, nearly killed me.'

The older man shrugged.

'It's usually hard to put meat on the table without putting blood on the floor, Rutilius Scaurus. And given that whatever it was that befell you hasn't blunted your customarily acerbic tongue, no matter how likely it is to cause offence, I suggest that you get on with sharing the results of those travails. I am in particular keen to understand the disappearance of an agent of mine, who seems to have vanished without trace after accompanying Vibius Varus here across the river in a mission to collect you from some tribe or other.'

The tribune replied without any sign of concern that his words might determine the futures of all three of the men before him.

'We played our part just as you asked, Chamberlain. The abduction of the Bructeri tribe's priestess was achieved just as we planned it. Ultimately, however, it was *your* man who decided that we should release her back to her tribe, as a means of fostering good relations with them.'

Cleander played a piercing stare on him for a moment before replying.

'I see. It was troubling enough to receive a communication from him telling me that he had been forced to abandon his cover in order to accommodate your change of plan, and that was *before* his subsequent disappearance. Am I to blame you for the death of such a valued servant of the empire?'

Scaurus shook his head, meeting the older man's piercing stare with a frank gaze of his own.

'No, Chamberlain. If you want to blame anyone, I suggest you look instead at the governor himself. Clodius Albinus persists in harbouring a grudge towards me that goes back to the death of the previous praetorian prefect, if you recall the circumstances involved?' Cleander nodded soberly at the reminder of the events that had catapulted him to power, a night in which Albinus's ambitions had been ruthlessly dashed by the man standing before him. 'Governor Albinus tried to intercept my party as we made our withdrawal, with the intention of taking the priestess off my hands so that he could send her to Rome in his own name. Which in turn compelled me to find another way to get her out of Bructeri territory, rather than surrender her to his somewhat uncertain motives, as I assumed that to do so would have run counter to your own expectations?'

'A change of plan which ultimately resulted in my agent's death, it seems. But only after he had somewhat uncharacteristically decided to release the woman back to the very people from whom we had expended so much effort to abduct her. Can you explain the circumstances of that decision to me?'

Scaurus shook his head blankly.

'I was as puzzled and dismayed as you are now when he announced what he'd made his mind up to do, given the pains we'd gone to in order to abduct her as ordered by yourself. Perhaps he did it because the priestess turned out to be the Bructeri king's half-sister, and he deemed that the diplomatic gains to be made outweighed her value to us? And the fact that the king and his men were between us and the safety of the Angrivarii tribe might also have been a factor.'

Cleander eyed him suspiciously, clearly not satisfied with the explanation.

'The man I sent to watch over Albinus would have fulfilled his orders by cutting her throat, and only then worried about finding a way to escape.'

'There was no way to escape, Chamberlain.' Scaurus shook his head. 'The combination of his plan and Governor Albinus's inter-ference had stranded us in the far north of the Bructeri lands, beyond the reach of any help, and we can be grateful that they chose to honour the bargain he made with them. Which was the case only because their king desires a peaceful relationship with Rome after all the years of enmity between us. Perhaps your man thought her life was a price worth paying for that?'

The chamberlain walked away across the room, deep in thought.

'Perhaps he did. Although it is Rome's long-standing practice to have at least one enemy across the Rhenus, to provide fertile conditions for diplomacy with the rest of the tribes. Why he would have made such a radical change without any instruction to do so is beyond me . . .' He turned back to Scaurus with narrowed eyes. 'How did he die?'

'He fell from his horse and broke his neck.'

'Where?'

'Close to the river during our return journey, while we were under the protection of the Marsi king.'

'And you can prove this?'

Scaurus shrugged, not taking his eyes off the chamberlain's glaring expression.

'There's this . . .' He passed Cleander a scroll. 'It's a letter from the king of the Marsi apologising for his death. Apparently the horse he was given was known to be a little skittish, and it's a fact that when it spotted a boar in the forest it was uncontrollable. And you can take it from me that he was no horseman, or he wouldn't have ended up with his head staved in by a tree trunk. Obviously the Marsi were suitably horrified at the loss of a servant of Rome, and have asked me to beg your pardon for such a disastrous accident.'

The chamberlain turned to look at Varus.

'Vibius Varus, you were also there when this accident happened, I believe?'

The young senator inclined his head in acceptance of the point.

'I was, Chamberlain.'

'And you're happy to back up the tribune's story?'

'Of course, Chamberlain.'

'I see.' Cleander walked across the room and looked out across the Circus Maximus, shaking his head slowly. 'I'm finding this all a little hard to believe – so hard, in fact, that I have ordered several men from the Camp of the Foreigners to head north and probe this story as closely as can be achieved without incurring the enmity of the tribes involved. Let's hope that they don't find any holes in your account, for the sake of all your families and friends. And you can be assured that if I didn't have a use for you and your men, you'd be spending the months that it will take them to report back in captivity. Yes . . .' He smiled humourlessly at Scaurus and Marcus. 'I thought that might get your attention. I have another mess for you to clean up. But before we turn to the subject of your next opportunity to die for the empire, let's discuss something a little closer to home.'

All three men waited while he considered his next words for a moment.

'As imperial chamberlain, I am well supplied with the city's gossip and rumours. I have dozens of informers, both great and small, who are well rewarded in their own different ways. This means that when a man of influence dies, the news invariably reaches me. A doctor, for example . . .'

He turned to look at Scaurus with a dangerously thin half-smile.

'A doctor who lived in one of the more exclusive districts of the city, catering to the health needs of a number of wealthy citizens. He also assisted a good deal of their fellows, who wished to be treated by a man whose hands had applied their healing skills to the richest members of society. A doctor who, somewhat unfortuitously, it seems, you visited on the very day of his suicide at his office in the Esquiline district. If that helps you to remember?'

Scaurus frowned.

'I need no assistance, Chamberlain, for I recall the event very clearly. A member of my familia was recovering from having been shot in the leg by Parthian archers not once but twice, and it occurred to me to seek medical advice as to the state of his fitness. The doctor, whose name I must admit I have totally forgotten, gave our man a clean bill of health, other than to recommend some stretching, and we took our leave of him.'

'And yet not long after this simple consultation the man's apprentice went to seek an opinion of him only to find him dead, an apparent suicide, clutching a pot of one of the deadliest poisons known to medical science.'

The tribune shook his head in apparent amazement.

'Which just goes to prove that we can never know what is happening inside a man's head, for he gave us no—'

The chamberlain raised a hand, shaking his head in grim amusement.

'Which just goes to prove that the one thing no man in the city can do without impunity is to wrong you or any of yours, I'd say. Well, *almost* any man . . .'

Cleander raised an eyebrow at Marcus, who met his stare impassively until the chamberlain nodded and dropped his gaze.

'As I suspected. Doubtless you would have performed the act of revenge with a good deal more bloodshed, Marcus *Valerius Aquila*, but your superior's rather more subtle approach very nearly succeeded in achieving that vengeance while going unnoticed, as I am sure was his intent. And so I asked myself, why would Gaius Rutilius Scaurus want an innocent doctor dead so badly that he would be willing to take such a risk? What could be the imperative for such a reckless act? And then I recalled to mind your wife's untimely demise.'

A long moment of silence hung over them before he spoke again, neither Scaurus nor Marcus deigning to answer the chamberlain's implication.

'Yes, better to hold your silence and see just how much I know. Although you already know the answer to that question. Gentlemen, I know *everything*. I had the dead man's freedman questioned at length, and it didn't take very long to discern the connection between a childbirth he attended on the Aventine Hill while you were away in the east – a childbirth that ended with the mother's death and the baby's survival – and you. A botched caesarean delivery, it seems. Apparently the doctor had delayed his departure from the dinner party he had been summoned from until he was somewhat less capable than usual. As a result, he managed to kill the mother while delivering her child. It happens, of course, depressingly frequently, but not every dead woman has a familia with such exacting expectations.'

He shrugged.

'That you killed the man mattered nothing to me. One less incompetent doctor in the city, that's all it meant, until of course I looked at the calendar and worked out the real significance of what had happened. The child, it seemed to me, was born a good ten months after your departure from Rome. But how could that be . . . ?'

Marcus stared at him levelly, with no sign of the rage that the chamberlain was looking for.

'She was raped.'

Cleander nodded.

'So I gather, from my questions of the emperor's favourite praetorian officer, the man who routinely accompanies him around the city when he decides to go out among the people in disguise.' He shook his head. 'It seems to be a common failing among royalty, this urge to put on a mask of anonymity behind which they can observe their subjects. He does it every now and then – puts on the armour of a praetorian and joins this centurion's detachment as a soldier – and you'd be amazed what he gets up to under that disguise. He went to your wife and graced her with his body, it seems. Their coupling wasn't entirely consensual, it has to be agreed – merely the preferable option to having her own child murdered – so I suppose you could call it rape. It was over in weeks, of course, he always grows bored and moves on to a fresh conquest . . .'

'*Victim.*'

'As you wish, Valerius Aquila. You have your own perspective and the emperor, of course, has his rather more nuanced view of the matter. After all, what woman could possibly resist the advances of a living god? And that, we all believed, was that. Except it wasn't, was it? A baby was conceived, and that baby survived the rather depressing circumstances of a botched delivery that killed his mother.'

He smiled beatifically at the two men.

'Yes, I know it's a boy. Once I realised what must have

happened, I set my best informers to watching your house, and to observing the woman who lives with your senior centurion. She cares for three children: her own daughter, Victoria, your son, Appius – your father's name, Valerius Aquila, very dutiful – and this imperial bastard, who she has been overheard to call Felix. An amusing choice of name, under the circumstances. So . . .' He looked at all three men in turn. 'Let's be clear. Whilst there is no law against harbouring the illegitimate son of an emperor, most emperors will tend to take a dim view of such a thing. A bastard is a difficult thing for any ruler to countenance, as the child will inevitably pose a threat, a potential rallying point for insurrection. The tacitly-recognised bastard child, of course, is often no threat at all, widely known about and trained from childhood to decline any idea that they might one day claim the throne, but the hidden bastard is entirely another matter. They grow to adulthood in the shadows, their potential destiny kept from them by the well-meaning people who raise them, but – and this is a well-evidenced fact from history – they almost always become aware of their parentage. Some fool or other just has to tell them the truth, rather than allowing them to live a quiet and unregarded life, and from that moment the fact of their conception weighs on them. The secret is a secret no longer, and word spreads. And then in the future, if the emperor dies childless, or with only a female child, the potential for a civil war for the throne becomes massive.'

'Surely, in that case, the senate will simply choose an emperor from among the best men in the city, Chamberlain, as was the case with Nerva and the men that succeeded him?'

Cleander shook his head at Varus.

'An attractive idea, but unlikely. For every peaceful transition of imperial power, there have been at least as many that involved the shedding of blood. Consider the example of the Year of the Four Emperors and then try to tell me that I'm wrong. Greed is a constant among the city's ruling class, and greed's constant companion, violence, is never far from her side. And tell me, who do you think would be among the first to die in the event of such an upheaval?'

The younger man thought for a moment.

'You.'

The older man nodded at Scaurus.

'Me. The man with all the previous regime's secrets. Too powerful to live, and therefore a target for murder by the agents of whoever fancies their chances of taking the throne but has not secured my backing. Bastards bring uncertainty, gentlemen, and men like me loathe uncertainty more than anything else.'

'So why is the child still alive? Surely you must have considered killing him the moment that you discovered his presence in the city?'

The chamberlain acknowledged the point.

'Perhaps I should have, Rutilius Scaurus. But men like me are also given to considering the options and the odds. And in your cases, the options and the odds make for interesting consideration.'

He pointed to the map of the world painted onto the office's wall.

'Where other, more carefree men allow themselves the luxury of a forest scene to decorate their walls, or frolicking nymphs, I make do with a constant reminder of the size of this monster I serve. Look at it, gentlemen. Look at the sheer mind-numbing size of it. One hundred million people. Forty-eight provinces. Hundreds of neighbouring peoples, all of whom eye our prosperity and consider their own relative poverty with sharp eyes and sharper ambitions. And not all of the threats we face are external.'

He tapped the painted representation of Gaul with a finger.

'There's a revolt of some sort brewing in the west, it seems. A praetorian deserter has gathered enough of his fellow traitors about him to form a private army, from the reports we've received.'

Scaurus stared back at him expressionlessly.

'A few deserters? Send a cohort of auxiliaries to . . .' His eyes narrowed at Cleander's knowing expression. 'You already have, haven't you?'

'Yes. A cohort of auxiliaries was ordered to deal with them. The bandits, which was what we believed they were at that point, simply ran away from them until they had them on more favourable ground and then attacked, using the sort of tactics that worked so well against our legions in Hispania during the conquest. Three days later, those few men who remained of the cohort were lucky to escape with their lives.'

'What did you do after that?'

The chamberlain smiled humourlessly.

'The emperor wrote to the governors of the provinces involved in something of a temper, when the news reached us. His ire was particularly aroused at the governor of Gallia Lugdunensis, a senator by the name of Niger, with whom I believe you have campaigned before, since it was his auxiliaries who had been humiliated. We decided that the best answer to the problem would be for his auxiliaries and those of Belgica and Aquitania to pool their forces and put these rebels, as we have come to realise they are, into a net so tight they could not escape. The result, of course, was depressingly similar to the first effort to bring them to bay, although they did display a new trick in evading the men who were sent. Can you guess what it was?'

'What force was ranged against them, and how strong were they?'

Cleander nodded approvingly.

'Good questions, as ever. We estimate there were by that stage a thousand or so of them, strength gathered from further desertions and the recruitment of slaves by a promise of freedom.'

'And vengeance for having been enslaved, of course. That and the chance to plunder the next farm or town they overran.'

'Exactly. And the forces pursuing them were three infantry cohorts and a squadron of horsemen. What would you have done under those circumstances?'

Scaurus shrugged easily.

'Not enough cavalry to comb the country for them, and the three cohorts were probably marching as separate entities, lacking much coordination and not daring to divide their strength into centuries that could be overwhelmed on their own. Which probably left most of the escape routes – from wherever it was they were supposedly trapped – wide open. After all, I doubt the man who leads them was simple-minded enough to let himself be bottled up. They separated into small groups, I'd imagine, and made their way to a pre-agreed point where they regrouped.'

'Yes, they did. They vanished, like smoke on the breeze, and left the cohorts sent to bring them to justice floundering. Clearly the provincial armies can't be relied upon when faced with hardened soldiers like that. So now the emperor has decided to make an example of these rebels, in order to demonstrate to all involved that he's up to the task even if they're not. The timing of your return from Germania is fortuitous, Tribune, because if you'd been a week later, your Tungrians would already have been on the march north, and under a new commander. As it is, I'm happy to let you lead them, and, since I suspect that Vibius Varus here has the strong potential to be yet another source of disruption for my carefully laid-out plans, you can take him with you as the commander of your Second Cohort. Perhaps your proven qualities of cunning and leadership will give you the edge when it comes to cornering these animals and putting them to death with the appropriate efficiency the emperor expects of his army. Or perhaps you'll all meet with a grisly end that will remove more than one problem from my list. Either will suit my purposes.'

Scaurus nodded soberly.

'As you command, Chamberlain. I presume that we're dismissed?'

'Not quite, Tribune. There's one other condition to your being allowed to leave the capital.' Both men waited expectantly while he walked to the office's window and looked out across the city with a half-smile. 'The emperor's bastard isn't housed in the safest or most discreet of locations, even if I have men watching your house, Valerius Aquila. We'll have him moved into the palace, I think. There are plenty of places where the emperor never ventures in this labyrinth of buildings, and the nursery in which certain illegitimate children are raised is one of them. You can deliver him to me before you leave, and go on campaign in the happy knowledge that neither he nor the other children are at any risk. Bring them all, and the woman who cares for them. That way I'll know I can be assured of your complete loyalty, no matter what the circumstances. Won't I?'

'Julius isn't going to like this.'

Scaurus shook his head, lips pursed, as he leaned on a low wall and stared across the Circus Maximus at the Aventine Hill where Marcus's house was hidden in the sprawl of rooftops. The three men had stopped on their way down through the Palatine's tiered terraces to allow the tension to leave their bodies, talking quietly as the unending business of the palace's day went on around them, the implications of Cleander's emphatic instructions sinking in as they considered their options.

'Isn't going to like it? He'll be furious. But I can't see that we have much of a choice. And it seems we're taking you with us to Gaul, whether or not either we or you like the idea, doesn't it, Vibius Varus?'

Varus stared down at the Circus's long, sandy track, watching as a quartet of chariots tore up the closer of the two long straights in the otherwise almost totally deserted stadium. Their pace too fast to be mere exercise; it was more likely a private race for rich clients. He nodded, shooting a wry glance at Scaurus.

'I can't say that I find the prospect anything other than a massive relief, to be honest with you. I'd expected my father to give me the silent treatment after an initial explosion or two, but since Cleander's messenger summoning me to that meeting got to the house before I did, he was already doing a fairly good impression of Vesuvius by the time I got back after dinner. Apparently I've disgraced myself, since my participation in your doings in Germania wasn't in any official capacity, and it seems that I could only have brought more shame to his house by running away to become a gladiator. All of which is probably linked to the fact that my cousin took it upon himself to lay out the full details of our activities on the other side of the Rhenus with his father, who in turn told mine. Which means that he's now accusing me of both treason and putting the family in mortal danger.'

'That last bit isn't entirely unreasonable, is it, if you consider it literally?' Scaurus fell silent as the chariots swept into the hairpin bend at the track's western end, one of the chasing pack driving hard in behind the leader and baulking the other two competitors in the pursuit. 'A good move. See how his nerve held and the other two backed off? Sometimes you have to forget your own safety in this life and do the one thing that nobody expects. That driver clearly doesn't have any time for half-measures. He knows that if you hesitate, you can die wondering what might have been.'

'And what's one more act of *treachery*?' Both men turned to look at Marcus, who was staring at the spot where the racing chariots had made their turn with an expression that both men had come to know all too well. 'You, Rutilius Scaurus, have committed one long act of treachery from the day you took me under your protection, strictly speaking. And you, Gaius, have done much the same, from the moment you realised who I was and yet failed to report my fugitive status when you had the opportunity. Our abandonment of the chamberlain's man to his fate in the wilds of Germania makes little difference. And besides . . .'

He fell silent as the racing chariots burst around the bend at the opposite end of the track. The risk-taking driver in second place had evidently taken the corner a fraction too tightly, and was thrown bodily from his perch as his inside wheel thumped into the track side wall, launching the chariot into the air. Landing awkwardly on the track's hard-packed surface he tumbled, coming to a halt in an unnatural sprawl of limbs, and lay still as the other three drivers raced away from the scene without a backward glance at the destruction his error of judgement had wrought.

'And besides?'

The young Roman looked down at the fallen driver, gesturing as the Circus's staff rushed forwards to remove the chariot's wreckage and his body from the track's sandy surface.

'We have no idea how this will all end. It could be another triumph, or we just might find that we, like him, have outmatched ourselves. But we have to be who we are.'

His eyes flicked to stare briefly at a praetorian officer walking up the stone stairs that led to the public gate below them. He gave the three men a cursory glance from beneath the gilded brow guard of his helmet as he went about his rounds, but if the guardsman recognised Marcus from his service with the imperial bodyguard there was no indication of it as he went on his way. Scaurus waited until he was out of earshot before speaking again.

'So, gentlemen, the facts are these. We have to lead our cohorts west to confront this deserter Maternus. It's either that, or watch our men march without us and then face the hard facts of Cleander's ire. And we have to do so in the company of two cohorts of the Guard, which, of course, raises the risk that Marcus may be recognised as the fugitive Valerius Aquila. But that we have no choice in the matter is beyond doubt. If we attempt to defy Cleander in this, I doubt it will end well for any of us.'

'And we have to leave Annia and the children behind us.'

Scaurus nodded.

'Yes, Marcus, we do. I know you made a promise to your son, but Cleander's discovery of the child's existence changes everything, I'm afraid. Not that I believe that leaving him to his mercies will make us any safer, given the nature of the men we'll be marching north alongside. Ultimately, though, Julius and the lady herself will have to make the decision, and with an understanding of exactly what it is that the chamberlain has decreed . . .'

He paused and smiled wryly at Cleander's very specific terms on taking their comrade's wife into the palace in their absence. The chamberlain had been unequivocal in his insistence on the point.

'The woman and children will move into the palace while you

are away. They will be well treated, you have my word on that, but I cannot allow them to remain at large any longer and neither can I let you spirit them away into Gaul, never to be seen again and forever a threat to the throne.'

'Your word.'

Cleander had simply smiled thinly at the acid in Marcus's tone.

'Yes, Valerius Aquila, my *word*. You may not trust me overmuch, but you can be assured that it's in my interests to make sure that this particular bastard remains safe. He will be granted the sanctuary of the Palatine, in one of the less grandiose buildings, tucked away from the public eye, along with the other two children. They will be well looked after, I promise you that, and when you consider the facts, you'll be forced to agree that it's in my best interests to keep him alive.'

Scaurus's bitter laugh had failed to trouble him beyond a raised eyebrow.

'Power broker you might have fleetingly been, Rutilius Scaurus, but you still fail to see the subtleties of the way a man like me is forced to manoeuvre if he is to keep his back safe from the knives his competitors would dearly love to plant between his shoulders. I need the child safe, gentlemen, not only as leverage to ensure your return but, to be frank, as my own means of ensuring the emperor's favour.'

'If the need arises, you'll sacrifice the child to keep your own skin intact.'

'Yes, Scaurus.' Cleander's tone hardened. 'Of course I will. What better way of proving my loyalty than to report the discovery of a bastard child, and to allow the emperor to determine his fate?'

Marcus stared out over the racetrack, watching as the strongest team of horses swept past the winner's post in a blur of pounding hoofs.

'He holds the power over us. And the power always wins until it is no longer the power. And on that day . . .'

'You'll make him pay.' Scaurus nodded his understanding. 'If, that is, we've not been quietly disposed of by the men we're being sent to fight alongside.'

Varus looked at the tribune with a raised eyebrow.

'You think that there might be potential threats among the praetorians?'

Scaurus smiled bleakly.

'Consider the facts, Centurion. We'd probably outlived our usefulness even before the unfortunate "death" of his spy on the governor's staff in Germania Inferior, which you can be assured he laid at our door the moment he learned of it, evidence or no evidence. Men like the chamberlain consider those they use for their most sensitive activities as resources, tools with a limited lifespan, and the conventional thinking among them is usually to dispose of those tools before their potential for failure is realised. I have no doubt that he considers us disposable, and until now it was only a question of when, not if, he would make the decision to have us dealt with. And now, I think it safe to say, that day is upon us.'

With Scaurus and his associates gone, Cleander stared at the map of the empire he controlled for so long that his principal secretary felt constrained to cough softly.

'I'm thinking.'

The scribe inclined his head.

'Indeed so, Chamberlain. I simply wished to remind you that the praetorian prefect and Centurion Lupinus are waiting upon your pleasure.'

His master nodded wearily.

'Send them in.'

The office doors were opened to admit the Guard's commander, who looked about him as he swept in, a swarthy faced centurion walking at his shoulder.

'This office of yours gets grander every time I visit, Chamberlain. I wonder if the emperor works in such splendour?'

Cleander raised an eyebrow.

'You wonder if the emperor *works*, Atilius Aebutianus? Whatever makes you think that our master would disrupt his constant enjoyment of pleasure with anything so mundane as the workings of the empire that exists only to provide him with the sources of his entertainment? And let us not delude ourselves that this is any sort of *visit*. This is business, Prefect, so I hope that you have come prepared to discuss the matter at hand.'

Aebutianus nodded dourly, ignoring the chamberlain's brusque put-down.

'My praetorians are of course ready to answer the emperor's call. Two cohorts of my men are readying themselves to march as we speak; Rome's finest soldiers.'

'Rome's finest soldiers.' The chamberlain allowed the statement to hang in the air for a moment, the silence doing his work for him. 'Possibly. Not that the title necessarily means all that much, given that the last time the Guard saw any fighting was a good ten years ago. Half of the men who fought alongside the last emperor are retired now, and the remainder have grey in their beards. Hardly worthy of the title "hardened in battle", although we'll spare no praise when your men march north. It does the city no end of good to imagine that your command have more in them than holding the populace back when the emperor decides to go out in public. And doubtless some of your men will prove themselves to be fit for their task, when they find themselves presented with it. Centurion Lupinus here, for example, has the look of a man whose backside won't be quivering when he draws his sword.'

He gestured to the officer, who had accompanied the prefect at Cleander's command, for reasons that he had led Aebutianus to believe were connected with the man's informal but highly sensitive role in palace life. The centurion, much as he had expected, stared back at him with the disinterested expression he wore most of the time.

'After all, he's clearly not troubled by my presence, and I've seen men struggling not to soil themselves at the slightest suggestion that my attention might be focused upon their affairs. Does nothing trouble you, Centurion?'

Lupinus shook his head, his voice a laconic drawl.

'No, Chamberlain. Any man who walks the streets with the emperor for long enough can be assured that Commodus will turn on him, eventually. But he's only done it to me once.'

Cleander nodded.

'I heard the story from the emperor himself. The version with which I was regaled was that you failed to express your amazement at his godly skill with the bow with sufficient sincerity. Which I'd have to say was a little unwise of you, given how much store he sets by his own martial prowess.'

The centurion shrugged.

'He's a decent enough shot. But when he told us for the third time that he was Hercules come back to earth again, it was all I could do not to laugh. Some hint of my amusement must have been obvious to the emperor.'

'And he put a sword to your throat.'

'Yes.'

The chamberlain frowned, raising an open hand in question.

'Were you not a little disconcerted? Afraid, even? He does have something of a reputation for violently impulsive behaviour.'

Lupinus shrugged.

'Afraid? Of course I was afraid. But I'm a soldier, Chamberlain. A centurion. The process of reaching that rank has a tendency to make a man either cautious or calculating. Cautious, for fear of losing what he has achieved, or calculating, as the result of working out the odds in every confrontation he had to win to get promoted. I am the latter.'

'And you calculated your way out of his putting that blade through you?'

The centurion nodded, his expression deadpan.

'I told the emperor that he wouldn't find another man like me to accompany him into the city anytime soon. And I looked him in the eyes as I said it; I showed him that I didn't give a fuck whether he killed me or not. And he lost interest in the thought of seeing my blood and started arguing with me that any other centurion in the Guard could do what I do for him without hesitation. I just laughed.'

Cleander's eyebrows rose in surprise.

'Now that's a first. You laughed at him and he let you live?'

'Not at him. Even I'm not that foolhardy. I told him I had to laugh at the idea that any of those tight-arsed sons of the aristocracy would last half a day without saying or doing something stupid, given the things Commodus gets up to when he's "in disguise", and after a moment he was laughing too.'

'Lucky for you that he was in a good mood.'

The centurion nodded.

'Possibly. But you know that old saying, don't you, Chamberlain? We make our own luck in this life.'

Cleander smiled.

'I've heard that said. And sometimes it's true. For a while.' He turned his attention back to a visibly-irritated Aebutianus. 'My apologies, Prefect. You were saying?'

'My men will be ready to march tomorrow morning, Chamberlain. We're just making the last adjustments to the composition of the cohorts in question.'

'I'm sure you're working assiduously to put the most warlike of your men into the field. After all, even a civilian such as myself knows that there are barracks soldiers and then there are real warriors, and it would of course be a dereliction of your duties were you to send any men less than perfectly suited to the sort of hardships and battlefield horrors that are likely to be required of them. Wouldn't it?'

The prefect frowned back at the man he considered a colleague, rather than a superior, wondering what lay behind his apparently supportive words.

'Yes. Yes, it would.'

'And I can imagine that you're more than busy enough with all that organisation and direction of the right men to the right positions without wasting time here talking to me. You are excused, Prefect; I only asked you here to ensure that you were on top of the task.' He smiled beneficently at the prefect's evident frustration at having his time wasted so blatantly. 'Your centurion can stay a while though. Perhaps he can illuminate the emperor's antics for me a little more clearly, and in so doing help me to ensure Commodus's safety. After all, with no heir, the last thing the empire needs at the present is a succession crisis if the emperor were to die without a son – much less the civil war that might result if one or more of the generals who command multiple legions were to take it into their heads to obey their soldiers' urgings to take the purple.'

Aebutianus nodded his agreement and withdrew with a narrow-eyed glare at his subordinate.

'I do so love to make the more powerful among us aware of the limits of their influence.' Cleander grinned at the remaining praetorian. 'I imagine you enjoy much the same emotions when you're out in the city with an emperor masquerading as one of your men?'

Lupinus shook his head.

'I'm usually more concerned with keeping one or two of my men between the unwashed scum and their ruler. He insists on taking us into the worst parts of the city, and the sort of people who live in the depths of the slums are more unpredictable than those who live on the hills. If they were to recognise him, they'd probably riot.'

'And either carry him on their shoulders or rip him to pieces. I can just imagine your nervousness.'

'Nervousness? More like readiness to use my sword.'

Cleander strolled away to the window, chuckling to himself.

'You're very much the man of action, aren't you? Don't you yearn for the chance to take that blade to a proper enemy?'

The centurion stared at him levelly.

'You want me to go on campaign.'

'How very perceptive of you. Yes, I want you to go on campaign.

I want you to march north alongside the auxiliary cohorts that I've allocated to this punitive expedition, and, when the time is right, I want you to take that blade you're so fond of and use it to kill a man for me. Or rather some men. Do you think you can do that? You will, of course, be very well rew—'

'Who?'

Cleander blinked at the interjection.

'Well, you're very sure of yourself, aren't you? Not many men get away with interrupting a man as powerful and, let's be clear, as alert to a slight as myself. And as to *who*, suffice to say you'll be clearing up a mess that the emperor – may his name be revered alongside that of the gods from whom he is so *clearly* descended – has contrived to create in one way and another. With, I might add, yourself as an active participant. He has, by contriving to seduce the wife of a very dangerous young man, both rekindled the flame of that man's enmity and sired a bastard son upon her. A son whom I intend to bring under the palace's wing in order to prevent his existence ever becoming known, lest every woman the man's ever shared a bed with come forward to claim money in return for their silence and have to be dealt with in their turn. And there are only so many people I can have killed before the rumour of there being dozens of imperial bastards takes hold of Rome. We'll have his illegitimate sons coming out of the woodwork for years. So I have decided that the best way to deal with this inconvenient birth will be to hide the child, along with the woman who has adopted him, and to liquidate everyone else who knows of his existence. The names are in this . . .' He passed the centurion a writing tablet. 'I suggest that you memorise them, seek them out, befriend them and then, when the time is right and if this man Maternus fails to do the job for you, kill them.'

Lupinus opened the tablet and considered the list of names for a moment.

'You're talking about the woman who lives on the Aventine Hill. The one he had me threaten with the death of both the children in the household.'

Cleander nodded.

'Lived. She died in childbirth, which has given her husband a double reason to hate Commodus, given that his father and family were murdered at the emperor's command in order to reinflate the imperial treasury with his wealth. He and his auxiliary protectors have been useful for the last couple of years, but every tool has a lifespan in even the most talented of hands, and this craftsman' – he put a hand to his chest – 'has decided to remove the risk that he and his comrades present.'

The praetorian stared at him for a moment.

'And when you say that I'll be very well rewarded, you do realise that I'll have to bribe a lot of men to make this thing happen?'

'Money really won't be the problem, Centurion. My secretary will ensure you have all the gold you need.'

'You must want these men dead very badly.'

Cleander nodded, his face lacking any emotion that the soldier could discern.

'Their service is no longer valuable enough to balance the danger they pose to the empire. Remove that danger for me and you may yet move upwards from the position of protecting Commodus from his own worst impulses. After all, we may make our own luck in this life but, as I can assure you from experience, no man's luck lasts forever, not where a man like Commodus is involved. I'm sure you'd find commanding a cohort a good deal less risky, quite apart from the financial benefits involved.'

The praetorian nodded.

'I will do as you wish, even though I suspect I may be exchanging a risk of one kind for another of a completely different nature. As you imply, Commodus may one day kill me in a fit of temper, but you, Chamberlain, would do it without even blinking, if you considered it essential. I see that same look when you consider my superior.'

The older man smiled slowly.

'Aebutianus? I put him where he is now, because I saw no

threat in him. And when the time is right, I'll pull the venal fool down from his pedestal and demonstrate how unwise he was to play a game for which he was not qualified. Tell me, he's busy selling exemptions from having to march north with the cohorts even as we speak, isn't he?'

Lupinus snorted a curt laugh.

'He's selling exemptions *and* the positions they leave open. The prefect's office is host to a series of men and their fathers, some of whom, as you suspected, wish to bribe him to post their sons to cohorts which will remain here in Rome, while others are willing to fatten his purse in order to secure a place in the cohorts that will march tomorrow.'

Cleander smiled.

'What an excellent piece of business, eh, Centurion? Selling an exemption only to then take another man's gold in return for the honour of the position opened up. One of these days I'll reel that fish in, once he's grown fat enough to make it worth the effort. But for now we'll allow him to have his fun, especially as it provides me with the perfect opportunity.' A dismissive hand gesture made it clear that the audience was at an end. 'Away with you, and make sure you take enough good men with you to get the job done. Tell the prefect to take it up with me if he has any problems with your being part of the Guard's vexillation and I expect you'll hear no more of it. Fool he may be, but he's cunning enough to know when to bluster and when to keep his mouth shut. As, I am quite certain, do you. And now you can be on your way.'

The praetorian turned towards the door through which he'd entered the room, a frown creasing his face as Cleander's senior secretary put a hand on his arm, seeking to guide him towards another, smaller door. The chamberlain smiled wryly, both at Lupinus's anger and the expression of fear it engendered in his assistant.

'You're best not laying hands on a man like the centurion, or he might decide to remove them. But he's right, Lupinus, we need you to leave by the alternative exit to that used by my usual visitors. It wouldn't do for my next appointment to see you. Tongues wag enough without that sort of provocation!'

'He's making me a *what*?'

'A prefect, First Spear. Or, as I'm now commanded to title you, *Prefect.*'

Julius stared at his superior in growing horror, flicking glances at Marcus and Varus who, forewarned by the tribune as to the Briton's likely reaction, kept their expressions carefully composed under his angry scrutiny.

'A prefect. Why the fuck would he name a rough-arsed barbarian like me as a *prefect*?'

'Because, *Prefect* – and you'd better get used to the idea because it isn't going to go away just because you don't fancy wearing bronze—'

'Like all those other useless bastards!'

'Like, as you so delicately put it, all those other useless bastards. And as to why, it's simple enough. Cleander intends to take the emperor's bastard son under his protection, so to speak, and the chance to add a hostage to that insurance is too good to resist. And since Felix can't safely be left to the whims of the ordinary palace staff, Annia will have to become a part of the royal household, even if they're kept in a remote part of the Palatine complex, probably alongside several other such children. For your wife to be quartered in the palace without exciting comment, she'll have to look the part of a noble woman, which is most simply achieved by promoting you to the equestrian rank and thereby instantly rendering Annia eligible for such distinction. The chamberlain signed the decree promoting you and granted you the base sum of money required without a minute's hesitation. And that means that from this moment' – Scaurus handed the stunned Tungrian a scroll and shook his hand – 'you are officially of exactly the same social status as I am. Colleague.'

Julius unrolled the parchment and read it from top to bottom before looking back up at his friends.

'But . . .'

'But nothing, you thick-headed fool!' Annia, who had sat in silence listening to Scaurus relate their meeting with Cleander with a face set in thoughtful lines, rose from her place and advanced on her husband with a finger raised, the usual sign that the roles traditionally observed between man and woman in their marriage were about to be reversed. 'For one thing, you're not being given a choice, and neither am I. Has that not sunk into your pea-sized brain yet, *Prefect*?' Her husband stared at her in startled bemusement as she continued without any apparent need to pause for breath. 'This bastard chamberlain is intent on getting control of little Felix, and if we try to avoid him doing it this way, we'll just end up being marched into the palace by a tent party of praetorians. And I can guess how that might end up being rather less enjoyable for me than the alternative. And besides, this way we get enough money to retire on in some quiet part of the empire when this is all done with—'

'If our throats haven't been cut!'

She stared at her husband for a moment with an expression that combined affection and irritation in equal parts.

'That's your part of the bargain, husband. I'll play the dutiful wife, suffer the hardship of being forced to dress and behave like a daughter of the city, and you can go off to war and work out how to avoid having your throat cut.'

Julius returned her gaze for a moment before nodding slowly and turning back to Scaurus.

'It would seem that I'm outflanked, Tribune.'

'It does, somewhat. Which means that I'll have to take you off into the city to get you equipped for your new position in society. But first I think we need to make some decisions as to who should replace you, don't you? After all, whoever it is will be wanting to go and acquaint his officers with his style of command, I'd have thought?'

Julius pursed his lips, gesturing at Marcus and Varus with a wave of his hand.

'Given that Cleander has ordered you to give Vibius Varus a cohort to command, and since you'll clearly need two men to fill my boots, I think you could do worse than make these two demonstrate some sense of responsibility for a change, instead of being allowed to run around causing trouble like poorly-trained children all the time.'

Scaurus smiled at his acerbic tone.

'You echo my own thoughts perfectly, Prefect. Centurion Corvus can take command of the First Cohort, while Centurion Varus can have the Second. It'll be a constant source of amusement for their men to see two sons of the aristocracy being told what to do by one of their own, I'd imagine. You two had better go and break the good news . . . and trust me, your officers are initially going to think it's the best news they've had all year, because they'll expect you both to be easier men to cope with than the prefect here. I suggest you both work out ways to prove that you're worthy of your new ranks without coming across as a pair of lunatics, and point out to them that the source of all that pain they've been suffering all these years hasn't gone anywhere other than upwards.'

'Which means that the weight of his disapproval just has further to fall, right?'

'Exactly right.' Julius stood, clenching his fists in a gesture of frustration. 'I think you're going to find me the most hands-on prefect you've ever served under, gentlemen. I will be setting exacting standards for my command, and you two will be dedicating yourselves to surpassing those expectations every day the gods grant me the breath to chastise you. Dismissed.' He inclined his head to Scaurus in a bow of respect. 'And now, *colleague*, I suppose you'll be wanting to take me on a tour of shopkeepers whose only goal in life is to extract large amounts of gold from the usually gullible ruling classes?'

Scaurus smiled beneficently.

'Correct, Prefect Julius. And I expect they'll all be delighted to see a brand-new member of the equestrian class darken their doorways. After all, you now have a different image to be maintaining than that of a man who sleeps with his vine stick. Speaking of which, I suggest you leave that sacred object in the capable hands of your wife.'

'A good idea.' Julius nodded, passing Annia the twisted and gnarled stick that had been, until moments before, his badge of rank. 'Look after this, my love, we never know when I'll be needing it again.'

His wife accepted his staff of office with a smile that, to Scaurus's eyes, signalled some less dignified fate for it other than to be carefully packed away and then conveniently lost.

'Go and spend some of our new-found wealth on the trappings of your new position in life, husband, but be warned that I'm expecting my share! Clothes, equipment and other campaign essentials are all fair game, but you'd better have enough left over for me to have my day in the silk market. Which means that you can leave the fancy swords to your new first spear.'

3

The guard centurion responsible for the security of the Palatine Hill's south-eastern gate called his chosen men to his side with a barked command, waving a hand at the guards standing stolidly on either side of the archway that crowned the steps up from the street below.

'Stay here and keep these idlers on their toes, Chosen; I'll escort the chamberlain's guests to the Domus Augustana.' He turned to look at Marcus and Julius with a dismissive expression that made it abundantly clear that they would not be accompanying Annia and the three children into the palace that would be their home for the foreseeable future. He raised the scroll they had been told to present on arrival at the palace. 'This pass specifies that the woman and children are to be admitted to the nursery in the private palace, and are to live under the care of the emperor's own household staff. It says nothing about anyone accompanying them.'

Shooting the two men a fierce warning glance, Annia stepped forward with a disarming smile that softened the centurion's demeanour by a fraction before she even spoke, her voice pitched low to further soften his resistance in a way her husband recognised all too well.

'What the pass doesn't tell you, Centurion, is that this man' – she pointed to Julius, who had the good sense to look suitably inoffensive for once – 'is my husband, and this officer' – Marcus inclined his head in a curt gesture of respect for the praetorian's authority – 'is the father of one of these children under my care, whose mother is now sadly deceased. They will both be marching north tomorrow, in the company of two of the Guard's cohorts, in pursuit of the bandit Maternus, and the emperor has been generous enough to take their loved ones under his wing while they are out of the city. The children and I are to be honoured guests of the imperial household, which is a source of great pride to all of us, as you can imagine. Under those terms, we were rather hoping that you might permit them both the pleasure and reassurance of accompanying us to our domicile? Quite apart from that, the two older children will need to be carried if we're to get them up all those stairs in less than a full hour.'

The praetorian looked the two men up and down, his eye lingering on their scarred faces and the thin purple stripes that adorned both men's tunics.

'I don't see any harm in it, as long as you mind your manners just as we're expected to. Can you manage that, gentlemen?'

Marcus nodded his head confidently in recognition of the point.

'I can assure you that we'll maintain the customary decorum that is expected of men of our rank, Centurion. My colleague here is a man of few words in any case.'

'Very well. And if we should come across the emperor, you are to follow my instructions immediately, understood? Don't make me regret this moment of soft-heartedness.' The praetorian turned away with a gesture for them to follow. Both men scooped up a child while Annia carried the baby, as they followed him into the palace grounds. Once they were out of earshot of his men, he spoke again, his tone less gruff than before. 'My apologies if I sounded a little terse, gentlemen, but you'll know how it is once you have a crest on your helmet. Standards have to be maintained, and soldiers like to know where they are with their officers.'

Marcus and Julius exchanged looks, the former first spear smiling knowingly at his successor. The younger man had found his officers in an ebullient mood when he had gathered them for their first centurions' meeting the previous day. Dubnus in particular had worn a smile that he had seemed unable to repress no matter how many pointed looks Marcus had shot at him. At length – tiring of his former colleagues' evident expectation that his promotion would result in an easier time of it for themselves and their men than Julius's regime of constant weapons practice and stamina training – his patience had finally been exhausted, and a barked imprecation had silenced them more abruptly than intended.

'Fuck *me*! Will you idiots just face the facts for a moment?' Waiting until the initial shock of his outburst had worn off, and been replaced by expressions of wary uncertainty, he had continued in calmer tones. 'What is it that you men are expecting from me? Because if it's honey cakes and wine, you're going to be sadly disappointed! Julius hasn't gone anywhere, or has that fact avoided you all? He's still going to be just as set on keeping us as fit as possible, and ready for battle at a moment's notice. So all the running and sparring that he's had you doing through the heat of the summer? It isn't going to change! Can you get that into your thick heads?'

The cohort's centurions had stared back at him with expressions ranging from mild disgust to stoic acceptance, a few heads nodding as the sense of what he was telling them sank in. Once he had issued orders for the cohort to parade at dawn the next day, ready to march for the northern side of the city and the praetorian fortress, he had dismissed them. He walked away towards his barrack to pack his chest, only to find Julius waiting for him.

'You were listening to that from behind the nearest barrack, if your amusement is anything to go by?'

His superior had nodded, his grin broadening.

'Not what you were expecting, was it? I guess I'm not the only man here having to adjust to something he didn't necessarily want.'

The younger man had nodded thoughtfully.

'It's a strange feeling. For years they've been my brothers, and even when I was temporarily a tribune, I still felt like one of them. But now . . .'

Julius had shrugged, his lips pursing in amusement at Marcus's realisation of the burden he had been passed.

'Now you're their father, mother and absolute ruler all rolled into one. And you might not have wished for the role, but you have it, so you'd better get on with doing it to the best of your abilities. I'd give you some advice on how best to manage them, but you know them just as well as I do. Better, in some cases. But keep them taut, *First Spear*, or you'll have a brand-new prefect up your arse from dawn to dusk. And while nobody will enjoy that, it's what will happen if it has to.'

The centurion led them through an archway into the palace's stadium, a sunken garden fully one hundred and fifty paces long by fifty wide, decorated with dozens of statues of gods and warriors; the occasional representation of a gladiator struck a discordant note that Marcus suspected reflected Commodus's obsession with the arena. The praetorian hissed a warning at them and raised an arm to halt their progress, recognising a burly, bearded figure holding a bow barely twenty paces distant, raised to shoot with an arrow nocked; an older man stood close by in an attentive pose.

'*Quiet.*'

Even as Marcus realised who the archer was, he released the first arrow. He reached for a second and fit it to the string while the first soared high over the garden, tipping over to fall towards the large straw target at the open space's far end. Marcus stared at Commodus with a hungry, calculating expression as he loosed arrow after arrow, each shot finding a home among the forest of fletching protruding from the closely packed straw. Shooting as fast as he could, the emperor emptied his quiver while the party stood in respectful silence and watched, the two older children kept quiet by the timely application of the cakes that Annia had brought with her for just such a moment. As the last arrow hit its mark, Commodus turned to the man beside him with a triumphant laugh, completely unaware of the onlookers standing quietly in the garden's shadows.

'There! I told you I could shoot all twenty without having to break my rhythm! And my style was . . . ?'

'Perfect, Caesar, as ever. You might have been inspired by Apollo himself.'

The younger man nodded knowingly, chuckling loudly as he gestured to the target.

'I might indeed. He is my half-brother, after all. Come, let us see what your tuition has done to improve my aim, shall we?'

The two men walked away down the garden with a senior praetorian officer trailing them at a discreet distance, his head constantly turning in search of any threat to Rome's master. The centurion lowered his arm and led them forward across the ground where Commodus had stood a moment before, speaking so quietly that his voice was barely more than a whisper.

'It pays not to distract the emperor when he's at his exercises. It's a good thing none of the children made a sound; he's not tolerant of any interruption.'

Annia smiled at the officer, whatever emotions she was feeling carefully disguised from him.

'As loyal subjects we know when our silence is required, Centurion. Shall we go and see our new quarters? Presumably they're a good distance from the emperor's private suite?'

As they climbed the long staircases that led up into the palace's higher reaches, Marcus caught glimpses of the view out to the south across the Circus Maximus, at first only obliquely but, at length, as they reached the highest floor of the massive stone building and the praetorian led them across to the edge of the balcony that overlooked the Circus, he found himself looking down into the huge arena from such a height that every seat in its sprawling structure was visible.

'It's quite a view, isn't it, gentlemen? And if you think it's impressive now, you can only imagine what it looks like when it's packed with a quarter of a million spectators.' He led them across the balcony to a door on the far side. 'And here's your accom-modation, madam.'

As the door opened, Marcus found himself staring in astonishment at what at first glance could have been taken for any nursery in the city were it not for the chamber's size and opulent decoration. Almost a dozen children between infancy and three years of age were to be seen, the youngest being tended in cots while those able to walk were playing with a scattered array of toys. The women, presumably their mothers, sat talking in twos and threes under the watchful eye of an older woman who was clearly responsible for the handful of young girls that were entertaining and caring for the children. Walking across the room to greet them she bowed deeply to Annia, who was careful to return the greeting in the more restrained fashion expected of a woman of her new-found rank.

'You must be Annia? I was warned to expect your arrival with these delightful children, although not, it has to be said, that of these gentlemen?'

Annia smiled winningly at her, shifting Felix to her other arm and taking the older woman by the hand in greeting.

'Indeed I am, and these are my children, Victoria and Felix, and my husband, Julius. And this fine fellow is Appius, the son of this gentleman.'

The men set their children down and bowed, drawing a smile from the nursery mistress.

'Greetings, Domina,' Marcus said, 'and our apologies for the surprise of our presence. My colleague here and I simply wished to see Annia and the children safely to their new home, and to reassure ourselves as to its suitability. Which is more than obvious. We can go on campaign knowing that our loved ones are in safe hands.'

The nursery mistress regarded him with a stare that, if not unfriendly, was at the very least calculating.

'Indeed they are, sir. I make sure that these ladies remain untroubled by the workings of the palace and are free to simply relax and enjoy the pleasures of motherhood. And now, if you're happy with all that you've seen . . . ?'

Taking their cue, the two men bowed and left, accompanying the praetorian centurion back down the stairs to his guard post and listening politely to him recounting his experiences in the palace.

'The one thing that we know never, ever to do is to distract the emperor when he's practising with his weapons. It could be a death sentence on the wrong day, knowing the way his whims come and go. And nobody but him gets to touch his weapons either, not unless he trusts them completely. He keeps that bow locked in a special shrine to Apollo at the other end of the stadium garden, and he's the only man allowed to so much as lay a finger on it – other than his master of archery, who has the job of keeping it in perfect condition, ready for Commodus to use whenever the fancy takes him.'

The three men walked out into the stadium and paused for a moment to enjoy its beauty.

'He considers himself to be a master of the bow?'

The praetorian looked around before replying to Marcus's question, despite the garden being empty other than a group of slaves manicuring the foliage at its far end.

'Caesar considers himself divinely gifted.'

He walked on, not giving the friends an opportunity to reply, ushering them through the gate and turning away without another word. Julius held his own silence until they were halfway down the steps to the street below.

'He was quite talkative until you asked that last question. Why did he go quiet, do you think?'

Marcus shrugged.

'The natural caution of a guardsman, perhaps. With an emperor like Commodus, I'd imagine the best thing to do is to forget what you've seen or heard just as quickly as you can, because I doubt there'd be any second chances given to a man given to gossip.'

His friend nodded dourly.

'And don't think I didn't see the look in your eye when you caught sight of him. Whatever else that witch gave you doesn't seem to have included the gift of forgiveness. I was half expecting you to go for him bare-handed. That would have made for an interesting last few moments for us both.'

The younger man shrugged.

'I rejected the idea before I'd even taken the time to consider how likely we were to get to him with a fully-armed tribune between him and us, not to mention the guardsmen littering the garden. It occurred to me that I was with a woman and three children, one of them my own son, and that was enough to stop any thoughts of revenge. If Gerhild didn't give me the ability to forgive what he did to my wife, she did do something to me that tempered my anger to the degree that I won't sacrifice those I love to kill him. And to be honest with you, all I felt when I saw him was disgust.'

'Do you still want revenge for what he did, then?'

Marcus shrugged.

'Revenge? Not as such. That would be a hot-tempered act, likely to result in my own death and most likely that of my friends. No, what I have in mind for the emperor, whether it was put there by the priestess or has simply grown from its own seed, is something much more subtle than simple revenge. And now, Prefect, I suggest we put all thoughts of such a thing from our minds and prepare ourselves to cope with the plans that the emperor's chamberlain has put in place to prevent our ever seeing our loved ones again. Thoughts of revenge will have to be delayed until we know we're not going to end our days in a ditch somewhere north of the Alps with our throats cut.'

'Here they come!'

The men behind Marcus fell silent from their usual, constant buzz of almost-inaudible commentary on the world around them – the complaints, witticisms and outright abuse that they considered their right as hard-bitten veterans of half a dozen campaigns – and stared with open curiosity at the leading centuries of the two cohorts marching onto the praetorian fortress's parade ground, upon which the Tungrians were already drawn up in an impeccably straight line. The young centurion's amused recollection of Julius's strongly expressed view that no barracks soldier was going to outdo him when it came to the sharpness of their respective unit's foot drills, was interrupted by the sound of a familiar voice close behind him.

'Praetorian Guard? I've had harder shits! They look like over-dressed arse-poking—'

'The First Century will be *silent!*' He turned on the spot to face the men of his new century, lifting his vine stick to point at a soldier in the front rank. 'You! Soldier Brutus! The next time I hear your voice between now and when we leave this parade ground, I'll give you a memory of today that you'll take to your grave!'

The front ranker stared at him for a moment in something approaching disbelief before raising a hand to his helmet in a belated salute, muttering something to the man next to him that, whilst inaudible, bore all the visual hallmarks of a shocked imprecation, and Marcus played a hard stare across the awestruck faces of his new century before turning back to contemplate the marching guardsmen.

'They might look like they spend all their time polishing their helmets, but having spent a good few months on duty in there . . .' he gestured to the fortress looming over the wide, open space onto which the two Tungrian cohorts had paraded after a long and complaint-strewn march around the city's walls, necessitated by the iron rule that no weapons could be carried in the streets, 'I would expect that those men will be every bit as good as we are.'

Varus nodded earnestly beside him, having strolled down the Tungrian line from his place in front of his new command to join his friend. He was still trying to accustom himself to filling the First Cohort's equivalent position and watched the oncoming guardsmen with a curiosity that was every bit as critical, if less vocal, than that of the men behind him.

'They're certainly well enough equipped. If a little . . . gaudy?'

The marching praetorians' turnout was a glittering splendour of rich colour and shining metal, their unmarked tunics a uniform shade of crimson, while the Tungrians were clad in a motley assortment of hues depending on their garments' ages. Where the auxiliaries were equipped with head protection from half-a-dozen different makers scattered across the empire's sprawling territory – each one subtly different from the next, but all starkly utilitarian in their brutalist design – the guardsmen were equipped with perfectly identical helmets, each topped with brass cross-ribs that rose to a central peak, their brow guards heavier than the usual pattern produced by the imperial armouries, with intricately decorated gilt and silver polished to a high shine. Varus shook his head at the contrast between the men before them and their own soldiers.

'Look at their armour.'

Each guardsman wore a leather-backed coat of tinned and polished scales, the thick metal discs each the size of a small apple in cross section and overlapped to put multiple layers of iron in the path of an enemy blade or point, their high shine making the Tungrians squint as the morning sun glittered almost painfully brightly from their mirror-like finish. Marcus laughed.

'Never mind their armour, it's their weapons that will have this lot behind us scheming about ways to upgrade their own iron.'

Every man was carrying a pair of sturdily constructed spears, their iron shanks double-riveted to the wooden shafts, wickedly barbed iron heads sharp enough to wink in the sunlight; but it was the swords they wore which were exciting comment in the Tungrian ranks. Every man had a long-bladed spatha on his left hip and a silver-inlaid dagger on the right, the weapons suspended by glossy brown belts and baldrics whose brass fittings shone with the same evident high polish that typified their overall turnout.

'Very pretty. But can they fight, I wonder?'

Marcus turned to find Dubnus strolling down the cohort's line from his place in front of the Tenth Century with his axe over his armoured shoulder, shaking his head in disparagement.

'Can they fight? I'd say so.' Marcus shrugged at his friend's bemused stare. 'Before you write them off as whatever it was that Julius called them earlier – "Palatine ponces", wasn't it? – consider this: every man in those ranks had to present proof of good character from men of genuine influence or responsibility before he could even enter selection, so there are far fewer thieves over there than there are behind us. And at least a third of the men who're accepted for induction are washed out before the end, usually because they can't stomach the hardships they're being put through. There's a training camp in the hills to the south of the city which turns out trained soldiers who aren't even allowed to set foot in the fortress until they're ready for service in every respect. And it's run by the hardest and nastiest centurions in the Guard, men at the end of their careers who aren't ever going to be tribunes but who are determined to make sure that—'

'Hang on. Their centurions can become tribunes?'

The young Roman nodded, smiling at his friend's open-mouthed amazement.

'It's not just a possibility, it's the rule even in these days of naked patronage. The emperor is guarded by men who are jealous of their traditions, and who make sure that he knows those traditions and supports their continuation. Cleander might be free to nominate his own man to command them as prefect, but the Guard appoints its own tribunes from within, and even then only after they've been through a selection that's arduous enough to put most men off the idea. And there'll be a good proportion of battle-hardened men in their ranks, I expect, given they were at war with the Quadi not so long ago.'

The second praetorian cohort was making its entry onto the parade ground in the wake of the first, and the hard-faced officer marching at their head cast an appraising eye across the Tungrian ranks as they passed the auxiliaries, his gaze alighting on the three centurions and lingering for a moment. His eyes momentarily narrowed as they met Marcus's stare.

'You know him?'

The young Roman nodded.

'I did, years ago. Whether or not he recognises me is rather more important.'

The officer in question snapped his eyes back to the front, bellowing a command at the men behind him that had Dubnus's head nodding in approval.

'He's got a good set of lungs on him, whoever he is. And I'll bet Morban wishes he was carrying a standard with that much silver on it.'

The standard bearer and trumpeter marching in their tribune's wake were resplendent in lion-skin capes, the beasts' snarling heads fixed to their helmets in a magnificent display, the former hefting a standard so heavy with decoration that it would clearly have been an effort for him to hold it aloft had he not been graced with the physique of a champion athlete. Varus laughed, shooting a glance at the awe-struck men behind him.

'Let's hope he sleeps with it cuddled up in his blanket, or he might find it somewhat less ornate come morning.'

'Not even Morban will be able to get within twenty paces of that much wealth, which is just as well because those boys have the look of men who wouldn't take the slightest insult to their dignity well.' Julius was strolling down the First Cohort's line toward them, dazzling in his new polished bronze armour, his face twisted by a wry smile at his men's bemusement. 'Tribune Scaurus and I are summoned to a commanders' conference by their senior tribune. And you, Prince Dubnus . . .' the muscular axeman rolled his eyes at his superior's customary reference to his long-defunct tribal status, 'and you, First Spear Varus, are also required. Dubnus, your role is to look fearsome without actually giving offence, so you can put that sneer away right now, and you, Centurion Varus, are to present an example of the centurionate's magnificence whilst being sure to inscribe anything worth taking note of into your tablet in your neatest handwriting. Not your usual scrawl, which resembles nothing better than the result of a particularly pissed spider trying to stagger home from the tavern.'

The young officer grinned, nodding happily at the good-natured abuse.

'Handwriting wasn't my first interest as a boy, Prefect, it must be admitted.'

Julius raised a jaundiced eyebrow.

'Evidently not. I'd imagine you were more interested in trying to get your leg over any of the female slaves who stood still for long enough. Anyway, the two of you can come with me to see what it is that these praetorians expect of us. And you, First Spear Corvus, can stay here, keep the men in order and most importantly avoid being spotted by anyone that remembers you from your time in their ranks.'

'I trust you'll agree that the cohorts look magnificent, Chamberlain?'

Cleander leaned against the fortress wall's parapet with a hard smile, watching as centurions roamed the line of their guardsmen, berating them for infractions both real and imagined.

'I can see that all the money we've poured into their equipment seems to have been well spent. And I can see the usual obsession with perfection on the behalf of your officers.'

Aebutianus raised an eyebrow.

'But . . . ?'

The chamberlain shrugged.

'All of that has its place, of course, in any palace guard. I was simply wondering how your men will perform in battle.'

His subordinate, too intelligent to take umbrage, smiled confidently.

'I have no doubt that they'll perform excellently. Half of them are veterans from the war with the Quadi, the other half are the very best men available from across my ten cohorts. And their leadership is first class. Victor is the cleverest of my tribunes, and will drive the campaign's strategy and planning like the Blessed Julius reborn, and Sergius is the most fearsome officer under my command. Once he and his men are allowed to slip their collars they'll make short work of this deserter.'

'Hmmm.'

The prefect pulled a pained face.

'You doubt my men's capabilities, Cleander?'

The chamberlain shrugged.

'Not at all. I'm sure those officers you've posted to join the cohorts in question weren't just chosen for the weight of their gold.' He paused for a moment to let the implications of the statement sink in. 'Doubtless they represent the cream of Roman manhood, superbly trained and equipped. And yet . . .' Aebutianus waited in silence for the man who was effectively his master to expand upon whatever it was that was on his mind. 'The thing is, Prefect, that the men of your command haven't seen anything more disturbing than a few drunken revellers at Saturnalia since they came back from Germania. They've had time to relax and get comfortable since their return – in what passed for triumph, when the emperor went against the advice of his generals and settled matters peaceably with the Quadi. You could almost wish that the war had continued and provided a training ground for your cohorts to be rotated in and out of. Instead of which they've had too many years of peace and quiet, standing guard on imperial palaces and slowly but surely losing their edge. Whereas those Tungrians . . .'

The other man shook his head in amusement.

'The auxiliaries? Please, Chamberlain, let's not try to compare the two.'

Cleander turned slowly to look at him.

'Did you see action in the German wars, Prefect?'

'I accompanied the legions—'

'That wasn't what I was asking you, was it? Did you actually get your sword wet? Did you face the enemy in battle?' He waited for a moment. 'No, as we both know, you did not. And neither did I. But as a diligent member of the imperial household, I made a point of seeking out those senior officers who had fought face to face with the Marcomanni and the Quadi. And the stories they told me, when I'd indulged them sufficiently in wine and women, were both chilling and deeply informative as to why men fight. And, more to the point, what makes them fight in the way that they fight.'

'Which means what, Chamberlain?'

Cleander held his subordinate's stare long enough that the other man started to become openly nervous.

'Which means, Prefect, that while you look at those auxiliaries and see men whose tunics, helmets and armour is mismatched, and whose presentation is in no way the equal of your cohorts', I see the men who fought and won in Britannia, and Gaul, and Dacia, and Parthia. They've been thrust into the fire so many times that they're perfectly tempered. The weak have either been killed or made stronger, and the strong have been made near-indestructible. When they fight, it won't be showy, but you can be assured that it'll be dangerous to whomever they face.' He shook his head to dispel the reverie. 'No matter, your tribunes will learn soon enough that the ragged dog they've been paired with has sharp teeth. You made sure that the officer I ordered to accompany the expedition was included in the roster, I presume?'

Aebutianus nodded.

'I did. Although I can't for the life of me understand what motivated your instruction.'

The chamberlain smiled.

'Those auxiliaries down there have a master who is, to say the least of it, a potential threat to the throne. So he needs to be dealt with, and prevented from posing any further threat. And yes' – he raised a hand to forestall any comment from the prefect – 'I could simply have ordered his death, but since I suspect that he is a major part of what has made them successful over the last few years, I want him alive until the renegade Maternus has been dealt with. So your man goes along for the ride and, when the task that Scaurus has been set to perform is done, he is to complete his own orders and liquidate the targets I've detailed to him. One way or another, Prefect, the Tungrians will be shorn of their upstart leadership and returned to their duty station in Britannia to get on with their lives under a new commander. Either that, or your man had better not come back at all.'

'Tribune Scaurus.'

The shorter of the two praetorian tribunes stepped forward and offered Scaurus his hand, a smile of genuine pleasure creasing his face. As Scaurus had already noted, both men wore exactly the same equipment as their guardsmen, eschewing the finer quality leather and precious metals that were frequently used in the equipping of the empire's ruling classes, with the exception of a decorative amulet hanging from a heavy silver bracelet on the tribune's right wrist. Scaurus noticed it as they shook hands, a golden scorpion the size of a man's thumbnail with eyes that glinted purple in the sunlight.

'I'm Quintus Statilius Victor, Tribune, and the commanding officer of this combined force that Chamberlain Cleander has seen fit to send after one of our own who has fallen from grace. And this . . .' he stepped to one side to make room for his more heavily-built comrade, 'is my colleague Sergius.'

The second tribune stepped forward and shook hands with Scaurus, looking at the other Tungrian officers standing behind their tribune with the sharp eye of a man adept at judging his fellows at a glance. Scaurus extended a hand to gesture his men forward.

'Allow me to introduce my officers. Prefect Julius is my deputy, and has filled that role since his predecessor died in Gaul defeating another bandit much like this man Maternus.'

Both he and Victor smiled as the two big men clasped hands, both of them looking the other in the eye to take the other's mettle. After a moment's silent mutual appraisal, the praetorian barked out a laugh that adeptly broke the growing tension.

'Put him down, Sergius, there'll be plenty of time for you both to work out which of you is the most manly later.'

Obeying his colleague's jocular instruction, the big man nodded at Julius and released his hand, both men stepping back with a knowing look at the other.

'This . . .' Scaurus indicated Dubnus, 'is the centurion of my pioneer century, Dubnus, a prince of the Briganti tribe in Britannia. The axe is supposed to be for use in field engineering work, but my pioneers seem to have come to regard it as a source of divinity in battle rather than a tool. And this is Gaius Vibius Varus, a young gentleman of the senatorial class who has chosen to attach himself to my command in search of experiences a little more challenging than those usually found at the foot of the *cursus honorum*. He commands my Second Cohort at the express command of Chamberlain Cleander.'

Victor nodded.

'We have heard your name, Vibius Varus. Your stories of these cohorts' exploits in Parthia have been the talk of the city's militarily-experienced men for most of the last few months.' He laughed at the younger man's bafflement. 'Don't look so surprised. Dinner table conversation on such a fascinating subject races around Rome faster than you might imagine. Tell me, Tribune Scaurus, did you really manage to hold off an entire Parthian army with a single legion on an open battlefield? If asked whether such a thing could be done, I would have considered it an impossibility.'

Scaurus nodded gravely.

'It was a happy combination of equipment and tactics that allowed us to send both their cataphract cavalry and their infantry away with their tails between their legs. Although had we not been able to take refuge in the city of Nisibis, I suspect that the eventual outcome might have been less fortuitous. The plains of Adiabene have seen more than one Roman army come to grief, and I was simply grateful not to have joined their number in the Underworld.'

The praetorian raised an eyebrow.

'It was my experience in Germania that skilled command is

usually required to make the most of even the best equipment and tactics. Perhaps you'll indulge me in the story of that campaign later, over a cup of wine? I'm always interested in the workings of such a victory, whereas my colleague here would probably prefer to closet himself with your prefect. His predilection, like yours, I suspect, Prefect Julius, is for valour in battle and the joy of leading men forward to defeat a wild-eyed barbarian horde.' He paused, looking around at the Tungrian officers with an expression that was abruptly business-like, giving the lie to his previous relaxed jocularity. 'But that, I propose, will be for discussion this evening once we've put some miles under our boots. Given that my guardsmen are garrison troops, and that your men have been sitting around in a transit barracks for the best part of the last six months, I'd suggest that we set a sensible pace for the first few days. Maternus has been plaguing the western provinces for years now, so it makes little odds whether we arrive a day or two later than if we'd flogged our men to the full campaign distance from day one and destroyed their feet for the best part of a week. Shall we make the marching distance fifteen miles today, Tribune Scaurus?'

Scaurus inclined his head in agreement.

'As you suggest, Tribune Victor.'

'Very well, gentlemen, let's give those idlers watching us from the walls something decent to watch, shall we? My cohorts will lead and yours can tuck in behind. We'll march at the standard pace for the first hour, and let them get accustomed to the feel of the road under their boots before we have an experimental few miles at the forced march. Oh, and feel free to encourage your men to sing as many of their doubtlessly highly-amusing marching songs as possible. My praetorians haven't heard any of the old favourites for years, so it'll be a reminder of days past.' He grinned at Scaurus knowingly. 'And be assured that you'll be getting the sentiment returned just as loudly as my boys can roar out *their* old favourites. Dismissed.'

As the Tungrians saluted, Sergius spoke again, his blunt statement delivered in an almost matter-of-fact tone of voice.

'And give my personal regards to Marcus Valerius Aquila, will you? I used to wonder where it was that he found to hide when he vanished from our ranks five years ago, and now it seems my question has finally been answered.'

The praetorian nodded tautly to Julius as he turned to follow his superior away, Scaurus and his men staring after them for a moment before the tribune spoke.

'Well, at least that's once piece of uncertainty out of the way. Get our men ready to march, Prefect. We'll worry about First Spear *Corvus* later, shall we?'

At Victor's barked commands, the praetorians were already on the move, turning from line to column of march in one perfectly coordinated movement that spoke of months of practice. The Tungrians hefted their shields and spears in readiness for Julius's order to follow their example, stamping to attention with a precision that told its own story as to the amount of parade ground work he'd enforced in the previous week.

'Tungrians . . . at the march . . . *march!*'

Scaurus nodded appreciatively, as the First Cohort's leading century ground past them in a cacophony of clattering hobnails and the rasp of iron armour against wooden shield boards, grinning at the fixed expressions of soldiers who knew that their prefect's eyes were upon them.

'Very nice, Julius. Let's hope they can handle a day marching in the dust kicked up by those peacocks.'

His senior centurion turned a hard smile on him, gesturing to the head of the column in obvious invitation for his tribune to take the position of honour alongside his leading troops.

'I think you'll find my men more than capable of tucking away a quick fifteen miles, Tribune. But then they've not spent most of the last three months on horseback, have they?'

'Ha! If I didn't know better, I'd take that as a challenge, Prefect! Don't you worry about me!'

Striding up the column to its head, Scaurus settled into the marching pace with the ease of a man who had covered thousands of miles alongside his men. Once the column had passed the last outskirts of the city, he turned to walk backwards and grin back at his subordinate.

'Do we have no songs, Prefect? I distinctly remember Tribune Victor inviting us to try out our repertoire on his men!'

Arching an eyebrow, Julius shrugged and shouted the first line of a song that was an old favourite whenever praetorians took the field alongside the rest of the army.

> *'Praetorian heroes, legends in the city . . .'*

The Tungrians roared out the second line with gusto, clearly having been waiting for their opportunity to make themselves heard to their gloriously armed and equipped comrades.

> *'Look down on us with sneers of pity,*
> *Armour of gold and equipment so fine,*
> *You can fuck off back to the Palatine!'*

He grinned at the men marching in front of the Tungrians, taking a deep breath for the song's chorus.

> *'Fuck off back to the Palatine,*
> *Help the emperor drink his wine,*
> *We'll reap the enemy with our spears,*
> *While you grab each other's ears!'*

As the soldiers sang the words 'with our spears' they rattled their spear shafts against the brass bosses of their shields, punctuating the roared words with a storm of sound.

> *'Praetorian masters of the world,*
> *Fawned upon by every girl,*
> *Gleaming armour with a dazzling shine,*
> *You can fuck off back to the Palatine!'*

They roared the chorus out again, the rap of wood on brass even louder than the time before.

> *'Legends on the battlefield,*
> *Last into battle and first to yield,*
> *Conquerors of the Parthian deserts,*
> *On the back of other men's efforts!'*

The last line of the final chorus was barely complete before the men marching in front of them responded, evidently ready to rise to the customary challenge.

> *'The emperor's bodyguard, once again,*
> *Proudly ignoring blood and pain,*
> *Battling the foe with all our might,*
> *Showing the rest of you how to fight,*
> *Proud praetorians have stood and died,*
> *Guarding your backs when you ran to hide!'*

With the day's battle lines swiftly drawn, the four cohorts marched away from the city happily swapping insulting verse until, growing tired of the bickering, Julius marched up the column to confer with Sergius, ignoring the jibes thrown at his back by the praetorians. He then waited at the roadside until the leading Tungrian century reached the spot.

'That's agreed, then. I'm bored to tears of hearing songs about praetorians and Sergius says that if he never hears his men giving voice to their disgust for anything *not* praetorian again it'll still be a day too soon. So from now on we're all going to sing the same songs, starting with an old favourite of mine that Sergius happens to favour as well.' He raised his voice to be heard by enough of his officers that the order would quickly be passed down the two cohorts' length. 'We will sing "The Centurion's Lament"!'

*

'To our success. Victory!'

Tribune Victor raised his wine cup as he proposed the toast, and the officers gathered around the fire followed suit before drinking. The four cohorts had made steady progress in their march north throughout the day, and as a reward for their efforts, the tribunes had agreed to forego the usual routine of digging out a marching camp. It was quite obvious, they had agreed, that no enemy was likely to present itself in the heart of the empire, that none of their troops was likely to attempt a desertion and, most practically of all, that the effort of digging out the usual ditch and turf walls would only have added insult to the injury already being suffered by the farmer on whose land their tents had been pitched.

Sergius refilled his cup and that of his superior before passing the jug to Scaurus. When the Tungrians had replenished their own cups, he raised his in salute to Marcus, who had accompanied tribune, prefect and his fellow senior centurion to the commanders' meeting at Scaurus's suggestion. The tribune had shaken his head when Julius had raised the possibility that the apparent acceptance of the younger man's presence might be some elaborate ruse to lure him out.

'If they had wanted to make his presence here known to the authorities, they would have done so before we left Rome, I'd have thought.' He turned to Marcus. 'And given that our praetorian colleagues are willing to overlook your presence, First Spear, I think under the circumstances they at least deserve your thanks.'

In the meeting, while Victor had watched the fugitive officer in silence, keeping his own counsel on the matter, Sergius had been openly welcoming to his former comrade in arms.

'And here's to your survival, Valerius Aquila. You're not the same man I once commanded, are you? The face is the same, if a little marked by experience . . .' he gestured to the scars across the bridge of the younger man's nose and cheek, 'but then you were little more than a youth – though blessed with divine talent when it came to blade work, it has to be admitted – when you disappeared from Rome. And now here you are, the warrior you must have needed to be to survive with these men, and yet at the same time, it seems to me, different in personality as well as in body. I recall a spirited young man, at ease with himself and the men around him, but now you seem more reserved.'

The Roman raised his cup in salute and sipped at the wine before replying, aware that Scaurus was watching them both intently.

'The scars that are visible on my body are not the only damage I have incurred, Tribune, both in the empire's service and at the hands of its rulers. When I left the praetorian fortress to ride north, I believed I was being sent to Britannia to bear an urgent and highly confidential message to the legatus of the Sixth Legion. If I had known what evil was intended towards my family, I would have stayed.'

The praetorian nodded slowly.

'I'm sure you would. And you would have died, of course.'

Marcus nodded.

'Undoubtedly.'

Victor broke his contemplative silence with a knowing look at the younger man.

'And, if you had suffered the same fate as your father, your mother and sisters, you would never have had the chance for revenge on their killers, would you?' The Tungrians looked back at him in silence, and he shook his head in quiet amusement. 'Come now, gentlemen, let's not be coy. There was a series of high-profile deaths in Rome quite recently, while I was serving my term in the vigiles and therefore in a good position to know the facts of the matter. An array of prominent men died, one after another, all apparently in unconnected incidents. One of them was one of our colleagues, a centurion of high reputation, but whose darker side was no secret to those who knew him, and whose close relationship with our own former prefect was poorly disguised from those of us with the eyes to see it. Another was a notorious gang leader, and the third a senator infamous for his predilection for preying upon those weaker than himself and his circle of depraved friends. Taken together, they seemed to typify a certain type of man, ruthless and without any scruple. And interestingly, both Sergius and I had seen all three of them together on occasion within the palace, albeit clandestinely, after our return from Germany. Even the less thoughtful among us were capable of putting the facts together and realising that our prefect had assembled a collection of murderers to do Commodus's bidding. Though in reality it was his own; he wanted to remove any perceived source of opposition to the emperor's inheritance of the throne, and as a useful consequence refill the imperial treasury – and of course to line our prefect's own purse by the same means. Their deaths, in short and violent succession, would have been enough on their own to signify that someone was exacting revenge for their past actions, but that wasn't all that happened in those few weeks, was it?'

He stared at Marcus for a moment, then shook his head in amusement at the younger man's blank face.

'You've become accomplished at the art of the blameless expression, I see. Very well, since you *seem* to be unaware of it, those murders were accompanied by the brief but brilliant career of a gladiator whose abilities are still discussed among the devotees of the arena. What was his name now? He was accompanied by a big brute of a man the games masters called Dubnus, which is something of a coincidence given that your pioneers are commanded by just such a man who goes by the very same name. But his name, this mercurially swift swordsman, what was it?' He waited a moment longer before nodding in apparent remembrance. 'Ah yes, I recall it now. This short-lived young hero took the name *"Corvus"*, didn't he, Sergius? He carved a path through the blade fodder that was thrown at him with the single-minded purpose of a man whose eyes were fixed on a greater prize, and then he disappeared without trace, although not before the two greatest fighters of the day – one of them the last member of the gang of assassins I was talking about a moment ago, the other his brother

– had met their ends within days of each other.' He leaned forward, fixing Marcus with a hard gaze. 'You came back for revenge, didn't you?'

Marcus nodded wordlessly, and Victor turned to Scaurus with a knowing look.

'And the curious thing, colleague, is that only weeks before all that happened, a small party of men were admitted to the palace by the man who now serves as the emperor's chamberlain. They were spirited through the secret ways used by the Palatine Hill's slaves and freedmen to move quickly and quietly behind the scenes, according to the officers who were on duty in the palace that night, to an audience with the emperor himself. And what they revealed to Commodus was that our own prefect was plotting to replace him, as a result of which revelation he met an end every bit as grisly as anything inflicted upon your centurion's family. You struck a bargain with Cleander, didn't you, Tribune? You provided him with the proof he needed to unseat the emperor's right-hand man, and in return you put him in that man's seat. And in doing so you made a bargain of the most dangerous kind, with a man as lacking in scruples as a snake.'

Scaurus nodded.

'I did. I believed that it was the only way to prevent Perennis from hunting us down and having my entire cohort either executed or exiled.'

'And now you find yourself used for one dirty job after another. Your mission to the east was evidently a brilliant success, but you weren't supposed to survive it, were you?'

'I suspect not.'

The praetorian shook his head.

'I *know* not. Our men hear everything that happens on the Palatine Hill, Rutilius Scaurus, and while they know how to keep their mouths shut, they also know that it is their duty to tell their officers everything they hear. Their centurions in turn pass that intelligence to their tribunes without hesitation, who in turn report it to the prefect. And when he thinks it fit, Aebutianus briefs selected members of our tribunate with the salient details of the way Cleander rules. I know the lengths he has gone to in his efforts to see you buried on a distant battlefield, and his growing frustration with your continued survival, even if you do provide him with the results he demands of you. Which leads me to believe that there will be men among our ranks who have been tasked with your deaths, once Maternus has been dealt with, even if our prefect has had no part in that scheming.'

'I suspected as much. But why would you . . .'

'Why would I be so frank with you? The Guard, Rutilius Scaurus, is a proud institution. We've had our moments of venality, of course, we've betrayed emperors and sold the throne to the men who succeeded them, but that was over a hundred years ago, and even Cleander hasn't managed to pervert us that badly. Not yet, at least. If there are would-be assassins within our ranks, then they have nothing to do with myself or Sergius. We are men of honour who have served Rome all of our adult lives, and we will not stoop to connive at the deaths of good servants of the empire. So watch your backs, gentlemen, and if you have cause to deal with such an assassin, then do so in a way that will appear either accidental or, at worst, a murder without an owner.'

Scaurus inclined his head in genuine gratitude.

'Thank you. I doubt that any such step will be taken before Maternus has been dealt with, but I appreciate your willingness to look the other way. And I suspect that bringing your former colleague to justice will not be the simple task expected in the corridors of the palace.'

'Simple? Maternus? Not likely!'

Sergius broke his silence with a barked laugh, shaking his head in dark amusement, and Victor nodded his agreement.

'Maternus is one of our own, the product of the hardest selection and training in all of the empire, a man who was one of the chosen few clearly destined to bear the rank of tribune. Take no umbrage when I tell you that, distinguished though your achievements are, Rutilius Scaurus, the route to the tribunate is a good deal easier for a man born into the equestrian class than for men like myself and Sergius. Men like us have to join the Guard as soldiers, and prove ourselves as both intelligent and fearsome enough to command a century, and for most of us that is enough to satisfy our ambitions. That wasn't the case for either of us, though, and so we chose to submit ourselves to the most precarious of challenges in seeking to command praetorian cohorts. We were selected to leave the Guard, once we had risen to the rank of senior centurion, and to join in the legions at the same rank, commanding cohorts, with the challenge of rising to the rank of legion first spear. Sergius went to Britannia to serve with the Twentieth Legion, commanding them for a year before he returned to Rome and presented himself for the next challenge. He was given the gold ring of the equestrian class by the emperor himself, and then served time commanding both a cohort of the vigiles and then one of the three Urban Cohorts. The intention, I'm told, is to ensure that the Guard is commanded by men who understand and have fellow feelings for the soldiers who safeguard Rome, to avoid unnecessary clashes between their men and ours. And after all that experience, having proven himself to be one of the best men in the empire, and worthy of the singular honour of his purple stripe, he, like myself, was awarded his last promotion, to command a cohort of praetorians.'

He paused and raised a questioning eyebrow at Scaurus.

'You are clearly a man who has earned your position, Rutilius Scaurus, but I would venture to suggest that there are many men of our class who, having inherited their place in the empire's hierarchy, fall short of the sort of excellence that you have demonstrated, and which Sergius and I have had to prove time and time again to be granted command of our cohorts.'

The tribune inclined his head in acceptance of the point.

'I could not deny your suggestion with a clear conscience, colleague. Clearly the road to your present rank is a good deal harder than that trodden by most men who wear the thin stripe. And perhaps this man Maternus might have admitted his own fallibilities to himself, and decided to follow another, less challenging path in life?'

Sergius spoke, his interjection weighted with a natural authority that made it evident he wore his rank easily.

'I was Maternus's comrade from our earliest days. We served as centurions in the same cohort, always competing to be the better man in whatever was put before us, but always as comrades rather than rivals. We had a friendship forged in the heat, the cold, the suffocating dust, and the spirit-sapping ice and rain of the training we had endured together as recruits, and we were as close as two men could be without sharing the blood of a common ancestor. We went to war in Germania together, both knowing that it was our best chance to show what we were made of. And the war changed us both. I became a different man and so did he, but where my experiences hardened me and made me even more sure of my chosen path in life, I could see that my friend was struggling with the things that we had seen and done.'

He paused, and Victor took up the thread seamlessly, as if this was a history the two men had recounted before.

'The campaign against the Quadi was the worst of the three German wars, not in terms of losses or battles, but simply for the blind, stubborn ferocity with which the barbarians resisted our advance into their territory, once we had bested them in a straight fight. They were incapable of facing us on a battlefield, but they proved to be masters of a war fought from the shadows. A sentry would vanish from his post, only to confront us ten miles further along the route of march, tied to a tree, with his eyes, tongue and manhood carved from his body, still alive but no longer a man, speechlessly begging for the mercy stroke from his comrades. If a village showed us anything but the most outright hostility, it would be burned out once we had passed, and its people mutilated, as an example to inspire greater resistance from the others. These horrors made every day a small but painful battle, often bloodless on our part, but with sufficient horror to slowly but surely erode our ability to resist. We were gradually but irrevocably changed by the experience, each man in a slightly different way. Every mile we advanced cost us a price in good guardsmen's blood, and it was our experience as centurions that even the best of soldiers will start to experience ever-greater fatigue of mind, the longer they are exposed to such a random and unpredictable risk. Some men react with nobility and strive to hold themselves above the horrors they have witnessed, and on occasion, been impelled to perpetrate. They manage to retain their humanity and their sense of self-worth. But others lose themselves to the continual slow drip of blood, and become as debased as the enemy that is inflicting such horrors upon them.'

His colleague spoke again, his voice as dark as the expression on his face as he stared into the fire's flames.

'We lost Maternus at the very end of the war. It was as if he had managed to hold himself together by force of will while his duty required him to do so, but he could no longer control himself once the need for restraint was removed. Late on, while the peace settlement was being negotiated, he took his century out on a scheduled patrol, with orders to maintain our wartime routine whilst giving the Germans no reason to refuse the emperor's generous terms. He and his men had every reason not to stray beyond their orders, which were to stay alert for trouble but to do nothing to provoke it. After all, who wants to be the last man to die in any war, whether its end has been negotiated or not? When he failed to return, his tribune was detailed to investigate, taking his first spear and a tent party of men to make sure that no disgruntled tribesman attempted any score settling.'

'And did they find him?'

'They did. And both officers paid for that success with their lives. He murdered them, having already burned out a village in total disregard for his orders. One of Maternus's men returned to our camp not long after, before the peace agreement was concluded and we marched for Rome. He was unwilling to risk the life of a brigand, it seems, and chose to throw himself on the mercy of his officers, hoping to buy his life with the story of his centurion's betrayal of everything the Guard stands for. He was executed in front of his comrades, of course, to demonstrate the fate that will befall any man who indulges in such treachery, no matter what remorse he might experience after the event. But Maternus and his century hid themselves away until the army had marched south, then followed behind us and forced a crossing of the Rhenus one night, cutting down the bridge sentries without compunction and vanishing into the countryside beyond. And for a while they vanished from sight, more or less. They must have been robbing and looting their way across the empire, of course, but knowing Maternus, he had a plan even then. The greatest likelihood is that he chose where to strike with care, always managing to make his depredations look like local slave revolts against their overseers, and adding to his strength in the process. And it was probably always his intention to head for Gaul.'

'Gaul? Why Gaul?'

Sergius replied to Varus's question.

'Maternus was born in Gaul. It would have been a homecoming for him, and he knew it was a province big enough for a small army to disappear without any easily followed trace. After all, the closest legions in Hispania or Germania are probably three hundred miles distant, and he'd have known all too well where to hide his men when troops were sent to find him. And for a while that was probably enough, a base from which he could strike out in any one of a dozen different directions and plunder at will. But it was only a matter of time before that was no longer enough for him, or for an army of the size to which his followers have swollen. And so, whether from a long-standing design, or just from simple necessity, he's started raiding larger settlements. After all, most towns in Gaul and the surrounding provinces are more or less unprotected, with nothing more than a few watchmen to keep the peace at night. And as long as his activities only impacted on private property, there was nothing to get the provincial governors too concerned. We all know that robbers and bandits have always been with us and always will be, and they weren't the only deserters to prey on the empire's soft underbelly. It was something that could be quietly written off as nothing more than what was to be expected, an echo of the events of the last ten years. Until he switched his focus to the larger cities.'

'Cities?'

Victor leaned forward towards the fire's flickering flames.

'Our former colleague seems to have played a clever game over the last two years. Moving his forces to each new target in small groups, he orders them to reform into larger groups of men, who fight together under the command of his deputies, men who deserted with him whom he knows and trusts. And then, just before mounting an attack, these . . . cohorts, I suppose you could call them, come together to form his army, thousands strong. Of course the men in command of the settlements in question would know he was coming – you can't move that many men across open country without there being some warning of their presence – but by the time their calls for help could reach the governor of their province, whatever brief resistance the townspeople could put up would already be over.'

'And what does he do, once his men are through whatever defence was set against them? He spares the defenders, I presume?'

The praetorian nodded at Marcus.

'You have the measure of it. Our former colleague clearly understands the difference between war and banditry, and his need to keep the population on his side if he is to swim in their sea. Once a man has thrown down his weapon, he's allowed to live. No women are raped, and what plundering takes place is restricted to the homes and businesses of the rich.'

'Because what's the point of ransacking the houses of the citizenry and creating enemies if there's little gain to be had?'

'Exactly. And he's become adept at making sure he has men controlling the roads in and out of the cities before showing his hand, to prevent the more astute merchants from getting their wealth to safety before it's too late. He's grown rich, and spends his money wisely, compensating the small farmers whose crops he takes to feed his men, always leaving them enough for themselves, thus effectively becoming their best customer.'

Scaurus leaned back and stretched his weary body.

'It seems to me that he's found the perfect modus operandi. He has enough strength to make his army difficult to overcome in a fight, enough skill to avoid a fight until he chooses to strike with sufficient strength to win, and enough open country to hide in that he's pretty much impossible to pin down. And he has the support of the people who might otherwise betray him. But all of this is hardly news. Why all this?' He waved a hand at the rows of tents surrounding them. 'And why *now*? What changed to merit this much force?'

Sergius drew his dagger and used the point to draw a curving line in the firepit's soft earth.

'What changed? I'll show you what changed. This . . .' he pointed to the line, 'is the river Rhenus. There's Bonna, there's Mogontiacum. And there . . .' he dug the point into the soil to the river's west, 'is Argentoratum. It's a legion fortress, home to the Eighth Augustan. And Maternus, it seems, has taken it under siege. The news arrived late last night, as we were making our final preparations to march.'

Victor smiled at their astonishment.

'So now you can see why it's so urgent that we deal with our former colleague before he starts chopping away at the props that hold up the edifice of the emperor's power. Because if he manages to capture a legion standard, it's probably safe to say that the matter of his brigandage will become something a good deal closer to an uprising. And, as you can imagine, the chamberlain who allows that to happen might not be chamberlain for very much longer.'

'Halt! Identify yourselves!'

Two armed men advanced from either side of the rough track that ran through the heart of the detachment's encampment, their spears raised, the polished iron of their blades gleaming in the moonlight. The Tungrian officers were walking the short distance back to their own section of the camp, so deep in conversation as to what might be required to defeat a cunning outlaw like Maternus that they failed to see the guard patrol coming. Julius stepped forward with a hand raised.

'Not so fast with the pig pokers, ladies, unless you have an ambition to find them deeply embedded where your boyfriends will never get them out again.'

The praetorian sentries bristled at the slur, but before they had a chance to properly take umbrage, a pair of centurions strolled up and defused the situation with a brisk command for the guardsmen to go about their business. The taller of the two stepped forward, his broad smile of amusement evident in the light of the closest campfire, his voice a lazy drawl.

'I can only apologise for those apes, gentlemen. It's not the usual way of behaving, but I suppose being allowed out of the city has gone to their heads.'

Varus started, staring at the praetorian officer bemusedly.

'Titus? Titus Flavius Titianus?'

The praetorian grinned and bowed theatrically.

'The very same. I was wondering how long it would take you to realise that it was me parading around in front of you.'

Varus grinned, delighted to see a man who was clearly a long-standing friend.

'Tribune Scaurus, it gives me enormous pleasure to introduce you to a man I shared my school days with. Titus Flavius Titianus, this is my superior, Gaius Rutilius Scaurus, and my colleague, Julius.'

Titianus put out a hand, and Scaurus shook it with an appraising stare.

'You're the son of Titus Flavius Claudius Sulpicianus?

The young centurion nodded, clearly utterly sure of himself.

'I am.'

'He's governor of Asia, isn't he? I would have thought he'd have taken you with him. After all, what better chance can a young man have to polish his Greek to perfection and see the ways in which the empire manages its provinces, than at first hand?'

The praetorian shook his helmeted head with an expression of horror that looked only partially feigned.

'My good friend Gaius will tell you that I absolutely loathed Greek throughout a long and, it has to be said, difficult education. And the Greeks too, if my teacher was any indication. So when my father offered me the chance to go to Asia with him, I declined and persuaded him to use his influence to get me a centurion's position with the Guard instead. Which, fortuitously enough, has brought me here to enjoy all this.' He waved a hand airily at the darkened camp, and the Tungrians smiled at his wry expression. 'Bad food, sore feet and the company of quite the most brutal colleagues the empire has to offer. Isn't that right, Lupinus?'

His fellow officer raised a sardonic eyebrow, his reply laced with acid.

'The Guard is used to welcoming the sons of the rich when they decide to come and sample military life. Sometimes they stay and decide to make a career of it, although it's baffling what they see in it compared to the life they could be living. Sometimes they don't last.'

Titianus grinned at him disarmingly.

'Centurion Lupinus has been given the unenviable task of being my mentor. Little by little he is hammering the lessons I need to learn into my admittedly thick skull, with a patience that can only be described as Herculean. Anyway, gentlemen, I'd say that we've kept you from your beds for long enough. Lupinus and I have the night watch for the next few hours, which, my colleague informs me, consists mainly of creeping around the camp in the hope of finding a sentry asleep so that he can be brutally punished in the morning as an example to keep the others on their toes! So I'll wish you all goodnight.'

Once the two men were out of earshot, Scaurus spoke, a musing tone in his voice.

'It never ceases to amaze me what the sons of the rich decide to do with their youth, or what they have thrust upon them. Would you have taken your friend as the type to have willingly submitted to the sort of discipline the praetorians specialise in?'

Varus nodded thoughtfully.

'It wouldn't have been my first prediction, I'll admit that. But he was telling the truth when he said that his education was a thing that happened around him rather than to him. His teachers tried everything to get him to learn, mainly because they knew his father would come down on them hard if he failed to progress, but anything other than the skills he thought he'd need for life as a Roman gentleman just didn't interest him. He was good with a sword, and he listened intently when it came to lessons that featured great men, and how they achieved that greatness, but everything else he simply set out to endure.'

'Strange, to meet a member of the city's ruling class that doesn't speak Greek.' Scaurus shrugged. 'It's the differences between us that define us, I suppose. He'll be worth cultivating afresh though, if only for the window he'll give us into their world.' He lifted the flap of his tent, raising a hand to cover a yawn. 'And now, gentlemen, I think we should all get a few hours' sleep. I doubt that Victor will set as easy a pace for the march in the morning.'

As predicted, with the continued fine weather the next day, Victor decided that a full marching distance would be appropriate, and the vexillation's men soon realised that energy spent singing would be better dedicated to the simple act of putting one foot in front of the other. The novelty of their ad-hoc pairing had already worn off, replaced by wary tolerance of their obvious differences and constant low-level mutual abuse. With their rest stops throughout the morning long enough only to adjust their equipment to mini-mise the discomfort of its weight and movement on the march, and to gulp down a mouthful of water, there was a genuine sense of relief when the order to stop for the lunch break was passed down the column. Leaving his chosen man to make sure that none of their men did anything rash like removing his boots,

Marcus strolled down the length of the relaxing soldiery, returning good-natured greetings and ignoring the occasional muttered 'Two Knives', as men who saw him as a talisman for the cohorts' continued success reflexively exchanged the verbal statement of their faith. Dubnus strolled out into the roadway to greet him, clasping hands in their usual way.

'I'm forgiven for taking up where Julius left off then, I presume?' Marcus asked.

The big man shrugged, a lopsided smile creasing his lips.

'You're nowhere near the bastard he was, no matter how much you might try, and in any case, this lot worship you, in their own way.'

'It's true.' Varus had walked from his place at the head of the Second Cohort to join them, exchanging salutes with Dubnus before he spoke again. 'See how many of them touch whatever they have for a luck charm as they call you that name?'

Marcus shrugged at the observation, reaching inside his tunic to fish out a gold pendant that he had worn since the battle on the ice in Dacia.

'We all have something that reminds us of a victory. And this is mine. A good man died, betrayed by the stupidity of his commanding officer, and in the moments before his death he wrote a message to me in his own blood. I wear this to remind me that even the best-intentioned of our leaders can simply get it wrong on occasion. As to the name they call me, we've been together since before their first proper battle in Britannia, so if it calms their minds to imagine that I'm some part of what keeps us all alive, there's no harm in it, I suppose. However much of a stretch of the imagination that idea might be.'

The men turned as they were hailed by a praetorian centurion strolling down the column as if he were taking his ease in the sunshine. Dubnus nodded a farewell and took his leave, returning to his cohort.

'Gentlemen! A good day for it, if a little too hot for comfort given all this iron we're forced to wear!' Titianus saluted his friend, stopping and arching his back against the stiffness engendered by the weight of armour and weapons he was carrying. 'I swear I'll be worn out by the time I'm thirty if I have to port all this iron across the mountains and back again. Perhaps our tribunes will reward our inevitable victory with a nice gentle march down to the sea at Massilia, and a ship back to Ostia, rather than having to trudge all the way back here.' He leaned closer to Varus and lowered his voice, although the grin plastered across his face didn't waver. 'Keep smiling and nodding, Gaius, as if we're just having the usual jocular discussion of life's trials between old friends. There's something I need you both to know.'

Varus smiled, nodding slightly as if in agreement with whatever point it was that his former school-friend had made.

'What is it that needs us to be so—'

'Shut up and *listen*.' The praetorian raised both hands as if in bemusement, his expression apparently inviting both men to join his wonderment at the ways of the world. 'That centurion I was with last night? Lupinus? He wasn't part of the cohort until two nights ago, and he simply arrived out of the blue, without any warning, to take command of the Eighth Century. And I know for a fact that the Eighth was supposed to be handed to another new boy like me from a different cohort, an officer from a well-off family who'd had his place in the vexillation bought for him at quite considerable expense. His father will have been incandescent with rage when he found out that his boy's chance for glory has been awarded to a social non-entity like Lupinus.'

Varus shook his head.

'He might be a nobody in the city, but he has the look of a man who knows the darker side of life.'

The young guardsman nodded, his artificial smile faltering.

'And that's what made me come to see you. The thing is, he has a bit of a reputation. One of the other centurions in my cohort took me aside last night, before I went on guard duty with the man, and told me, very quietly and with the threat of a beating if it gets back to Lupinus that he told me, that the man was until very recently the officer entrusted with escorting the emperor around Rome when he decides to disguise himself as a commoner.'

'Disguised as a guardsman?'

Titianus flinched at Marcus's vehement interjection.

'Yes. And in the name of all the gods, put a *smile* on your face. He also warned me that the man has killed dozens of times at Commodus's command, and makes no secret of it. An indignant husband, an over-zealous bodyguard, or just an innocent slave or child, to persuade the emperor's intended victim to do as she's told and get on her back to avoid further bloodshed.'

The Tungrian smiled slowly, baring his teeth mirthlessly.

'You'll understand better why I'm finding it hard to smile, Centurion, when I tell you that I suspect your friend Lupinus to have been with the emperor when he raped my wife, murdered a member of my familia and threatened my son with death as the leverage to make her submit to him. And it was Lupinus who was wielding the blade that killed my friend. So if he's been inserted into your cohort at the last moment, then it can only be with the intention for him to remove the threat we pose to Cleander in our knowledge of the bastard child that resulted from that rape. A child he has quietly secreted away in the depths of the imperial palace as a form of insurance against the uncertainties of his position.'

Titianus stared at him, aghast, before mastering his amazement.

'I had no idea. I'm . . . sorry . . .'

Marcus shook his head brusquely.

'It's what it is, and no amount of regrets can change it. And, without any disrespect in your coming to tell us this, what of it? So he's part of the emperor's depraved circle, and close enough to Commodus to claim the favour of being sent to take revenge for the praetorians' lost honour; that means nothing to us.'

'But it does.' Titianus looked out over the ordered rows of vines that stretched away on both sides of the road north. 'You see Lupinus wasn't the only man to join the Eighth two nights ago. He came with a complete tent party of men, all pretty much from the same mould. They keep themselves to themselves and ignore anyone that tries to engage them in conversation. I think they're the men who accompany the emperor around Rome, remorseless killers who wouldn't think twice before putting a dagger to an innocent's throat. And I've seen them watching *you*, Centurion. So be warned.'

He turned and walked away with a cheery wave, leaving Marcus and Varus looking at each other in bemusement.

4

'We've been on the road for the best part of three weeks, gentlemen, and every step from here will be uphill as we start the climb into the mountains. I think a rest day is probably called for.' Victor made the announcement over dinner in the city's transit barracks' officers' mess to the general approval of his officers, who nodded with equal vigour at his next suggestion. 'And given the continuing undercurrent of rivalry between my men and your Tungrians, I suggest that we give them something to cheer about. We're going to have a boxing tournament, our champions against yours, and the overall winner's cohort will be excused from guard duty tomorrow night. How does that sound?'

Scaurus nodded his agreement.

'I think the men will appreciate the entertainment. We have two cohorts each, so I presume your intention is for us to run a competition between our own units to select a champion and then have our champions fight each other to determine the overall victor?'

'Exactly. And the ideal result once we get to the last of my men and your overall winner would be a draw. We'll have to be careful who we get to adjudicate the last bout, for fear of accusations of favouritism.'

'I have just the man.' Both tribunes turned to look at Julius. 'A centurion who spent twenty years fighting for his cohort – and his belief in the rules of what he considers to be an art is stronger than any loyalty other than to his military oath. And trust me, any man who dares to suggest that he's anything other than scrupulously neutral when it comes to adjudicating a bout – any bout – is likely to find himself counting his teeth with his tongue.'

After breakfast the next morning, the four cohorts were marched from the barracks to the city's amphitheatre. Each man had been issued with a bronze sestertius with which to buy the refreshments that were on offer from the vendors, who, knowing a good thing when they saw it, had turned out in force to cater for a wide variety of tastes in both food and drink. Ignoring the arena which, while impressive in size for a provincial town, was nowhere near as big as the Flavian arena in Rome where they had watched the finest gladiators in the empire compete, the soldiers made straight for the various stalls selling alcohol and hot food with the look of men determined to enjoy their day no matter what the consequences might be later. A German vendor of beer found himself surrounded by an eager group of Tungrians who started work on consuming his stock while loudly complaining about its flavour and dissimilarity to what they considered beer should taste like.

'Well if you don't like it, then you can all fuck off and buy that rough dog piss that's being sold as the finest amphora-aged Falerian!' Tapping the barrel behind him the beer seller nodded confidently, raising an admonitory finger. 'This is the real thing, boys, made the old-fashioned way like we do in Germania!'

Sanga shook his head in disgust, grimacing into his mug in distaste.

'Like we do in Germania? When were *you* last in Germania? I was there a few months ago and the beer didn't taste anything like this filth. I'll bet you've never even been north of the mountains, have you?'

The vendor bridled at the suggestion that his beer might be anything less than authentic.

'You must have been drinking some watered-down tribal muck! This beer is made with the finest malts and pure mountain spring water, and—'

'Pure mountain spring water? More like whatever came out of

the local bathhouse! This smells worse than a barbarian's crotch, and it tastes like horse shit!'

Warming to his subject, the Tungrian took another mouthful of the despised brew to be sure that it was still as bad as his initial perception. He was about to appeal to the men around him to back up his complaint, in total disregard of the way they were eagerly consuming the German's swiftly diminishing supply, only to be distracted by the sight of a dozen women making their way into the arena with an escort of almost as many burly bodyguards.

'Hello! Looks like the entertainment's arrived!'

The beer vendor grinned at the chorus of cheers that erupted from the men around him at the sight of so many prostitutes.

'Take my advice, soldier, if you've got the coin to spend and the urge to sample their wares, I'd suggest that you do it early. Those girls are in for a tiring day, I'd imagine. And don't try telling the lads that keep an eye on them you're not happy with the taste, eh? Being thrown down the arena stairs could spoil your entire day.'

Sanga shook his head knowingly.

'Nah, I've got a better idea. I'm going to put some money down on a soldier from my century to win the tournament today, and when he's smacked seven shades of shit out of whatever loser the praetorians put up against him, I'm going to collect my winnings and spend them in the comfort of a nice, quiet brothel, in the company of someone a bit more exclusive, a woman who's not soaked with the sweat of two dozen men who've already climbed on top for a quick ride.'

The vendor raised an eyebrow.

'You're that sure your comrade can win?'

'I've seen Plug put away men twice his size. He's so hard that just punching the bastard is like hitting the side of a barn, only this barn can knock you out clean with a single backhander. He's deadly, is my man, and I've already got a silver on him to win at fives.'

'Fives?' The other man raised an impressed eyebrow. 'I wouldn't mind a piece of that, if your gambling man's anywhere near!'

Sanga grinned.

'As it happens, he's one of the boys busy drinking their way through your beer. Morban!'

The standard bearer strolled over to join them with a mug of beer in his hand.

'Sanga, you animal.'

'Man here wants to get some money on Plug.'

The older man nodded sagely.

'A good choice. He's the best we have, no doubt about that. Only question is what those palatine ponces can put up against him once he's won our side of the bout. They can't all be as effeminate as they look.'

The vendor opened his purse and pulled out a gold aureus, holding it up to gleam in the warm autumn sun.

'So how about I put this down on him at fives, eh?'

Sanga sucked his teeth dubiously.

'Too much risk, my friend. What if he wins? I don't have that sort of money to hand . . .' Morban ignored Sanga's raised eyebrow, 'which means I'll have to lay it off with someone else. Best I can do is twos.'

'Twos?' The incensed beer seller gestured to Sanga, who was grinning happily at him and nodding. 'But you gave him fives!'

'I gave him fives on a silver, but even that was an over an hour ago and an act of charity for an old comrade. There's so much money coming in now that word's got around that fives ain't the price any more. Look, I'll do you a favour, seeing as this beer isn't too bad.' Morban ignored Sanga's cynical grin and the German's irritation at such faint praise. 'I'll take your gold, promise you two gold and two silver if Plug wins it, and I'll even undertake to return it in the event of a draw. Can I say fairer than that?'

'Done!' The aureus vanished into Morban's purse with the speed of a man long accustomed to making money disappear, plucked from the vendor's fingers even as the word was uttered. 'But how will I find you to claim my winnings?'

Morban grinned.

'That's easy, friend, I'll be just over there by the main entrance when this is all done with. Right, Sanga, I feel the need of some of that hot sausage they're selling down the road. Come on!'

'Fighters . . . are you ready?'

Both of the pugilists standing on either side of Otho nodded curtly, eyeing each other warily from behind their raised fists as the battered Tungrian officer raised his voice to bellow hoarsely at the soldiers packed into tiered seats encircling the sand on which they stood. Sitting in blocks allocated to them by cohort, the detachment's four fighting units were separated by gaps patrolled by their centurions, whose vine sticks were held ready for vigorous chastisement of any man attempting to express his frustrations with a bout's result in the customary physical manner.

'This will be a fight over three rounds timed by sand glass, and governed by the rules of pugilatus! Victory will go to the man who puts the other down for a count of ten, or who I judge to have rendered his opponent incapable of resisting! No blow is forbidden, but the commanding tribune has ruled that any bone or joint injury inflicted on an opponent will be punished by scourging!'

The day's fighting had proceeded with brisk efficiency from its mid-morning start; each pair of fighters were marched into the arena as the previous combatants had walked, limped or been carried away at their fights' end. Every century of all four cohorts had put up a champion, even if some of the men were not entirely willing in their participation. Then the fighters paired off against men from their own half of the detachment, Tungrian or praetorian, to fight against each other in bouts selected by lot. By the lunch break, at the completion of the first twenty bouts, the midday meal was celebrated with gusto by all parties other than those facing a fight in the afternoon. Praetorians and Tungrians mixing happily in the arena's environs despite their previous hostility, as the heady pleasures of alcohol and bloody violence inflicted by others and upon others inculcated a happy mood among soldiers whose days had consisted of staring at the backs of the men in front of them for the previous three weeks. By mid-afternoon, another two hours of fights had whittled the remaining pugilists down to one man from each side of the draw. Their excitement at the final bout of the competition was evident, both for the spectacle itself and their imminent release to an evening's continued drinking in the streets of the city. The veteran Tungrian centurion who had officiated throughout the day, his voice hoarse despite the regular sips of wine he had been taking to keep it lubricated, gestured for the first of the two fighters to take his place in the circle and shouted his name above the crowd's hubbub as he did so.

'On my left, fighting for the Tungrian cohorts, the soldier known as Plug!'

The Tungrian stepped forward, studiously avoiding Otho's raking stare, and raised his gloved hands to accept the raucous cheers of his fellow soldiers. He bounced lightly from one foot to another in a shuffling dance intended to demonstrate his nimbleness and stamina. Short and squat, his lack of commanding height was compensated by arms and legs bulging with muscle; his arms, unnaturally long, sported fists big enough that a well-placed punch would blacken both of an opponent's eyes. Stepping back, as the applause and abuse alike died away, he brought the leather-wrapped knuckles of both fists together several times in the customary signal that he was ready to fight. Otho nodded, gesturing to the other contestant to step forward.

'On my right, fighting for the praetorian cohorts, the guardsman known as the Beast!'

His nickname every bit as appropriate as his opponent's, the guardsman nodded determinedly as he too raised his hands to acknowledge the roared adulation of his comrades. A good head taller than the Tungrian, he was rangy and sinewy where the other was compact and muscular. His face, like Plug's, bore the evidence of half a lifetime's pugilism, his eyes equally devoid of any sign of emotion as he turned to stare down at the shorter man, repeating the raised fists signal that indicated that he too was ready to fight. Otho pushed him back into place, stepping forward to roar his final instructions at the waiting audience.

'This fight will determine who is the champion pugilatus of this detachment!' Otho paused and looked around the arena, turning in a slow circle with an expression any of the men who served under him would have instantly recognised as his fighting face. 'And my decision will be *final*! I serve no master when my beloved sport is in question, no master other than the gods of pugilatus! And any man who questions my decisions can take his chances with *me*.'

A momentary silence fell over the audience as every man present contemplated the prospect of facing off with Otho, even with the years of his prime unquestionably behind him. The Tungrians' tales of his casual brutality, calculated violence and outright bestial ferocity when even only gently provoked had been the talk of the lunch break, and there were few men present not in awe of his legendary reputation. The fighters exchanged glances; both men wanted to get on with the ordeal facing them rather than stand listening to Otho's bristling threats, although neither of them was willing to show any sign of impatience and risk arousing his legendary ire. A praetorian pugilatus fighting in the early rounds had summoned the nerve to question a decision which most of the onlookers agreed had been questionable at best, and had been backhanded by the big centurion with such force that – despite the sweat-soaked padded leather helmet protecting his cheeks and temples from his opponent's gloved fists – he had spat a pair of bloody teeth onto the sand. Otho had waved him away from the bout with a look of disdain and raised his opponent's hand in victory.

'One moment, Centurion, if I may?'

Victor had walked out onto the sand while Otho had been laying down the law, and it was with almost palpable relief that the gathered soldiers saw the older man snap to attention and salute, growling at the fighters to follow suit.

'Tribune, sir!'

Smiling wryly at the veteran's parade ground bark, the praetorian officer looked around at the soldiers seated around him, raising an eyebrow at the occasional patch of discordant colour where both Tungrians and his own men had been spirited back into the arena by their counterparts.

'Guardsmen! Soldiers! Today you have enjoyed a pugilistic feast, and had the chance to do something more than march and count your blisters!'

Laugher rippled across the stands, the more waggish among the cohorts pointing to their tent mates and then the palms of their hands. Victor simply waited until the amusement had died away under the silent but meaningful stares of his centurions.

'Today you have discovered that the men you have been insulting with such vigour are in fact just like you! You have the same hopes and fears, the same bravery and the same will to defeat the empire's enemies!'

Cheers replaced the laughter, even if a jocular undercurrent of irony ran through the reaction to his words.

'You are about to witness two men fighting for the honour of their comrades. No matter who wins their bout, I am sure you will agree that each of these two men has fought his way to the top of his cohort and his half of the detachment, and we can all be proud of them both! I'm sure I don't need to point out that no matter the outcome, I expect you all to make your ways back to barracks in an orderly and comradely manner, *if* you wish to enjoy the pleasures of an evening's liberty to enjoy the city! That is all!'

He signalled to Otho, who saluted crisply and then turned back to his fighters, beckoning them both in to hear his final instructions.

'Fine words. Which do *not* fucking apply to you pair of cunts. I expect you bastards to fight like wild animals, for the respect of your comrades, the glory of pugilatus and so that I don't have to give either of you an encouraging tickle. Got that?'

Both men nodded, backing away and locking eyes as the big centurion raised his hand to the timekeeper.

'First round . . . *fight!*'

The two fighters closed, a flurry of blows flying as they set to the determination of men who knew that the victor would be well rewarded by his tribune for the honour that would accrue to that man's cohort. Otho strode around them to maintain his unobstructed view of the punches flying in both directions, a happy smile on his face as they closed to knife-fighting distance and continued exchanging vicious jabs and hooks at a furious rate. Neither gave any ground to the other as both sought to dominate the bout in the face of their opponent's obdurate resistance. The praetorian fighter, taller and clearly an accomplished pugilist, was attempting to box tactically for all his willingness to match the Tungrian for bravado, but if Plug was at a height disadvantage, his freakishly long arms allowed him to match the guardsman's reach and power. Neither man was seeking the protection of his raised elbows, as was usually the fighting style in the first round, as men sought to work out each other's abilities; each instead sought to impose himself on the other in a mutual deliberate bid to win the fight through a swift knock-out. But for all their furious effort, it was clear that neither man harboured any vulnerability to a well-thrown punch, and the round ended with both fighters panting for breath, their faces already freshly marked by each other's vicious assaults.

The bell was sounded as the first sand glass ran out and the timekeeper nodded to his assistant. Both fighters backed leaden-footed away from the blood-spotted circle of bootprints where they had fought toe to toe, both momentarily uncertain of which direction to walk to their seconds. But the respite granted to them by their unbending taskmaster was momentary at best, a brief moment to rinse and spit bloody water and steady their breathing, in the short time that Otho gave them before he called them both back to renew the fight in a tone that brooked no delay. At the command to fight, the two men closed with looks no less determined than had been the case a moment before. This time, however, rather than step into immediate and unremitting close combat, both belatedly decided to use their feet to determine the course of the fight as they shuffled and swayed around the central locus of the bout at the spot where their fists met.

Perhaps advised by their seconds that there was no way they could fight at the furious pace of their previous engagement and hope to last three rounds, both men were now boxing more calculatingly, their styles more defensive, either ducking away from punches or using their elbows to block. But despite their mutual decision not to persevere with the suicidal tempo the first round had set, both continued to fight with unwavering commitment, landing telling blows that left the praetorian with a bloodied eye from a knuckle strike and his opponent with blood pouring from a broken nose. Each further punch elicited a grunt of pain that was the only sign that the injury troubled him. Both started to tire, flicking glances at the timekeeper as his sand glass ran down. They stayed toe to toe until the last moment, both grimly determined not to back away, even if their stamina was approaching its limits, to judge from their increasing lack of mobility. The men of the four cohorts bayed for blood as each attacked in turn. The last grains of sand ran down from the upper half of the sand glass and the command to stop fighting was barked out for a second time, releasing the pugilists to stagger back to their seconds, chests heaving and faces pouring blood. Both men's supporters screamed at them for one last Herculean effort to snatch the victory while the watching soldiers roared their own support and invective in a deafening cacophony.

Called back to the circle for the final time, both men were now clearly heavy-footed to the point of shambling, slow to raise their fists as they shuffled inside arm's length, each shepherding his dwindling energy and eyeing his opponent in the hope of an opportunity to finish the fight with one killer punch. They ducked and bobbed with each threat, their own blows little more than ineffectual jabs against the other's raised defences. But if the state of near-stalemate was effort enough for two men who had poured all they had into the first two rounds, and had little left to give unless some golden opportunity presented itself, the same was clearly not true of their arbiter. Otho strode forward to roar a warning at both men, but as he drew breath to shout, the unthinkable happened.

Opinions differed as to exactly how Otho came to find himself on his back, his nose streaming blood and broken for what must have been the twentieth time in his life. The inglorious incident happened too fast for some men to follow, especially as, with drink taken, few were paying close attention to the fight's finer points. But Saratos, who had partaken lightly and whose interest in the bout had been keener than most, given that he might have been forced to participate had not Plug been from his century, and consequently Otho's choice, later described it to Sanga and Morban with admirable accuracy.

'Praetorian, he slip on bloody sand. He chin wide open, see?' He jutted his own chin out in a demonstration of just what a tempting target the guardsman's unguarded face must have made, as his arms rose to each side involuntarily to maintain his balance. 'Plug, he see last chance to win fight. He go for knock-out, like this . . .' he drew his fist right back and in the process threw his elbow out behind him, 'and he not know Otho stupid enough to be so close.'

The swiftly raised elbow smashed into the unsuspecting centurion's face, sending him reeling backwards onto the sand while both men stared aghast at the sight of the stricken arbiter, knowing instinctively that the veteran centurion's reaction would not be a happy one. Springing to his feet with a blood-curdling roar, Otho gripped his own soldier by the shoulder and spun him round, smashing a straight right into his face that lifted him cleanly off his feet and threw him into the praetorian. The back of the Tungrian's head connected with the guardsman's chin with a click that, in the sudden awe-struck silence, was heard by every man in the arena as his jaw broke. Silence reigned for a moment before the watching soldiers erupted into hysterical laughter, men bending double and in at least one case actually vomiting, such was the onset of hilarity at the sight of an abruptly-abashed Otho standing over two unconscious men with his fists clenched. His face was creased in bewilderment at the unexpected turn of events, as Julius strode onto the sand flanked by a pair of his biggest and most robustly-minded officers. To the relief of all concerned, except perhaps the thousands of men who would have been delighted to watch the veteran pugilist take on his own comrades, the dumb-struck centurion chose instead to leave the arena quietly, shaking his head in continued bafflement as to how it was that he could have brought such ignominy down on himself.

'He not going to be a happy man for next days, that for certain.' Sanga and Saratos exchanged glances, knowing that as his watch officers they would probably be among the first to feel his wrath, once it resurfaced from the temporary sea of confusion into which it had sunk, but Morban had a more immediate concern to deal with.

'Fuck Otho, what am I going to do with all the money I took on Plug?'

Sanga grinned at his discomfiture, looking around to confirm that at least a dozen men were staring at the standard bearer with looks ranging from calculation to outright hostility, their angst at the chances that Morban would refund their wagers well-founded in the soldier's expert opinion.

'You want my advice, Morban old son?' He grinned, ignoring the other man's raised hand. 'You're getting it anyway, like it or not. I suggest you pay back every last copper that you took on Plug winning the contest, 'cause if you don't then I reckon you'll get it taken out of your leathery old hide one dark night. Besides, think what the men will say about you if you do pay them back?'

'I don't know.' The standard bearer shook his head unhappily. 'They'll probably call me Morban the soft-hearted. My reputation will be destroyed overnight.'

'No!' Sanga shook his head with a laugh. 'They'll love you for it. They'll call you Honest Morban! The man you can trust with your coin! You'll do more business on the back of a small moment of pain than you can imagine!'

'And no part of this oiling you're giving me is to do with the fact that you and the Dacian here had money on him?'

'I let you into secret.' Saratos leaned closer, lowering his voice conspiratorially and exchanging glances with Sanga. 'That money we put on Plug? It not all ours to gamble. Some of it was given to us by a centurion.'

'Which centurion?'

Sanga stared down at the bemused Otho standing with Julius on the sand beneath them, and Morban followed his gaze in horror.

'The fucking *arbiter* had money on his own man?'

The soldier shrugged.

'What can I say? There's none of us perfect, is there? Certainly not good old Otho, he managed to half-kill both fighters including the man his gold was on! And if you ever tell anyone about it, then I imagine he'll tear your ears off and put them where the sun will never shine. And ours. So then me and the Dacian here will have to do the same with whatever's left of you.'

Morban shook his head in amazement.

'Now I've heard it all. So I can't tell anyone that the arbiter was gambling on his own man, and if I don't return his stake, he's likely to make my life misery. *Shit.*'

He thought for a moment before drawing breath to shout at the men around him.

'Honest Morban will refund all monies paid out on Plug! You know you can trust your old comrade Morban with your coin!' Raising his arms in acknowledgement of the cheers of the men who had been glaring at him a moment before, he shot Sanga a look that spoke eloquently of his frustration, hissing a comment intended for their ears alone. 'And that's half my takings on the day going straight back into the pockets of those fools. And that's before I find half the vendors in the city queuing up for their refund, once word gets out. The next time you pair place a bet with me, it'd better be your own money!'

Saratos shrugged.

'Why word need to get out? You tell soldiers that refund depend on they stay quiet. They not stay quiet, I take you revenge. Is fair?'

'Yes . . . but how do I get out of the promise I made to that beer seller? I told him that I'd refund on a draw, and he looked like the type to take disappointment badly.'

Sanga laughed, shaking his head.

'You should have been watching more carefully, Morban. That weren't any sort of draw, Otho knocked Plug out before the praetorian went down, so as far as you're concerned, Plug lost. Simple, eh?'

The standard bearer stared at him for a moment before bowing his head in genuine admiration.

'And to think I took you for simple-minded muscle. You devious bastard . . .'

'All things being considered, I'd say that's a decent day's work. Would you agree, Rutilius Scaurus?'

Scaurus looked at Victor over the edge of his wine cup for a moment before responding, his lips pursed in a half-smile. The two men had repaired to the praetorian's tent to raise a cup of wine to the day's proceedings, having left Sergius and Julius to ensure that the evening's entertainment in the city stayed light-hearted enough to ensure that all four cohorts would be able to march without any more loss of fighting power than had already been inflicted in the course of the pugilatus competition. Praetorian tribune and Tungrian prefect had both equipped themselves in their finest walking-out uniforms, then gathered their centurions and warned them that they would be taking a cup or two of wine in the city and were expecting to see nothing more challenging to their sense of well-being than happily inebriated soldiers.

'After a fashion, Tribune, yes, I would. Our men found

something to talk about other than each other's manifest short-comings, and they bonded just as well as you'd hoped, once the alcohol was flowing. There weren't any fights of any note and we only lost two men to serious injuries.'

The praetorian grimaced back at him.

'One of them, ironically, incapacitated by a blow inflicted by the arbiter of his final bout.'

'Yes.' The two men shared a moment of wry amusement. 'Although I find myself compelled to admit that not only was the resulting draw the fairest result possible, considering how evenly matched they were, but the sheer comedy of the moment seems to have done more good for relations between our men than everything else put together!'

Victor nodded his agreement, taking a sip of his wine before speaking again.

'So, we march in the morning, doubtless with half our men nursing hangovers of epic proportions. From here it's all uphill to the mountain passes, and we'll have to push on if we're going to get through the Alps before the first proper snows fall. Your men are good for twenty-five miles a day, I presume?'

'More, if needed, if we can cut back on the non-essentials, like taking four hours a day constructing a marching camp to the centurions' exacting requirements.'

Victor grunted his agreement.

'It's two hundred and fifty miles from here to Vindonissa, and I'd like to be knocking on their gates no more than ten days from now.'

'And after that?'

'Hopefully we'll be incorporated into the army of the legatus that's commanding the relief force that's being gathered from along the Rhenus and can get on with dealing with Maternus. The sooner we either have his ankles in chains or his head in a jar, the better.'

'And you think it'll be a straightforward task, from the sound of it.'

The praetorian drained his cup and poured them both a refill.

'I think that Maternus's army is a fearsome thing to face if you're a farm owner with only a dozen armed men. But he'll find four cohorts of this sort of quality, plus whatever strength has been gathered from along the frontier, hardened troops without any fear of deserters and escaped slaves, something completely different. And I fully intend to take maximum advantage of that mismatch in expectations. My former colleague Maternus, Tribune, is already as good as done.'

'So did your man Otho eventually snap out of his funk?'

Julius grinned at Sergius's baldly stated question.

'You're not much for subtlety, are you, Tribune?'

The praetorian shook his head.

'Cut the shit, Julius, and call me by my name. I was a centurion less than a year ago, and even now I have to fight the temptation to look around when someone calls me tribune, and find the person they're really talking to. I was born to be a centurion, just like you, and if I'm totally honest, I think I preferred it when I didn't have this image to maintain.'

He waved a hand at his fine tunic, belt and boots with a slight shake of his head.

'I know.' Julius nodded his agreement, sipping at the beer he'd purchased at their first stop of the evening and pulling a face. 'Gods, but the boys were right when they said this stuff tastes like cat's piss. You . . .' He waved a hand at a passing server. 'Take this away and bring me a cup of the wine my colleague is drinking.'

He cast a hard glare around the tavern into which the two men had stepped for their first stop of the evening in the full and justified expectation that the soldiers who were now apparently enjoying a quiet drink would remain docile until the two senior officers walked off to their next stop.

'At least our combined forces are bright enough to keep the noise down when we're around. Although the evening is young. But seriously, I know what you mean. As a centurion I had all the money I could ever realistically spend, all the power I could ever have wanted and none of the responsibilities that come with being the man in charge of two cohorts of these idiots.'

The two men nodded simultaneously, Sergius laughing tersely at the look on his comrade's face.

'And so here we are, victims of our own success.'

'That's a truer statement than you might think in my case. Except that it's not me that's the victim.'

The praetorian bowed his head in acknowledgement of the point.

'Indeed. And my apologies for seeming to make light of the matter of your woman. I doubt she'll come to any harm.'

'Not for the time being. But when the time comes for the child that she's sworn to protect to die, as it surely will with a calculating bastard like Cleander, I doubt very much that he'll be willing to leave any witnesses to the boy's existence. Do you?'

Sergius shook his head slowly.

'No.'

'And there you have it. Having regained the woman I left behind when I joined the army, I've lost her, probably forever, because I joined the army.'

'I feel your anger. But don't abandon all hope just yet. Who knows what might yet happen?' Sergius eyed his cup of wine with thinly-disguised amusement. 'Do you really think this is going to be all that much better than the beer?'

'To be honest, no.' Julius sipped, his face contorting at the taste. 'Presumably this grows on a man, given the way this lot are throwing it down their necks as if it were the finest Falerian.'

The praetorian tipped the rest of his cup down his throat, grimacing in disgust.

'Well, it's not growing on this man. Come on, put that down your neck and let's go and see if the application of a little more money can procure something a bit more tolerable, shall we?'

They strolled out into the street, studiously ignoring the drunken salutes offered by those of their men who felt too exposed to be able to join in the low-level abuse being muttered by those who felt more secure deeper in the ranks of drinkers. They had almost completely desegregated from their previously tribal rivalry by now and had taken over both the tavern and the street outside.

'So . . . Maternus.'

'Yes?' Sergius shot a glance at Julius, who continued talking even as he raised a finger in admonishment at a Tungrian who was standing with his hands on his knees and showing a clear and apparently undeniable need to vomit. 'You appear on parade tomorrow with puke on your boots and it'll be five strokes of your centurion's best friend for you, my lad!' He turned away in disgust as the soldier noisily retched up a gut full of alcohol onto the cobbles, liberally spattering his own legs with the results of a day's drinking. 'So, this Maternus was a good soldier, was he?'

'Good? He was better than good. He could easily have been the man here talking to you instead of me. He was all the things a first spear loves in his officers: brave, meticulous, cautious when necessary. But he also knew when to take a risk and make it pay off.'

'And you respected him?'

'Hugely. I was sure he was centurion material from the first day I met him, and by the time he made centurion, I knew he had tribune in him.'

'So you – a man with more experience than most in what it takes to rise high up this particularly greasy pole – think he had the right combination of guts and brains to make it to your rank. And yet your comrade Victor puts him down without a second thought. It stands to reason that one of you has to be wrong, doesn't it?'

Sergius answered without hesitation, and with the certainty of a man who had spent half a lifetime being proven correct in almost every judgement he'd ever made as a soldier.

'Yes, it does. And it's not me that's wrong, I can tell you that much. When we finally catch up with my former comrade, he's likely to give us somewhat more of a dancing lesson than my colleague Victor expects.'

Julius stopped walking.

'So why, if you know better, are you not telling him so every time he talks about the swift schooling that he's going to give the man?'

The praetorian turned to face him.

'If you disagreed with your tribune, would you tell him so in front of us?'

'Fair question. I'd certainly tell him in private.'

'And there you have it. I've tried to make it clear to him just what a clever opponent I expect our former colleague to be. And on every occasion I've made that point, he's found some way to put me down without making me feel he thinks any less of me for holding such an unwelcome view. I've tried, Julius, and I've failed. And I'll keep on trying . . .'

'But you'll keep on failing?'

'I feel it likely. So when we finally do manage to catch up with our former brother-in-arms, we'll find out who's right, won't we?' He nodded, signalling that the conversation was, as far as he was concerned, done with. 'And now, since we both probably need a decent drink to cheer us up, here's an establishment that looks more likely to sell us a drink that wouldn't peel the paint off a boat's back end. Shall we? One or two in here and then we can go and see how good a job our centurions are doing on the other side of the city, eh?'

5

'Of course this would all have been much simpler a hundred years ago. In those days the infamous Twenty-first Legion was based here, and they would have been the natural candidates to be sent to deal with a threat like Maternus.'

'The Rapax?' Victor laughed tersely at Scaurus's assertion. 'Those animals would have ripped through Maternus alright, but only after they'd killed every man, woman and child within a fifty-mile radius of his camp. The population of whichever province he was hiding in would have been as defenceless as that sacrifice whose liver made our men so happy last week.'

The two men were marching side by side, as had become their habit during the long slog north through northern Italy and over the towering Alps that were the barrier between them and the northern provinces. Crossing the mountains without incident only a week before the usual date around which the high alpine passes were traditionally rendered impassable by the first heavy snows of winter, with no more than a thin dusting of minute flakes to redden their cheeks, the cohorts' men had been quick to declare their easy passage a sign of divine favour. It was a gift from the gods that, Tungrians and praetorians united in their observation of the traditional soldiers' superstitions, had been pleased to see repaid by the dutiful sacrifice of a goat to Jupiter, whose temple stood at the highest point of the road through the mountains. And even if it had been a scrawny and ill-favoured-looking animal, sold to them by a farmer who clearly made much of his income selling his reject animals to passing travellers who were eager to retain the god's favour, both heart and liver had been blameless, leading to much nodding as the news spread among the waiting centuries. The older sweats had made great show of letting their junior comrades in on the secret that it was a mistake to judge the quality of the sacrifice by its exterior, while the younger men rolled their eyes at each other having already heard much the same from their fathers on more occasions than they could remember. The two tribunes' faces and arms were tanned by the sun, and, like their men, they had long since failed to find the punishing marching pace that allowed their cohorts to cover twenty-five miles a day troubling to either their legs or feet. They had taken to discussing the things they had seen and done, the empire's military history, the best way to face a multitude of tactical situations and whatever else was inspired by the land through which they were marching, as the detachment had progressed steadily northward.

'The bloody Rapax . . .' The praetorian snorted his derision again, in the open manner the two men had adopted with each other as they recognised kindred spirits. 'Everything I've read paints them as an undisciplined collection of thieves and murderers. I'd imagine that the inhabitants of Vindonissa breathed a sigh of relief when they were destroyed by the Roxolani during Domitian's reign.'

Scaurus grinned at his acerbic turn of phrase.

'Doubtless they did. Although I'm pretty sure that there would have been many among them who would have mourned the loss of their gold, even if they weren't going to miss the men themselves.'

Victor shrugged.

'They would have been fast enough to move to the closest fortress, lower their rates and go into competition with the established population of leeches. Although I expect there will be enough of them here to keep our men entertained for a few days.' He pointed to the fortress looming over the vicus buildings that had gathered under its walls, already imposing with more than a mile remaining before they would reach its walls. 'There's at least one legion cohort in residence, and where there are legionaries, the whores and tavern owners won't be far away. And now, if you'll excuse me, I'm going to drop back and make sure my men resemble the empire's finest warriors they're supposed to be and tell them not to ogle the local whores, if they know what's good for them. Coming?'

Scaurus shook his head.

'I'll stay up here at the front if it's all the same to you. Julius's threats as to what he'll do to any man caught displaying himself to the women usually find a more responsive audience without my presence impeding his style, which I doubt will be hampered all that much by his new rank.'

Suitably chastised in advance of their nevertheless-inevitable lapses of discipline in the unaccustomed presence of the female sex, the four cohorts marched through the settlement's vicus, bawling out one of the less obscene marching songs in their collective repertoire. The column's head stamped to a halt twenty paces from the massive wooden gates of the stone-walled legion fortress that had stood beside the Rhenus for two centuries, re-inforcing, sometimes brutally so, the *Pax Romana* in the hills and lakes north of the Alps. A legion centurion was already waiting on the wall above them to shout down the challenge that both he and the detachment's tribunes knew was only a formality, given that their approach would have been communicated to the fortress days before by passing postal riders.

'Identify yourselves!'

Looking to either side, he gestured for the bolt throwers that stood on platforms built into the walls to be manned; the swift and business-like way that their crews took up their positions and started cranking the heavy strings back was clearly intended as a demonstration of competence rather than any sort of threat. Victor strode forwards and raised a leather tube for the centurion to see.

'I am Praetorian Tribune Quintus Statilius Victor, and I have been ordered to march over the mountains and bring the emperor's finest troops to reinforce your own strength. I carry a message for Legatus Augusti Pescennius Niger from the imperial chamberlain.'

He waited in silence as the centurion was joined by a figure dressed in the tunic and shining leather belt and boots of a legion tribune; but while the former looked every inch the grizzled veteran, his nominal superior was clearly barely out of his teens.

'How do we know you're really praetorians? The rebel Maternus claims to have been a praetorian, before his mutiny, and has been known to disguise himself and his men to gain an advantage.'

Scaurus stepped forwards to join his colleague.

'I am Gaius Rutilius Scaurus, recently returned from the east where I defeated the army of the Parthian king Arsaces, and my Tungrian cohorts have accompanied these men of the emperor's guard north over the mountains with express orders from the imperial chamberlain to assist with the destruction of the man Maternus's rebel army. When were you last in Rome, Tribune?'

The young officer looked down at him for a moment before replying.

'I left Rome to join the Eighth Legion six months ago. And I have heard of you, Rutilius Scaurus, if you are who you say you are. Tell me, has your family always been part of the equestrian order?'

Scaurus shook his head.

'No. My ancestor chose the wrong side in the Year of the Four Emperors, and was demoted from senatorial status as his reward for loyalty to an emperor who ended up on the losing side.'

The tribune turned to his colleague and gestured decisively.

'Open the gates, Centurion. This man is Roman war hero.'

His subordinate turned away and barked an order for the gates to be unbarred, leaving Victor regarding his colleague with an amused smile.

'"This man is a Roman war hero"? Gods below. Although it's

a good thing you're with us, or we'd have been left waiting outside while I lost my dignity and quite possibly my temper arguing with a boy barely old enough to shave.'

The twin gates, each wide enough to admit a pair of armoured men, were thrown open, and the centurion strode out first, snapping to attention and saluting the tribunes. Victor returned the salute and stepped forward to offer his hand, which the other man took after a moment of confusion.

'Forgive me, Tribune, it's not customary for centurions to shake hands with their officers in the Eighth.'

Victor smiled easily.

'There's no apology needed, Centurion. In the Guard all officers have risen from the rank of soldier, just like you, and all ranks share a healthy respect for each other's position.'

The young legion tribune emerged from the gate, approaching with the look of a man not entirely sure of his footing, and Scaurus flashed Victor a glance.

'If you'll permit me, Tribune? I was in that young man's boots not all that long ago.'

The praetorian gestured his assent, and Scaurus stepped forward to face the younger man, snapping a meticulous salute that brought the legion officer up short as he realised that the object of much of Rome's military gossip over the previous year was offering him the traditional gesture of respect for a superior.

'Greetings, Tribune. At moments like these, when the established hierarchy is turned upside down, it can help a man in your position to have the niceties of rank explained.' He waited until the younger man nodded before continuing. 'I am a tribune commanding auxiliary cohorts, and so I must salute both yourself, as a legion tribune, and Tribune Victor as a praetorian officer, even though we are all of the same rank. And you, Tribune, must salute Victor and accept his orders, not simply because he is of greater seniority and experience than yourself, but because as a praetorian, he outranks you. Your centurion here, of course, must salute all three of us whilst remaining completely convinced as to his innate superiority, for such is the way of centurions throughout the empire.'

The legion officer smiled at the joke, some of the tension leaving his face.

'Thank you, Tribune Scaurus.' He turned to Victor and saluted. 'Tribune, welcome to Vindonissa. The fortress is usually manned by a detachment of two cohorts from the Eighth Legion under the command of a thin-stripe tribune like myself; I have been left in command while Legatus Niger summons reinforcements from the auxiliary forts to the north.'

'And you shall remain in command, Tribune. You and your officers understand the locality and its population better than I, and it would make no sense for me to take control of a fortress with which your legion is already very familiar. I'm assuming that you have barracks space for my detachment?'

'We have more than sufficient space, Tribune. The legion might have moved to Argentoratum, but the fortress has always been maintained in good condition by retired veterans. They are allowed to live within the walls in return for their service, as a fall-back position in the event of a serious barbarian incursion. If your men follow me, I'll have them allocated to empty barracks blocks and order the stores to prepare an issue of food and beer for them.'

Victor smiled his gratitude at the centurion.

'Thank you, Tribune. I look forward to seeing how my men react to the taste of that beer. Nothing could be more calculated to remind them that we are no longer in Italy!'

'Your cohorts can bed down in this run of barracks, Prefect; each one's big enough for two centuries so these ten blocks ought to house you well enough. And let me know if you have any trouble from the neighbours.'

Having led the column deep into the fortress's gloomy depths and indicated the buildings in which the Tungrians were to be temporarily housed – the praetorians already having been allocated to a different part of the sprawling maze of stone – the centurion gestured over his shoulder at the adjacent buildings. Dozens of inquisitive men were watching the Tungrians from doors and windows as they waited to be directed to their quarters, apparently lacking anything better to do than watch the newcomers and speculate as to their abilities. With the unerring instincts of a time-served centurion, he had swiftly deduced that Julius was a man with a background like his own, and the two men were already conversing more like peers than their respective ranks would normally have dictated.

'Trouble from the neighbours?' Julius smiled, shaking his head. 'I doubt it. They look like a docile enough herd of bullocks to me. Have they seen any combat recently?'

The centurion shrugged.

'The Eighth hasn't had a fight any bigger than an argument over whose first go it is to get their dicks wet on payday since half the legion went away to fight the Marcomanni with the last emperor. And that was nearly ten years ago. Just to make it worse, all of the cohorts that marched north back then are bottled up in Argentoratum . . .' he hooked a thumb over his shoulder, 'which means that all our veterans are cooped up under siege. Meanwhile, this lot are probably looking at your men and wondering what they'd be like in a fight, just like all unblooded troops do when they meet men with scars they didn't get from not paying enough attention in training.'

'You fought in the German Wars?'

'Yes.' The older man grimaced. 'I was part of that long, slow goat fuck. A handful of glorious victories after another on the battlefield, when the tribes could be tempted to come out and have a go at us, or when we managed to put them in a corner they couldn't get out of without fighting. But the rest of the time, it was mostly weeks of boredom with the occasional moment of terror thrown in just to really screw us up.' He paused for a moment, reliving the memory, before continuing. 'I hear rumours that this man Maternus deserted at the end of the war, while the peace treaty was being negotiated. The story goes that he was unmanned by everything he'd seen and done, and descended into bestial madness. Or at least, that's the way the legatus put it when he was briefing us, although I was nearly asleep by the time he got round to actually telling us what was driving the maniac to lay siege to our fortress.'

'That's the story we've heard too. The praetorian tribunes were his comrades, and they say Maternus was among the best of them until the war broke his mind.'

'Until the war broke his mind? I doubt it did that, Centurion, not if his reason had survived intact to the end of the war. *Changed* his mind, more like. I saw it in my own comrades, and I'm sure you have too. A man marches away to fight, steeling himself to face the enemy in the line of battle like we're trained for, and instead of that, he finds himself hunted from the shadows, his friends mutilated and murdered by men he will never have the chance to take revenge on, and the war fought in a totally different way than what he'd expected – not as battles with winners and losers but more like . . .' He stopped to think again. 'Imagine that you're in a forest. You can hear the sound of axes chopping at trees. It's never in one place for more than a moment, and never for long enough to fell any of them, but suddenly all the trees around you have axe marks, and sap bleeding down their trunks. And then, out of nowhere, there's an axeman in your face with his blade ready to split your skull. That's what I dream, when it comes back to me, and that's what it was like. Weeks of boredom interrupted by moments of unpredictable horror.'

Julius nodded.

'And do you dream often?'

'Used to be every night. Now it happens every now and then, just when I least expect it. You?'

'Off and on. I can go a month without a problem, until my woman . . .' Julius paused for a moment, shaking his head at the reminder of Annia's plight, 'thinks I might have seen the last of it. And then something or other will start it off again, and I'll have the same dream every night for a week. And what I see in my sleep is wave after wave of eastern cavalry, horses and men all clad in shining iron armour, advancing up a long slope towards my men on a desolate plain. We kill them with arrows and bolts. We kill them with volleys of spears. We kill them with rows of fire-hardened wooden stakes, men and beasts screaming in agony as they ride onto the points. We kill them with our swords and shields, and our daggers and our bare hands. And we kill them, and we kill them, and we *kill* them, and they still keep coming, until I wake up soaked in sweat and trembling with the image of the man who's just about to run me through with a fucking great sword still in my mind.' He shook his head. 'Not that I'd admit that to another man, but since you mentioned it . . .'

The other man smiled wanly.

'It's our secret, Centurion. Between two men who've seen the other side of the coin, and can't forget the shit-eating grin on that evil bitch Victory's face while they pile the spoils of war around her feet. War makes us hard, while at the same time stripping away our defences against the things we are ordered to do, and the horrors that we see.'

He walked away, briskly collaring a pair of idlers to clear away an eyesore that was besmirching his vision of a perfect fortress, leaving Julius smiling at his cheerfully brutal stream of invective. The Tungrian turned back to face his waiting men, pointing at the nearest row of barracks.

'First Cohort, First Century, you're camping in that barracks for the night. The rest of you follow me, and try to look a bit more like proper soldiers and a bit less like road-menders, will you? Straighten your fucking backs and stop leaning on your spears or I'll have you out on the road for another ten miles just to remind you who you are! Senior centurions, get your men into their rooms and then gather in my quarters for a briefing!'

Left to their own devices by the absence of their officers, the men of Marcus's First Cohort swiftly adapted to what was apparently expected from them – which, being nothing, they were happy enough to deliver. Sanga and Saratos, to whom Otho's temporary absence felt like an unexpected gift, quickly decided to wander over a few blocks and see what was what in their former century.

'We might catch that old bastard Morban in the act of emptying out the younger lads' purses before they get the chance to waste it on the local whores.'

Saratos shook his head brusquely, his Latin still a rough edged growl in comparison with the older man's lively vernacular.

'I hear he go by name of "Honest Morban" now, and not the man he used to be. Or maybe he century finally get tired of being temporary owners of they pay on way to he purse.'

Sanga shrugged.

'Just as well he's got a new fortress of boys still wet behind the ears to terrorise then, ain't it? Come on, you dirty-arsed Dacian lump, let's go and sniff the air for gossip.'

The two men strolled easily along the row of barracks, ignoring the stares and occasional pointed comments aimed at them by the Eighth's soldiers, to find Morban, already hard at work on a half circle of men from across the road that divided the auxiliaries' temporary barracks from those occupied by their legion counterparts.

'You see that's the thing with combat soldiers, which you clearly aren't—'

The apparent leader of the legionaries shook his head and raised a hand.

'I'm not having that, friend. We're combat soldiers, alright!'

Morban looked around the faces gathered about him.

'In name, perhaps, but you don't look it to me. There's not a scar to be seen on any of your faces. Whereas . . .' He turned to indicate the men standing behind him, pointing to each one whose cheeks, chins and eyebrows were marked by the thick white cicatrices that had resulted from battle wounds repaired in haste. 'See? One in three of our boys has tasted his own blood at one time or another. Nice and tidy, mind you, most of them sewed up by our doctor when she was alive, and none of them bad enough to put a woman off their coin, but there all the same. That's Britannia, that is, and Germania, and Dacia, and Parthia . . .' He smiled, shaking his head at the legionaries. 'I could go on, but why embarrass you? The farthest any of you lot have been from home is here, for fuck's sake! And the worst that's happened to any of you is getting caught out by the three cup trick, right?' He pointed at the beautifully inlaid handle of the legionary's dagger. 'I'll bet that knife's never been used for anything more challenging than making the fortress pimps mind their manners, eh?'

Now thoroughly irritated, the legion man shook his head vehemently, gesturing to the muscular specimens lurking behind him. Testament to months with nothing better to do than condition their bodies to peak physical strength, they sported the sort of swollen biceps and rippling chest muscles that would have put a frown on the face of any athlete.

'So fucking what? We could still have you scrawny collection of rejects any day! You look like you couldn't hold up your own dicks in the bathhouse!'

Morban's slow, lazy smile was all the confirmation the two newcomers needed to know that, with his hook taken, he was about to reel in his latest catch.

'It's a common mistake, and we'll forgive you for it. After all, you all probably sleep like babies, untroubled by the sort of things we've had to do, and the horror that's happened on the other side of our shields. Mostly to the men trying to best us, of course, or else we wouldn't be here, would we? So never mind, girls, come back for a chat when you've got your blades wet and then we can talk seriously.' He turned away with a slight shake of his head, then looked down at the hand on his tunic's sleeve. 'Is there something I can help you with, *friend*? Only I was under the impression that this conversation was over. There's nothing more to be said—'

'My arse!' The blunt rejoinder narrowed the standard bearer's eyes, a simulation of anger that Sanga knew from experience was just Morban doing what Morban did best, but the legionary facing him, as intended, was getting a little more angry with every tiny gesture of contempt. 'You think you're all that? Any one of us could have any one of you in no time. *Any* one of us!' He gestured to the men behind him, some of them nodding with equal vehemence. 'Not that any of you women will have the balls to—'

Sanga flicked Morban a glance, catching the return blink that told him the time was right, and gestured to Saratos, whose face was apparently blank with a total lack of concern, or indeed interest in what was being discussed.

'You lot? There's not one of you muscle queens that could take my mate here.'

In the silence that followed his interruption, the legion men looked at each other, disconcerted at having their manliness challenged in such forceful terms.

'Him? That scrawny sack of shit?'

Morban grinned, tapping his purse.

'I'd back that scrawny sack of shit against any one of you. And as it so happens, I'm flush with silver at the moment, on account of having met some especially stupid locals in Mediolanum. I emptied their purses and then we were ordered to march before I got the chance to spend the dozy bastards' money.'

'And it's burning a hole in your purse, is it?' The leader of the group of soldiers gathered around Morban grinned down at him. 'I think we can do something about that, can't we, lads?'

His comrades voiced their assent, delving into purses with the eagerness of men who knew that when a golden opportunity presented itself, a man either grabbed with both hands or forever regretted his moment of hesitation. Morban looked about him with the happy smile of a man who was either deluded or supremely confident, nodding eagerly as the pot being collected in the legionary's cupped hands grew.

'So what's that, twenty denarii? If that's all you have, then let's . . .'

The legionaries' ring leader raised a hand.

'Not so fast! I'm not in yet. Here, Titus, get a hand in my purse and pull out a gold. And keep your sticky fingers from the rest of it.'

The auxiliary inclined his head in respect for the bold move.

'An actual gold aureus? You don't see many of those, and the ones you do see you're not allowed to touch as a rule.'

'You can match it?'

He grinned at the soldier's suspicious glare.

'I can match it, sonny, never you mind that.'

'I'll match it too!'

Both men turned to look at Sanga, Morban with a glare that spoke volumes for his disgust at his comrade's evident urge to get in on the action, the legionary with fresh amusement.

'You want some too, eh ugly?'

'Yes I do. I want that pretty little knife you're wearing. This . . . gets that, when my mate here leaves your man puking his guts up on the cobbles. Or is that rich for your taste?'

The other man shrugged.

'One gold piece will feel as good in my purse as any other. You're on.'

Morban shook his head in irritation.

'If you two have finished with the side bets I suggest we get on with it. Let's see this champion that's going to risk his life for your money.'

The biggest of the legionaries stepped forward, clenching his knuckles and squaring his massive shoulders. He looked down contemptuously at Saratos with a good head's height advantage, but the man with the handful of coins shook his head in puzzlement.

'Risk his life? He's going to put your man on his back once or twice and then wander off for a nice nap to get him over his efforts.' He grinned at the Dacian, shrugging as he backed away from the spot where the fight would play out. 'It's nothing personal, friend, you understand that, don't you? So let's get on with it, eh? I've got better things to be doing, once your tent mate here's coughed up the coin he's going to be owing us. Let's face it, he volunteered you for the wrong fight.'

Saratos laughed, shaking his hands as if to loosen the fingers and then looked down to examine his knuckles critically, wryly turning them to display them to his opponent. Their skin was flecked white with the marks of previous fights, which should have been enough to make the other man wary.

'Hah! He always doing that, is why hands have so many scar. But he not my tent mate. *This*' – he gestured to Sanga with a sneer – 'my tent mate, and he smell like pig most of time. He fart so bad you can cut with knife. Once he even shit heself after too much wine, and the shit *this* big—'

He stepped forwards with his hands raised as if to demonstrate the size of the offending item, Sanga grinning as his friend ghosted within arm's reach of the big legionary. The move went unnoticed by the men, who were genuinely amused by his bitter complaints. The big legionary was nonplussed by the apparent lack of any aggression from his opponent. He flicked a confused glance at his friends, and that was all the opportunity the Dacian needed. Changing his demeanour in an instant from that of a world-weary victim of his tent mate's gastric emissions to hard-faced executioner, he lunged in fast and low to spear a rising half-fist up under his hapless opponent's ribs, knocking the wind out of the legionary with an explosive whoosh, then stepped back and waited while the big man slowly doubled over in agony. He raised a fist and picked his spot as the winded soldier's head sank towards his chest, then stabbed a swift jab into the side of his jaw and felled his victim, dropping the insensate soldier to his knees, his head shaking in stunned bewilderment as he swayed on the edge of collapse. The Dacian turned away to face the astounded legionaries, opening his hands in an untroubled shrug.

'You hit him before he was ready!'

Saratos paced towards him, looking contemptuously to either side as the legionary's comrades backed away a pace.

'I hear you. You say "Let's get on with it". Is not signal to fight?'

'Yes, but—'

Sanga shrugged, his expression a parody of sympathy.

'I think what my mate's trying to get through your thick skull is that you told him to fight. Just because your man was too slow-witted to see the punch coming doesn't let you off the fact that he lost. And that you owe us. So either pay up or get ready for a proper kicking, not the gentle tap that this lump gave your man. And yes . . .' he grinned as the legionaries looked at each other in trepidation, 'you might get away with it if you fight like men, but the difference between us is that you're not much more than recruits, whereas we've all killed. *All* of us, and more than once. So handing out a beating to you lot is a holiday by comparison.'

Morban stepped forward wordlessly, and after a momentary hard stare, the legionary tipped the handful of coins onto his open palm, white-faced with anger.

'You bastards had better—'

'Sleep with one eye open?' Sanga shook his head in amusement. 'The day one of you tries to catch any of us unawares, is the day you'll discover just how quick men like us are to reach for our blades first and wonder who it is we're stabbing later.' He tapped the knife on his left hip as he turned away. 'Try me and find out.'

Sanga stepped close to the legionary, staring expressionlessly into his face.

'And you can take that dagger off your belt before you go. Unless you want to find out just how upset I can get when a wet behind the ears recruit calls me ugly.'

He grinned as the other man freed the weapon's scabbard from the frogs fastening it to his belt, taking it from him and pulling the blade from its leather protection, tossing it into the air and allowing it to turn a full circle before catching it expertly by the hilt and re-sheathing the sharp iron.

'Nice balance. I bet you paid good money for this, didn't you? At least you can comfort yourself that the next time it gets drawn it'll be tasting blood before I put it away again.'

★

'Tribunes, brother officers, welcome to Vindonissa.' The governor of Gallia Lugdunensis opened his arms in greeting. 'Your four cohorts are as welcome to me as any legion. You, Tribune Victor, at the head of two thousand of the best-disciplined men in all of the empire, and you, Rutilius Scaurus, I remember your Tungrians very well from your exploits in Dacia against the Sarmatae while you were under my command.'

Scaurus inclined his head in recognition of the praise, allowing himself to be embraced in the manner that was customary among former comrades of war. Gaius Pescennius Niger was as dour as the tribune recalled him, lacking any of the rhetorical flourishes that were usually popular with men of the exalted senatorial rank, who more often than not sought to both portray their own self-importance, and inspire their followers to share that sense of wonder.

'Thank you, Legatus Augusti. Although we might have preferred to renew our acquaintanceship under somewhat less troubling circumstances.'

The fortress's headquarters was lit by the flames of dozens of lamps, Niger having marched back into Vindonissa at the head of a thousand auxiliary soldiers an hour before, just as dark was falling. He had wasted no time in calling for his officers, his boots still flecked with mud thrown up by his horse's hoofs. Victor took his offered hand, then stiffened to attention and snapped a crisp salute, holding out a message container with his other hand.

'I am instructed to deliver this message from the imperial chamberlain, Legatus Augusti.'

The older man smiled grimly.

'A message from Cleander. I know my feeling of well-being was too good to last.' He looked at the proffered leather cylinder for a moment like a man offered a live scorpion, then sighed and took it, snapping the seal and pulling its contents out, holding the scroll up to the lamps' dim light. 'Greetings Gaius Pescennius Niger, and the emperor's felicitations on you and the men of your command . . .' He shook his head dubiously. 'I doubt the emperor even knows my blasted name. Anyway . . .' He read on, raising an eyebrow as he reached the bottom of the message's tight script. 'As I thought. Cleander gives with one hand and clenches the other into a fist, ready to deliver the inevitable punishment that will be mine in the case of a failure. I am commended to make the best possible use of the reinforcements that a beneficent empire has provided, and to bring this matter of Maternus's rebellion to an end as swiftly and ruthlessly as the empire expects. So it's a *rebellion* now, is it?'

Victor nodded.

'All the talk in Rome is of just that, Legatus Augusti. In progressing from his depredation of farms and isolated settlements to laying siege to a legion fortress, my former colleague has showed his true ambition, it is being said. He challenges the emperor himself, and must be brought to the emperor's justice.'

'And you, Tribune Victor? Do you believe that he seeks the overthrow of the state?'

The praetorian shook his head.

'In truth, Legatus Augusti, I cannot say with any truth that I comprehend the man's actions. Not when he mutinied against the Guard and murdered his tribune, nor at any point since then. And I fail to see why it is that he should change his tactics now, after such a long run of success in evading the forces sent to bring him down. Why do such a thing and expose himself to the full weight of Rome's retaliation, and why now?'

Niger nodded.

'Well put, Tribune. Why now indeed? But whatever the reason for his change of tactics, my orders are very clear. I am to topple him from this throne he seems to have constructed for himself and to bring him to Rome so that he can be seen to be punished, and in such a way that will make clear to anyone who sees or hears of it that the empire will not tolerate such an insurrection. Not even one so obviously doomed to fail.'

'And do you have a plan to unseat him, Legatus Augusti?'

Niger turned to the map painted on his office wall to answer Victor's question.

'I do, now that you and your men are here to reinforce my own, Tribune, and it's as straightforward as it has to be. Maternus has made a disastrous mistake in concentrating his force here, at Argentoratum. In taking a legion fortress under siege, he has pinned himself to a location and effectively lit a signal fire, daring us to come and get him. Which we will, gentlemen. His plundering of the Gallic provinces played to the strengths of the forces at his command, and helped him make a fool of our thinly spread forces. With hundreds of thousands of square miles to hide in, and lacking any fixed camp to which he might be tracked and bottled up, he was able to roam the western end of the empire more or less freely, even crossing the Pyreneii mountains into Hispania to raid that province in addition to those to its north. But now I scent his blood, and I intend to finish him quickly, before he has the chance to slip away again.'

He pointed to the centre of the map.

'We are here, with two legion cohorts totalling a thousand men, two cohorts of praetorians adding another two thousand, and three cohorts of auxiliaries – one of them admittedly a scratch force put together from centuries pulled from the border cohorts – making another three thousand trained and disciplined soldiers. With your four elite cohorts we have as much fighting power as a legion, gentlemen, and I intend to use it in the way that the emperor would expect of me.'

Victor stepped closer to the map.

'From here to Argentoratum is five or six days' march. But there appears to be more than one way to make that approach, presuming that Maternus intends to continue his siege that long. I'm assuming that you plan to keep our force together, legatus, rather than try to deploy the cohorts separately?'

Niger nodded his agreement.

'We're hardly in any position to fight as anything other than one force, not with most of the Eighth Legion trapped inside their fortress and with our own cohorts so disparate and lacking the practised coordination of a legion. And Maternus will have men watching all the potential approach routes, you can be sure of that. The man seems to have an almost divine gift for knowing when an enemy is at hand.'

Scaurus nodded.

'Good scouting must be the first essential that his survival has rested on all these years. And there are three approach routes, which means that whichever direction we come at him from, he has two ways to escape.'

Niger pointed to the besieged fortress.

'Indeed so. For those of you who don't know the place, Argentoratum is here, on the upper reaches of the river Rhenus, in a wide valley between two ranges of hills. To the west we have the Vosegus range and to the east the Abnoba mountains, both crossed by roads suitable for swift movement of troops. Which means that we have three potential routes of advance: up the eastern side of the Abnoba and then west through the mountains, up the western side of the Vosegus and an easterly approach, or, most directly, up the valley of the Rhenus between the two ranges. It also means that, as Tribune Scaurus points out, there are multiple routes along which Maternus can withdraw without any difficulty, no matter which direction we come from; too many for us to make any attempt to bottle him up.'

He pointed at the road to Argentoratum's south.

'If we advance up the river valley from the south, he'll know we're coming when we're still more than a day's march away, which means he'll have the advantage of choosing whether to disengage and melt his force away into the Vosegus hills and back into Gaul, or come at us head-on with more strength than we have, and with room to manoeuvre.'

'Won't the Eighth sally from their fortress if they realise we're close at hand, Legatus?'

The senator shrugged at Marcus.

'That's a gamble I'm not sure I wish to take, First Spear. Maternus has enough men under his command to overwhelm us in a straight fight on an open field simply by turning a flank and getting a mob of his men into our rear. And the Eighth's legatus may well be too cautious to make any sort of aggressive move, if the besiegers simply march away without any sign of a relief force. The legion has already sent four cohorts north to reinforce the army on the lower reaches of the Rhenus, which means he only has two thousand men inside the fortress. Maternus's departure will be a cause for celebration, but the man in command may suspect a gambit designed to draw him out from behind his walls. I'd certainly wait a while before coming out if I were standing in his boots. As a result, I expect that we'll have to face his army with what we have here, and I'm unconvinced that what we have here will be enough in a straight fight. Even if we anchor a flank off the river, he might well have enough strength to turn the other one and envelop us. If there is a battle to be fought, it must be fought in a way that favours our strengths, and not his.'

Victor was staring at the map thoughtfully, and after a moment he pointed to the fortress's position.

'If my former colleague had set out to pose us a difficult question, I doubt he could have done any better.' The men gathered around him waited for him to explain, and the praetorian pointed a finger at Argentoratum. 'The complexity lies not in the approach march, or which route Maternus might use to retreat his army, but more in the question of what it is he thinks he can achieve by attacking the fortress. I'll show you what I mean.'

He moved to the sand table, drawing lines with his finger.

'Let's assume that an approach from the south is too easily spotted, and will lead to a battle that we might well lose, as it will provide Maternus with ample time to manoeuvre his army on a broad plain that will, as the legatus augusti says, allow him to outflank us. So that's not really an option. But what about coming at them from another direction? Say we march north on the eastern side of the Abnoba range. When we come out of the mountains we'll be less than ten miles from the Rhenus, so there's no way that the garrison won't know we're there given the elevation of their walls. And consider the local geography.' He sketched a swift rectangular shape with a finger and then a line that bifurcated around it and then rejoined on the far side. 'Here's Argentoratum, about a mile to the west of the Rhenus. It's situated on an island between two branches of a tributary of the Rhenus which joins it a few miles to the north. The Rhenus itself is bridged, here . . .', he drew the larger river and its crossing to the fortress's east, 'with plenty of room to manoeuvre our cohorts between the two rivers. So let's say we approach from the east, through the mountains. If Maternus didn't see us coming with enough time to get his men over the river, and into position to attack us during our approach march, then he'd either have to move a significant force to defend the bridge over the Rhenus or retreat. And he'll know that if he tries to stop us crossing the river, he runs the risk of having legionaries at his back, if the legatus in Argentoratum has any spirit.'

He shook his head in bewilderment, staring at the map.

'But that still doesn't answer the question that's troubling me. Why would he come all this way east from Gaul and lay siege to a legion fortress? Why attract all this attention, only to take up a position that means he'll have to run away at the first threat of attack, if a strong enough army comes after him? I just can't see what it is that's made him take such a bold step after so long masterfully avoiding any serious confrontation.'

Niger walked around the sand table to stand alongside him.

'And what of the western route, on the far side of the Voseges?'

'It's too open. Any scouts would see us coming miles away, whereas the road through the Abnoba foothills is much closer. If we're going to make any sort of covert approach, it's going to have to be the eastern route.'

The legatus nodded slowly.

'So I see. But what's to stop Maternus from posting scouts on that road, too? He must see the vulnerability.'

Victor shrugged.

'Absolutely nothing. I'd certainly do it. Tribune Scaurus, where would you post your lookouts if you were intending to spot an approach march across the Abnoba mountains?'

Scaurus stepped forward, stared at the map for a moment and then pointed decisively at a spot where the road that ran north alongside the mountains was joined by the route through the range from Argentoratum to the west.

'There. That's the point where a relief force would unmistakably be heading for the fortress. Put a few horsemen there and be ready to ride at the first sign of hostile troop movements and Maternus could count on having at least a day's warning of any approach.' He looked at Niger and the other tribunes levelly. 'If, of course, the message rider actually manages to get back to warn him.'

'There's nothing like getting out of bed in the small hours to make a man know he's alive, eh, First Spear?'

Marcus shot a glance at his companion, but if Silus was expressing any frustration at having been woken less than four hours after getting to sleep, his face was showing little sign of it in the light cast by a pair of blazing torches that were illuminating the stable block.

'You're genuinely enjoying this, aren't you, Decurion?'

'What do you think?'

The cavalryman grinned at him, proffering his cup of wine and honey and waiting until Marcus had taken a sip and returned it before continuing in the same soft tone that night operations always seemed to inspire. The silent darkness pressed in closely around the quiet bustle of activity as the troopers of the Tungrian horse squadron, attached to the First Cohort years before in Britannia and never reclaimed, busied themselves preparing for a night march that was to be conducted under wartime rules, tying sacking to their horse's hoofs to muffle the sound of their exit from the fortress.

'While you lot were mincing around the German forests and kidnapping witches, me and this lot were left to rot in Rome with the rest of your muddy-footed rabble, weren't we? Which meant we had nothing much better to do than drink ourselves half to death and run the risk of the local bar girls finishing the job. It's questionable which of us was taking the greater risk.'

Marcus twitched a small smile at his comrade.

'My apologies, Decurion. If I'd known the dangers we were exposing you to, I would have begged Tribune Scaurus to have brought you along with us. Although when we got back from kidnapping witches, it seemed to me that you'd managed to cope with the adversity well enough. And quite possibly fathered more than one little bastard to leave your mark on the city.'

Silus stared at him for a moment before speaking again; his eyes had narrowed at the last word he would have expected to hear from the younger man's mouth.

'There's no gentle way to put this, my friend, so I won't try to coat it with honey. You left the city and went north a broken man, seemingly lost to us. But you came back almost completely healed.'

'Almost?'

'I see you staring away into the distance sometimes and I know your spirit is with hers. But given that we feared you were lost to us forever, your return is nothing short of miraculous. What did the witch do to you? How did she pull the man we knew back from wherever it was you had gone to hide?'

Marcus shrugged.

'What did she do? I have no idea. I wasn't myself, and those days are something of a blur to me now. But I do recall falling into a sleep so deep that I might never have woken again with the touch of her fingers on my forehead as my last conscious memory. I dreamed, Silus, a dream more real than the world I had temporarily left, my ennui falling from my mind like a worn out cloak. I was sitting by a river, wide and dark and still, too wide for the other bank to be clear to me, and I knew that what I wanted most in all the world was waiting for me on that distant shore. I was considering easing myself into the water and swimming out into the darkness when someone spoke to me, and I turned to see a woman standing at my side. I cannot remember her face, but I know that an overwhelming sense of peace descended on me. I was overcome by the feeling that nothing really mattered, and that my life was little more than a dried-up leaf resting on her palm. It was the same feeling as extreme exhaustion, or inebriation, but without any of the emotions involved in either. I was simply nothing, and of no consequence to the world. It felt . . . serene.'

He shot a glance at Silus, but the other man simply tipped his head in a silent gesture to continue.

'She spoke to me, and her voice seemed to come from far away and yet with total clarity. I still recall the words, which is strange when I've forgotten almost every other dream I've ever had within a moment of waking. "This is the Great River," she told me, in a voice so gentle it seemed to soothe my spirit, and yet strong enough to bring me to my feet beside her. "It is the border between your life and the life that follows. You may cross it, but if you do so you will lose this life, and all that you love in it. And yes, she lies across that river, but there are others still alive who will depend on you in the years to come, those of your blood and those with whom your spirit has become entwined. Will you abandon them to be with her?" And I knew I could not bring myself to turn my back on our son, or even on the unfortunate child that had been forced upon her by another man, and even as that realisation struck me, she spoke again, her voice harder than before, purposeful and majestic. "And there are wrongs to be righted, justice to be delivered. If you cross over now, these insults to what is right will endure long beyond your time, and harm the spirits of those you love. Will you surrender to the hurt you have suffered, or will you fight?" I stared across the river for a moment longer, wondering how it would feel to be joined with her again, and then replied to the woman's question. I gave her the only answer I could.'

'You told her that you would fight.'

Marcus nodded at his friend.

'I did. And as the word left my mouth, her face changed. The serene goddess of peace disappeared, and in her place was someone different, a hard-faced and noble warrior priestess armed and arrayed for battle, and she roared a single word at me, seemingly loudly enough to split stones, the sound of it resonating in every bone and muscle of my body, raising my choler, my teeth baring in a snarl even as I slept.'

'What was the word?'

Marcus smiled again, recalling the memory of what had followed.

'*Wake*. Just that. And with that one word I regained consciousness from whatever sleep Gerhild had entranced me into, so abruptly it was as if a thunderclap had snatched me back to life. I was on my feet without thought, my hands on the hilts of my swords, and even before I realised that our party was under attack and in danger of being overrun, I was moving, my blades in the air and hungry for blood. I was death incarnate for that short time, more warrior than I have ever been before or ever will be again, fighting as if I was possessed by some daemon of vengeance, my previous torpor burned away to leave my spirit incandescent with fury.'

'And the thoughts that had troubled you?'

'Are gone. Never to be considered again, not even when I think about my wife and the wrong done to her. I cannot recall what was troubling my mind because I am consumed with one purpose and one purpose alone, to protect my familia. At any cost.'

Silus nodded.

'A man can have worse ambitions in life. And it's good to see you whole again. Or nearly so?'

The younger man nodded.

'Yes, *nearly* is a fair description of where I find myself. I still yearn to have revenge for what has been inflicted upon those I love, but not in the same hot-blooded manner, and not at any price. I will take that revenge, but when I do so I will walk away from the cooling corpses of my tormentors unchecked.'

'And that will be a trick I'd pay good money to witness. But for now I suggest we limit our ambitions to the job in hand. Are we ready to march?'

The question was directed at his double-pay man, who had approached silently with his hobnailed boots muffled in the same way as their beasts' feet.

'Yes, Decurion. All of our men have completed their preparations.'

'Very well, let's get their faces into the oats and be on our way.'

Placing a nosebag of fodder over each horse's head as their last act before leading the animals out of the stable block's concealment from the fortress around them, the squadron proceeded out into the torch-lit gloom in single file, walking their mounts out through the opened gates and into the darkened street beyond in almost total silence. The fortress gate was watched by the lone figure of the legion's senior centurion, his men having been ordered into their closed, shuttered guardroom. The grizzled veteran exchanged salutes with Silus and Marcus as the two men brought up the column's rear in the company of several men of a more nondescript appearance than the cavalrymen. Watching as they disappeared into the gloom, his lips twitched into a knowing smile at the sight of their worn cloaks and hard faces.

'Good hunting, gentlemen. Take no prisoners.'

6

The army marched north on the road for the municipium of Arae Flaviae the next day, with the Eighth Legion's cohorts leading the column as suggested by Scaurus. Heading north at the standard march pace of twenty miles a day, and digging out a marching camp each night, with the full wartime security routine in force, they reached the city before dark of the third day. They camped close to the river Nicaros in plain view of the sprawling settlement's elevated position on a promontory beside the river. The city's magistrate, alerted to their approach by the army's outriders, came out to meet them and paid his respects to a suitably dignified Niger. After a brief discussion, the legatus issued his orders.

'Since the city has two good-sized bathhouses, the army will bathe, two cohorts at a time.'

While his men took their ease sweating the dirt of three days' marching out of their pores, he called his officers together, serving the usual wine and contemplating the copy of the Vindonissa fortress's map he had had drawn up before their departure from the fortress.

'We're going to need a slice of good fortune if this plan of yours is to work, Rutilius Scaurus.'

The tribune's mouth twitched in a smile.

'My experience, Legatus Augusti, has long been that we make our own good fortune in this life.'

The senior officer nodded dourly.

'True. And Fortuna, as I'm sure you were about to add, favours those with the courage to demand her favour by means of their valour. But the fact remains that we're investing all our hopes for making this attack work in the abilities of a handful of your men. As the Divine Julius said all those years ago, the die is indeed cast. You think that Maternus's scouts will already be watching us?'

'No. If I were him I'd put my watchers on the road between this municipium and Argentoratum. After all, we might simply march on to the north and pose him little threat. He'll want to be sure we're definitely committed to an approach from the east before making any changes to his tactical dispositions, though; a lookout posted in the valley would give him more than adequate warning, I'd imagine.'

'Do you concur with this opinion, Tribune Victor?'

The praetorian nodded.

'I do. Maternus always was a logical thinker, and that fits with what I'd expect of him.'

'Very well, gentlemen, I tend to agree. But let us consider the possibility that we are all mistaken, and that a messenger is already riding west with the news of our presence here. What would you do, if you were in command of his army, and warned that this many men were camped here, only two days' forced march away?'

'I can answer that question, because I know Maternus the best of all of us.' Victor considered the options available to their enemy for a moment. 'He'd manoeuvre his army to prepare for an attack from the east, and have the bridge across the Rhenus ready to fire at the first sign of our approach. But he wouldn't make those changes to his tactical disposition until he knew for certain that we were moving west – however much he might suspect this as being the most propitious approach route – because he won't want to lose his freedom to respond to any other threat. And when he sees the signs of an army on the march to his south, he'll know that his decision to keep that flexibility was the right thing to do. He'll throw everything he can spare south to confront what will look for all the world like a relief force. And, if we have our timings right, that will be the moment of our maximum opportunity.'

'I hope you two gentlemen are as justified in your confidence as you seem.'

Scaurus and Victor exchanged a wry glance, both men well aware of the pressure that their superior was feeling. Victory over an army of bandits was nothing more than was expected of him, whereas defeat would end his previously successful career in ignominy.

'I have every confidence that my men will play the part expected of them, Legatus Augusti.'

Niger nodded.

'And so do I, Tribune Scaurus. I recall how well they fought in Dacia, and the stories of your exploits since then have done nothing other than to burnish your reputation – even if you do seem to have dabbled in politics a little more than might be appropriate for a man of your class. My concern is not with your men, or whether they will succeed in their role in this plan of yours, but rather with the unknown here. Will this man Maternus play the part we have written for him? That's the question on my mind. Because if he fails to do so, we may find ourselves in a difficult situation that's entirely of our own making.'

'You want my firewood?'

Silus nodded, pointing at the cart standing beside the farmer's barn.

'All of it. And I want to rent that waggon for a few days, and the horse that pulls it.'

'And what am I supposed to do for a fire once winter starts to bite?'

The decurion swung his leg across his mount's back and dropped lightly to the ground, reaching into a leather saddlebag and pulling out a small purse that caught the farmer's attention exactly as he had intended.

'You sold your harvest about two months ago. And ever since then you've had little to do other than get ready for winter. Slaughtering and salting your beasts, gathering plenty of wood: all important, but secondary to having that crop in and sold, right? And you'll have made a decent price, because it's been a good enough year, enough rain, enough sunshine. But a man can never have too much gold, can he? After all, firewood can be replaced easily enough.'

He held up the purse on a flat palm, tossing it into the air a few inches to land with a reassuringly heavy thud.

'How much?'

Silus turned to his double-pay man with a smile.

'See? I told you they always see sense the moment they hear the gold. How much?' The decurion cast an expert eye across the farm's stacked cordage, pursing his lips. 'I reckon you'd pay a neighbour two . . . perhaps three in gold . . . for this much wood. You rent me that cart, and a man that knows the horse to make sure all goes well – and to bring it back to you once we get the wood to where it's going – and I'll pay you five.'

'Ten.'

Silus grinned and walked forward to stand toe to toe with the farmer.

'A nice start to negotiations, my friend, and displaying all the cunning of your kind. Congratulations on exceeding my expectations. But you're missing one crucial fact, I'm afraid.'

The burly bearded man stared into his face with an expression of disdain.

'And what would that be?'

'Two things. This.' The decurion held up a scroll, smiling again as the farmer shrugged. 'I know, you can't read. It says that the province of Germania Superior – that's where you live, in case the fact had passed you by – is hereby placed under wartime law. *Military* law. Which allows me to take whatever I want from you and pay you what I deem to be a fair reparation for your loss. And at the moment I'm setting that very fair price at five in gold. Not very long from now I'm going to reduce the price to what it's actually worth, and not long after that I'm going to take what I want and tell you to go fuck yourself. Which will mean that you'll have to go and join the queue at the fortress in Argentoratum, once we're done chasing off the bandits who've got it under siege, and see just how generous the legatus in command there is, given that it was probably the same bandits who bought your grain that have him bottled up in his own fortress. It's true, isn't it? You and all the other farmers round here have had a good year, first with a no-questions-asked purchase of all the grain you could spare by strangers from the north, and now us, offering to pay double for your winter fuel.'

The farmer nodded, his obdurate expression surrendering to one of reluctant resignation.

'And then there's this.' Silus tapped the hilt of his sword. 'This, whether you realise it or not, is wartime. And what with you having supplied an enemy of the state with food, I'd be totally justified in airing my iron and arresting you as an accomplice, or just opening your throat here and now. So. Let's try that negotiation one more time, shall we? The price I'm offering for your firewood – all your firewood, since you've irritated me more than was sensible, including whatever's waiting by your hearth – and for the loan of that cart and a decent horse, and a man to bring them back here when we're done with them in a day or two, is now *four* in gold, and it'll be four until I've had time to count to—'

'Four. Done.'

'Wise of you.' The decurion turned to his second-in-command. 'Get the cart loaded and make sure we leave nothing behind. And check the beast he tethers to that cart, I don't want some poor fucking nag that drops dead between the shafts before we've covered a dozen miles.'

The double-pay man saluted neatly and started shouting orders, galvanising the waiting column of troopers into what was evidently well-practised action. The farmer stared at the scene in undisguised disgust, shaking his head at the four gold aureii Silus had slapped into his palm.

'I'm not your first, am I?'

The decurion grinned at him, slapping his brawny arm in commiseration.

'Not hardly. There's another half dozen carts of wood waiting back there on the road where you can't see them, just so's you weren't encouraged to make this even harder on yourself. And now you're wondering why your neighbours didn't warn you we were coming. Part of it's the obvious fact that you'll already know well enough, which is that no man likes to imagine his neighbour escaping the fate that's overtaken him. But just in case you've got blood ties to the next man we'll be having this little chat with, I'll say the same thing to you I did to your neighbour to the south: if I find any of the farms I'll be doing business with ready for my visit, with their cordage suspiciously light and their waggons not to be seen, I'll assume that they've been warned by one of you. And in the event that I think that's happened, I'm going to kill all your carthorses, set fire to all your waggons, and then I'm going to ride back down the road and torch every farm I've visited. Which means that not only will you lose your livelihood, but when your neighbours find out that it was you who caused their hardship, they'll be after you with blood on their minds. That clear?'

The farmer nodded glumly.

'Clear.'

'Good.'

Silus turned away, smiling to himself as big man blurted out the question that he'd been asked at every farm.

'But why do you need so much wood that you'll pay over the odds for it?'

He turned back to face the other man with a hand on the hilt of his dagger.

'You'd be wise not to speculate, friend. Let's just say that I've got a fire to build. A big fire. Is that enough to satisfy your curiosity?'

'Here. This is the perfect spot.'

Qadir looked up and down the road, squatting beside Marcus in the cover of the dense undergrowth that flourished beneath the canopy of trees tiered up the hill behind them. The road below them swept around the edge of the hill they had cautiously advanced down before straightening up to run for several hundred paces alongside the river, whose steep-sided valley provided a convenient passage through the Abnoba hills. At the bend's midpoint, a massive boulder the size of a small house rose above the road, its pockmarked sides testament to the close attentions of military engineers before the decision had presumably been made to leave it in place rather than expend any more energy to little benefit. It was equally clear that the usual, yearly task of clearing the vegetation away from the roadside had been ignored for at least a decade, to judge from the scattering of bushes and trees along the verge. A copse had sprung up in the rock's shadow, half a dozen young trees rising over a profusion of bushes to form the perfect conditions for an ambush.

'Yes. My men can cover the road to take down any men that evade us.'

The small party had parted company with Silus's cavalry squadron at dawn three days before, working their way carefully up the eastern edge of the Rhenus's wide valley, although there had been no sign of the rebel leader having set any of his men to patrol that far out from the besieged fortress. Making their way up and over the broad valley's side, rather than simply turning left onto the road through the Abnoba hills and risk running into the very messengers they had been sent to intercept, they had cautiously eased their way through the forested folds in the land using hunters' paths. They emerged at length at a point overlooking the narrow valley through which both the army and the men riding ahead of it to alert Maternus to its presence had to pass.

Arminius slid into the bush's cover behind them, appraising the scene before them with equal expertise.

'A bend to slow them down, a copse for concealment and then a straight road to let the easterners' arrows fly true. Where will we camp?'

Marcus gestured to the treeline's edge.

'Right here. We'll grub out enough of this low stuff to give us space for a few men to sleep, and cut steps into the hillside large enough for a man to roll up in his blanket and close his eyes on level ground. I want a pair of bows two hundred paces down the road at all times, one man watching the road in from here and another on the other side with the rope. When anyone passes heading east, we'll show no sign, so make sure your archers find good places to conceal themselves, Qadir.'

'Where do you want me and this monster?'

Marcus smiled at Arminius's description of the enormous Briton Lugos, who was now looming behind them, his face as imperturbable as ever.

'You can both go and fashion yourselves a hide on the other side of the road, then grub out a trench between the cobbles to hide the rope where it crosses the road. When the time comes, I want strong hands on it, and men who won't be afraid to wade into whatever chaos results without hesitation.'

'Perhaps we should have brought some of the Hamians' boyfriends with us, if you're expecting a brawl?'

'Perhaps. But Dubnus and his men aren't naturals when it comes to stealth, and I want us to be undetected until the moment comes to spring our trap.'

'And then you want whoever comes down that road to be scared shitless?'

The Roman shook his head.

'And then I want whoever comes down that road to be dead before they even know what's hit them. On this occasion, brothers, we're definitely not taking prisoners.

'It will be a grey day, it seems. Perfect weather for marching, if this rain keeps up.'

Scaurus nodded at Sergius's opinion, looking up at the clouds scudding through the dawn sky and pulling his cloak more tightly about him to keep out the wind nagging at its corners.

'Yes, a little rain will be a good thing, if we're to make the sort of march distance that will be required today. Our men will appreciate the cooling effect, once they've got over the discomfort of having water running down their backs.'

Sergius grinned his wry acceptance of the point, but before he had the chance to reply, a movement behind Scaurus made him snap to attention and salute with punctilious precision.

'Good morning, Legatus!'

Niger waved a salute at him in reply, looking around at the ranks of soldiers formed into column of march and ready to move.

'Good morning, gentlemen, although quite what's good about this infernal drizzle eludes me. Is everything ready for our departure?'

Niger had made his appearance at just the right moment; Scaurus flashed his colleague Victor a swift glance, to find the praetorian looking as if he shared his fellow tribune's amusement at the legatus waiting until the last possible moment to join them.

'All cohorts ready to go, Legatus, and the men carrying a double ration of bread to get them through a day's hard marching. All you have to do is issue the command and we'll get on the road.'

'Very well.' The senior officer turned to the man holding his horse's reins and took them from him, hauling himself into the saddle with the look of a man who would have preferred a mounting stool but knew that appearances needed to be maintained. Looking down at them from his vantage point, he shook his head in confusion, perhaps feigned, perhaps genuine. 'Are you sure you intend to march thirty miles today? Surely it would be better for you to be fresh and clear-headed at the day's end?'

Victor shook his head with a smile.

'I've ordered the Eighth's young gentleman to ride, as he's not had anywhere near enough conditioning to manage that sort of distance without his feet cutting up, but the rest of us will share our men's hardships, as should be the case when we're demanding more from them than they usually have to give. And besides, Tribune Scaurus has a theory . . .'

Niger raised an eyebrow at them.

'Which is?'

'Knowing the way of soldiers – some of whom would bet on which man's urine will run out first in a pissing competition – I have every expectation that money will already have changed hands on the question of whether we officers can make the distance today, especially since it's raining. I'd hate to disappoint those men who were sensible enough to place a bet on all of us reaching the other end of the day on our feet.'

Niger inclined his head in a slight bow.

'Then I can only admire your commitment to your men's morale, gentlemen. Shall we?'

Victor nodded to Sergius, who promptly bellowed the order for the praetorians, whose turn it was to lead the order of march, to pick up their grounded shields and ready themselves to move, and commands echoed down the formation a moment later. Setting out from their camp at the battle march, the incessant rattle of thousands of hobnailed boots in their ears as century after century made their way onto the road's cobbled surface, Victor and Scaurus led the column through the town and up into the hills to its west. Any thought of a marching song was swiftly forgotten as heads were thrown back to suck in the air demanded by bodies working hard to maintain the brisk pace, grimly grateful for the drizzle's cooling scatter of droplets.

'You're sure about this plan not to build a marching camp tonight?'

Victor nodded at Scaurus's question.

'There won't be any open space wide enough to take a camp, not once we're up in those hills, and I'd rather use the time marching as far as we can today to minimise the distance we have to cover tomorrow. The men can sleep in their blankets at the roadside and be on their feet at first light, ready to move, without all that time spent taking tents down and getting them on the carts.'

'We'll have to hope that the rain stops by then or it'll be an uncomfortable night, to say the least.'

The praetorian shrugged with a grin.

'If it doesn't, then we'll all be that bit keener to get off our backs and onto the road again, won't we? A bit of rain is nothing compared to what Maternus and I were put through in basic training. We camped out in all weathers, with nothing more than as many tunics as we could wear and our cloaks and blankets to give us some semblance of warmth. Pouring rain, freezing wind and snow, storms . . .' He smiled again, a rueful remembrance of simpler times. 'Yes, the old bastards who were training us made sure we knew how to survive whatever weather the gods saw fit to throw down on us. A little bit of rain would be a small price to pay to remind Maternus that I for one never forgot those lessons. And now, Tribune, I think we need to provide these animals following us with an example of Roman leadership. Shall we up the pace just a little and tow them along for a few miles before we allow Julius and Sergius to take their turns at being the rabbit?'

'So, me and the others are wondering . . .'

Silus looked up from his place by the cooking fire, regarding the self-appointed leader of the young men who had been sent by the farmers to care for their waggons and the beasts that were pulling them with a questioning expression. Chewing vigorously at the mouthful of meat he'd taken a moment before, he swallowed, drinking from his beaker of water before replying. The farm boy's face was wan with exhaustion from a day of unremitting hard labour, he and his comrades having been roped in to assist the horsemen with a long day's brutally hard labour, but the curiosity was evident in his eyes as he waited for a reply from the hard-faced decurion.

'Yes?'

'We were wondering . . .'

'What all this is about? Why a squadron of cavalry, who've probably got better things to do, goes on a tour of the local farms buying up their firewood for generous prices? That's what you're all wondering, isn't it? And then there's the question as to why, now that we've got enough wood to heat a legion bathhouse for a month, we didn't just cart it back to the fortress we came from? What's the point, you're wondering, in building half a dozen bonfires out here in the middle of nowhere?'

The squadron had worked at a relentless pace through the day, unloading the waggons of firewood at one-mile intervals, sufficiently far from the road that ran alongside the Rhenus to be invisible to casual passers-by. The wood had then been fashioned into towering piles, expertly constructed to allow air to penetrate to the heart of the pyre where kindling had been carefully placed. The speculation as to why such strange preparations needed to be made had been evident in the youths' faces, and Silus had been expecting the question ever since he had turned the waggon train around and driven it back south to the first of the unlit structures, leaving a guard of four men to watch each of the other five. To the youth's evident surprise, the cavalryman patted the ground beside him.

'Come and sit down here and I'll tell you what's going on.' He laughed at the sudden look of caution in the boy's eyes. 'It's alright, I'm not that sort of man. One or two of my men wouldn't think twice about rolling you over, but we're not that sort of unit, either. So either come and sit next to me so that I can talk to you without having to bend my neck or piss off and remain ignorant. Your choice!'

After a moment's calculation, the German eased himself down onto the spot indicated.

'So, why build a load of pointless bonfires out here in the middle of nowhere? You clever lads haven't guessed it yet?'

'Well . . .'

'Now that you're sat here next to me, with me waving this about . . .' Silus raised the dagger with which he was spearing pieces of meat from the pot in front of him, 'you're worried that if you have guessed it right, I might just cut your throat. Which makes you wise, because I've known a lot of men who would already have left you all dead under a hedgerow for the crows. But that's not the way we work. So come on, what have you guessed?'

'They're a signal?'

'Yes, of a sort. But not the sort you might be thinking. What do you know about what's happening at the fortress?'

The youth shrugged.

'Not much. The rebels came and bought our grain, respectful-like – paid a decent price too – which my old dad said made them better than the soldiers because they always drive a hard bargain and pay as little as they can.'

Silus nodded, talking through the mouthful of meat on which he was chewing.

'They're clever bastards, those bandits. They have you thinking they're alright, when what they are is murdering scum who've been preying on innocents like you for years. And now they've laid siege to a legion fortress, which is like declaring war on Rome itself. Which makes them brave too. Or stupid. I'm not sure which it is yet. And so we've been sent here to chase them off, and put them down if we can, and these fires . . .', he gestured to the tower of wood a dozen paces from them, its dark bulk silhouetted against the stars, 'are, as you have guessed, a part of our plan. But they're not a signal, not in the way that you're thinking.'

The youth stared at him in puzzlement, and Silus continued his explanation.

'We're going to wait until an appointed time, and then we're going to light this one, make sure it's burning properly and then move on up the road to the next, and light that. And we'll keep doing that all the way to the last one, by which time there'll be half a dozen plumes of smoke reaching up into the sky, each one looking as if there's a burning farm at its base. So what will that look like?'

'Like someone's burning farms out one at a time?'

'Exactly. I told the lads that you were the clever one. And why would we do that?'

'I . . . I don't know.'

'We're going to do that so that the men besieging that fortress will look south, see the smoke from the fires, and tell themselves that there's an army marching north to challenge them. What do you think they'll do then?'

'I don't know.'

'Good answer. Neither do I. Perhaps they'll decide to run away and avoid a fight. Or perhaps they'll come south looking for one. Or maybe they'll just send their horsemen down here to find out what's behind the fires. They might even react in some way that we haven't thought of. But I know the one thing they won't be doing, and which we don't want them to do.'

'What's that?'

'Look somewhere else, sonny. For a very short time, we don't want them to look anywhere but south, and all the excitement that these fires will spark up ought to be just the thing to make sure that they don't.'

The farm boy stared at him apprehensively, and Silus laughed out loud at his pensive expression.

'You think now that I've told you all that I'm going to kill you. I told you, we're not that sort of men. Tomorrow morning we'll send you back to your farms with a tale to tell of how you were part of the trick that led to the defeat of the bandit Maternus. But for now we'll have to tie you up, I'm afraid.'

The youth started as he was pulled to his feet by men who had approached in silence while his attention had been on Silus. Binding his wrists and ankles, they laid him on the ground, rolling him in a blanket to keep out the cold before making their way back to the fire and leaving Silus looking down at him.

'It's nothing personal, boy, all you carrot crunchers will be getting the same treatment tonight. There'd be no point us going to all this trouble if one of you little buggers was to slip away and warn Maternus what's planned for tomorrow, would there?'

'What if they come looking for you, too many of them to fight off?'

The cavalryman laughed softly.

'Then we'll run, boy, like the good soldiers we are, and live to fight another day. All that will ever come from battle that can't be won and isn't run from is crow-picked bones and grieving widows. And I don't plan on being anyone's sad memories for a while yet. You get some sleep and we'll set you free in the morning when it's time for the fire to be lit. And then we'll see just how this man Maternus thinks.'

Marcus awoke from his doze with a start as Qadir shook his arm with a hissed warning. The sun was not yet high enough to cast its light directly into the valley, and mist from the river was hanging over the landscape in a grey blanket that cut visibility to less than twenty paces.

'Riders.'

Rolling swiftly to his feet to crouch beside Qadir in the cover of the foliage they had used to disguise their hide, he stared up the valley to the east, searching the impenetrable wall of mist for any sign of their quarry. The sound of hoofs that had alerted the Hamian to their approach was getting steadily louder; the clattering sounds of several horses were muffled by the fog but still perfectly clear to both men.

'Six of them. Perhaps eight.'

The invisible horsemen riding towards the copse were pushing their mounts to a fast canter from the sound of their progress, a pace clearly intended to cover ground as swiftly as possible without exhausting the beasts.

'Our column can't be too far distant, to judge by the speed they're making.' His face hardened at the prospect of a fight. 'Give the signal to Arminius and Lugos, and then get ready to shoot.'

The two men on the other side of the road responded immediately, rising from the cover of their own hide to signal their readiness. Lugos took a firm grasp of the rope and turned to look across the track at Marcus, waiting for the signal to spring their trap. The Roman drew his swords one after the other, laying both carefully on the ground before him and peering cautiously around the massive boulder through the cover of the roadside vegetation. He tensed as the approaching horsemen rode out of the grey curtain that had obscured them, close enough that he could see their grim expressions and the water beading on their armour. Returning his gaze to the two barbarians facing him, he raised a hand beside his face, turning it to show them the white palm and drawing a nod of confirmation from Arminius. The riders drew close enough that he could hear their raised voices over the clatter of hoofs, the jocular tones of men whose work was all but done, no doubt anticipating the reward that would be bestowed on them for providing their leader with the warning to reorient his army and meet the Roman attack from the east head-on. Keeping his hand perfectly steady, Marcus waited for the final few, critical moments, as the riders covered the last ten paces to the barely-discoloured line in the road's surface where the rope lay buried. He heard snatches of conversation over the tumult of their passage, one man's voice, louder than those of his companions, catching his attention as he tensed to issue the signal.

'. . . he'll tear them a new arse just like every other—'

Marcus whipped the hand down, reaching for the hilts of his swords as Lugos burst into motion, his upper arms bulging with the effort of tearing the rope free from its concealment and snapping it taut in the path of the oncoming riders, hurling himself to his left to pull it hard against the trunk of a tree. The leading horseman was lifted bodily from his horse with a choking grunt of surprise as the line snagged beneath his chin and ripped him from his saddle, dumping him onto the road's surface in the middle of the pack of men following. The next two riders raised their hands in an automatic reaction as they found themselves being forced backwards over their mounts' rumps.

'Go!'

Storming onto the road's cobbled surface, Marcus raised his swords and advanced on the men to his right, while Lugos and Arminius dropped the rope and snatched up their own weapons. The rebels who had been dismounted were still on their backs, struggling to comprehend what had happened through the shock of their impact with the unyielding stone surface, one of them lying in an apparent state of unconsciousness. A mounted man Marcus took for their leader raised his spear and pointed it at the Roman.

'There's only three of them! Into th—'

He stiffened convulsively as an arrow loosed from above tore down into his neck, its fletching almost lost in the soft flesh and the long shaft protruding from the side of his chest, glistening with his blood. Rising momentarily out of the saddle as his thighs spasmed, he toppled onto the road head first in his choking death throes. The horsemen beside him flinched defencelessly as Qadir loosed a second shaft down into them from the rock's flat top, felling another rider with the same precision and reaching for a third arrow with the fluid speed of long practice.

'*They're ours!*'

The Hamian nocked the missile to his bow, but obeyed the command and simply watched as his companions stormed into the milling horsemen. Marcus led with his spatha, dodging around a riderless mount and putting the long blade under the ribs of a man still staring up at the waiting bowman in terror. He thrust the sword home into the hapless bandit's heart and lungs before stepping away to make room for his slumping body, as it collapsed headfirst onto the cobbles and lay still in a rapidly spreading pool of blood. Arminius and Lugos were making their own terrifying assault on the group's other side, the German fighting with his usual slit-eyed intensity with sword and shield, ruthlessly cutting down first one and then the second of the two dismounted bandits who were attempting to defend themselves, while his monstrous comrade threw himself into the milling horses without any concern for his own safety. Swinging his beaked war hammer, he staved in a rider's armour, catapulting him from his saddle, then looped the weapon high over his head, turning it expertly in his hands to present the flat hammer face, in readiness to swing it down onto a horse's head. The beast's rider drew back his spear to throw it at the barbarian's massive chest but the cast flew wide as Qadir pinned his thigh to the horse's back with a swiftly-taken shot that left the rider contorted in agony. Not pausing in his attack for an instant, the Briton slammed the hammer's heavy iron head down onto the hapless animal's face, breaking its skull with an audible crack and dropping it lifelessly onto the road with a bellow of victory as Arminius put his sword through its helpless rider's throat, the horrific assault the last straw for the remaining two riders. Abandoning all hope of fighting their way out of the ambush, they turned their horses and spurred them back the way they had come. A mount staggered to its knees and threw its rider as Marcus hamstrung the beast with a swing of his spatha. Watching as Qadir dropped the last man from his saddle, hand scrabbling futilely at the arrow buried deep in his back, the Roman caught a flicker of motion to his left, as the momentarily-stunned rider who had been the first man plucked from his saddle by the draw line staggered to his feet. He regained his wits just in time to jump back out of the arc of Lugos's swinging hammer and, after a moment's indecision, turned to hare away through the copse towards the river.

'*After him!*'

The barbarians gave chase. Arminius swiftly outstripped the lumbering Briton, but the bandit, seemingly given wings by his terror, covered the twenty paces to the fast-flowing stream ahead of him and threw himself bodily into the water, striking out powerfully as he was whisked away by the river's flow.

'I have no shot!'

Marcus nodded at Qadir's warning, sheathing his swords and grabbing at the only horse that hadn't bolted, restrained from doing so by the dead weight of its rider hanging from its reins. Mounting it with a leap, the Roman pulled the reins free from its former owner's death grip and put his booted heels into its flanks to spur it down the road to the west, racing towards the remaining two Hamians and shouting a warning to stop them shooting at him. Reining in the horse, he leaned out of the saddle and extended a hand towards the waiting archers.

'*Give me a bow!*'

Snatching up the swiftly-raised weapon and a quiver full of arrows, he looped the container's strap over one shoulder and the bow across his back and chest, then spurred the beast onward down the road in swift pursuit of the bandit floating downriver, the swimmer already lost to view. Hearing hoofs clattering behind him, he looked back to find Arminius gaining on him, having managed to capture another dead man's mount, his horse's eyes bulging with the effort being demanded of it. Slowing to allow his friend to catch him, he spurred the beast back to the gallop once they were riding side by side.

'Perhaps he drowned!'

Marcus shook his head.

'He looked strong enough to me! If he can stay afloat, the river will take him all the way to the fortress!'

They rode on, both men shooting glances at the river to their right in the hope of seeing their quarry's head bobbing in the stream, but for several minutes they saw nothing. Just as their mounts were beginning to flag and Marcus was about to give up hope and call off the chase, his companion pointed at the river-bank in front of them.

'There he is!'

Clearly exhausted even when viewed from a hundred paces, the weary fugitive had staggered out of the river and was standing with his hands on his knees at the water's edge. Lifting his head to stare at the oncoming riders in disbelief, he turned and waded back into the flow, allowing the water to pull him away and floating on his back, clearly too spent to make any effort to guide his course.

'See if you can hit him with an arrow!'

Not waiting to see Marcus rein his horse in, leap from the saddle and run for the river bank, Arminius spurred his own mount on down the road at a breakneck pace, wringing every last iota of strength from the flagging beast. The Roman steadied himself, nocked an arrow and let it fly, cursing as the shaft hit the water five paces short of the swiftly receding target. He nocked and loosed again, the shot's distance accurate enough but dragged to the right of the helpless swimmer by a gust of wind. Estimating that he had one last chance, he raised the bow to its maximum elevation and pulled the arrow back to his ear. His eyes narrowed in concentration as he estimated the distance to where he expected his target to be when the shaft arrowed down onto him, but held the shot as Arminius came into view, galloping his exhausted mount towards the river's edge. One last mighty kick at the beast's flanks achieved what the Roman would have believed impossible, catapulting it out across the stream in a mighty leap that brought its huge weight down directly on top of the swimmer. Releasing the horse's reins, the German vanished beneath the surface for long enough that Marcus was starting to feel concerned when he surfaced again. He struck out for the left bank and crawled up onto the sandy shore to where his horse had already found its footing, staggering out of the water to stand, legs shaking but triumphant, at the water's edge.

Waiting for Marcus to walk the two hundred paces to join him, leading his own tired mount by the reins, the German looked up at his friend with a tired but jubilant grin.

'I knew you weren't going to hit him at that range. I doubt even Qadir could have put a shaft into him given the circumstances. So I did the only thing I could think of.'

'You're sure you killed him?'

Arminius laughed, pointing at the river's bank; the bandit's decapitated head was lying on its side where the river's water lapped at the shore.

'Unless he can live without a head, yes, I'm sure I killed him. His body might get that far downstream, but without his head, he's just another corpse.'

The army arrived an hour later, with Victor's magnificently arrayed men at the head of the long column. Marcus saluted as Legatus Niger, Victor and Scaurus reached the spot where the ambush party was waiting.

'This is all of Maternus's scouts?' Niger stared down at the line of corpses dispassionately. 'None of them got away?'

'These are the bodies of all but one of them, Legatus. And this . . .' the Roman gestured to the severed head at his feet, 'is the last of them. He made it into the river but Tribune Scaurus's slave jumped a horse onto him and then cut his head off.'

Scaurus turned to Arminius with an eyebrow raised.

'You jumped a horse onto him? While he was in the river?'

The German inclined his head to affirm the question.

'It was either that or watch him drift away on the current. He would have been close to the fortress by now.'

'And our advantage of surprise would have been lost.' The legatus nodded, his face creased in thought. 'I understand. So if you came up the valley to get here, I presume you hugged the foothills until it was time to turn right. Which means that you will have seen the fortress, First Spear?'

Marcus nodded.

'Yes, Legatus. We watched it for an hour or so from the hills the day before yesterday and it appears that Maternus has Argentoratum properly under siege. The fortress appeared to be completely encircled.'

'As I'd expect. But how is his army deployed? Which direction is it facing?'

'They were camped around the fortress for the most part, with a small part of their force covering the eastern bridge. A thousand men, no more.'

The senior officer pursed his lips.

'A thousand men to resist our crossing the river. And the remainder close enough to put us in the most difficult of positions if they catch us in the act of crossing the river. We'll just have to hope that this ruse of yours works, won't we, Tribune?'

Scaurus nodded.

'Indeed. And if my decurion manages to make what we planned come to pass, then it will start to play out from midday. Which gives us a little time to get our men into position for the approach march.'

'Very well, it seems that the success of our attack is now dependent on the actions of this man Silus. First Spear Corvus, you're the man here with the best understanding of the local geography. How far are we from the crucial bridge?'

Marcus came to attention.

'It's two miles to the end of the valley, Legatus, and another ten miles to the bridge.'

'And how quickly can our men cover those ten miles?'

Scaurus answered the question, his face carefully composed to avoid any hint of superiority over his praetorian colleague.

'My Tungrians are trained to run long distances, Legatus. Without their pack poles, they can do a ten-miler in well under two hours and still have the stamina to fight a battle at the other end.'

'And your praetorians, Statilius Victor?'

'I am forced to concede that my men are not as fast across the ground. I'd say their best pace would have them at the ten-mile mark in two hours.'

Niger nodded.

'With the Eighth Legion's cohorts right behind them, I'd imagine, and the auxiliaries bringing up the rear. Very well, gentlemen, re-order our column of march to put Rutilius Scaurus's men at the head, and once it's clear whether this idea of his has actually worked, we can let them off their rope to show the rest of us how it's done. Let us hope that this ruse of yours succeeds, Tribune, and that your men aren't running headlong to their deaths.'

'Well, this is the day, and this is the time.' Silus looked up at the sun one last time and nodded decisively. 'Midday on the fifth day, that was what we agreed, so let's keep our end of the agreement, shall we, boys? It's time to see just how well this wood will burn!'

The four men gathered around him huddled in closer to form a wind-break, as their decurion put his torch into the small fire that they had kept burning overnight, smiling in satisfaction as its grease-laden fleece, steeped in sulphur and lime, caught fire. Stepping back, he gestured to his men to do the same.

'There you go then, get on with it. It's not going to light itself.'

Taking their own torches, all four men lit them in the fire's flames and turned to the carefully constructed tower of wood they had built the previous day, fire logs painstakingly placed around a frame built from longer branches to form a chimney that would allow the tower's base to burn as quickly as its extremities. The bottom of the tower was liberally salted with forest debris from the nearby woods to encourage it to catch light quickly.

'Remember what I said, one torch on each side, and get them as deep into the wood as you can without snuffing them out.'

Waiting until all four men had their brands in the tower of wood, and the logs were starting to smoulder, he lowered his own torch and allowed the flames to lick up the handle until fully half its length was alight, then, carefully judging the distance before making the throw, tossed the blazing torch high into the air to fall down into the chimney and onto the waiting kindling. He grinned as the fire roared into life, a tongue of flame licking up the chimney to flicker at the tower's top with an angry roar that would not be subdued until all the wood had been consumed, the blaze sending smoke billowing into the air high above the field.

'And that, my lads, is how to do it. All we have to do now is saddle up, go and find the boys at the next pyre and do the same.' He pointed to the column of greasy smoke rising high into the calm air. 'Let's hope that the men besieging the fortress are scratching their heads and trying to work out what that means. Just imagine how much more puzzled they're going to be when there's five more of these to ponder. Let's go!'

They mounted their waiting horses and turned north, Silus gesturing to the farmer's son waiting on his now-empty cart that he could go home. The youth had been sullen and uncommunicative since being cut free that morning, but Silus hardly felt he could hold that against him given the indignity he'd been unavoidably subjected to.

'You've had a lucky escape, youngster! Just be sure to warn your old dad that the next time he supplies an enemy of the state with anything more than the steam off his piss, we won't bother taking the wood out of his barn before we set light to it!'

7

'This is it. Once we pass these hills, we'll be in plain view from the high ground between here and the fortress, if they've posted scouts this far out.'

Scaurus nodded at his centurion's observation.

'And while you'd have thought they wouldn't waste the manpower, given they had the road through the mountains watched, Maternus doesn't seem to be short of labour. And he doesn't sound like the sort of man we should underestimate either.' He turned to Niger. 'Perhaps First Spear Corvus and I should take a look at what's happening on the other side of that hill before we commit to running all the way to the Rhenus? It would be disappointing to charge out onto open ground and find his entire army waiting for us on the other side, to say the least.'

The two men climbed the hillside with their swords drawn, alive to the potential for enemy scouts to be roaming the countryside, in an attempt to discover the direction from which the inevitable Roman counter-attack would be launched. But when they reached the ridge overlooking the wide valley in which the Rhenus ran north from the mountains' foothills, there was still no sign of Maternus's men. The two officers stood looking out over the patchwork of fields between the hills and the river as they got their breath back, enjoying the feeling of the sun on their backs after the long climb up the hillside.

'Well, there's the fortress.' Marcus pointed across the plain to where the Eighth Legion's base loomed over its vicus, the white-painted walls standing out against the drab colours of its surroundings exactly as intended, a bold statement of imperial presence and power. 'It didn't look much like a siege to me when we got closer in, though. No trenches, no catapults, nothing you or I would recognise as the means of reducing the garrison to the point of surrender.'

Scaurus nodded.

'True. But it's still completely surrounded, earthworks or no earthworks. And with only two thousand men within its walls, they're as completely trapped as if they were inside a triple line of ditches. Let's see what else there is to be discerned from up here. Ah, look . . .'

He extended an arm and pointed to a spot ten miles south of Argentoratum.

'Do you see it? Smoke!'

Marcus looked at the valley floor for a moment before replying. 'Silus has done as he was asked, it seems.'

Thin plumes of smoke were rising from a number of points in the valley, and as the two men watched, a new fire sprang to life, another thin, twisting line of black rising into the air a mile north of the closest blaze.

'It looks for all the world like the signs of an advancing army announcing its presence by burning out everything in their path to prevent it being used as a defensive strong point.' Scaurus turned back to the fortress, staring intently at the ground between the while walls and the main course of the river. 'The only question now is whether Maternus takes the bait or decides to hold off making a move until it's clear whether he's really got an army to his south. And what about this little buttock of a hill between us and the river?'

Both men stared intently at the thin ridge of raised ground between the river crossing and the waiting cohorts in the valley below. If there were scouts positioned in the trees that grew thickly along its mile-long protrusion, they were not evident.

'So providing that's not been garrisoned, it will conceal us from the men besieging the fortress until we're less than five miles distant.' Scaurus stared at the feature thoughtfully. 'I suppose that's the big question, isn't it? If they have men in those trees, we'll be spotted the moment we leave the cover of this valley, but if they don't, then we're going to be within five miles before they spot us. And now, First Spear, I'd say that we've seen enough, wouldn't you?'

'That's the last of them, and here we all are together again, eh boys?'

Silus grinned around the circle of his men, the squadron complete with the firing of the sixth and last pyre to add its plume of smoke to the others still burning behind them to the south, the lighting of each fire in the chain having added five men to his gradually reforming squadron with their progress north.

'And with a little bit of luck, all this skulking about in the hedgerows won't have been wasted. Even now the man that leads those bandits will be staring this way and wondering who it is that's burning out the farmhouses to his south, which is what he'll think he's looking at. Which means that he's going to do two things: firstly, he's going to pull men from his positions to the east of the fortress watching the river – or at least that's what the tribune's hoping for. And secondly . . . any guesses?'

'If it was me, I'd send someone like us to find out what the fuck's going on.'

The decurion pointed a finger at the speaker.

'Exactly. He'll send some scouts out to have a look. And what do we do with enemy scouts?'

Another of his men answered the question, his face split into a grin.

'We kill the bastards!'

'How eloquently put, Trooper. We do indeed kill the bastards. Now, given that we're still ten miles short of their lines, and that it will take them a while to get their shit into a neat pile and decide who to send out, I reckon we have a bit of time before they'll be coming for a look at this particular little bonfire. Even so, we need to get mounted and find somewhere we can keep an eye on it without being seen. Nobody is to make a sound, or show any sign that we're here, until we know that we're up against, right?' He looked around the circle, meeting each man's eyes. 'Anyone who so much as twitches their dick at the enemy before I say so will have me to deal with once this is all over, because the only sort of fight I believe in committing to is an unfair one. We can leave the heroism to the officers and those dumb grunts who follow them round, just waiting for their next opportunity to get their spears wet, right? We, my lads, follow the old cavalry tradition that the best place to put a long blade is in the square of a running man's back! So, get saddled, follow me, and keep it *silent.*'

'I'm happy to report that the trap we set for Maternus has been set, Legatus. Whether he'll put his leg in it or not is a different question.'

'You were unable to see any sign as to whether the enemy has reacted to the fires you had your cavalrymen set?'

Scaurus shook his head.

'No, sir. The ground around the fortress is too far away for us to be able to discern troop movements. We either proceed as planned and take the chance that he's refused to take the bait, or we withdraw in fear of the unknown.'

Niger nodded decisively.

'Then there's no choice in the matter whatsoever. We must attack! As we planned it, Tribune, you must take your Tungrians in as fast as they can run, and the remainder of the army will follow up behind you at our best pace.'

'Yes, Legatus.' Scaurus saluted and turned to Julius who was waiting impassively behind him. 'Very well, Prefect, you know your orders.'

The big man saluted gravely, turning to Marcus and Varus with a wry smile.

'This is the moment we get to see if you two have big enough balls for the roles you've been given, much as I'd rather you were wearing the striped tunic and I was still carrying a vine stick. Get to it, gentlemen, and let's go and take that bridge.'

The two men nodded to each other and strode away down the line of their cohorts, Marcus barking orders that galvanised the Tungrians as their centurions echoed his commands in stentorian tones.

'Drop your pack poles by the side of the road! Make sure your valuables are either in your purses or up your arses, because you don't know if you'll ever see them again! Check that your boots are properly laced, triple-knotted and the ends of your laces are woven though the holes in your boots! Any man who falls out of the advance with a boot problem will have to sprint to catch up and will be on the receiving end of five with the short whip when this is all done with! Put your helmets on and tie the cheek guards shut! Get your tent mates to check that your armour is secured and that no buckles have been left open to let the air in! And you can leave your shield straps with your pack poles, this is an advance to battle, not an afternoon stroll around the countryside! I want you ready to *fight*!'

He waited while his officers encouraged their men through the few short minutes of preparation to march, pacing up and down with the air of a man eager to be elsewhere, waiting until the last of his centurions signalled their men's readiness before continuing his harangue.

'We will advance the first five miles at the run! Once we're past those trees in the far distance, we're going to make it simpler for you by running the remaining five miles! At the far end of the run, there is a bridge for us to take! With a little luck it'll have been left unguarded, but there's every chance that we'll have to take it from unpleasant men who would rather we didn't! And even if we do get across the river without a fight, you can bet that the enemy will have a good try at taking it back from us before the rest of the army arrives!'

Marcus paused and allowed his words to sink in for a moment before continuing.

'We're fighting today, there's no two ways about it! And we're *winning* today – that's not in doubt either! So you'd better be ready to be sharp, even after a ten-mile speed march, because the animals we're facing are honourless dogs who won't give a moment's consideration to cutting your throat and leaving you for the crows! Let me put this simply so that no one's in any doubt as to what we're going to do this afternoon. We're going to march! We're going to fight! And we're going to *fucking* win!'

The Tungrians stood in silence waiting for his next command, while the young first spear stalked back toward the senior officers with a grim expression that Scaurus knew wasn't any sort of affectation.

'No calls for a cheer or two, Rutilius Scaurus?'

The tribune turned back to Niger with a tight smile.

'We tend not to bother, Legatus. That sort of thing is all very well for men who need their spirits raising before a battle, but my men have been doing this for years now. They don't need to be reminded what they're fighting for, or to have heart put back into them. They know how to fight and they know they will fight, and that's all that matters. Are we ready, First Spear?'

Marcus saluted punctiliously, snapping to attention.

'The First Tungrian cohort is ready for battle, Tribune!'

'Vibius Varus?'

'The Second Tungrian cohort is ready for battle, Tribune! Will you be leading us into the fight?'

Scaurus shot Niger another amused glance.

'Young men, always thinking they can get away with unbridled impertinence, eh? Although on this occasion, they happen to be correct in that belief. The price of all that competence is that their tribune has to submit himself to the same hardships and dangers as his men.'

None of the men within earshot dared to express even the traditional cough, knowing that their first spears would be on them with their vine sticks in an instant were they to risk even the smallest attempt at humour in front of the legatus, and the tribune played an amused glance over their mute ranks before turning back to his subordinate.

'Thank you, gentlemen. And yes, I believe I ought to at least show willing. Will you march with First Spear Corvus and myself, Prefect Julius?'

The three men walked to the head of the two-cohort column, Marcus raising his vine stick in a clenched fist and pumping it up and down vigorously three times as a signal to those of his officers out of earshot that they were about to advance.

'Tungrians! At the run! *Run!*'

The waiting centuries lurched into motion in swift succession, and within half a dozen heartbeats the entire First Cohort was on the move at the exhausting pace they had been practising all summer, with the second close behind.

'You really think they can do this all the way to the bridge?'

Julius grunted a laugh at his tribune's half-jest, looking back to make sure the cohorts were completely in motion before responding.

'Half of them might be fit to puke, but they'll make it.'

Scaurus shook his head, a wry note in his voice as the first ache of straining muscles started to punish his legs.

'Just as long as the other half are fit to take the damned thing from whoever they have guarding it. Let's just hope there aren't too many of them for us to handle.'

'There.'

The squadron's double-pay man nudged Silus's arm, tipping his head fractionally to indicate a minute disturbance in the hedgerow fifty paces distant from where the two men were lying in the cover of an overgrown bush.

'Could have been the wind.'

The gnarled veteran shook his head in flat rejection of any possibility that he might be wrong.

'Wind ain't that strong, brother. That's them and I'll put gold down if you want to doubt it.'

The decurion grinned without taking his eyes off the spot his deputy had indicated.

'What's your fucking name, Morban? No, I won't be putting any gold down, not least because I can see him now.'

'Told you.'

Both men watched as a single man pushed his way cautiously through the hedge, the polished iron flicker of a drawn sword held low glinting as he looked around the field for any sign that the men who had set the fire were still in the vicinity. After a long moment's silence, he turned and called back at whoever was waiting in the hedge's other side. The two cavalrymen watched as half a dozen men in ill-matched tunics and an assortment of armour forced their own openings in the hedge and stood staring at the now half-burned pile of blazing wood in bemusement.

'Any second now those morons are going to realise that this is nothing more than a distraction. And I think we'll know when they do, because—'

Silus fell silent as another man struggled through the thorny barrier in the wake of the others, his crested helmet taken, the decurion surmised, from the corpse of one of the bandit's victims, now some sort of rudimentary badge of rank in the rebel army.

'Here we go. This looks like the brains of the unit, such as it is . . .'

After a moment spent staring at the pyre, the newcomer started shouting orders, pointing back the way the scouts had come, and Silus grinned at the urgency in his tone.

'Yes, all you bastards need to mount up and ride back to Maternus with the news, don't you? Except that ain't going to happen. Come on, let's deal with these fuckers before they piss off and leave us here holding our dicks.'

He wriggled backwards out of the hide and strode the two dozen paces back through the copse behind which the squadron were waiting, standing by their horses, issuing his orders as he swung his body up into his mount's saddle.

'They're here, probably no more than a dozen of them, and

they'll be running away to tell their leader that this is all a big lie unless we stop them!' He pulled his spear free from the soil into which its butt-spike had been driven to keep it upright. 'So we need to ride them down! All of them! But keep your eyes open for more, this ain't the kind of army that operates in tidy-sized units so there could be another five hundred of them not far behind that lot. So no horns and no cheering, just into them and let them work out for themselves that they're being fucked!'

Putting his booted feet into his horse's flanks he cantered it out from behind the trees and then pulled its head around to the right, spurring the beast at the hedge. The rangy stallion soared over the four-foot-high barrier in a graceful bound and hit the ground on the other side at the gallop, the presence of an out-thrust spearhead by its right eye all the horse needed to unleash its ferocious pace. The last of the scouts had stayed to urinate on the flames, perhaps simply from dire need, or possibly a basic desire to express his disgust at the ruse inflicted on the bandit army, and the fire's crackling roar prevented him from hearing the horsemen bearing down on him until the last moment as he tucked his manhood away. Turning away from the fire, he gaped at the oncoming wall of horseflesh and iron and fled, screaming a warning to his comrades, but whatever despairing cry for help he let out in his moment of terror was lost in the thunder of the detachment's charge. Silus rode him down without slowing his mount's gallop, spearing him in the back of his neck and tearing the blade free even as its impact punched his victim's corpse aside. Looking back to make sure his men were close behind, he set his horse at the next hedge and grinned as the beast put its ears back and gathered itself for the leap. On the obstacle's far side, the scouts were still in the process of mounting, their faces blurred by the shaking of the decurion's charging steed as they turned to face the wave of horsemen washing over the hedge through which they had forced their way moments before. The helmeted man roared a challenge and spurred his mount forwards only to be punched out of his saddle by a pair

of spears thrown by the men on either side of Silus, his stricken
body somersaulting over his horse's hindquarters to land heavily
in front of his men. Bereft of their leader, they turned and fled,
spurring their horses away, but the Tungrians had the advantage
of fresher mounts and rode them down without either compunction or difficulty. The last of them – the first to make a break
for it and blessed with a horse that, while obviously tired, was
game enough to give him everything it had left – was barely ten
paces ahead of his pursuers when he smashed through the next
hedge in a shower of broken branches. Silus winced at the wounds
the beast must have incurred, but as he set his own mount to
jump the obstacle, his concern gave way to alarm at what he
could see on the far side. Pulling back on the reins, he dragged
his horse's head hard to the left, grimacing in pain as its right
flank dragged his leg through the hedge's debris. Raising his
spear, he pointed to the south and roared a frantic order over
the thunder of his men's hooves.

'Retreat! Ride for your fucking lives!'

Spurring his mount back towards the plume of smoke still
rising from the fire, he looked back as his men pulled their horses
around to follow him, the rearmost among them flinching as a
torrent of horsemen poured over the hedge behind him in full
cry. A dozen horns sounded as the thorny barrier disintegrated
under the weight of successive ranks of riders. The slowest to
react among his men were ridden down unceremoniously, over-
whelmed by the roaring tide of riders tearing across the field
behind the fleeing squadron, but Silus could see that the oncoming
mass of horses were already close to being blown after what must
have been a swift ride south in the wake of the initial group of
scouts. Another moment took the squadron clear of their threat,
leaving the bandits' advance to slow inexorably from a gallop to
a weary canter. Silus's double-pay man closed in on his right side,
close enough to shout a shocked question at his friend.

'Where the fuck did they come from?'

The decurion shrugged helplessly at his deputy, the absurdity of their rapid juxtaposition of circumstances making him laugh despite the narrowness of their escape.

'That has to be every fucking horseman he's got! Clearly he took our bonfires seriously enough to send them down this way and put a dent into whatever it is he fears might have lit them. And if they're here . . .'

'They can't be getting in the way of our boys!'

'Exactly . . .' Silus raised a hand to gather his men around him. 'I think our work here is done. Let's fuck off and see if we can't find a farmer with some beer.'

'There!'

As the Tungrian column burst from the trees crowning the small hill halfway to the river, the men marching at the column's head had their first proper view of the fortress they had been sent to relieve, its twenty-foot-high white walls looming over the vicus that surrounded it. At such a great distance, the presence of a besieging army was almost invisible but for the smoke rising from dozens of campfires and the blackened buildings in the settlement that spoke of an undisciplined army at work. Julius shot a questioning glance at Scaurus, who nodded grimly. As the leading centuries had approached the hillock, and the lack of any lookout guarding the approach to the bridge had become obvious, tribune and prefect had exchanged glances.

'We're undetected, Julius. We need every little bit of speed they have in them now.'

The prefect nodded, sucking in a lungful of air and roaring a command loudly enough to be heard at the First Cohort's rear, not that any of his men needed to be told what was expected of them.

'Tungrians, give me everything you've got!'

The soldiers responded as one, lengthening their strides fractionally as their prefect led them forward at the run, just as he had done over and over again through the heat of an Italian summer until it was second nature. The occasional outbreaks of rough humour that had marked their swift passage from the valley's end to the forested outcrop that was the last cover for their advance died away to nothing. The only sound to be heard, other than the wind whistling through the trees, was the unmistakable grinding crunch of thousands of hobnailed boots on the road's surface, the rattle of equipment as the soldiers pushed themselves to their best pace and the rasping of their breath as the faster pace began to take its toll on legs and lungs. The officers ran in silence, eyes fixed on the road ahead and the farmland on either side for any sign that the bandit army had noticed their presence. To the south, the plumes of smoke from Silus's deception were still rising into the cloudless sky, but if Maternus had ordered his men south to investigate, there was no obvious sign, other than a faint haze of dust with the appearance of that sometimes left in the wake of fast-moving horsemen.

'That's a mile! Keep running!'

Groans from behind Julius made both prefect and tribune grin despite their own discomfort; none of the men in the cohort's leading ranks were capable of anything more acerbic as they threw back their heads to gulp in the air their bodies were demanding. The tribune grimaced as a sharp pain lanced through the right side of his abdomen, grunting involuntarily at the discomfort.

'Side stitch?'

Scaurus nodded, fighting to stay at the running pace as the sensation swiftly doubled in its intensity; Julius dropped into step with him, muttering fierce instructions at his tribune as the younger man's eyes rolled with the pain.

'You can't stop, you know that . . . concentrate on matching my pace . . . and breathe to the same rhythm as me.'

Grunting his gratitude, the tribune forced himself to focus on the pattern of his subordinate's breathing, a slow and more controlled respiration than his own harsh panting breaths, and after another five hundred agonising paces, the pain started to subside, allowing him to take his eyes off the road in front of him, on which he had been single-mindedly focused. He raised his head to look at their objective again, the white walls a mile closer but still seemingly floating on the skyline as far distant as before.

'Better?'

'Better.' Scaurus nodded his thanks, settling into the distance-covering stride and luxuriating in the absence of the enervating, stabbing pain. 'Any sign of them . . . preparing to meet us?'

Julius shook his head.

'Nothing.'

As if to mock him, a trumpet blew away to their south, and all three men swivelled their heads, looking for whoever it was that had spotted them.

'There!'

A pair of horsemen were closing on them from the direction of the river, spending their mounts' strength extravagantly to close the distance as fast as possible. They reined the beasts in two hundred yards distant from the oncoming Tungrians, sounding their horns again as their horses skittered and danced at the sight and sound of the fast-moving column, then turned away and made for the bridge at the gallop.

'There goes the element of surprise.' Julius shouted a command back over his shoulder. *'Keep running, you bastards! Run as if your lives depend on it!'*

The road to the bridge crested a gentle ridge and settled into the most gradual of downward gradients, the slight elevation finally allowing them an uninterrupted view of the crossing they had to take if the attack were to succeed. Distant figures were already moving at the span's far end, dozens of armoured men being mustered into a defensive formation by an officer whose shouts were all but inaudible over the thunderous rapping of the Tungrians' headlong advance. Julius shook his head in undisguised professional disgust.

'Whoever's leading those poor fools just made a big mistake.'

Scaurus followed his stare to look at the rebels.

'What mistake?'

'You defend a bridge on the near side of the river, and make an attacker pay in blood for every inch if you're pushed back across it. They're inviting us to join them on the other side free of charge.'

The tribune nodded grimly.

'Then let's make them regret their generosity, shall we?'

Having struggled for most of the speed march, the Roman suddenly found himself running so lightly that he could almost have been floating across the ground, and Julius laughed at him as he drew his sword.

'Got that kick in the guts, have you? Your body knows it's time to fight. First Spear Corvus!'

Marcus ran forward the half dozen paces to join them.

'Prefect!'

'They'll have archers, their sort always has a few. When we get to two hundred paces, I'll call a halt. Get your men ready and then go in fast to clear them out before they get time to sort themselves out, and I'll come in hard behind you with the second.'

The Roman nodded his understanding, and Julius raised a hand to halt the column's advance at precisely the moment that the first speculative arrows lofted across the river and slapped down onto the road's stones a dozen paces short of the leading men of the leading century. Still breathing hard, Marcus turned to face his troops, drawing his swords and raising them over his head with the blades crossed to ensure he had their full attention.

'Reorder your ranks to eight abreast!'

He waited while the century swiftly doubled its frontage, switching formation from four men wide by sixteen deep to eight by eight, a compact block of muscle, bone and iron whose members had the look of men who knew that the moment of life or death was upon them. Once their shuffling manoeuvre was done, he stalked out in front of them, close enough to smell the sweat soaking their tunics, scanning their ranks for any sign of doubt or fear and finding neither in their level gazes.

'We've known each other for long enough that I consider every man here to be my brother, in arms if not in blood. And we, my brothers, are the point of the spear! There are seven cohorts behind us, all ready to hold this bridge once we have it, but for that to happen, first we have to take it from those ragged-tunicked murderers! When I give the order to advance, we go in fast, shields raised, not giving them anything to aim at! Keep your shields up and your spears low, and when we hit them we hit them *hard*! Are you ready?'

The men of his century growled their answer, their eyes fixed on the line of armoured men waiting for them on the bridge's other side, and Marcus shouted one last instruction as he turned to point his gladius at the waiting enemy.

'These men you are about to scatter are not soldiers. They are no better than murdering scum, the armour they wear nothing more than the spoils of their treachery! They deserve to die! And I want the men who come to try to take this bridge back to march past their scattered, bloodied corpses so that they can be clear how we will serve them out in their turn! There will be *no prisoners*! First Century . . . *advance*!'

Sweeping his swords down to point at the waiting enemy, Marcus stepped aside, allowing the leading ranks of his century to sweep past him as they made purposefully for the bridge, stepping in alongside his chosen man at their rear. The Tungrians went forward in a shuffling march as they had been trained to do against archers, moving as fast as they could with their knees bent to allow them to cover both their bodies and legs with the shields that were wrapped with layers of leather and silk to make them more resistant to arrows than simple wooden protection. Only their booted feet and the minute gap between shield rim and helmet brow remained vulnerable as another ragged volley of arrows lanced down into their formation, the iron heads ricocheting off shields and helmets, a single loud curse the only sign of any damage to his command. A soldier in the rear rank beckoned Marcus into the shelter of his shield, but the Roman shook his head with a smile of thanks.

'They'll lower their aim as we get closer, I'm safe enough back here.'

The rattle of hobnails on stone abruptly changed to the softer-edged sound of iron on wood, as the compact formation's head reached the eastern end of the bridge. The din of the soldiers' passage was punctuated by an irregular toc-toc-toc of arrows pecking at their shields and armour, a sudden agonised scream announcing that at least one missile had found its mark. The century's ranks shivered as each successive line of men coped with the unexpected obstacle, the men in front of Marcus parting to pass to either side of the stricken soldier, as he lay on his back groaning with the pain of an arrow that had punched through the leather of his boot and driven deep between two of his toes. Blood was flowing to fill his boot, leaking from its lace holes, his comrades grimacing at a wound that was likely to end his military career. As they hurried across the bridge, ducking their heads under the cover of their shields and pushing on almost blindly, the horizontal sleet of arrows seemed to increase in its volume. Shouted commands goaded the archers to loose their missiles as fast as they could at the rapidly approaching soldiers before battle turned the enemy's tidy line into a whirling melee.

With a vengeful roar, the front rank was on the defenders, smashing into the flimsy line with their heavy shields and reaping the scattered bandits with spear thrusts to their throats and thighs. Raising his head to look over the rest of his men, shooting a glance back at the Second Century following up fifty paces behind, Marcus realised that the enemy archers were repositioning sideways, looking for shots into the attacking Tungrians from the flanks. He tapped hard on his chosen man's arm, pointing to the soldier's right.

'Archers on the flanks! You go right, I'll take the left!'

The other man nodded, and the Roman raised his voice to bellow a command.

'Rear rank, four with me and four with the chosen man!'

Rounding the formation's end, he sprinted forward, heedless

of whether his men were on his heels, his swords flashing in the early afternoon sun. Picking a man in the faltering enemy line, he charged straight at the unnerved bandit, roaring a challenge as he shrugged the man's spear aside with his spatha and then opened his throat with a swift stab of the eagle-pommelled gladius. Barging the dying man aside he swung the long sword backhanded into the next man's face, teeth flying as the heavy blade shattered the hapless rebel's jaw, then pushed through the gap created into the open space behind their line. His men crowded in behind him, the threat of their spears further opening the hole he had carved in the enemy line. Ten paces to his right, a tall burly man wearing the tarnished but recognisable armour of a praetorian, heavily bearded and with the tell-tale facial scars of a veteran, was staring at him in amazement, while to his left several archers were taking up position to start shooting into his century. Making an instant decision, he snapped an order to the men behind him, throwing out the gladius to point at the bowmen to their left.

'Deal with them! I'll take the officer!'

Turning back to the praetorian, he stepped into a defensive stance as the big man ran at him with his sword ready to strike; he parried the first powerful blow wide and stepped back, giving his assailant all the encouragement he needed to raise the weapon to attack again. As the sword rose high, the Roman stepped in, darting the spatha's long blade into the other man's thigh, and then stepping back as his opponent stared down in puzzlement at the blood running down his leg, fighting to stay erect with the muscles of his leg torn open. Smashing the sword from his hand with a casual flick of the spatha's heavy blade, Marcus turned back to the archers to find them already in flight, running from the vengeful Tungrians as two of their number died noisily on spear blades that had been thrust through their looted mail shirts. The crippled officer dropped to one knee, and then was sent headlong by the men reeling from the disintegration of his command, as the Second Century joined the fray with the eager speed of men who knew their enemy was on the verge of collapse, turning the already unbalanced contest into a rout.

'*No prisoners, First Century! No prisoners!*'

Marcus's chosen man was hot in pursuit on the other side of the melee, hurling his spear into the back of a running man, then ripping his sword from its scabbard and chasing down another, cleaving the bandit's head open with a savage blow that dropped him, insensate and dying. All around Marcus, the Tungrians were obeying his command of a moment before, running amok in pursuit of the fleeing defenders and hacking them down wherever they were brought to bay in ones and twos.

'You fucker.' The officer spat wearily at Marcus's feet, shaking his head in disgust. 'No prisoners? Most of these boys have been prisoners all their lives, you fucking Roman pon—'

His eyes widened as the point of his captor's gladius whipped out and came to rest on his throat.

'Call me what you like, I never broke my oath of loyalty.'

The big man shook his head, laughing in the face of his impending death.

'We'll do a lot more than break our fucking oaths before we're done, I promise you that. On the day that the bull bleeds for the great—'

A thrown spear, its trajectory so badly misjudged that for an instant Marcus thought it was going to strike him, sailed out of the fray and took the praetorian in the throat, dropping him choking and gurgling to the road's cobbles with blood spurting around the wooden shaft. Julius walked up the column of men, stopped behind the Second Century and looked about him with a nod of satisfaction.

'It seems you've won us a bridge, First Spear.'

Marcus shrugged.

'It was more like being given a bridge, but I'll accept the plaudits.'

'Make the most of them, they'll be trying to reclaim the gift soon enough. Keep your century here in the centre where it's going to get the warmest. You can fill the time the rest of the cohort will spend deploying getting your wounded back to the medic for treatment. I think they've killed every bandit that wasn't too fast for them to catch.'

The younger man nodded wearily, calling his men back to join the line.

'Get them back into order, Chosen. Have them clean their weapons and check their boots are still laced, we'll be fighting inside the hour! How many wounded do we have?'

The other man pointed at the small group of men gathered at the bridge's end, a pair of bandage carriers doing what they could for them with the supplies they had to hand. Marcus walked across to the huddle of stricken soldiers and the men treating them with the usual mixed feelings that accompanied a victory for which his men had shed blood.

'What do we have?'

The more experienced of the two saluted and pointed to each man in turn, starting with an unconscious soldier who was barely breathing.

'He's dying, so I've made him comfortable and put a coin in his mouth.' He moved onto a glum-looking man with a long slashing cut down the front of his thigh. 'He's got a wound that needs bandaging, which is what I'm about to do, but he can't walk on that leg for several weeks unless it's a matter of life and death.' A third man was speculatively probing a steady trickle of blood from a shallow wound in his neck with a grubby finger, seemingly untroubled by the cut. 'He's got a scratch and can fuck off back to his mates to pretend he was wounded. Whereas this one might never march again, unless the cohort doctor's some sort of magician with arrows embedded into small bones.' The man with the arrow in his foot was groaning quietly to himself and examining the missile's protruding shaft with an expression of disbelief. 'It'll be barbed, and there's so many bones in there that I'm fucked if I can see how it's going to come out. And this one . . .' he pointed to the last of them, who was standing patiently with an arrow's fletched shaft buried deep in his thigh, a bloody bandage wrapped around the wound to soak up the blood, 'needs to go to the medic, too, so that he can have that pulled and the wound cleaned like your wife used to do for us, sir.'

He nodded respectfully and Marcus gestured wearily for him to carry on, realising with a start that he had not thought about Felicia for several days.

'Perhaps the scars really do fade.'

'What's that?'

He turned to find Julius behind him.

'Nothing important. My losses are minimal, one dying, two out for the next month, one who needn't have bothered the bandage carriers and one whose foot will probably have to come off.'

The prefect nodded, then turned and saluted as Scaurus approached alongside the ranks of soldiers trooping across the bridge.

'It looks as if we're it for a while, gentlemen, the praetorians are a good three miles back. I suggest that we put a double thickness line across the bridgehead and get ready to repel the counter-attack that Maternus must make if he hopes to hold his position.'

'Already ordered, Tribune.'

'Good. Casualties?'

'Light, sir.'

The tribune nodded in satisfaction.

'Then so far we've had the best of the day. Let's see if we can keep that up when they come to ask for their bridge back.'

Quickly deployed into an eight-man-deep defensive line, the two cohorts had only just been allowed to remove their helmets and expose their sweating scalps to the breeze when a loosely organised mob of men appeared through the hedgerows that divided up the fertile farmland between the two rivers. Advancing with obvious purpose in several groups, each one several hundred men strong, they came forward at a pace that told Marcus this was no feint. The men around him were already pulling their sweat-sodden arming caps back on when he started shouting the orders for them to prepare for combat.

'*Get your piss buckets on! Get your shields up! And start making some noise!*'

He stalked along his cohort's line, eyeballing each front ranker in turn as the Tungrians rapped spear shafts against the rims of their shields in a rhythmic challenge, seeing wary determination in the faces turned to his. He reached the place where Varus stood at the head of his own cohort just as Julius stepped out from behind the line, staring balefully at the bandit war parties being harangued by their leaders just outside of bow shot.

'I have to fight this one from behind the line, I'm told. Apparently gentlemen don't indulge in combat until it's absolutely necessary. So it falls to you two to provide our men with the leadership they'll need to beat these animals soundly. To them you are as kings, gentlemen, with the power of life and death over each and every one of them. The decisions you make today, and the way you inspire your troops to fight like the heroes we know they can be, will be what decides whether we win a real victory here or just stand and bleed to hold that bridge like any other cohort in the empire probably would. The men leading those deserters and escaped slaves are going to throw them at us like wild dogs, probably focusing on one spot in the line and hitting it with as many men as they think will be needed to break it. Your task, you pair of warrior kings, is to hold them, to react to whatever tactics they choose, and then to rip them limb from limb with all the aggression and savagery you can inspire in these men. But don't allow my cohorts to bleed needlessly, gentlemen, not if you want to avoid a difficult conversation when the fight is done. I think we've all come too far to lose a single man more than we have to fighting undisciplined scum like this.'

With a collective roar of intent, the bandits were on the move again, the officers leading them dressed and equipped in the same manner as the man Marcus had bested moments before, men drawn from among Maternus's original comrades.

'I'll give this man Maternus his due . . .' Julius stared at the oncoming counter-attack with something approaching approval despite its disorganised nature, 'he hasn't wasted any time making his move, and his men don't seem to be shy either. Do me proud, gentlemen, or at least have the good grace to die well in the trying. And don't make me come out here, because if I do, the tribune will probably give me another lecture on what my new position entails and that won't endear you to me one little bit.'

He turned and pushed his way back through the line of soldiers, ignoring the amused glances and muttered comments provoked by the unusual sight of their war leader turning his back on a fight. The two men stared at him for a moment before sharing a swift glance of comradeship.

'Feels lonely, doesn't it, watching him leave us to it?'

Marcus nodded, shooting a look at the oncoming war bands.

'Time to earn our pay, Gaius. Whichever one of us gets the main thrust is the anvil.'

Varus nodded, immediately understanding what his friend was telling him.

'And the other the hammer. Let's hope we're not both going to be playing at being the anvil all afternoon.'

They tapped fists and parted, each pushing his way into the ranks of his First Century and taking his place at their rear. Looking out over the rows of helmets, Marcus realised that the enemy were already starting to focus their effort on Varus's Second Cohort. Four large groups of men at least five hundred strong were running side by side, with the biggest and strongest men in the lead, while a pair of smaller groups were facing off to Marcus's First Cohort with the evident intention of pinning them in place while their comrades went to work on the other half of the line. Qadir's archers were shooting, lofting a constant stream of arrows into the oncoming mob of men; Marcus knew from grim experience it would be creating small pockets of chaos among their ranks as the falling missiles found their mark.

'First Cohort! Ready spears!'

The soldiers in front of him reacted automatically, reversing their grips on the shafts of their spears in readiness for the next order. The bandits came on. Some men shouted and screamed defiance at the waiting auxiliaries while others ran in white-faced silence, goaded forward by the imprecations of their officers and the bolder men in their ranks. The Hamians had shifted their aim lower at the one-hundred-pace mark, shooting with flatter trajectories intended to put their arrows through shields and into the gaps between them, looking to unman those of the enemy unlucky enough to stop one of their shots and cause further confusion in the ranks behind their victims. Suffering under the sleet of flying iron, the war bands struggled forward until they reached the distance from the Tungrian line that Marcus had been waiting for, inside the range of his next means of disrupting their attack.

'Spears, volley by rank, throw!'

The first volley of spears whipped across the twenty-pace gap and into the attackers, dozens of bandits staggering as long iron blades punched through their looted mail. Along the front rank, men were falling to the ground, writhing in pain with blood spurting from horrific wounds, but even as they drew breath to scream out their agony, the Tungrian second rank stepped forward, past their comrades who had taken a collective knee and ducked their heads to ensure that any misplaced butt spikes would only find the iron plate of their helmets. They hurled their spears into the men struggling around the obstacles formed by their dead and dying comrades, adding to the chaotic scene playing out before the Tungrians. Going to ground in their turn, they made room for the third and fourth ranks to hurl their spears consecutively, as the bandits closed ever more slowly with the line. As the next rank stepped forward, Marcus, judging that the grievously weakened enemy were at the limits of their courage, roared a fresh order.

'Cease volleys! Reform and advance to combat!'

Without breaking step, the new front rank paced forwards, shifting their spear grips to position the weapons for stabbing rather than throwing, while the remaining three ranks who also still possessed their spears followed them into the fight. Marcus turned to look down the line to his right, shouting a command at the centurions standing behind each century.

'Flank them! I want these bastards penned for slaughter!'

With a clash of iron, the front rank was into the fight, tearing into an enemy still not recovered from the shock of successive volleys of spears that had reduced their previous resolve to bloody turmoil. The enemy officers cursed and railed at their men, but faced with the deadly threat of spearblades darting out from an impenetrable line of shields, to reap yet more lives without any effective means of reply, it was only a matter of time before the enemy front began to unravel. Individual bandits turning to flee rather than face the savagery being visited upon them by Marcus's incensed soldiery. Then, suddenly confronted by the entire right flank of the cohort pivoting to take them in the flank, Dubnus's axemen striding forward eagerly to begin the task of slaughter, the remainder of the two war bands took to their heels. Their leaders followed after a momentary pause to digest the undeniable reality that to stay would be to die without any good reason.

'Make sure they're all dead! No prisoners!'

While his men carried out the grisly task of putting the enemy wounded to the sword, Marcus switched his attention to the Second Cohort's defence, realising that his colleague's command was under fearsome pressure, their line bowed in several places under the weight of two thousand men hammering and driving into their shields. The savagery of their assault battered at the Tungrian front rank with a single-minded ferocity that was starting to tell even against the veteran soldiers.

'Let me lead from here.'

He turned to find Dubnus beside him, the handle of his axe wet with blood.

'You've notched your blade.'

The big man shrugged.

'One of those praetorians that was leading them didn't run fast enough, but his brow guard was too thick for my axe. Perhaps I need to get a hammer like Lugos. Seriously, Marcus, let me lead. There's no point you risking your skin against dregs like those.'

'There's every point, brother.' Marcus grinned at his friend, putting a hand on his shoulder. 'I know you mean well, and I'll have you fight at my shoulder in an instant, but I am a first spear now, and a first spear either leads or he is worthless. These men know that, I know it and so, my friend, do you. And that's enough delay, I think . . .' He turned to his trumpeter. 'Get me their attention. Sound the Stand To.'

The horn's mournful notes rang out sonorously, both Tungrians and those enemy soldiers on the edge of the closest war band turning to stare as Marcus barked fresh orders at his officers.

'First Cohort, form battle line!'

The disordered Tungrians hurried to follow his instruction, their officers encouraging them with shouted orders and swings of their vine sticks, while chosen men used their brass-bound hastiles to put their centuries into some form of alignment, not caring if the men they were pushing into formation were theirs or from another century. Blades dark with the blood of their enemies, armour blasted black with drying gore and still panting with the exertion of the fight, the cohort put itself into order and fell silent, awaiting instructions from their grim-faced first spear.

'First Cohort, our brothers are fighting for their lives! There is a time for fighting in line, like the disciplined men we have trained to be! And there is a time to run wild, and show our enemies that we will never be beaten, to break on them in a wave of iron and rip them to ribbons! And this is that time! *First Cohort, with me!*'

He turned and swung his long sword to point at the enemy pressing into the Second Cohort's line, roaring a battle cry that was on every man's lips an instant later.

'Tungria!'

The entire cohort was on his heels as he started running at the open flank of the closest war band, Dubnus's axemen at their head as the hulking centurion grunted with the effort of keeping pace with his friend.

'I knew you'd do this! I told my men to get close to you because I knew you'd never resist the temptation to fly into them!'

The bandits on the fringe of the war band were screaming over their shoulders at their comrades, trying in vain to alert them to the threat bearing down on them. But even as the men pushing at their comrades' backs to drive the war band deeper into the defenders' line began to realise the danger they were in, Marcus's men tore into them, led by Dubnus's Tenth Century, their choler fully aroused by their first victory. The impact of their charge threw the closest of the four war bands into chaos as the Tungrians hacked and stabbed their way into the heart of the tightly-packed formation with Marcus and Dubnus at the point of the attack. The rebel formation was so compressed by their efforts to drive the Tungrians back, that even once they were aware of the deadly threat on their left, they were unable to turn and face their executioners. Maternus's men died without ever really knowing what was happening as the vengeful auxiliaries ripped into them without any thought of mercy. Unable to manoeuvre, the bandits shouted and struggled against their own tightly-packed ranks in terror as Dubnus and his fellow pioneers waded into them, axes rising and falling in deadly arcs, blood flying with each stroke. Every swing inflicted another horrific wound or simply killed its recipient where he stood, with a head cleaved open or a body split from clavicle to sternum in a shower of iron, blood and bone. With a sudden, convulsive heave the formation ruptured, panic-stricken men frantically seeking an escape from the blood-soaked killers in their midst. Marcus stood for a moment, watching as several hundred men obeyed the ancient instinct of self-preservation. He held back his sword when easy targets presented themselves in the form of routing men; they had no idea who they were running at until he raised his blades and instantly became an island in the flow of panicking men, their reason totally lost other than the need for survival. He raised an arm to hold Dubnus back from pursuit, shaking his head at his friend's surprise.

'There are too many of them, and they're beaten. They won't stop running until they puke with the exertion. And we, brother, have other business.' Looking around, he found the trumpeter close at his shoulder, nodding his appreciation at the soldier's devotion to his role. 'Sound the Stand To again.'

As the war band's fleeing bandits thinned to a handful of desperate men, wounded and struggling to walk, Marcus ignored their entreaties for mercy and raised his sword to point at the next war band, whose warriors were for the most part, as unaware of their plight as their scattered comrades had been a moment before.

'Again, brothers! Raise your swords and give me another charge to show those honourless bastards what it's like to fight against real soldiers! *Tungria!*'

The cohort went forward across the fifty-pace gap and into the new enemy, centuries now intermingled to the degree that any thought of a battle formation was abandoned. Men from the Second Cohort's right-hand centuries joined the attack at Varus's shouted command. Again the axemen were in the lead, the pioneers pushing their bodies to the edge of their endurance and given fresh strength by the joy of fighting shoulder to shoulder, hacking their way into the enemy formation in a repeat of their victory a moment before. Fighting on instinct alone, so weary that it was an effort even to lift their weapons, they fell onto their opponents with the simple ferocity of men whose exhaustion reduced their assault to a series of swift murders. Each fresh victim was dispatched with brutal economy of effort, their blood soaking the ground over which the desperate struggle was being fought, the boots of the successive ranks pounding the earth into a muddy red-tinged froth that would stain their boots for weeks to come. As men reached the limits of their stamina and came to a breathless, panting halt, hands on their knees as they fought for breath, fresher soldiers pushed past them and took up the task of slaughter. Until, just as with their comrades, the terror reached men who could turn and bolt, at which point the horrifically one-sided battle ended in just the same way as the last, with bandits fleeing for their lives across the open farmland. The remaining two bands turned to run without having to be engaged as they realised that the fight was already lost.

Marcus stood with his swords hanging at his sides, held by hands barely capable of retaining their grip on the blood-slicked hilts, and laughed exhaustedly at Dubnus as the big man's axe handle, too slippery with the blood coating its polished wood, slid from his grasp to lie half-submerged in the gore-spattered mud.

'That seems conclusive enough.'

'Eh?'

The Roman pushed the blade of his spatha into the soft ground, raising an arm wearily to point at the fleeing enemy, unpursued for the most part by Tungrians too spent to make any such effort, able to do no more than throw curses after them, although Qadir's Hamians were taking a steady toll of the runners with their bows.

'And here come the reinforcements we no longer need.' They turned to find Scaurus and Julius picking their way around the worst of the puddles of blood scattered across the ruined ground. The first of the praetorian cohorts was crossing the bridge to their rear with Victor at its head, and the Tungrian tribune shook his head in unfeigned dismay. 'I had seriously hoped that he might bring his men to the battle in time to take their share of the credit, but it seems we've done it all by ourselves. Which means that my colleague isn't going to be a happy man. And neither, I suspect, is he going to be content to sit on this gain for very long. Warn your men that we'll be marching in the morning, gentlemen, because I also have a strong suspicion that his unfinished business with Maternus is about to assume a new level of importance to him.

8

'You know that we're not going to find them?'

Victor looked at Scaurus for a moment before replying, sipping at his honeyed wine. The three tribunes were breakfasting together in accordance with their usual routine, chewing on the same toasted bread and cheese that had been their fare for the previous five days' march. Their four cohorts had marched west from the fortress the day after its relief, in the wake of an officer's conference that had left Victor more than a little perturbed as to the combined judgement of Legatus Niger and his praetorian colleague. In the wake of Maternus's swift withdrawal from the vicinity of the fortress – without offering any further resistance once his initial counter-attack had been so comprehensively broken, apparently wrong-footed and thrown off his ground by the army's unexpected approach from the east – Niger had shown every sign of resting on the laurels he had already secured. Seemingly keen not to risk any resumption of the siege, and evidently equally wary as to the risks of leaving the German frontier any less well-defended than necessary, the legatus had swiftly decided to order the praetorian and Tungrian cohorts to hunt down and deal with the remaining bandits without any further reinforcement. He had waved away Scaurus's concerns that such a reduced force might find itself outnumbered, with the observation that his Tungrians had easily seen off close to twice their own strength, a victory which surely indicated that the remainder of the rebel army would collapse under any sort of attack.

'I'll detach enough cavalry for you to be able to scout for miles around, and I've every confidence that you two fine officers will find a way to bring this to a swift conclusion. My priority has to be to guard this fortress and prevent any recurrence of the near disaster that Maternus threatened us with, and I have written to Cleander with exactly that analysis, making clear my confidence in you both.'

Scaurus, knowing all too well that Niger was happily passing them the responsibility to snuff out the bandit threat that had been looming over his own career, had had little choice but to accept the challenge in the face of Victor's prompt and sanguine agreement with the proposal. His colleague's apparent over-confidence had only increased over the succeeding days, as the four cohorts had marched deeper into the hills of Gallia Lugdunensis in pursuit of their elusive quarry.

'Are you listening, colleague, or just worrying about the threat we face from a ragged army of slaves and deserters?'

He bowed in apology, smiling in the face of Victor's only partly-feigned irritation.

'I'm sorry, colleague, my thoughts were indeed momentarily elsewhere. Forgive me, what was it you were saying?'

'That I firmly believe you to be underestimating our chances, Rutilius Scaurus. With half a cavalry wing at our disposal, we can hunt my former comrade with a good deal more efficiency than you're giving us credit for.'

The younger man conceded the point with a tilt of his head.

'Horse scouts are a bonus, I'll admit, but all they've found so far are his army's tracks, and faint tracks at that. We're following a trail that could run dry at any time, and our marching speed is no better than his, so our horsemen can only scout thirty or so miles ahead of us. And Maternus has thousands of square miles of empty country to hide in if he wants to avoid contact with us. It's my opinion that he'll simply vanish into the countryside and wait for us to get tired of looking for him. Although that still leaves unanswered the question of what he thought he could achieve by laying siege to Argentoratum in the first place.'

Victor shook his head, looking across the fire at Sergius who, sitting on the other side of the fire's embers was keeping his own counsel, methodically feeding bread into his mouth and chewing vigorously, eating as efficiently as he did everything else.

'And that's because you don't know him like we do. The Maternus I remember was a proud man, certain of his own supe- riority over the rest of us. He was always going to make it to the top, precisely because of that drive never to be second best. And he'll be sitting at a fire like this, somewhere not as far away as you might be if you were in his boots, plotting some way to get his own back on us for humiliating his army. We won't have to look for him because he'll come to us when he thinks the time is right. And when he does, our cavalry will see him coming while he's still miles away. He'll find us ready and waiting to serve him out the humiliation he has so clearly earned. We put his rabble to flight at the bridge and we'll do it again, because with your men and mine we have four cohorts of the best-disciplined soldiers in the empire. He underestimated us before and I'm certain he'll make the same mistake again.'

Scaurus conceded the point with studied good humour, finished his breakfast as the three officers discussed the day's order of march, and walked back to the Tungrians to find Julius eating his own breakfast and casting envious glances at the nearest centurions.

'Good morning, Prefect. How are our men this morning?'

His deputy raised a sardonic eyebrow.

'Exactly as you'd imagine, Tribune. Bored with field rations and wondering how long it will be before our senior officers realise that we're chasing a greased pig around the farmyard in the darkness. Our boys will march another thousand miles if you tell them to, but they know that we're wasting our time out here just as well as you do. Sir.'

The Roman shook his head in mock dismay.

'Now I know it's bad. My first legatus was a clever man, and decent enough with it. Where some of the senior officers I've known would have been keener to drink themselves into insensi- bility, he always made the time to pass on his experience to the younger tribunes. And the lesson that I recall the most clearly was the first he ever gave me.' He paused for a moment and looked around at the buzzing activity as his men prepared for another day's march. 'He pointed to his own first spear, a soldier so ferocious that I considered him the most terrifying man in the world, not having yet seen battle with the Germans, and he told me a fact that has stayed with me to this day.'

'Which was?'

'"Gentlemen," he said, "when you come to know the habits and behaviours of the average senior centurion as well as I do, after all these years working with them, then you'll know that the time to be most concerned about your first spear's opinion is when he pauses meaningfully, gives you that look we all know so well, and then calls you *sir* in a tone of voice you will quickly come to recognise." A prefect you may be, but I have little doubt that the same rule applies, even with your elevation to the equestrian class.'

Julius shrugged.

'What can I say . . . *sir*?' They shared a moment of mutual amusement before he continued. 'Tribune, this is our enemy's ground, and he knows it well enough that we could chase him around the hills for a month and never find him, much less bring him to battle. And that might be a good thing, because there's more than twice as many of them as there are of us. And you know my view of what happened at the bridge. We might have battered their attack to pieces, but for the most part we didn't defeat Maternus's army, they withdrew. And they did it under pressure without losing their cohesion. They might look like a gang of savages, but this man Maternus has them well enough drilled for his purposes, even if they don't form tidy formations while they're doing it.'

Scaurus nodded.

'I know your view, First Spear, and while I respect your opinion as much as ever, I know how strongly my colleague Victor would disagree, were he here. He believes that we drove them off their ground through the simple superiority of the Roman fighting man, and my gentle hints that Maternus's men seemed to be withdrawing to some sort of plan have totally failed to gain his acceptance.'

'So we're to continue blundering deeper onto ground that our enemy has been fighting on for years.' Julius raised a hand to forestall his tribune's rejoinder to his gloomy comment. 'Yes, I know, it doesn't feel like blundering with six squadrons of cavalry to scout ahead of us, but I doubt those donkey wallopers will see anything that Maternus doesn't want them to see.' He shook his head and shrugged. 'But if you can't change Victor's mind with logic, then I'm not likely to do so by complaining at you, so I think it's time to shut up and soldier. What does Sergius think of all this?'

'Sergius? I don't know. As far as I can tell, he's just getting on with shutting up and soldiering as well. Why do you ask?'

'Because for all the fact that he's the junior of the two of them, and despite the appearance that he likes to give off that he's still just the best centurion in the Guard, underneath it all, I know there's a good deal more to him than that. And I think he knows the risk we're taking in chasing Maternus onto his own ground just as well as you or I. The question is, when is he going to *stop* being a good soldier and start telling his comrade a few home truths?'

The cohorts left camp without fanfare, leaving behind them the same rectangular field defences built of turf that they built every evening, the ashes of their watch fires still smouldering in the chilly morning sunshine. As they marched west along the valley of a river, following the directions of the scouts who had reported coming across what looked like the day's old tracks of a large formation to the west, Julius looked up at the sun and thought for a moment.

'We rose before dawn, we were on the march pretty not much more than an hour later, and yet we've probably only got ten hours of usable daylight left. Assuming we cover three miles an hour, then by the time we've followed this latest report of Maternus's footprints to the spot where the cavalry say they found them, it'll be pushing on towards the time when we'll have to be thinking about making camp ag—'

'*Horsemen!*'

All three officers turned to look back down the marching column. Marcus reacted first and ran back down the ranks of soldiers to the Second Century, in the line of march where a man on the rightmost file of men was pointing at the valley side, Scaurus and Julius hard on his heels.

'What did you see?'

The veteran he was addressing, a man who had been with the Tungrians since well before their battles in Britannia, pointed up at the valley's edge.

'I saw a rider, First Spear, watching us from up there.'

'How clearly?'

The soldier looked at his officer with the untroubled eyes of a man who was utterly sure of what he'd seen.

'It was a horseman, alright, armed with a spear and shield. I saw him as he crossed the crest, as clear as the day but only for a moment.'

Julius looked at the men around the soldier questioningly.

'Did anyone else see anything?'

A chorus of muttered negatives was his answer, and Marcus nodded to the man who had made the momentary sighting with a look of respect.

'Well spotted. And well done for having the balls to call it out. There'll be a double ration for your tent party tonight.'

The three men trotted back up the marching column to their place at its head, Julius speaking urgently as they ran.

'If that's not enough proof that we're being led by the nose, then I'm not sure what is. They're watching us as we march, and providing us with just enough incentive to keep going forwards.'

Scaurus considered his words for a moment.

'If I go to Victor with this, it's not going to change his mind on the subject, you know that. He'll say that one man making a fleeting observation of a horseman that nobody else sees could easily just be case of over-imagination, or that even if there was a horseman, it could simply have been a farmer keeping well out of our way.'

'Will you tell him anyway?'

The tribune nodded at Marcus's question.

'Of course. He can't be expected to make the right decisions unless he's in possession of all the information we have. Just don't expect him to suddenly start seeing what we're trying to counsel him about.'

Victor proved to be just as unconvinced as Scaurus had predicted when briefed on the sighting.

'One man sees a single horseman? A sighting that nobody else can attest to? My guess would be that it was just a farmer. You're not expecting me to act on this, are you, Scaurus?'

The younger man shook his head, holding his superior's eye.

'No, colleague. But neither am I prepared not to provide you with both the information and my opinion as to what's happening here.'

'Which is?'

'I agree with my prefect. He thinks we're being slowly but surely teased onto ground that Maternus knows intimately, ground where he can use the terrain to put us at a disadvantage.'

The praetorian turned away, raising a hand to point out at the landscape before them.

'Look at it, colleague. Open farmland. Maternus won't get within twenty miles of us without our scouts seeing him coming. And trust me, when we bring him to battle, when he runs out of places to hide, we'll see just what a mess four elite cohorts can make out of an army even twice their size, when the latter is composed of deserters and freed slaves, men with no guts accompanied by men with no skill at arms. It will be a massacre, Rutilius Scaurus, just like *your* battle with them at the bridge, and you and I will return to Rome with Maternus either dead or in chains. We will receive the grateful thanks of the empire, and my former colleague will submit to the justice that's awaiting him.'

Scaurus saluted and turned away with a sense of foreboding that stayed with him throughout the rest of the morning, scanning the brooding landscape around them with fresh eyes now that he was convinced of the hidden threat that Julius believed was lurking somewhere close to hand. He sat with Marcus and Varus at the lunch stop, eying his men as they joshed with each other and chewed on their bread and dried meat.

'There's no smoke without fire, and Maternus's scouts won't be watching us if his army isn't sufficiently close for him to be waiting for an opportunity to exploit. I can't make Victor see it no matter how I approach the matter. He seems to be fixated on what he calls *my* victory at the bridge, which, it appears, he is determined to better.'

Varus nodded his understanding.

'Our victory over them at Argentoratum seems to have been all too easy. After all, we killed over a thousand men for the loss of less than a hundred of our own. It's allowed him to convince himself that he has the beating of his former colleague under almost any circumstances. And that level of confidence feels dangerous when the enemy outnumbers us so heavily.'

'I know. I find myself looking at the men of my cohorts and wondering whether everything that we've weathered over the last few years has just been a cruel jest on the gods' part. They've allowed us to taste the sweet wine of victory, only to whip the cup away and offer us the bitter gall of defeat and death at the hands of an honourless army of outcasts.'

With the midday meal taken, the praetorian trumpets sounded the command to restart the march, and Scaurus waited pensively while his centurions chivvied their men back into formation, once more looking out at the surrounding country with a sense of deep foreboding. Julius gave the order to march in his customary stentorian tone and joined his superior and Marcus at the column's head as they followed the rearmost praetorian rank along the rough track that was taking them gradually west across farmland. It wound through the terrain in a way that they were unaccustomed to seeing after years of marching on roads built by the empire. The afternoon's march was uneventful until the column reached the tracks that had been reported by their scouts; the tribunes and their senior centurions went forward to look at the evidence of Maternus's recent passage. Victor nodded, the unmistakable trail of his enemy's passage enough to bolster his fierce expectation that he could find and destroy the bandit army. He consulted with the decurion commanding the cavalry detachment and then announced his opinion to his colleagues.

'They passed this way two days since. Possibly three. This won't take us to him, but it's proof that we're hunting in the right direction.'

Scaurus looked at the battered turf with a thoughtful expression.

'And of course they lead away to the west, deeper into Gaul.'

The praetorian shrugged dismissively.

'Which simply means, colleague, that we must *follow* them deeper into Gaul. And in respect for your concerns, we'll double the number of flank scouts, so as not to be caught unawares.' The matter decided, he turned away and signalled to his officers to resume the march. '*Onwards!*'

The column marched west until dusk, following the further intermittent traces of Maternus's army. They dug out the usual marching camp and spent the night with sentries doubled and kept alert by patrolling centurions, woke at dawn, breakfasted and rejoined the road west, such as it was now that the military road had given way to a thoroughfare created by less rigorous minds. Its lazy meandering around the impassable features that littered the increasingly hilly terrain put Scaurus even more on edge as they passed one potential ambush position after another. After two hours' march, the signal was given for a break to allow the soldiers to drink, and while his men sipped at their canteens with the discipline of soldiers who had marched across deserts and knew the value of water, Scaurus walked away from the road a few paces to stare down the track along which the detachment's four cohorts were taking their temporary ease.

'Oh for a decent road, built in a straight line by legion surveyors. This damned footpath could be taking us anywhere.'

Julius laughed at his irritation.

'Cheer up, Tribune. You look like a man who's discovered that his wife has run away with his banker. I'm supposed to do the glowering while you remain composed and confident.'

Scaurus raised a sardonic eyebrow.

'That was the deal, was it? Me cheerful, you dour? Well, I have news for you, Prefect, which is that I'm about as worried as I've ever been, and yes, that does include the moment when a Parthian army rode over the horizon and threatened to leave our corpses to decorate the Persian desert with yet more bones. And my greatest frustration is that I simply can't get that sense of foreboding through to my colleague Victor. In one breath, he's telling us what a fine soldier his former colleague was, and in the next he's decrying the man's army and promising to put them away with a few minutes' fighting. The two statements just don't feel as if they join up at any point.'

'I had a good long talk with Sergius while we were both making our rounds last night.' Julius ignored Scaurus's raised eyebrow, knowing very well that the tribune disapproved of him continuing to behave as if he were a senior centurion, rather than with the reserve and decorum expected of a member of the equestrian class. 'And I found his opinions to be a little better rooted in reality than those of his colleague. So you can trust me when I tell you that he's worried too.'

'In which case I'm forced to observe that he's keeping those reservations to himself. Not once has he ventured an opinion when I've raised my concerns with Victor.'

Julius shrugged.

'I asked him when he plans to express his concerns, and his answer was as straightforward as the man himself. He's a praetorian, Tribune. He's been trained from the age of sixteen to do as he's told under any and all circumstances. You've seen them close up, so you can see that they're a shining example . . .' the big man grinned at his own analogy, 'a *gleaming* example of discipline above anything else. They do what they're told, they do it quickly and neatly, and all their thinking is done for them. In a line of battle, they could be terrifying for the enemy because they shine like gold, and under the right circumstances, they'll fight to the death without questioning the order. But I have yet to see how they'll cope with something unexpected. So we can't expect Sergius to contradict his superior, no matter how small the gap between their opinions might be, because that's not what praetorians do. And since we've exchanged roles, let me try on your usual mantle of optimism. After all, we're not exactly in a desperate position, are we? We have a cavalry screen out, so the odds of them catching us unawares are pretty slim. We ought to have plenty of warning before we face them, which means that we ought to be able to choose the where and the how of taking our spears to them.'

The tribune pulled a dubious face.

'There are still at least twice as many of them as there are of us, and yet the onus is on us to bring them to battle. So unless Maternus does something monumentally stupid, we're going to have to attack them on ground of their choice, and with a numerical disadvantage. Which makes even the question of catching them somewhat moot, because if we do find them, we're probably not going to know what to do with them.' Scaurus shook his head. 'And *every* damned time I've raised the subject with my colleague, all I've got back is the usual bravado about how one praetorian is worth three of Maternus's men.'

'He's deluding himself.' Both men turned to look at Marcus, who had walked up the cohort's long column to join them with Varus at his side. 'I've served with them, remember, and I'd say that while they're well drilled and equipped, their lack of experience means that they're not all that much better than any other legionaries. And those bandits are fighting for their lives, because they will know only too well what Victor intends to do with any men that he captures.'

'Indeed, First Spear, not to mention that they'll have been taught a salutary lesson by your own ruthlessness at the bridge. Although perhaps I'm seeing the gloomy side of all this too clearly. Perhaps given that Maternus has the whole of Gaul and Hispania to withdraw into, he might just keep retreating from us forever. Victor may not get the chance to match his men against this rebel army any time soon.'

As if to mock his rumination, a blare of trumpets from the head of the column had the men of the cohorts securing their water bottles and snatching up weapons and shields. The stand-to was followed by the order to march in no more time than the trumpeters would have needed to regather their breath.

'Something clearly has Victor's attention.' Scaurus stared up the line to where the leading praetorian cohort was already on the move, driven forward at the battle march by shouting centurions. 'And we seem to be going *somewhere* in a hurry.'

A guardsman was running down the column towards them, and Scaurus went forward with his officers to receive the panted message.

'Tribune's compliments, sir, we've had a report of enemy troops less than ten miles distant! Tribune asks you and your senior officers to join him for orders!'

He saluted again and turned back towards the head of the column at the run, leaving Scaurus staring after him.

'I suppose we'd better go and see what this means, hadn't we?'

They found Victor and Sergius deep in conversation as they marched at the column's head, the former greeting them with a triumphant smile.

'See, Rutilius Scaurus? I told you that if we had faith, the gods would deliver Maternus to us, and so it has proved!'

'We've found them?'

'We've found some of them, from the sound of it. The cavalrymen report that they came across a cohort-sized force camped ten miles west of here and showing no sign of moving. Better still, it seems that our horsemen went unobserved. So if we move smartly, we can be on them before they have time to run. This is the beginning of the end for Maternus, because when his men hear of the havoc we'll wreak on this detachment, they'll soon enough decide to abandon his lost cause!'

'I see.' Scaurus thought for a moment. 'Do we know the tactical situation on the ground?'

Victor waved a hand airily.

'Flat ground, more or less. Wooded hills to either side which will deny them any escape other than into the spears of our horsemen. I'm sending the scout squadrons around behind them to deny them any means of retreat.' Scaurus and Julius exchanged uneasy glances at the insouciant way in which Victor was denying himself any further reconnaissance as he approached the enemy position, but the praetorian officer was too bound up in his impending victory to notice. 'My orders are simple enough. We'll make the fastest possible approach march, deploy into battle line on the march once we have them in sight, and then go for them fast and hard. I expect our men to slaughter every piece of scum that dares to offer us resistance, and to make prisoners of the cowards who try to run. Does that work for you, Rutilius Scaurus?'

The tribune nodded tersely with a hard-faced grin that looked to his officers as if he had deliberately composed his expression to suit the praetorian's expectations.

'How could the opportunity to smite our enemy be anything but a thing of joy, colleague? I'll march with you in the vanguard and enjoy the spectacle of their discomfiture when they catch sight of us.' He turned to Julius with the same grim smile. 'Make sure our men are ready for battle, Prefect, and bring them into action as a second battle line while the Guard take their spears to the traitors. Today's glory should rightfully belong to Tribune Victor and his men. First Spears Corvus and I will re-join you when the time has come for our cohorts to mop up any survivors and take prisoners. Unless, of course, you would prefer my Tungrians to take the lead, colleague?'

Victor smiled happily.

'No, Rutilius Scaurus, you have the right of it. The Guard allowed this abomination to spring up and it is the Guard that must deal with it, if we are to expunge the stain on our proud reputation. There will be other opportunities for your men to demonstrate their undoubted prowess, I'm sure of that.'

'There it is, gentlemen.' Scaurus shot Julius and Varus a meaningful glance. 'Our orders are to follow up as a second line, and at whatever distance you think sensible. Dismissed.'

The two men saluted and turned away, leaving Scaurus and Marcus marching alongside the praetorians. Victor extended a hand to indicate the track snaking away into the distance around a hill.

'We march to victory, gentlemen! Victory, and the restoration of praetorian honour!'

'What do you think he meant by that?' Varus looked up the column to where Scaurus and Marcus were marching alongside the praetorian officers with a puzzled expression as he and Julius waited for their own cohorts. 'Follow up at *whatever distance you think sensible?*'

'It's obvious enough to me.' Julius raised his crossed arms over his head, fists clenched, the signal for his centurions to gather for their orders. 'The look on his face said it all. His colleague Victor has allowed his thirst for revenge to get the better of his common sense, and intends to drive his cohorts straight into an unscouted enemy position. Under the circumstances, we'd be wise to maintain enough separation between our cohorts and the praetorians that we can manoeuvre freely, in the event that things don't go quite as smoothly as he's expecting.'

'You think that this might be some sort of trap?'

The big man shrugged.

'I have no more idea than you do, First Spear. But I do trust

Tribune Scaurus's instincts. As, I expect, do you?' Varus nodded in silence. 'So there it is. We follow his orders as *we* interpret them.'

They reached the head of the leading Tungrian cohort and rejoined the march, the command group swelling as a succession of centurions ran up the long column to join them. When all twenty officers were marching around him, Julius issued his instructions in a matter-of-fact tone that concealed his concern with the swift turn of events.

'As you've probably guessed from the fact that we're covering ground like charging bulls with burning branches up our arses, the horse fuckers say they've found some of the bandits lazing about a few miles that way.' He pointed to the column's head. 'The decision has been made to get stuck into them without hesitation, delay or any further scouting, with the cavalry being sent around behind them to jump out and shout boo if any of them try to leg it. The Guard will form the first line of attack; we'll follow up as the reserve. Questions?'

'What's the ground like?'

Julius nodded approvingly at Dubnus's question.

'Flat apparently, more or less, with the enemy camped between a pair of hills which are forested to some degree that's not clear to me.'

'Which means—'

Varus interrupted with the air of a man equally as frustrated as the big centurion.

'Which means, Dubnus, that we don't know how heavily wooded they are or how much cover they might or might not give. So we know practically nothing worth knowing. Which is the reason why Tribune Scaurus issued the prefect and me orders that are very much open to interpretation, and which we intend to interpret to the degree necessary to ensure that we avoid any disaster that befalls the praetorians. We are to follow up behind the Guard at a sensible distance, depending on the circumstances.' He shot a glance at Julius, who gestured for him to continue with a slightly surprised expression. 'So warn your men, all you centurions, that we might be taking it nice and careful or we might be going straight in behind them like old sweats with a sniff of a bar girl's cunt.' Eyebrows raised at the spectacle of a man considered by his men to be far too much the gentleman to use foul language. 'All will be revealed once we've got eyes on the enemy, it seems. In the meantime, make sure your men are ready to drop their packs and fight, because we might be balls deep in bandits before much longer. Tell them to eat whatever they've held back for a special occasion, because that time is here, and not to bloat their guts by guzzling water just because their mouths are dry. Anyone that needs a piss moves to an outside file and does it on the move, anyone that needs to defecate falls out, drops off their burden and then runs to catch up. But I don't want anyone with his hand in the air once we're in line, is that understood?'

Silence greeted his terse instructions, and he turned to Julius with a half-smile.

'Did I forget anything, Prefect?'

'No, I'd say you covered what needed to be said quite comprehensively, First Spear.' The big man looked at his goggling officers with an expression of disgust. 'Right, you've got your instructions, now fuck off and carry them out! Dismissed!'

He waited until the centurions were out of earshot before speaking again, a sardonic note in his voice.

'Like old sweats with a sniff of a *bar girl's cunt*? If I didn't know better, First Spear, I'd have to wonder if you're not trying a bit too hard at this "being a professional soldier" thing.'

Varus shrugged.

'I don't think it's entirely fair for you to have all the fun, Prefect. After all, if I follow your somewhat dolorous line of thinking, we could all be dead or imprisoned before the sun sets. Under circumstances like that, I think it's good for a man to try new things, don't you?'

Julius snorted a laugh.

'Just when I think I've heard it all, here's my new first spear telling me that we centurions have all the fun because we're allowed to swear. And yes, Varus, to answer your question, I do think it's good to try new things. And if we can limit that pushing of the boundaries to your saying the word "cunt" and not have it include us all getting killed today, then I think we've struck just the right balance, don't you?'

A horseman rode up to the column's head an hour or so later, the decurion in its saddle pointing back the way he had come as he leaned down to impart the latest intelligence to the praetorian officers raising his voice to be heard over the noise generated by thousands of marching men.

'They're still where we found them, Tribune, just sitting in their camp begging to be attacked! You're within a mile of them, so best not to sound any horns!'

Victor nodded, turning to Sergius.

'Let's allow the men a short stop to get a mouthful of water. We'll leave our packs here too, rather than toss them aside at the last moment. The last thing we want after fighting a battle is men coming to blows over who owns what.'

The cohorts' noisy progress was replaced by an unusual quiet while the soldiers made their last preparations, men placing their pack poles at the track's side in tidy piles ordered by century and tent party under the instructions of their centurions. Some of the guardsmen took one last opportunity to take a whetstone moistened with spittle to their blades before tucking the precious blue stones away again, while others simply closed their eyes and offered silent prayers to their gods. A few even fell asleep in the time-honoured soldier's reaction to a moment of peace while Victor chafed at the delay, pacing up and down until he deemed that his men had had long enough to have made their preparations.

'Come on, then, let's get them on their feet and get at the enemy before we lose the opportunity!'

He led the reformed column forward with the decurion walking his horse beside him, the cavalry officer pointing out the signs of the enemy's passage when they reached a section of softer ground.

'Do you see, Tribune? Bootprints. At least a cohort's strength. They marched down this track, set up camp and they've been sitting there ever since. You do have to wonder why, though . . .'

'I know why, Decurion.' Victor nodded confidently. 'It's because they're stupid enough to think we're still back in Argentoratum, toasting our success and sitting on our backsides just like they are! They don't realise that the emperor has unleashed the men who hate them most in all the world, or the lengths we'll go to in order to make them pay for their treachery. How long until we see them?'

The cavalryman raised his hand to point at a stand of trees silhouetted against the skyline, barely half a mile distant.

'Once you're past that copse, you'll be in full view of them. They're another half mile further on down a bit of a slope, camped by a stream between two woods.'

'And as far as you can tell, there are no other forces in the vicinity?'

His answer was a firm shake of the decurion's head.

'There's nothing to be seen for miles, sir. No tracks nor traces of anything bigger than a farmer's cart. The only place we haven't been able to scout is the immediate vicinity of the enemy camp, but then we've not needed to, because we know they're all over those woods looking for anything they can burn. I've seen them moving round in there, at the edge of the trees, looking for fire-wood most likely. But apart from that, we've combed the ground for ten miles in all directions, and we've not seen a thing.'

Victor looked to his colleagues, nodding at the decision he had evidently just made.

'In which case, gentlemen, I suggest we make the best of what we're offered? My plan is to pass that copse up ahead in column, then to sound the horns and deploy into line of battle as we advance on them! That should put the fear of the gods into them, given I doubt they'll even be able to tie their own shoelaces, much less actually perform any battlefield manoeuvre more complicated than a mob charge! We'll pin them in place while your Tungrians follow up and perform an envelopment, eh, Tribune?'

Scaurus nodded.

'I'll order my cohorts around their flanks once your men are engaged and the shape of the battle is clear.'

Victor took a deep breath.

'Very well! If we all know what we have to do, it would seem to me that all we need to do is get about doing it. Follow me!'

He led the column towards the stand of trees with the determined pace of a man hurrying towards his destiny, not breaking stride as the level path began to slope away from them. It opened up a view that would stay with Scaurus for the rest of his life. The bandit camp was a half-mile distant, and as the leading praetorian cohort came over the crest, Victor raised his hand in the pre-arranged signal for his trumpeters to sound the advance with all their might. An instant later, their Tungrian counterparts added the brassy squeal of their horns to that of the guardsmen's instruments, and the combined blare of their ire sent a sudden flurry of panicked activity through the enemy camp as men ran for their weapons and began equipping themselves to fight. Sergius barked an order which was echoed down the column by his centurions, and the lead cohort's First Century abruptly began turning right two files at a time, the column of march starting to extend sideways in the process of becoming a line. Saluting Victor, who had taken up a position to watch his own men deploying to the left side of the column, the taciturn tribune turned away and stalked down the line of marching men with a critical eye.

'It might not be soldiering as you and I would know it, but by the gods, I'm forced to admit that it's impressive.'

Marcus nodded at Scaurus's musing.

'As long as nobody manages to break their formation, then they'll be formidable enough.'

The two cohorts completed their transition from column to line with the precision of long practice, and their tribunes stepped forward in front of their men. They raised their arms in salute to each other before turning in unison to point down the slope, both men roaring the order to advance. Stepping behind the advancing double line of soldiers, Scaurus looked back at his own cohorts, who were deploying in much the same fashion, even if their manoeuvres lacked the parade ground precision of their praetorian colleagues.

'Well then, here we go. It seems that the enemy has decided to stand and fight rather than simply making a run for it.'

The bandit force was hurrying to form something approximating a battle formation capable of resisting the advancing praetorians, the mongrel appearance of their mismatched equipment lending their unpractised haste to get into line a darkly comedic aspect that wasn't lost on the two men.

'If appearances are to judge, then those men are already beaten. But why would they choose to fight, rather than do the sensible thing and run?'

The advancing guardsmen began to sing as they closed with their discomfited enemy, and Victor raised his sword to the sky in salute.

'You have answered my prayer, Lightbringer! We have them now, brothers, we have them at our mercy!'

Barely a quarter mile separated the two forces, and as his centurions looked to Victor for any sign that he intended halting their advance to allow for the usual pre-attack routine, he simply waved them forward with urgent gestures of his sword.

'There's no time for speeches or adjusting the line, we just need to get into them and finish this!'

Looking out to the marching guardsmen's right, at the forest edge less than two hundred paces distant, Marcus was unable to shake the feeling of foreboding that had gripped him from the moment he saw the bandit force trapped so completely.

'This is too easy. They should have taken flight the moment we came into view in such numbers.'

'And yet there they stand, just waiting to be put to the sword? I know. But my colleague's choler clearly has the better of his judgement.' Scaurus looked back at his own cohorts, advancing down the hill in the praetorians' wake at what appeared to be a less than determined pace, allowing a gap to open between the two forces. 'At least one man on this battlefield is exercising a little caution.'

The praetorian advance was speeding up, as the guardsmen vied to be the first to take their iron to the waiting enemy. Their leading rank was less than two hundred paces from the bandits' hastily formed line, the enemy seemingly determined to offer the onrushing guardsmen battle despite the odds stacked against them. They braced themselves to accept the attack, their officers shouting orders and beating those men who were wavering back into their places as their nerve failed in the face of the oncoming rush of their implacable enemy. As the praetorians closed to within a spear's throw of the waiting enemy, close enough for the pale faces of the bandits to be visible above the line of their mismatched shields, Victor pointed with his sword and roared an order which would unleash his men at their quailing foes.

'*Now, guardsmen, now is the moment we make these animals pay! Ready spears . . .*'

The praetorians already had their spears held ready to throw, and at the command, the rear rank stopped marching, in readiness for the command to unleash their deadly rain of iron at the doomed bandits. And then, as Victor drew breath to shout the order, a peal of trumpets unexpectedly split the air. The praetorian reflexively turned to look back at the oncoming Tungrians, but even as he pivoted, the real source of the horns' abrupt braying calls to battle revealed itself. Bursting from the trees on the right side of the advancing praetorian line, hundreds of men clad in the motley combination of different colours, mismatched armour and weapons, stormed towards the exposed right-hand end of the advancing praetorian line. Their ragged formation advanced swiftly across the two-hundred-pace gap towards their shocked opponents.

'*Shit!* We've been deceived!' Sergius turned and ran for the right-hand end of his cohort's line, shouting back at his colleague over his shoulder. 'Victor, disengage your men and pull back to join the Tungrians!'

But even as the praetorian commander fought to master his surprise, the enemy line facing his men was in motion, their passivity converted into hard-eyed attack in an instant as their leaders sought to take advantage of the moment for which they had been waiting. Charging forward with a ragged cheer, they were suddenly face to face with the discomfited praetorians, but as the Tungrian officers watched from behind the guardsmen, the attack's real purpose was already clear. Scaurus turned to shout at his colleague, who was still reeling at the unexpected turn of events.

'Victor! They're trying to hold us in place while their main force rolls up the line from the flank! You need to use your rear rankers to support Sergius's men, and give my cohorts a chance to get into them on the right!'

Rousing himself from his momentary state of shock at the unexpected attack, Victor started shouting for his centurions to disengage their second line guardsmen and join Sergius's cohort. But orders that might have been feasible on the parade ground were of little use when his men were face to face with a determined opponent and fixated on their own survival. Realising that only his personal intervention stood any chance of rescuing the situation, he made for the rear of his own cohort with Marcus and Scaurus at his heels, shouting commands at the nearest of his centurions as he ran.

'Give me your rear rankers and hold that rabble with the rest! We can still win this fight!'

The bandit horde hit the outermost century of Sergius's cohort with an audible clash of iron, and in the space of half a dozen heartbeats, the entire right-hand side of the praetorian formation was transformed into a bloody melee. The guardsmen fought for their lives against their assailants' superior numbers, unable to prevent themselves from being beset on both sides as increasing numbers of the enemy pressed forward around them. With two or three attackers for every guardsman, the endmost century's fight for survival was short-lived, dozens of men falling under their enemy's spears as the bandits pressed their advantage. The next century in the line was already starting to lose its cohesion as the guardsmen eyed the havoc being wrought on their comrades, individuals stepping backwards in a reflexive attempt to form some sort of flank defence. Victor shouted a command at the nearest of his officers, trying to rouse him from the shock that seemingly had him paralysed where he stood.

'*Disengage your rear rank!*' The centurion turned to stare at him with unfocused eyes, and Victor realised that he was over-whelmed by the sudden onset and fury of the ambush. The praetorian tribune pushed him away with a curse, striding to the men at the century's right-hand end and screaming the command again. '*Rear rank, disengage! Move, you fuckers!*'

The guardsmen and their officers were reacting at last, still gripped by the torpor of men in a state of shock at the horror unfolding to their right as the last remnants of a second century vanished into the oncoming bandits' remorseless advance. The ranks of men who were next in line for the bandits' murderous onslaught tripped over each other in their attempts to escape the advancing enemy spears, their formation unravelling under the imminent threat of slaughter. Shuffling backwards in obedience to their tribune's roared orders, Victor's rear rankers were being pushed and cajoled into a new line, perpendicular to the front rank which was fighting back against the motley force that had been the bait on Maternus's hook. Victor stalked along the line of his men shouting commands and attempting to steady the unsettled guardsmen.

'Get your shields up and get ready to fight! We *can* still win this!'

While some of his men obeyed the command with the instincts drilled into them in long years of service, just as many were still lost in their own private struggle between fight and flight. They stared in amazement at the advancing enemy horde as it fell on another century and tore it to pieces, the enemy's battle-frenzied howls as they ripped into the praetorians and the anguished screams of the wounded filling them with dread. The remaining centuries in Sergius's cohort increasingly resembled nothing better than a mob of men who were yet to decide in which direction to run, their line reduced to little better than a terrified straggle of soldiers. A praetorian in the impromptu formation turned to run and found himself looking down the length of Victor's sword. 'Get *back* in line, guardsman!'

The man in question reluctantly turned back to face the enemy, his fear of the tribune's threat temporarily overriding that of the desperate danger they faced, but around him men were increasingly looking back up the slope at the Tungrians standing in line two hundred paces behind them. Victor wheeled angrily to face Scaurus, pointing at the immobile Tungrian cohorts.

'Why aren't your men advancing, Scaurus? Without them we'll be outflanked!'

'Because I told Julius to do whatever he thought best under the tactical circumstances. And because of *that*.' The tribune pointed at another rush of men charging out of the trees further back down the valley, another war band at least a thousand men strong, clearly intending to bypass the enemy camp that had lured them onto Maternus's carefully chosen ground and assault the left-hand end of the praetorian line. 'They're going for an envelopment, Victor, and if Julius commits his cohorts, then those men will brush what's left of your men aside and destroy my cohorts as well!'

'But without them—'

'We're lost?' Scaurus's patience snapped. 'Look around you, Tribune! We're *already* lost! They're going to pen us up and slaughter us like the *fools* we are to have blundered into such an obvious trap!' Victor stared at him in dismay, unable to gainsay his fury. 'All I can hope is that my prefect can get his cohorts extricated from this mess! Because we, Victor, are already dead men!' Drawing his sword, he nodded with approval as Marcus unsheathed his twin blades. 'All that's left to us is to make a decent job of dying.'

9

Varus stared, wide-eyed with amazement, down the slope at the praetorians' increasingly hopeless position.

'Surely we have to attack? We can't just march away and leave our comrades in the hands of that rabble!'

Julius replied to Varus's impassioned outburst without taking his eyes off the chaotic scenes playing out, shaking his head as the rebel right flank swept around the praetorian left, forcing the defenders' line to bend back until the First Cohort was little better than an encircled mob, quiescent under the spears that so drastically outnumbered them. The Second Cohort, grievously ravaged by the loss of at least three centuries, was now being driven remorselessly into the same pocket, its capability to resist completely broken by the horror of the rebel assault that had killed hundreds of men and left the remainder cowed. The legion cavalry were retreating too, cantering away rather than face the threat of the superior force of enemy horsemen who had ridden over the hill to confront them.

'Yes, we can. And we have to. Partly because we have a duty to preserve these two cohorts to fight another day, and partly because that fight is already lost. Trust me, First Spear, nothing we can do will change that, in any other way than making the defeat even worse. And Tribune Scaurus gave us both a direct order, before he went to try to persuade that fool Victor not to stick his head in that noose. You heard him tell us to make sure that we don't allow a defeat to become a disaster as clearly as I did, and that's exactly what I intend to do.'

'But—'

'No.' Julius raised a hand, his face set hard against whatever argument Varus might be about to make. 'Absolutely not. My decision is final. Denounce me to the first senior officer we meet if that's what you have to do, but I won't send my men into that fight. Doing so wouldn't change anything, other than getting them killed. And besides that, it's clear enough to me that they plan to attack us next, so the fight will come to us soon enough. So hold your water, First Spear Varus; your chance to piss yourself will come before very long!'

'We're being enveloped!'

Scaurus nodded grimly at Marcus's shouted warning, following his pointing hand to where the bandit attack had washed so far around the praetorians' right flank that Sergius's men no longer had an escape route, even though their courage had clearly deserted them.

'Yes. It appears that Maternus is penning up his former comrades for slaughter.'

He turned, assessing the speed with which the fresh wave of attackers were streaming around the left-hand end of the embattled praetorian line and performing the same manoeuvre as their comrades on the right. The praetorians were being pressed on both flanks, their previously immaculate battle formation swiftly being compressed into a seething mob of desperate men held at bay by the threat posed by enemy archers who were shooting down any man attempting to flee. A mounted man was trotting his horse up the hill in their wake, and as he closed on the melee, the two men realised who he must be.

'Maternus.'

Scaurus nodded, watching as the rider made his way around the edge of the fight, evidently searching the praetorian ranks for someone.

'It must be. Although it seems to me that he may be more interested in capture than butchery.'

'Tribune Gaius Statilius Victor!' The horseman was still staring intently into the cauldron of captured praetorians, most of them unable to raise their arms, so tight was the space into which they had been penned by the surrounding wall of shields. 'Your command is trapped, Victor! This battle is lost! And so I present you with two alternatives, either of them equally acceptable to me. You can either surrender your command to me, with the guarantee that no more guardsmen will die, or you can choose to fight to the death, and I will order my army to take their spears to you like sheep in a pen, until every last one of you is dead.'

The guardsmen around them seemed to promptly lose any remaining will to resist, staring up at the mounted man in combined hope and terror.

'Clever. With a few words, he's beaten all thought of resistance out of them.'

Scaurus nodded at Marcus's quietly voiced opinion, shaking his head in disgust.

'I should have gone back to command my own men when I had the chance.' He turned to search the crush of guardsmen, looking for his colleague's plumed helmet, then pushed his way through them towards it.

'Victor!'

The praetorian tribune squeezed through the disordered ranks of men to join them, his unbloodied sword held impotently with the point uppermost, his eyes empty with the realisation of his shameful defeat.

'That, as you will have realised, is Maternus. And he's right, my choice is a stark one. I fail to see what alternative I have.'

Scaurus appraised him for moment, shaking his head angrily.

'You have the choice of ordering us to attack!'

'Ordering you to die fruitlessly, you mean.'

The look in Victor's eyes was that of a beaten man, and his reluctance to meet Scaurus's gaze spoke eloquently as to his state of mind.

'You would be ordering us to die with some measure of honour.'

The praetorian shook his head.

'An honourable death is still death, Rutilius Scaurus. And what right do I have to condemn the rest of my command to such a meaningless sacrifice? I will pay the price for this disaster, but they do not need to share my fate.'

'You intend to surrender?'

The praetorian nodded soberly at Marcus.

'Yes, First Spear. I can only hope that if we lay down our weapons, Maternus will allow the rest of my men to live. I won't go to my death with the spirits of hundreds of needless casualties on my conscience.'

He dropped his sword, turning to his men and shouting an order for them to stand down, turning away as his stunned centurions repeated the order with a combination of incredulity and relief and dropping something to the ground, pressing it into the battlefield's battered turf with a twist of his booted foot. Maternus rode closer to the trapped mass of guardsmen, staring down at the officers for a moment before calling out a command to his men.

'Cease fighting! This battle is over! Back away from the prisoners and hold them where they are! Archers, any man that tries to escape is to be shot without hesitation!' He looked down at Victor with a pitying expression. 'You'll keep here a while, Statilius Victor. I have a more pressing matter than your surrender to deal with.' He turned his horse away and spurred it up the slope towards the spot where the Tungrians were under attack by the remainder of his army, shouting back over his shoulder as he kicked the beast into motion. 'You can use the time to reflect on how brutally our positions seem to have been reversed!'

'Here they come! Prepare to repel attackers!'

Sanga hefted his spear, spitting on the ground at his feet in disgust, as much as at Otho's shouted order as at the sight of the bandits running towards them up the shallow slope.

'Like I can't fucking see the bastards in front of me.' He glanced to either side, glaring at the men beside him. 'I ain't worried about them. All I'm worried about is you two. We fight together, right? I go forward, I expect you pair of women to come with me. And in case you're wondering, I ain't planning on stepping back, so if I see you even thinking about it then this . . .' he tapped the ornately decorated dagger at his waist, 'is going where the sun won't ever shine.'

The bandits were shouting and whooping as they came on, taunts and imprecations clearly intended to unnerve their would-be victims, but the waiting Tungrians stood in silence, each man knowing what was expected of him. Julius had issued a flurry of orders as soon as the bandits' ambush had become apparent, pulling the four centuries at each end of the line back at right angles to create a three-sided box to resist any attempt to outflank them. The ragged, undisciplined line was washing up the slope towards them, individual men loping forward ahead of their comrades with swords and axes held high in a display of their determination to be first to the spoils of victory, and the glowering prefect shouted over the clamour of their advance to steady his men.

'We stop them, we hold them, and then we start killing them! There'll be no retreat until I say so, because you don't run from a wild dog, you put your fist down its throat and rip its guts out! If we fight, we'll live to fight again! If we run, we'll all die! It's that fucking simple!'

'Hah! He not one with hand in dog's mouth!'

The men around them grinned at Saratos's muttered complaint, then tensed at their centurion's barked command.

'That's enough chatter, you animals, get your spears ready!'

The steady patter of black humour dried up in an instant, the men around Sanga hard-eyed as they waited for the order to loose their spears, eyeing the oncoming bandits dispassionately. Julius waited until the enemy were twenty-five paces distant, then barked the one-word command that would unleash his men's frustration on the advancing enemy.

'*Throw!*'

The centuries facing the bandit line stamped forward as one, lofting their spears in arcs that would drop them into the advancing attackers in a shower of sharp iron. Their adversaries' advance faltered momentarily as the volley struck, dozens of men screaming their agony at the sky above as the long, evilly-sharp iron blades sliced deep into their exposed flesh or punched through their mail, leaving them kicking and thrashing with the cold iron's brutal intrusion. Their bladders and bowels reflexively emptied to add a sharp smell to the air, and they fell, dead or insensible, to be trampled under their comrades' feet. Driven forward by the threats and blows of their officers, the bandits came on despite their growing uncertainty in the face of their opponents' obdurate defence, and Sanga shook his head wearily as the century unsheathed their swords.

'Here we fucking go, then. Remember what I said, you two, or you and me'll be having words once these cunts have run away to mummy.'

Setting himself to resist the impact of their charge, he stared dispassionately at the men running at him over his shield's rim, making a practice stab with his sword's rough-sharpened blade as if to subconsciously remind his muscles of the action that would shortly be demanded of them, then leaned into the shield as the bandits covered the remaining few paces and ran onto the Tungrian line. Suddenly face to face with an adversary, he punched out with the shield's iron boss, feeling the shock of its impact on the bandit's shield, instantly stepping forward a pace to stab his sword over the top of the other man's board and into his throat; a fine spray of blood and a gurgling cry told him that the strike had found its mark. The Tungrians fought in silence, as had become their habit over years of campaigning, rear rank men staying close to the soldiers in front of them as they went about their deadly craft, filling gaps in the line when a man fell without having to be ordered or thrust into the fight, as both sides fought for the supremacy that would enable them to impose their will on the battle. Another bandit came at Sanga shieldless, his eyes wide with the madness of bloodlust, and the veteran allowed him to hack overhand at his own raised shield twice before striking back into the teeth of the third attack and slamming his blade's point through the ragged mail that was his opponent's only protection. Shrieking with the sudden enervating pain, the dying man snapped his blood-flecked hands onto the rim of the veteran soldier's shield, perhaps reflexively, perhaps with the intention of ensuring that his killer met the same fate, and pulled it down and away with the last vestiges of his fading strength. Faced with the choice of fighting for the shield and taking a spear blade from behind the stricken bandit, Sanga made the instant decision to release it, leaning forward to put his gladius's blade into the mortally-wounded bandit's mouth and through the back of his neck. A swift snatch at the shield's handle found it to be locked in the dead man's grasp, and he stepped back barely fast enough to evade a questing spearhead as the men behind their slaughtered comrade bayed for his blood. Grinning at the men facing him as they looked down at the two corpses still twitching on the ground at their feet, he drew the dagger from the scabbard on his left hip and raised its ornate, patterned blade for them to see clearly.

'We change?'

Sanga shook his head at the suggestion from behind him, his ire suddenly aflame with the stink of blood and the fear he could sense in the men before him.

'Not yet! I got a thing or two to show these cunts! Watch my back!'

He stepped forward a pace with the knife still raised and his sword held low, casually chopping the sword blade down into the dead man's fingers and severing their death grip on his shield's rim. And then, while the bandits were staring at him aghast, he went at the man to his right, parrying his sword wide and stabbing in with the dagger to open his throat while he was still focused on the long blade. The dying man's comrade raised his own blade to strike, then staggered back with blood streaming from his chest where Saratos's spear thrust had punched iron through his mail and between his ribs. The third man was frozen where he stood, staring at Sanga through a mask of hatred as the Briton sheathed his knife and picked up his shield before stepping back into his place with a hard grin. The two battle lines were drawing apart as the bandits realised that the auxiliaries, still formed and more than able to fight on, were not going to be as easy to defeat as the praetorians behind them. Even as both sides paused for a moment before renewing the fight, a man on horseback rode up behind the bandits, his voice carrying unmistakable authority as he roared a command at his officers.

'Leave them! We have what we need! Front three ranks, hold position, watch them and keep them honest! Rear three ranks, break formation and come with me!' Raising his head to stare across the battle line, he spied Julius and Varus in their place at the centre of the Tungrian line and rose in the saddle, astonishing the watching auxiliaries by saluting. 'Well done, brothers! At least some men in this so-called army can fight!'

Wheeling his mount away, he rode back towards the encircled praetorians, barking orders at the men running alongside him to strengthen the ring of iron that had them surrounded. The bandits left behind stepped back a dozen paces and grounded their shields, to the Tungrians' amazement.

'Is that it, then? One quick bit of blade play and then they fuck off and leave us holding our own dicks?'

Saratos pushed forward into the front rank, pointing at the encircled guardsmen.

'You hear him. He got what he want. And he got our officer.'

'Greetings, vaunted warriors of the emperor's guard! I am pleased that your commander has chosen the wiser of the two options that I put before him!' Maternus had ridden back down the slope from where the Tungrians stood to address the penned guardsmen from the vantage point of his horse. 'Drop all of your weapons and rid yourselves of your armour and shields! It's boots, tunics and belts only from here, and you can offer a prayer of thanks for my beneficence in allowing you to retain your daggers and your dignity when next you stand before an altar. Leave your gear for my men to collect, and have your purses ready. Any man not presenting a purse will be beaten! Any man caught attempting to hide the contents of his purse about his body – anywhere about his body – will be beaten to death! Senior officers, you are to gather here . . .' he pointed to the ground in front of the horse, 'bringing with you all your equipment! Chosen men and watch officers, divide your wounded into two parties, those who can walk and those men whose wounds prevent them from walking! Walking wounded may be supported by their tent mates, as long as they are able to leave this place on their feet. Those too seriously wounded are to be put out of their suffering without delay!'

The rebel leader paused for a moment, and when he spoke again the amusement in his voice was evident.

'So, are you waiting for something? You have your orders; I suggest you carry them out before I'm forced to consider the alternative! Do it!'

Victor shook his head in disgust, then took a deep breath and roared the command he knew was needed if a massacre was to be avoided.

'Men of the praetorian cohorts, do as you have been ordered by the rebel Maternus! Retain your dignity and discipline, and leave this battlefield as a formed body of men, but obey the instructions you are given! Centurions, to me!'

He waited as his officers gathered around him, his stature seemingly diminished by the shocking defeat, saying nothing to his officers as they gathered around him in silence. The last man to join the group was Sergius, his helmet already removed to reveal a long cut across the skin above his eyebrows that was bleeding down his face and neck, his bloodied face blank with barely-suppressed fury. Unfastening his wide leather belt, he unstrapped his sword, then removed his dagger's sheath and purse from their places on the leather strap and dropped them beside the discarded blade, looking up to find Maternus appraising him from his elevated position.

'How very dignified of you, Tribune. Stoic even in the depths of your misery. But then, we always were trained to obey the orders of those with the power to issue them, weren't we, comrade? A senator murdered, a wife procured for unwanted sex with the emperor . . . a war abandoned . . . yes, all orders are to be obeyed without thought, aren't they, brother?'

The hard-faced tribune shook his head at their captor, the knuckles of his clenched fists white with undisguised anger.

'I'm doing as you've told us because if I don't, you'll order your men to finish the rest of us. My commanding officer . . .' he spat the words out without taking his eyes off the bandit leader, 'has ordered our surrender in order to spare the lives of those men not already dead or too badly wounded to march. And I am obeying his order, because that is what soldiers do, *brother*. We follow the orders of those with the authority to command us, no matter what our personal opinion on the matter might be.'

'Sergius? Is that you under all that blood?' The rebel leader grinned, evidently delighted at the discovery. 'The hardest of the hard men, the centurion we all secretly admired for your poise and couldn't-give-a-shit attitude? And here you are, with your sword at your feet alongside your pride. That's what mindlessly following orders will do to a man, colleague. It feels comfortable, doesn't it, letting someone else do the thinking and trusting them to do the right thing? Right up to the moment when their orders stop making sense and you find yourself with your expectations in ribbons and your beliefs torn apart. Which is where you find yourself now, isn't it? It's a familiar feeling, I can tell you that much. I felt it for the first and last time the moment that Commodus abandoned the spirits of the good men who had died in his father's wars and sued for peace.'

Sergius looked back at him with stone-like eyes, shaking his head slowly.

'I told you, I follow orders because that's what soldiers do, Maternus. And when those orders don't make sense, I follow them anyway, because without respect for authority, we have nothing.'

The bandit leader dismounted, pushing his way through the defeated guardsmen until he was toe to toe with the grim-faced tribune, heedless of the fact that the praetorian officers all still had their weapons close to hand.

'And there's the difference between us, isn't it? You're willing to do whatever you're told, no matter how much you might not agree with those orders, even if it leads to something like this. Your career is over, Sergius. All those years spent working your way up from the rank of guardsman to the peak of your profession, rendered a complete waste in a single moment, and all because you allowed your superior to lead you into a trap. But we'll talk of this more later. For now, you officers can concentrate on doing what you're told, and not getting your men killed out of hand with any unwise acts of resistance.'

He stepped back, and gestured to the weapons and equipment that the centurions had piled at their feet.

'Let's have this finery removed, shall we?'

Maternus waited in silence while the officers' equipment was carried off under the attentive eye of one of his own centurions, his face creasing into a lopsided grin as the man swung his vine stick with vicious force to smack a hand that one of the watching bandits had unwisely extended to touch the gleaming cuirass that Scaurus had deposited in front of him.

'Of course, when one commands an army formed almost entirely of thieves, deserters and slaves, one has to exercise discipline just a little more robust than that usually employed in more selectively recruited bodies of men. Bring that armour here!' He examined the fine metalwork, nodding appreciatively. 'Quite beautiful, Tribune . . . ?'

'Scaurus. Gaius Rutilius Scaurus.'

'Scaurus.' Maternus thought for a moment. 'Your name is familiar to me from the stories we hear from Rome. No wonder your armour marks you as a gentleman, and not a centurion who's managed to fight his way to the tip of the pile like my former colleagues here. What brings you to be marching with the Guard?'

He flicked a glance up the hill to where the Tungrians were standing in line, unbeaten and ready to fight again.

'You've already guessed, I'd imagine. Perhaps you're waiting to see if I'll try to lie to you?'

'Perhaps I am. There are clues to be had as to a man's character in this sort of situation. So yes, I wondered if you'd lie to prevent me ordering them to surrender in return for your life.'

The Roman laughed tersely.

'Unlikely. Feel free to walk up there and try it yourself, if you think it's worth the wasted effort. I expect my prefect will laugh at you, and I wouldn't get too close because as a former front ranker, he's liable to try putting a spear point between your eyes. But by all means, give it a go if you think you can charm him into ordering his men to lay down their arms.'

The two men shared a moment of amused mutual appraisal before Maternus shrugged and replied.

'No, clearly that wouldn't work. And besides, I see no reason for your men to lay down their arms.' Maternus turned to Victor and Sergius with a tight smile. 'After all, *they* didn't stop fighting, did they? No, we'll allow your cohorts to make their exit in a dignified manner, I think, carrying their shields with pride, as long as they withdraw at least five miles and guarantee to take no further part in this matter. You can go and issue them with the order if you like, Rutilius Scaurus. I know you'll come back, because if you don't, this young centurion of yours will pay a heavy price for your freedom. Do I need to elaborate?'

'No.'

Scaurus walked up the slope, past the waiting ranks of bandits who had tried to overrun his command, ignoring their murderous stares as he stepped over and around the scattered corpses of their dead and dying comrades which littered the ground in front of the Tungrian line. Julius stepped out through his men's shields to meet him with Varus at his shoulder.

'We were right. It was all too easy to be true.'

'It was.' Scaurus turned to look down the slope at the praetorian cohorts whose men were being herded away at spear point a century at a time. 'And now Victor is paying the price for his over-confidence. It would have been better for him to have died in battle, but Maternus didn't really give him the chance. It was all too well planned and swiftly done for any thought of a glorious last stand. Even if he'd had the gall to order such a thing.'

'I presume you've come to tell us to leave?'

'Yes. Maternus seems to have been impressed by the fact you didn't fold when his men came at you.'

The first spear barked a terse laugh.

'Their hearts weren't in it once we'd shown them which end of the stick they were really holding. But I'll take that. How far away does he want us?'

'At least five miles. And you know he'll have horsemen watching you. You're to take no more part in this matter, that's his only condition.'

'And you?'

'Marcus and I are to remain prisoners. I have no idea what he has in mind for us senior officers, but he seems to be releasing the praetorians once they've been disarmed.'

'Why hold them prisoner?' Varus shook his head at the sight of another century of dispirited guardsmen being led away past the jeering men still facing off with the Tungrians. 'After all, he'd have to feed them, wouldn't he? I'd imagine his supplies won't be generous all this way from any sizable town, whereas their supply carts have enough food to get them back to Argentoratum.'

'And imagine the impact when two cohorts of guardsmen walk back into the fortress without their weapons and equipment. Maternus will have sent a message back to Rome that he's not to be trifled with.'

Scaurus nodded slowly.

'Yes. But all that will do is bring Rome's full strength down on him. Instead of a few mismatched cohorts, he'll have two or three legions hunting him. And that can only end badly.'

'Perhaps that's what he wants?' Both men looked at Varus, who spread his hands and shrugged. 'It's a thought I've been pondering ever since you posed the question of what it was that he could possibly hope to gain from besieging the Eighth Legion, Rutilius Scaurus. Why do such a foolhardy thing as to pose as a rebel, rather than the brigand he clearly is? Why bring such unnecessary attention onto himself, rather than simply maintaining his bandit lifestyle in the shadows of Gaul? And this latest exploit only makes that question more intriguing, does it not?'

Scaurus nodded.

'True enough. And who knows, perhaps I'll get the chance to find out over the next few days. As for you, Prefect, your orders are these: you are to withdraw as far and as fast as you can, until you're no longer under threat should Maternus change his mind or just be attempting to bluff you into letting your guard down.' Both men saluted, and Scaurus turned away down the hill with his final words called back over his shoulder. 'And just this once, do as you're ordered? We've already lost two cohorts of praetorians as far as their combat effectiveness goes, and I'll be damned if I'm going to add my cohorts to that tally!'

They watched him walk down the hill until he reached the waiting group of officers, who were then marched away under guard towards the west.

'So, do you intend to follow our commander's instructions?'

Julius contemplated the question for a moment before responding.

'Every order given by a tribune appointed by the imperial chamberlain is to be obeyed to the last detail. So yes, First Spear, I do plan to do as he told us and march east for the rest of the day. Once we reach a defendable position, we can dig out a marching camp and work out our next steps. But that, Centurion, is where my obedience to his orders will end.'

'What is that you want with us, Maternus? What possible purpose can our capture serve? Or are you only interested in humiliating the Guard and proving yourself . . .' Victor paused, staring at the rebel leader with a gentle shake of his head. 'Proving yourself to yourself, that is.'

Maternus smiled back at him, sprawled in a heavy wooden chair with every sign of still being immensely amused by the fact that he had managed to deceive his former colleagues so completely. Half a dozen armed and armoured men had taken up positions to either side of him, each with a hand on the hilt of his sword, the same men having accompanied the prisoners on their short march to the spot where the rebel army had made their base, a turf-walled facsimile of a legion marching camp. Maternus had introduced them with evident fondness as the last survivors of the men who had deserted with him, turning his brooding stare on Marcus as he did so, tapping the eagle-pommelled gladius that now hung at his hip.

'There used to be more of them, of course, but you, First Spear, and this rather splendid blade, are responsible for having thinned their numbers somewhat of late.'

The Roman stared back at him impassively, and after a moment the rebel leader laughed bitterly.

'You're not denying it, then? The men who ran from your assault on the bridge . . .' He paused, smiling wryly at Scaurus. 'You have my congratulations for the diversion you threw me to get me to take my eye off that potential axis of advance for just long enough that you had a free run at it, by the way. My men told me that one of my original comrades was killed by a centurion with two swords.' He turned back to Marcus. 'You have two swords, Centurion, do you not?'

'I *had* two swords. Now I have none, thanks to your thievery. That sword is a family heirloom that is my only remaining link to my father, a man who died in battle as the consequence of his betrayal.'

Maternus shrugged.

'The empire turned my hand to *thievery*, and so now I thieve with the best of them. And more fool you to have brought such a fine weapon to battle, especially if it is genuinely your last link to your father. So, first you killed one of my oldest comrades and then, in the fight to stop our counter-attack, you and your men managed to kill another two of my brothers who had accompanied me in my struggle to survive; they had attended me all the way from the wastes of Germania to Gaul, then helped me to build the army that brought you so low. I'm told that you and your Tungrians tore into my men like wolves, slaughtering men who were too tightly pushed together to even raise their arms. Whereas, you will have noted, I spared your men out of fellow feeling. After all, it's hardly their fault they were led into such an obvious trap, is it? So tell me, killer, why should I not deal out my friends' revenge to you here and now?'

Marcus shrugged.

'Why not? The man who holds the sword is the one who decides whether to wield it, stolen or not. There are worse ways I could die than on my birth father's blade.'

The rebel leader smiled slowly, nodding his head in recognition of the point.

'Indeed there are. And I think I'll keep you intact for the time being so that, when the time comes, you can look back at this moment and wish I'd given you that honourable release from this life.'

Maternus turned his attention to the praetorians, staring at them for a moment before speaking again.

'And you have no congratulations for me then, Victor? No honest reflection on a deception that completely fooled you?'

The tribune shook his head.

'No, Maternus. I can't find any way to praise a man whose treachery has terrorised three provinces for years, and whose actions have brought the Guard into such disrepute.'

'Disrepute? I doubt that one man in a thousand in Rome has the faintest clue that I was once a praetorian. But that, *colleague*, will change overnight, when my plan comes to its bloody completion. I'll make the Guard infamous for all eternity!'

The two men stared at each other in mutual enmity for a moment before Scaurus interjected.

'You'll forgive me for interrupting this reunion, but I'm curious as to what your purpose in such a carefully planned ambush might be? You can't be hoping for any reduction in the empire's iron resolve to see you crucified, because you must know only too well that Pescennius Niger won't hesitate for a moment to do whatever he has to do to bring you to justice. He'll consider our fate for just as long as it takes to commend our spirits to the gods and move on with his plan to destroy your ragtag army. So if you think that holding us hostage will—'

'Hostages?' The bandit leader grinned back at Scaurus. 'I have no thought of using you as *hostages*, Rutilius Scaurus, none at all. Rome doesn't often show that sort of regard for those among its commanders who are unwise enough to find themselves in captivity, does it? But the loss of Victor's men, that will be entirely another matter, which is exactly why I was so quick to retreat and provide Niger with a question that he answered perfectly, by allowing you to come after me and drive your men into a trap. Left with not much more than half a legion and a pair of auxiliary cohorts with which to repel a potential renewal of the siege on his fortress by an army with six thousand men, I would expect him to swiftly come to the conclusion that with winter drawing on, he has little option but to ensure his food stocks will see him through to the spring and consolidate his gains. He'll wait for reinforcement before he takes the offensive. And when he does come looking for us, he'll find nothing. My army will have melted away like the snow itself, leaving only isolated bandit gangs formed of those of my men who were too stupid to take the chance this hiatus has provided them with, too greedy to give up the life of living off the suffering of the less well-favoured.'

'You're going to break up your army? Why?'

'And why *now*, you're asking yourself? After all, I might not have managed to break into Argentoratum, but I do still hold much of Gaul and Hispania in my fist, if I choose to squeeze it closed. And if only it were that simple, I could probably keep on evading the lumbering fools the empire sends after me for another few years. But all good things, Tribune Scaurus, as I'm sure you know, come to a natural end. If I were to carry on with this way of life, I would eventually make a mistake and find myself in a trap of my own making. Or more likely, someone within the group of men I've come to trust would betray me to buy their own safety and a life of luxury for the rest of their years. The life of a bandit leader rarely ends with a death of any other kind than violent or protracted, and a place in history that records my crucifixion isn't quite what I had in mind when I decided to leave the ranks of the emperor's Guard, and seek a different path.'

The captured officers stared at him in silence, and after a moment he stood up, crossed the tent and tapped the tribune's scale armour, which had been placed on display, suspended on a cross-pieced armour tree along with his weapons and helmet.

'I always thought our equipment was a little too gaudy to be taken seriously by men like these.' He extended an arm to point at the Tungrians. 'Did you see the way their cohorts defended themselves against my men? It was masterful, Victor, peerless. I thought we had you all bottled up, but whoever was left in command of those auxiliaries wasn't going to lie down and surrender, was he? I walked the field after they'd extricated them-selves from my trap, and counted the dead left behind, theirs and my own. There were twenty-seven corpses left by your cohorts, Tribune Scaurus, and over two hundred of our own men. Given a legion of that quality, I could hold Gaul and Hispania for as long as I wanted.' He smirked at Victor. 'Not like your guardsmen, eh? From the moment they realised they were caught in the jaws of my full force they were lost, pitifully stumbling around in an ever-tightening net until they only had one choice, to surrender or to die. Most of them chose to give up the fight disappointingly quickly, and stood quietly like lambs waiting for the butcher's blade. Their armour and weapons might be of the highest quality, but the men themselves lack the genuine hardness that comes with battle, after battle, after battle. Your men were soft, Victor, and so were you, when it came to the point of decision. You surrendered them because you knew that the only alternative was their slaughter. And trust me, Rome would have preferred the latter. Dead heroes, as they would have been termed, always beat live cowards.'

'And that was why you released them?'

Maternus shrugged at Scaurus's question.

'What else could I have done with them? I don't have the supplies to feed that many captives. And in sending them back east to the fortress at Argentoratum without their armour or weapons, I sent a far louder message than if I were simply to have had my men put them to the sword.' He grinned at Victor. 'Far better to have them parade their shame back into the fortress and demoralise the Eighth Legion further still with the exaggerated story of how they came to lose in battle to a mob of thieves and deserters, and in the telling of it, convince the soldiery that they face an enemy who knows no fear. Pescennius Niger will send for reinforcements rather than risk the rest of his army, and by the time he feels safe to sally in pursuit of us, his efforts will be of complete irrelevance to the fate of the empire.'

'What do you mean . . . the fate of the empire?'

His captor grinned back at him.

'Yes, Tribune Scaurus, you heard me correctly. The truth of this game we're playing is that it will be decided far from here, and not in any province.' He turned his attention back to Victor. 'That armour you gifted to me, colleague, was your badge of office. Your finery was what saw you waved through most guard cordons and gates without a word of challenge. But of course, for the most rigorous of security, there must always be some further means of proving that you are who you say you are. After all, a man with sufficient determination and money could probably fake your everyday appearance without too much trouble. And so it is, as we both know, that you carry a badge of office that you never remove. A badge given to you by the emperor himself, as is the custom with new tribunes, something that ties you to him and makes you utterly loyal. You know only too well that the grant of the trinket in question comes with the most thorough of investigations by the men who live in the Camp of the Strangers. The Grain Officers identify your family, your friends and even those people you have loved in the past, and they detail all of those names to the imperial chamberlain's office, since he now has responsibility for the Guard. And so it is that in return for your position of power and favour, you place the lives of everyone you've ever loved in the emperor's hand. It is the ultimate surety for your devotion and fanatical loyalty. And the symbol of that trust – and your right and duty to go anywhere, and to command any man in the city to do your will – is invested in something small and unremarkable, and yet imbued with all the power that the emperor sees fit to bestow upon you.'

Victor was staring at him through slitted eyes, and Maternus nodded at his sudden realisation.

'Yes. That talisman you were wearing on your wrist until the moment before we captured you. A gold scorpion with jewelled eyes, a gift from the emperor himself. But of course, it's so much more than just a symbol of your trusted position. Did you really think you'd be able to simply throw it away?'

He opened a clenched fist, showing them the intricate, beautiful design nestled on his palm, at once familiar to Scaurus as having previously hung from the tribune's wrist.

'I told my men that the one to bring it to me would receive twenty gold aureii and his release from my service. And I warned them that the man to hide it from me would die slowly and in torment. Which meant that they combed the battlefield, such as it was, and put it in my hand within an hour of your capture. Which in turn means that all the power carried by this insignificant piece of jewellery is now mine, and that I am now, to all intents and purposes, *you*, Tribune Victor. Think on that tomorrow, while you listen to the sound of my army celebrating the most important victory of its short, disreputable life.'

'So what is it that he's planning, do you think?'

Victor sat back against the tent's central pole with his eyes shut, his face a mask of control that flexed as the muscles in his jaw worked. His answer to Scaurus's question was almost acerbic, but more tinged with self-loathing than sarcasm. He had been brooding in silence ever since Maternus had dismissed them to their makeshift prison, a tent alongside his own with guards stationed at front and rear to ensure there was no attempt at escape.

'Isn't it obvious? He lured us into that trap with only one aim – to take my armour and my badge of office – and now he has it, along with enough of our equipment to turn as many of his followers as he sees fit into praetorians. He can walk anywhere in Rome with impunity. *Anywhere.*'

'But surely someone will realise that he's not a real tribune?'

'How?' The praetorian officer looked at Marcus's dim figure in the tent's near darkness. 'We hold the post for a year, no more, not unless the emperor takes a particular fancy to one of us and keeps him around for longer. There's a new tribune appointed almost every month, making it impossible for the guardsmen to keep track of their comings and goings. Which is why we wear the scorpions. And even if a sentry did wonder if the man demanding passage was a fake, is he really going to challenge the uniform and authority? Men have been executed for far less. No, now that Maternus has that scorpion, there's no place in Rome he can't walk into at will.'

'One of your guardsmen might recognise him.'

The tribune shook his head.

'I doubt it. That's not the Maternus I knew at the end of the German wars. Yes, he's recognisable if you're looking hard enough, and knew him well before his mutiny, but the years he's spent preying upon the western provinces have changed him almost beyond recognition. And if a man did think he saw his former comrade, a swift barked denial would be enough to silence him, trust me. The Guard's discipline is absolute. He can go anywhere in Rome, gentlemen, and when I say *anywhere,* I literally mean it. If a praetorian tribune demands access to the emperor's bed chamber in the middle of the night, then even the German body-guard won't think twice to admit him, simply because of his status.'

A heavy silence fell over them, broken at length by Scaurus voicing the fear which Victor seemed unwilling to make real by explicitly naming.

'You think he plans to murder Commodus?'

The reply was no more than a tired whisper.

'I know it. Why else go to such outlandish lengths to lure us out here? The calculated insult to the empire's dignity of casting a spear at a legion fortress, an act he knew must result in the empire stretching every sinew to bring him to a very public justice, including the use of our conveniently available cohorts. The clever retreat, forever just within reach but using country he'd been getting familiar with for years to keep us at arm's length, always luring us on. The bait dangled so enticingly in front of us that like a fool I couldn't resist taking it . . .' He sighed deeply, slumped back against the heavy wooden pole. 'This whole charade of his being a bandit, and his campaign of freeing slaves and recruiting deserters has been a total sham to build an army strong enough to draw Rome's forces out and put one person within his grasp. *Me*. He's probably been planning this since the moment he made the decision to kill his tribune and walk away from the Guard, and now there's nothing and nobody that can stop him. He's going to take the ultimate revenge for what he sees as the crime Commodus committed when he took the throne and ended the war with the Marcomanni and the Quadi.'

'We can stop him.'

Marcus's statement, voiced into the quiet that followed Victor's flat statement of what he knew were facts, drew a chuckle of dark amusement from the other praetorian tribune.

'*We can stop him?* Have you not realised how deep in the shit we are, First Spear? Maternus commands an army of deserters, freed slaves and criminals that he's given the option of either joining his gang or dying. They're hardly the most loyal of men, and if they realise that he plans to ditch them and head for Rome

– which I can assure you is exactly what he's planning – they won't take it well. Which means that he'll need a distraction to take their eyes off him. With the entire army drinking itself into oblivion in this celebration of his, when the time comes for him to make his exit with his oldest and most trusted comrades, there'll be nobody conscious to argue the toss, or even to see which direction he takes. We're likely to be the centrepiece of the celebration of this mighty victory that will render this pack of dogs incapable of even noticing when he takes his leave, and I doubt that what he has in mind for us will be all that pleasant a way of leaving this life. My choice would be crucifixion, if I were Maternus. A long, drawn-out death which will have them watching us in rapt attention as they drink themselves stupid and offer each other odds on which of us will choke to death first.'

'What my young colleague is trying to say is that our friends won't be far away, Sergius. We've developed some skills at moving quietly, not being noticed and – when the time comes that being noticed is inevitable – being so indisputably part of the normal way of things, that the beholder never even thinks to challenge what he's seeing.'

The tribune's reply to Scaurus's explanation was terse to the point of anger.

'We're in the middle of an army of renegades, colleague! Do you really think that a few men can stroll in here, free us and then stroll out again?'

'That's to be seen, isn't it? But I guarantee you that the men I have in mind will walk through this camp without anyone giving them a second glance.'

IO

'We know we can't take them on frontally. That's clear enough, I'd say.'

'We can't?'

Julius turned a questioning eye on Varus, staring at him over the fire around which the Tungrian officers had gathered to count the costs of their narrow escape from Maternus's trap.

'No, *Centurion*, we really can't. Maternus has several times our strength, he knows exactly where we are, and they've already sent half of the men we had back to mummy in tears, in case it had slipped your mind.' Julius pointed at the watch fires that formed the praetorian half of the camp. 'They're not going to be any use to us, not now they're depending on us for protection from anything more fearsome than a bad-tempered farmer. And we're only here because Maternus seems to have a soft spot for soldiers who know what they're doing. But I'd expect that his patience with regard to us will only last for as long as we keep marching east. So, all things considered, I'd say the omens couldn't be all that much clearer if Jupiter himself were to illuminate them with a shower of thunderbolts.' The two men eyed each other for a moment while Julius composed himself and adopted a more conciliatory tone. 'Any sort of attempt in force is doomed to bloody failure, no matter how clever we think we might be.'

The younger man thought for a moment before responding.

'I realise that I'm very much the junior partner to Rutilius Scaurus in this matter. And to yourself, Prefect, in terms of my limited experience of soldiering. And I'm not trying to tell you anything you don't already know . . .' His face hardened. 'But we have no choice but to get them out of that camp, and quickly. Because I can't see any good reason for them to have been kept prisoner.'

Julius inclined his head in respect for his subordinate's frank statement, gesturing for Varus to continue, and after a further moment of thought, the tribune started speaking again.

'It's pure chance that our colleagues were with the praetorians when they put their heads into that trap. If Rutilius Scaurus hadn't been so convinced that there was something wrong with the whole situation, and so determined to point that out to Victor and Sergius, he'd be here now and we'd be thinking through our next steps with a good deal less weight on our shoulders. And it's clear to me that Maternus was looking to snare the praetorians, and not us. Once we'd showed them that we weren't about to roll over for them, they lost interest in us, and allowed us to back away with no more than a few dozen horsemen to keep an eye on us and make sure we don't try anything clever without them knowing about it.'

'Which means?'

'Which means, Prefect, that they set that trap for the praetorians, and that they must have done so for a reason. But the stranger thing is that they let them all go again, all bar their tribunes.'

The men around the fire went quiet, brooding on the shame that had so evidently descended on the tattered remnants of the Guard cohorts that had straggled along behind them on the march east from the scene of their defeat, shorn of their officers, their equipment and, for the most part, any hint of their pride.

'Two elite cohorts of guardsmen have been sent home to spread misery and fear. Isn't that enough of a victory for it to have been Maternus's plan all along? Perhaps our escape was just a combination of the tribune's good sense and a lot more fight than they were expecting.'

Varus brooded for a moment.

'I don't think so, Julius. If that was what Maternus intended, then why keep the officers prisoner? Those guardsmen would be just as useless with Victor and Sergius as they are without them, because they've got no means of fighting. No, it's clear to me that he wanted the officers, and even if I can't work out why, I'm damned sure it won't be without some purpose. But I'll tell you what's worse than any suspicions I might have, whether they're founded in truth or not: those bastards have our friends captive. And while they do, you know as well as I do that we can't just fall back to Argentoratum and wait to see if they're released, or held for ransom, or just have their throats slit because they're not required and those animals can't be bothered keeping them.'

Julius nodded slowly.

'So what do you propose?'

Cotta spoke up from his place with the First Cohort's centurions.

'We have to rescue them, don't we? Because Maternus either wants them for some purpose that has to be prevented, or he doesn't actually want them, and their lives are already a debased currency. Either way, we're going to form a scouting party, go in, find them, free them and get them out of there. I'll go alone if I have to. I'd imagine that Arminius feels much the same way.'

Julius held his stare.

'"We have to rescue them"? Just like that? You do realise that this isn't going to be like sneaking through an empty forest towards a bunch of sleepy German tribesmen who'd no idea you were out there? Nothing you've done before will have any relevance to what you're proposing.'

Varus nodded slowly.

'Yes, I think we all know that. But I also know that Centurion Cotta is right. We can't just do nothing, which you know as well as I do. And let's face it, I'm not really a first spear, just as you'll never be truly comfortable in that purple-striped tunic you've been forced to wear. If I go out there and never come back, then these cohorts have lost precisely nothing.'

The prefect smiled slowly.

'I was waiting for you to get round to that. And it's true, these men will follow me without hesitation while you're still something of an unknown to most of them. Half of them think you're slumming it with us until you get bored and the other half think you didn't have any choice in the matter. But that's not important right now. You're the senior centurion commanding a cohort of the best infantry in the empire, and you need to do your duty.'

His subordinate shrugged.

'And I think I'm doing just that in seeking to rescue my superior from his captors. So I suppose we'll just have to accept that we have differing opinions, won't we, Julius? After all, there'll always be another man waiting for a command like this.'

'And the men you take with you? What about them?'

Varus nodded, his face set hard.

'Volunteers only. I won't take anyone with me that doesn't know the risk he's taking.'

Julius shook his head.

'When you know only too well there's not a man in either cohort that wouldn't join this mad scheme in a moment.'

The younger man shrugged.

'That's the nature of this beast, Julius. They know their officers would do the same for them, if need be.'

'And you're set on this, despite my advice that it's likely to kill you and anyone you take with you?'

'I am.'

The prefect nodded, turning to the oldest and most obviously battered of the centurions.

'Very well. Otho, send for those two idiot watch officers I keep lending you. Tell them that they've just volunteered to go to their deaths in the company of the first spear here. Dubnus, I'm going to want your ten bloodiest maniacs. This isn't Germany, and I'm not looking for subtlety, just enough blood lust to charge a thousand angry bandits if they're told to do so. And you're going to need scouts.'

Qadir nodded at his unspoken command.

'I will ask for volunteers from among my archers. I know that every man will consider it a matter of his personal honour to volunteer for such a task.'

'Good. And of course you can take my favourite regicide with you as well. I'd swap him for my first spear in an instant.' Julius raised an eyebrow at Cotta, who simply inclined his head in reply, then glared around the fire pit. 'You're all dismissed. I want those men here before the next guard change, kitted up and ready to march. And that includes you, First Spear Varus, so you'd better go and get yourself ready.'

The younger man nodded and turned away, leaving his superior staring at his back.

'Admit it, you want to go along as well.'

Turning his head, Julius found Dubnus standing alongside him.

'Of course I do. But you know as well as I do that he's probably going to get himself killed playing the hero. Young fools like him are raised to believe all those bullshit myths the Romans like to pretend are the reason their empire will last forever, because it's "their destiny" to rule the world. Doubtless in his head he's already holding off a dozen of those bandits while the rest of you escape from them . . .'

'He's young, Julius. We've all been that age . . .'

'And that stupid. Yes, we have. The gods know that I did some idiotic things when I was that old, and I know you did because I was the centurion that kept having to point out to you that you weren't a prince any more. But he's seen enough of the real world with us to know better. Which means that he'll need the foolishness beaten out of him, one way or another. Either by seeing the men he commands die or by dying himself.'

The big centurion nodded.

'I'll do my best to keep either from happening.'

Julius shook his head.

'Who said you were going with him? I've got you in mind to replace him if he stops a spear.'

The big man shook his head dismissively.

'I'm a pioneer, Julius. We're not a century, we're a warrior brotherhood. Titus made me his successor with his dying breath, and that's not something a man can walk away from. No, you'll have to find someone else, because whatever idiot plan the boy comes up with is only going to work if I'm there to make sure it does.'

'Gods below . . .' The reluctant prefect shook his head in disgust. 'I swear you were inhabited by the Bear's spirit when you picked up his axe; you've got the same infernal sense of your own self-importance that . . . are you even listening to me, you bastard?'

Dubnus shook his head.

'Not really, but you don't expect me to, do you? And you're going to let me go along with the boy for one very good reason.

'Yes. I am. Because while I have every respect for his courage, I have very little confidence that his scheme stands any chance of success. So in the event that he proves me right in thinking that he's determined to throw his life away in some noble act or other . . .'

'I save the rest of the party?'

'Absolutely. Whether you've managed to get the tribune and Marcus out of there or not, when Maternus's rabble realise what's happening, you order whoever's left standing to start running and you don't look back. Because when several thousand angry bandits realise what the game is, they won't hesitate to kill you all to put an end to it.'

'Keep your heads down! If we get spotted now, then not only are we all probably dead, but my wager with Morban will be a total waste!'

Varus shot Dubnus an indignant look. The two men were lying flat behind a fallen tree twenty paces from the forest's edge, hiding from the searching eyes of the mounted scouts who had been ordered to follow the Tungrians and their hapless praetorian comrades back towards Argentoratum, and who were poking over the remains of the abandoned camp for anything of value before riding east in the defeated army's wake. The other members of the rescue party had concealed themselves further up the hill, with only the two officers and a pair of soldiers to confirm that the previous night's camp was no longer under observation before leading the detachment back to the west.

'Morban's taking *bets* on our chances of success?'

The big Briton raised his eyebrows in a silent, jaundiced reply, putting a finger to his lips. The closest of the horsemen had dismounted and was pacing toward the forest in a purposeful manner, staring about him with the intensity of a man who was looking for something.

'He's either spotted something he doesn't like or . . .' Reaching the forest's edge, the bandit selected a good-sized tree and squatted behind it, lowering his leggings to reveal the reason for his brisk walk up the hill. 'Or that.' Dubnus averted his eyes. 'He's clearly been holding that in for a while. I just wonder what he's going to wipe with.'

Realising that the forest floor was devoid of anything with sufficiently broad leaves to serve the desired purpose, the scout had no choice but to shuffle back out into the open and gather handfuls of grass with which to clean himself, while his comrades kept up a non-stop flow of amused abuse. Tossing away the last of his impromptu toilet, he remounted and rode away down the track left by the four cohorts of marching men an hour before, shouting for his comrades to follow him.

'That went about as well as could have been expected. We'll still stay in cover for a while yet, just in case they've left anyone behind.'

'Did you actually say that Morban's taking bets on this mission?'

Dubnus grinned knowingly at the Roman.

'Every cohort has someone like Morban, First Spear. Someone who'll place a bet on which one of two men can piss higher up a tavern wall, or who's got the bigger balls under his tunic or, in this case, how likely it is that a handful of men, including the most degenerate oaf in the entire cohort, are going—'

'I heard that, Dubnus.'

'You were supposed to hear it, Sanga. Now keep your mouth shut and your head down, in case shit man's friends are lying in wait for us to reveal ourselves.'

Ignoring the muted grumbling from behind him, he continued.

'How likely it is that a handful of men are going to be able to march into the enemy camp, find our officers and then march out again without being spotted and ending our days as heads on sharpened sticks.'

'Well, if you put it like that, I'm not sure I want to—'

Varus snorted his amusement at the indignant soldier.

'Shut up, Sanga. You were the first to volunteer.'

'Second.'

Conceding Saratos's point graciously, the Roman continued.

'Indeed, almost the first to volunteer. And it's too late to be changing your mind now just because Dubnus has pointed out that the odds being given against our success are . . . what are they?'

'He's offering one gets three that we make it back with the tribune. He started out at fives but the betting was a bit too brisk for his liking.'

'And the odds against us?'

'Two gets one.'

A low groan of disgust behind them made Sanga's view all too clear.

'So every bastard in camp has money on us not coming back? I wish I'd known that before I crawled up this fucking hill in the dark.'

'I know.'

The voice was unmistakably the Briton's Dacian comrade in arms, Saratos.

'You fucking knew?'

'Yes. I put bet with Morban. Gold aureus that we come back with gentlemen alive. He give odds of five.'

'Fuck me, no wonder he wound his neck in to threes. But what made you place such an idiot bet with our money?'

Saratos chuckled quietly.

'First, is my money, not our. And second, I hardly going to bet we die, right?'

'Well, if you put it like that . . .'

Silence fell, only to be disturbed after a further period of patient waiting by the sound of a horse cantering past their hiding place. Varus edged his head up for a glance as the last scout rode away in pursuit of his fellows.

'It's an old trick, but there's a reason for that. Shall we?' Dubnus stood, brushing leafy detritus from his armour and putting out a hand to pull Varus to his feet. 'We've got five miles to cover before we can get eyes on their camp.'

'Well now, distinguished colleagues, I trust you spent a comfortable night?' Maternus walked into the tent in which the three captives were being held with a cheery air, handing each of them a hunk of bread stuffed with what smelt like roasted pork. 'The farmer whose land we're camped on keeps pigs in pens on the hill beside his fields, so we bought them off him and set up fire-pits to cook them in.'

Famished from a night and most of a day without food, the prisoners started eating without waiting to be bidden, and the bandit leader grinned as they wolfed down the cooked meat.

'Good, isn't it. And just as well. Every condemned man needs a decent meal to set him up for the ordeal to come.'

Scaurus stopped eating and looked up at their captor in disdain.

'So you intend to execute us. No more than I expected from a man who renounced his honour so completely when he decided to abandon his vow of loyalty to the emperor. You did swear to serve Commodus when he succeeded his father, I presume?'

Maternus nodded disinterestedly.

'I did. We were herded out onto out what passed for a parade ground, in that part of the world the gods long since forgot and left to the barbarian scum of the earth to populate with their forever-warring peoples, and were ordered to swear allegiance to the young fool. We knew what he'd do as soon as his arse was on the throne, of course, it was obvious to anyone who'd spent any time on guard duty around the royal family. We knew that he'd be away back to Rome like a rat scurrying for the sewer it came from. He needed to "consolidate his rule" as the official announcements had it, but in reality we knew he just wanted to get away from the filth and blood of the war. Fighting was good enough for the rest of us, but he'd never seen it any closer than on the back of a horse surrounded by a ring of iron at the side of his father Marcus Aurelius. He proved us right, of course, and sooner than we expected, to boot. No sooner was the oath complete than our prefect announced that the new emperor had sent for the tribal leaders and was making peace with them. He promised us that we'd be back in Rome in time for Saturnalia, not that I could have given a shit about that. All I wanted was for the legions to be turned loose to burn out every village and kill every man of fighting age for a hundred miles, because that's the only thing that works with the Germans and their like.'

'Depopulation. The last resort of the desperate.'

The bandit leader snorted his disgust at Scaurus's acerbic response.

'And that's exactly the sort of view I'd expect from a man who hasn't seen what they're capable of.'

The tribune shook his head tiredly.

'Oh, I know what the barbarians are capable of, Maternus, I fought in the same war as you. And since then, while you've been busy robbing and killing the innocent, I've seen it on the frontiers of Britannia and Dacia, and in the forests of Germania too. We've seen everything you've suffered and more. But despite all I've experienced over the last few years, I've never sunk as far as to believe that wiping out innocent peoples is the answer to the problem.'

Maternus shrugged with the expression of a man whose mind was not for changing.

'And your soft principles are beside the point. We wanted to be turned loose, to take revenge on the scum that had lost to us in battle and resorted to murder from the shadows. Instead of which, we were told to forget all that and march home, the memories of our dead utterly forgotten. But this is all so much wasted breath, isn't it? I have consulted with my men and their answer is clear, you must die.'

Victor stirred, leaning back against the tent's central pole with a yawn.

'And we're to die slowly, I presume? Something to hold your army's attention while you slide away unseen? After all, how would they react if they discovered you were about to discard them, now that they've served their purpose? You know what'll happen, of course, because you know them better than anyone.'

The bandit leader nodded sanguinely.

'They'll disintegrate, naturally. Without purpose, with no one to tell them what to do, they'll argue among themselves. Men will die, fractures will quickly open between the cohorts, and within a month they'll have been reduced to dozens of gangs fighting each other for the food they need to survive. The local population will suffer, of course, but that's always the way of it in a war. And finally, when your legatus Niger realises that there's no meaningful resistance left in them, he'll march out from Argentoratum and mop them up, or enough of them to justify him returning to Rome to accept the thanks of a grateful senate. His reputation will be burnished to a shine by having been the man who rescued first the Eighth Legion, and then Gaul, from the predations of a bandit turned rebel.'

He paused, a knowing smile on his face, and Marcus spoke from his place in the tent's shadows.

'But that's all somewhat peripheral, isn't it? You spoke of Niger being lauded by the senate, but you don't mention the emperor. Because you plan to murder Commodus, don't you?'

Maternus nodded levelly in the tent's half-light.

'Yes. His death is the only fitting repayment I can take for the honour of the thousands of dead soldiers whose sacrifices he threw into the gutter, when he sued for peace and ran for Rome.'

'And the chaos that will result? There'll be a civil war, and you know what that means. It will be a repeat of what happened when Nero committed suicide and left the empire leaderless.' Scaurus stood, his hands held open before him as the bandit leader put a hand to the hilt of his dagger. 'I even know the pattern it'll follow. The senate will put some poor fool on the throne who's neither ready nor able to rule, a compromise candidate acceptable to all in the short term, then fall to plotting behind his back. Powerful generals will ponder having their men elevate them to the purple, with the appropriate show of reluctance, of course, and before we know it, every soldier in the empire will be on one side or the other. It'll be the Year of the Four Emperors all over again, and those barbarians you're so disgusted by will be the only winners, encouraged to raid our land by the absence of legions who have withdrawn to fight for the throne in far-off lands. Or is that what you want? Is that your final gift to the empire?'

The bandit leader shook his head.

'I have no concern with the fate of the empire, Tribune. All peoples get the leaders they deserve, I'd say, and for a fool such as Commodus to find himself on the throne, a good many of our more influential men must have been negligent in their duties over the last ten years. Let *them* deal with what falls out of what I plan to do.'

'You think that even the most powerful of senators had any choice in the imperial succession?' Marcus was on his feet, his eyes blazing with anger. 'My father was one of the best men in Rome, and he could no more have prevented Commodus becoming emperor than any other man, because the senate is awash with cowards and men whose fortunes depend on the palace!' He shook his head, looking up at the tent's ceiling. 'And he died at our *glorious* emperor's hands, as did my wife, because ultimately we are all powerless in the face of the naked power exercised by men like the imperial chamberlain on his behalf.'

Maternus stepped forward to look him in the eyes.

'In which case, you should wish me well, or even join me in my mission to take revenge on him for what he did. There's no need for you to die here if you'll put your considerable talents alongside my own. Leave these fools to pay the price for serving such a man, and take payment in blood for what he's done to your loved ones.'

Marcus turned, his teeth bared in a snarl.

'You cannot begin to imagine my hatred for the man. I have sworn to have my revenge on him. But it will be *my* revenge. Not *yours*. If you manage to kill him, then I will put that hatred aside unfulfilled, but it would be better never to see the life leave his eyes than to betray my comrades. If you're set on murdering the best man I know, then you can forget any idea that I'll buy my own life at the expense of my honour. Plan to do your worst to us, but be warned, you'll spend the rest of your days looking over your shoulder, and just when you least expect it, you'll find me behind you. With my iron in your back.'

Maternus sniggered in unconcealed amusement.

'I'll spend the rest of my life looking over my shoulder, will I? Possibly so, Centurion Corvus, but it won't be you I'll be looking for. Because tonight, once my men have eaten and drunk their fill, I'm going to have the four of you crucified. Your choking, writhing death spasms should be enough to keep that rabble out there distracted, while I and those of my century who've survived these years in the wilderness make our exit and turn our horses towards Rome. You've had your chance to avoid such an inglorious end to your life, Centurion, so now you'll have to face the cross and its horrors. So prepare to die well. Because that's all that's left for you. But you will not die without the appropriate words being said on your behalves.'

He turned to the tent's doorway.

'I will pray for you, when next I see an altar.'

'There they are. In all their ragged glory.'

Sanga and Saratos shot each other a swift glance, the older man rolling his eyes at Varus's turn of phrase. The Dacian nodded almost imperceptibly as his hard eyes took in the sight laid out before them. In the cover of a bush, at the very edge of the forest covering the hill that rose to the south of the bandit army's camp, they had a perfect view of the untidy sprawl of tents inside turf walls that were a direct copy of those used to protect similarly-sized Roman formations in the field. The smoke from fifty fires was rising into the still, early afternoon air, Maternus's men evidently enjoying the luxury of a day free from the sort of routine that would have dominated a legionary's waking life.

'You two know what you have to do?'

The Dacian replied for both of them, his stony gaze fixed on the enemy encampment laid out before them.

'Yes, Dubnus. Is simple. Is not *easy*, but is simple.'

The centurion pointed down at the camp's centre, and the cluster of larger tents that formed the camp's focal point.

'You see the command tents? That's where they'll be, in one of those, most likely.'

Sanga nodded, tapping his fellow watch officer on the arm.

'We can stare at them all we like, but it ain't going to get our gentlemen back, is it? Come on, you Dacian meathead, let's go and see what we can see.'

The two men backed away from the vantage point until they were sufficiently far back into the trees to avoid being seen, and then stood, picking up the heavy bundles of firewood the party had gathered earlier. They made their way down the hill's eastern flank until they came across a hunter's path that ran to the treeline's edge. Sanga regarded the smoke rising from the sea of tents for a moment, spitting on the ground in disgust.

'Was a time when I thought all this sneaking around was nothing but a bit of fun. A good way to avoid all the bullshit we're part of day in and day out. Looking at that lot I'm suddenly not so sure . . .'

Saratos followed his stare, shrugging with his customary lack of concern.

'Is easier for me. I was prisoner, remember? I was already dead man; slave or gladiator is all same. But now I have new life, and I got a new skill I never know I have. And you have same skill. You the best I know.'

The older man grinned at him, shaking his head in amusement.

'Go on then, what's this skill we both have that I'm the best at?'

'We liars, Sanga, we *very* good liars. Now we tell lies to save friends. Is simple.'

'It's always simple to you, isn't it, you dozy Dacian prick? Tell a few lies, smack someone around a bit, drink a few beers. March a thousand miles and do it all again. Does it never bother you that every time we do this, we get closer to some bastard seeing right through us, and all this fun and games will end up with the pair of us being burned alive or nailed up for crow meat?'

The muscular soldier turned his gaze on the bandit camp, clenching a fist until the knuckles turned white.

'Is possible. And if that happen, I take man who catch me with me to meet ferryman, I make self that promise. But not today Sanga, you ugliest of men . . .' He grinned back at his comrade's reaction to his unexpectedly jocular turn of phrase. 'Not today. Today we lie like gods themselves, eh?'

Hefting two bulky bundles of firewood onto his shoulder, he turned and started walking, leaving Sanga staring at his back in disbelief.

'Fuck me. You're actually enjoying this shit, aren't you?'

The Dacian replied without turning back.

'Is simple. We lie, we find officers, we rescue. Now come, I hungry.'

Sanga lifted his own burden, staring at the camp for a moment longer before following his comrade.

'He's hungry. Now I've heard it all.'

The two men crossed the open space between the forest and the camp's edge at a steady walk, Sanga steadily complaining about the weight of the wood he was carrying, the state of his feet, the cold of the day and a half dozen other topics in a relentless monologue that he continued as they approached the camp's eastern entrance and the lounging men who passed for a guard at the break in the turf wall that encompassed the encampment. Saratos called out while they were still twenty paces distant from the waiting guards, his voice loaded with weary exhaustion.

'You hear he? He never stop complain. Someone kill he and put me out of misery!'

Smirking, the two men strolled forwards, looking the newcomers up and down, taking in their bare heads and the mail they both wore, each with a rent where Dubnus had punched a hole with his dagger to enhance their credibility as battlefield looters.

'I don't recognise you, and you ain't come out of this gate this morning. Who are you?'

'We're camped on the other side, friend, where the firewood's already been stripped out like the hair on my old man's head. So we thought we'd try it over this side . . .' Sanga tapped the firewood with his free hand. 'Which turned out alright.'

The taller of the guards stared at them calculatingly.

'And that's all very well, but this side of the camp is ours, right? So if you want to take our wood back to your side of the camp though our gate, you have to pay a tax. Half.'

'Half? Fuck you. How about we pay nothing and my mate here doesn't give you both a good fucking hiding.'

Saratos dropped his bundles, stretching out his cramped arms and flexing his biceps before shaking them out and experimentally clenching his hands into fists. The guards both stepped back involuntarily despite the manifest advantages of their spears over the daggers that the two men before them wore.

'Steady, friend. It was a suggestion, alright? But if it comes to a fight, you're two blokes on your own. And there's fucking hundreds of us.'

Saratos shrugged off the sentry's attempted threat.

'Either of you call for help, or raise you spear, I break both your right arm. I break both your right arm, you useless. And useless men left behind when army march, no? So why we not trade, eh? Is better than you try to steal and we all be dead.'

The guard nodded, evidently preferring the Dacian's suggestion to the alternative.

'What do you want for the wood?'

'Breakfast.' Sanga stepped forward, tossing his bundles on the ground in front of them. 'I could smell the pigs roasting from a mile off, and it smells right tasty. So you give me and the lump here a proper feed of pork and bread – not the short rations we'll get if we go back to our own century – and we'll give you *one* bundle of the wood we've been gathering while you were standing round here scratching your hoops. Or we can just walk all the way back around the camp instead, going hungry that much longer, and you don't have any more wood than you do now. You choose.'

The two men looked at each other.

'Sounds fair to me. Come on then, bring it in and we'll see what we can do about getting you fed.' He looked at the Dacian's face, frowning in frustrated half-recognition. 'You look familiar, and yet you're not from this cohort.'

Saratos shrugged.

'Is small army. You see me before, I see you before, is obvious.'

The bandit nodded.

'I suppose . . . come on then, and bring that wood with you.'

Sanga muttered an imprecation under his breath, lifting the bundle back onto his shoulders with an affected grunt of weariness.

'Fuck me, I sell you the wood but I get to carry it home for you. Feels like I'm the one with the shitty end of the stick here.'

He followed the enemy sentry and his Dacian comrade into the camp still muttering bitter complaints, while his eyes flicked from side to side taking in the men lounging at their leisure to either side of the path that led to the centre of the mass of tents.

Fifty yards into the tented city, their guide pointed to a fire surrounded by men dressed and equipped in the haphazard manner that was prevalent in Maternus's army.

'Here we go, boys! Just when you thought you were about to run out of firewood, here's a new supply! Cut these lads a slice of that pork apiece and wrap it in bread and they'll keep us warm for the next few hours!'

The two friends were greeted with a chorus of drunken cheers, the bandits clearly having been drinking for hours. The fire flared into fresh life as several inebriated men applied the firewood to it at such a rate that it was unlikely to last for more than an hour, and pressed generous hunks of bread and meat into their hands. Sanga fended off a man who was attempting to relive him of his second bundle, clearly intent on increasing the blaze still further.

'Just the one bundle, friend, this one's still ours!'

The drunken bandit's comrades laughed as he staggered away and slumped by the fire, and the sentry, clearly disappointed still to be sober, looked down at him wistfully.

'Trust me to draw guard duty the day after we beat the arse off an imperial army. This lot have been on it since first thing, Maternus's orders, and I've had nothing better than a cup of water all day. But at least I'll be off duty when the time comes to put their officers to death.'

Sanga and Saratos shared swift glances of professionally-masked concern, as the man who had walked them in from the gate waxed lyrical about their leader's predilection for mass executions through a mouthful of steaming pork.

'Remember that shower of useless auxiliary bastards we ambushed south of Vesontio? A whole fucking cohort of cowards who ran for it the moment they saw us coming for them. I'll never forget the way the chief gave the men we captured a choice. Join us or burn, he told them, and bugger me but about thirty of them told him to go and piss up a tree. Perhaps they thought he was having a laugh with them. Mind you, the screaming when he had them coated in pitch and set alight one at a time could have been heard for fucking miles.'

He'd looked at Saratos questioningly, and the Dacian had nodded approvingly.

'Is one thing to scream when you think you going die. Is another thing when you burning, eh?'

'Too right it is, mate, too fucking right. But Maternus has something a bit more drawn out in mind for tonight from what we've been told.'

Sanga shrugged, chewing vigorously on another piece of hot meat.

'What's wrong with burning them?'

'Nothing at all, but it's over before you know it. The bodies burn for a while, of course, but they're dead inside a minute so there's not much sport to be had from it. Whereas a good old-fashioned crucifixion gives the lads hours of fun.'

'Yeah.' Another man staggered across to them. 'And it's good for the wagering too! How long they'll last, how many times they'll heave themselves up on the heel nails to stop themselves choking, how long before they start begging for the mercy stroke . . .'

'I'm a bit traditional that way, too.' Sanga nodded vigorously. 'Here, give us a sip of that.' He swigged from the other man's cup, warming to his subject. 'And serve the bastards right, eh?'

The men around him growled their assent, and the man whose cup he had swigged from nodded vehement, drunken agreement.

'They're the ones who put us where we were before Maternus saved us and made us soldiers. The bastards with the money and the power, and now they get to pay for the things they done to us!'

Saratos turned to find the sentry staring at him with a look of frustration.

'What you problem, friend?'

'I know you from somewhere, I know I do. I just can't put my finger on where from.'

The Dacian shrugged.

'I tell you, is small army. We meet before without even know.'

The other man shrugged, his face still creased in the frustration of a mislaid memory.

'Perhaps . . . I'd better get back to the gate before our fucking centurion turns up and finds me missing. That fucker's going to get his stick rammed up where the sun don't shine one of these days.'

He turned and left, and Saratos relaxed inwardly with his departure, unable to put his finger on why the man's presence disquieted him. He put a hand on Sanga's shoulder, pulling the older man away from his new friends.

'We need go. This wood not going to walk itself over to other side of camp. We got men depend on us, right?'

Sanga's drinking companion raised his cup in a cheery salute, lurching slightly with the wine's disorienting grasp on his senses.

'Stay and have another drink! That wood will burn just as well here as it will over there!'

'I'd love to, mate.' Saratos grinned as his comrade wrapped the other man in a bear hug, lifted the cup from his hand and drained it. 'But the lump's right. We have to get this wood to our tent party. We've got this right bastard of a centurion. Otho's his name, knuckles harder than a whore's heart, and he'll paste the pair of us if he finds out we shared it with you.'

Bidding their new friends farewell, they stepped out onto the path through the tents that led to the camp's centre, Sanga looking about him at the rebel army's collective state of inebriation.

'So this collection of pissed-up halfwits are going to crucify our officers unless we get them out of here, and pretty soon from the sound of it. We ain't got long, mate, not long at all.'

'I told you. We're going to die. The only choice we have is whether to die badly or to go out with some dignity.'

Scaurus shook his head at Victor's muttered opinion.

'If you decide that the end has come, then it most assuredly has. Keep some hope, and stay ready for any opportunity.'

The praetorian smiled wanly at him.

'You're a prisoner in the middle of a legion-sized enemy force whose members have no regard or respect for your position, and a positive hatred of mine. As far as they're concerned, we're just like the men who were their masters before Maternus freed them. On top of which, their leader – a man so deeply severed from his service to Rome that he's terrorised three provinces for five years, and who most recently had the balls to lay siege to a legion fortress – has told us that he intends to use the sideshow of our executions to distract these animals, while he makes good his exit and leaves them to their own devices. Which means that when they discover his absence, they are more than likely going to run amok and murder us, if we've not already choked out our last breaths on the crosses they'll have nailed us to not very long from now. So tell me, Rutilius Scaurus, what part of that doesn't spell your death, exactly? Slow and agonised or quick and bloody, it's all the same other than the manner of our passing.'

Marcus answered for his tribune from where he sat in the tent's shadows close to the wall, raising a finger to tap his ear.

'The camp is already well past the halfway point to inebriation, if I can trust the evidence of my ears. And the sentry outside this side of the tent is asleep, to judge from his snoring.'

'And that's all very well, but it means nothing without any better means of getting out of this tent than our fingernails. Or disguising ourselves as anything other than what we are, for that matter. We wouldn't get ten paces without being recognised.'

He stared at Marcus for a moment, his eyes narrowing at the younger man's total lack of concern.

'And yet you look like you don't have a care in the world. So what is it that you know and I *don't*?'

The Roman shrugged, a half-smile touching his lips.

'I have every expectation that there are men close to hand who intend to get us out of this predicament.'

'And if your expectation is unfounded? Or your friends are spotted and put to death?'

'All of these things are possible. And it might be that I will indeed end my life on a cross before the next dawn.'

'Which doesn't seem to trouble you.'

Marcus shook his head.

'It doesn't. If today is my day to die, then it will also be the day I am reunited with my wife. I do not seek death, although I have in the past, but neither will I shrink from it. And besides . . .'

'What?'

'There's a camp full of inebriated halfwits out there, Tribune, and I know at least two men who'll swim in that sea with the greatest of ease.'

'We keep wandering around this camp with a single bundle of firewood between us for much longer and someone's going to ask us just who we think we're fooling. We need to shit or get off the pot.'

Saratos grunted his agreement, dropping his burden to the ground and arching his back in relief at its removal.

'We close enough to tent.'

Sanga gestured to the sky above them, a delicate shade of gold as the sun sank towards the horizon.

'But it's not dark enough. If we try to get them out now, some bright boy will see us doing it and that'll be that.'

'I not so sure. See?' The Dacian stared hard at the cluster of tents, directing his friend's attention to the space between them, in which a single man was sitting cross-legged, his head nodding in half-sleep. 'We see him from here. But if he take two step to the right he not seen.'

Sanga nodded dubiously.

'True. But so fucking what? If we just pole up to him, the first thing he's going to do is start shouting, because that's just what he's been put there for!'

The Dacian shook his head.

'You wrong. He put there to stop men escape from tent. Is no threat of rescue, not with all these men around us. And perhaps he been there long time with no pork except what he smell.' He looked around him, nodding slowly. 'Half camp asleep with belly full of pig and beer. They sleep now, because want be awake later.'

'Half the camp asleep with a gut full of pork and beer. Yes . . .' Sanga mused for another moment before speaking again. 'And that bloke's going to be hungry, right, and he'll fancy a drink, too.'

Saratos nodded, rolling his eyes.

'Yes. Is good thing you have such good idea. So we need pork and beer?'

'Yeah, but that's not all.' Sanga cocked his head in the direction of the nearest fire. 'I can see something else we need, now you mention it. You ain't the only one with good ideas, you hairy bastard. Follow me.'

He strolled towards the nearest fire with a grin fixed on his face, putting both hands on his hips and waiting until the men around the slowly dying embers noticed him.

'Looks to me like you men need some wood. And as chance would have it, here I am with my last bundle.'

The tent party's leader stepped forward, looking him up and down with a pugnacious attitude clearly at least partially born of the amount of drink he'd consumed in the previous few hours.

'And what's to stop us just taking it off you, eh?'

Sanga smiled evilly, stepping in close and going face to face with the drunk, patting the ornately decorated handle of his dagger.

'The fact that I'll carve your fucking ears off and make you eat them?'

The other man retreated a step, his face still hard but clearly unsettled by the failure of his threat.

'You threatening me?'

The Briton grinned broadly.

'Nah, mate, I'm just joking with you the way you were joking with me! You wouldn't try to rob me, not with a nasty bastard like that at my back.'

The bandit refocused his bleary gaze on Saratos, his eyebrows rising as the Dacian tossed the bundle of wood aside and flexed his biceps.

'You want me kill he?'

Sanga raised a hand in mock restraint.

'Not just yet, you dirty bastard.' He leaned in towards the other man with a conspiratorial air. 'I let him fuck the men he kills. That's what all those eastern bastards are like. So how about I just sell you some wood for a nice big piece of that pig you lot are trying to force down your necks, now that you're all bulging with it and wondering if you're going to puke. And I might have some gold, if you want to sell me some gear.'

The other man's expression went from aggression to calculation.

'Gold? For what?'

The Briton waved a hand at several mail shirts draped over the men's spear-propped shields in an obvious invitation to buy.

'Obvious, ain't it? Look at you in your lovely new praetorian armour while there's blokes in my tent party wearing mail that's more hole than rings. But we do have gold that we took off the men we killed yesterday, so they sent me and the lump here out to buy some new gear for them, me to negotiate and him to beat the shit out of anyone trying to relieve me of the coin I'm carrying. When I saw your display there, I just thought that you lads might fancy getting a piece of it. But no worries if you're not bothered, we'll take our trade somewhere else.'

He turned to leave, winking at Saratos as the leading man put a hand on his arm.

'Whoa! Not so fast, friend! Sure we can do a deal! See those mail shirts? Not a hole in any of them, as you can see. We'll turn them out to you for a gold piece each. How many do you want?'

'A gold apiece? I don't fucking think so. There's lot of mail on the market right now what with the number of blokes poncing around in their new praetorian gear. Four shirts for one gold, that's my offer. And the pork, of course, you can throw that in to sweeten the bargain.'

'Four shirts for a gold? Are you some sort of madman?'

Saratos shook his head in bemused amusement as Sanga and the bandit fell to bargaining, the Briton lifting one of the mail shirts from its resting place to examine it critically.

'Thin rings, for a start. This is the cheap stuff they make the urban guards wear, isn't it? I bet you took it in some shithole town back in Gaul, and you've been desperate to get rid of it ever since. And now look at you, all fine and manly in armour that was being worn in Rome until a couple of months ago.' He pulled a face. 'Tell you what, I ain't even got the time to waste, 'cause they'll be nailing up them officers soon and I don't want to miss that. Two golds for four shirts and a belt and dagger to go with each. How's that?'

II

'What's that?'

Marcus gestured to his comrades for silence, bending closer to the leather wall and putting a finger in his other ear. The camp's clamour formed a faint aural backdrop to the apparent silence, and after a moment he shrugged and straightened up, shaking his head in disappointment.

'I thought I h—'

All four men spun back to the tent's rear wall as a dagger pushed through the leather at shoulder height and then sliced downward with brisk efficiency, opening a long slit through which its owner stepped with the weapon held ready to strike. Marcus stepped forward to greet him.

'Sanga!'

Putting a finger to his lips to forestall any further talk, the Briton passed Marcus a mail shirt and belt, then reached back and procured more from outside the tent, handing the equipment to the other officers.

'Put them on, and try to look like pissed-up soldiers rather than what you are, got it?'

'You can't really hope to . . .'

Sanga raised a hand to silence the praetorian.

'I'm rescuing you, Tribune, and there ain't much time to do it in either. So put the mail on and get ready to go. No, not like that, us dumb bastards wear our knives on our left hips!'

Recognising the voice of a man in control of the situation, the officers pulled on their mail and adjusted the belts to put the daggers on the correct sides of their bodies as instructed.

When Sanga deemed that they were ready to go, he pointed to Marcus.

'We've all had a few drinks, right, and now we're going out to get some more firewood before it gets too dark, out through the gate me and the idiot here came in through.' He took the meat and bread from Saratos. 'Here, get these in your faces and keep chewing them. It might stop someone recognising you, so don't eat it all at once!' He gestured to Marcus. 'We've all had a drink, like I said, so we're a bit tired and not all that steady, and I'm totally pissed as it happens. You go with Saratos, Centurion, sir . . .' he pointed to Scaurus and Victor, 'and you two gentlemen each get an arm round me and hold me up. And you, sir' – he gestured to Sergius – 'you look handy, so you bring up the rear and be ready to get stuck in if it all goes to rat shit. If anyone has a good look at us, they'll mostly be laughing at me. And no matter what you see or hear, keep them grins on your faces. You've had a few drinks and you couldn't give a shit what anyone else thinks.'

He beckoned them out of the tent through the rent his dagger had opened in the canvas, all four men blinking at the evening sky's rosy light after a day in the tent's darkness. Lolling against Marcus with the practised ease of a man well-experienced in the finer points of excessive alcohol consumption, Saratos steered him out from behind the tent's cover. He headed into the camp's celebratory hubbub, leaning on Marcus and muttering in his ear.

'Is simple, eh, Centurion? I take us where we need go, you hold me up, eh? And eat food, yes? You starving drunkard, not tight-arse officer like Sanga say.'

Grinning despite the extraordinary gravity of their situation, the young Roman did as he was told, relaxing into the role and taking a mouthful of the greasy pork. The Dacian looked at the fat running down his chin and onto his mail with a smile, and nodded enthusiastically.

'Is perfect. But you never get that out of tunic.'

Staggering along the road that led to the eastern gate, the small party went pretty much unnoticed in the camp's general state of inebriation and pre-execution ferment. Scaurus and Victor looked about them with expressions of amazement despite Sanga's warning to expect the worst. On their left, a century-sized group of men were being harangued by their commander, a mug of wine in his hand, over some unidentified offence or other, while on the other side of the road, a group of fifty or so men were incoherently singing a marching song around the embers of their fire. As the gate drew nearer, both soldiers straightened up and began to walk unaided, keeping their gait slightly unsteady until the last moment, as the guards, still unchanged from an hour before, swung round from their bored contemplation of the empty countryside around them.

'You again? I thought you'd be away getting tucked into the wine by now.'

The same sentry who had escorted Sanga and Saratos to his century's fire an hour before was standing before them.

'I thought you'd be doing the same.'

He shook his head at Sanga's reply, apparently just as relaxed as before.

'Not me. I'm stuck here for another hour or so. Don't tell me you're going out for more wood?'

'You know how it is. Find a willing horse and load the bastard up. My officer sent these four with me to bring more wood back, so we'll have the same agreement as last time, yeah?'

The sentry laughed, looking at his comrade and nodding.

'Seems fair enough. Alright, lads, off you go, but don't stay in the trees after dark, there's been something moving around up there that's made the birds right uneasy. A boar most likely, and that's make some good eating if you can catch it.'

Sanga laughed dismissively.

'I ain't going to kill a boar with this little thing, now am I?'

The Briton put a hand to his dagger, and suddenly the blade was in his hand, its distinctive patterned blade gleaming in the late afternoon's golden sunlight. The sentry stared at him, his facial expression slowly hardening with the shock of recognition as the knife's pale iron bar jogged his memory.

'You're . . .' A horn sounded in the camp behind him, an urgent call to arms that brayed out across the tents and carousing soldiers and silenced them in an instant, and the sentry's face hardened as the realisation of who he was talking to hit him. '*Fuck!* It's him, from the battle, the bastard with the dag—'

Sanga was on him with the same speed he had displayed on the battlefield the previous day, punching the weapon's evilly sharp point into his throat and ripping it out sideways. Saratos sprung onto the other man as he turned and drew breath to shout a warning to his comrades, driving a punch into the back of his neck that snapped his head forward and dropped him to the ground. Turning back to the officers, he pointed at the hillside before them and barked an order above the sudden tumult.

'*Run!*'

Men were shouting and pointing on the other side of the camp's turf wall barely a dozen feet away, the less inebriated among them snatching up their swords and spears as they realised that something was amiss. Their cries of alarm redoubled as they realised that the trumpet calls were connected with the men sprinting away from the gate. The Tungrians ran for their lives, breathing hard as the slope began to steepen, and Marcus looked back to see dozens of men pouring out of the enemy camp behind them. Sanga shouted an instruction from behind them, panting for breath.

'To the right! Into the trees and then follow Saratos!'

They plunged into the forest's gloom, straining their eyes to see the Dacian's back as he led them up the narrow path as far as the branch he'd broken earlier in the day, and then veered left up the hill towards the place where the rest of the detachment were waiting. A dozen paces up the slope, he sank down onto his hands and knees, below the level of the bushes, hissing at them to follow his example.

'Stay low, move slow!'

With a sudden explosion of noise, the first of the bandits burst into the trees behind them, and Marcus realised that if they had stayed upright, they would still have been visible to their pursuers, who – lacking any indication that their quarry had done anything other than follow the path deeper into the forest – hared off down the track in hot pursuit. While increasing numbers of the enemy flooded into the confined space, the Tungrians followed Saratos's slow, deliberately careful path through the undergrowth, the Dacian staying low to the ground until he judged that they were over the crest and out of sight.

'Now we *run*.'

Sprinting through the trees in his wake, they covered a quarter mile before falling breathlessly into the detachment's waiting circle of axemen and archers. Dubnus greeted Marcus with delight, clapping Sanga on the back in congratulations.

'It's about time. We were starting to wonder if you'd decided to stay for dinner.' Dubnus sniffed audibly, his eyes narrowing as he detected a familiar smell. 'Is that . . . beer? Have you been drinking, you pair of—'

'What you think? Sanga smell beer, he drawn like to woman.'

The centurion nodded at Saratos's acerbic statement, raising an eyebrow at the Briton's protests.

'What did you fucking expect, Dubnus? I was hardly going to say no thanks, not when we were trying to blend in.'

'He blend in perfect. Blend in several time.'

'This is all very well, Centurion, but what's the plan from here? Where are the cohorts?'

Dubnus turned to Scaurus and saluted.

'Tribune, sir, our cohorts are camped ten miles to the east and waiting for us, along with the praetorians.'

'So all we have to do now is escape that mob of wild animals?'

'We need to be away before they work out that they're looking in the wrong direction. Lead us, Qadir.'

The Hamian uttered a hissed order that had the detachment's men on their feet, then pointed through the trees in the direction from which they had made their approach march. His archers moved out first, assuming a half-moon formation that would be their eyes and ears, but they had covered no more than fifty careful paces when the distant sound of pursuit abruptly increased. The first of the men hunting them appeared over the crest of the slope they had climbed moments before, evidently casting about for any sign of the fugitives. The Tungrians sank into cover, their presence undetected in the forest's late afternoon murk, but any chance of the party making a stealthy escape was evidently rendered impossible by the rebels spreading out into the forest's gloom.

'*Fuck.*' Dubnus rubbed his face wearily. 'I suppose I always knew it would end in some miserable spot like this.' He turned to Scaurus. 'Make it worth my while, eh Tribune? Me and my brothers will sell ourselves to buy a few dozen of them; you use the distraction to disengage and get out of here.'

'I'm with you.'

The Briton shook his head at Marcus.

'No, not this time, brother. If you're with me, then they'll all be on you, and that's not the game we need to play here. Go and find your revenge, and think kindly of me when you have a blade in the emperor's guts.'

'But—'

'*No.*' Sergius pushed forward through the ferns, his tone vehement. 'This is on me, for not speaking out when my colleague was leading us to disaster. And *I'm* the dispensable one here.' He turned to Victor. 'I have two words for you, Victor. Make amends. And you, Centurion Dubnus, can give me that sword.'

He stood, taking the blade and turning away, striding determinedly through the trees in silence, using their cover to close with the searching bandits without being detected.

'He's going to sacrifice himself to help us get away!'

Victor nodded grimly at Marcus's astonished statement.

'Yes. He is. So let's not have him die in vain. Move!'

They made as much haste as was possible bent double beneath the luxuriant undergrowth, weaving around patches of thorns and pressing through ferns, regardless of the risk that their movement might be spotted. Varus took the lead as he recognised the path they had left on their approach march.

'Follow me! There's a gulley this way and once we're down it, we can run properly without being seen!'

Behind them a shout interrupted the calls of the searchers, and Marcus turned, peering over the tops of the foliage to see Sergius step out from behind a tree with the sword held two-handed in a wide-legged fighting stance.

'Come on then, you gutless bastards! Come and fight a real soldier!'

'It's what he was born for.' He turned to find Victor at his side. 'And I'd give everything I have to be alongside him to regain some honour.'

They watched as the tunic-clad tribune dodged his first assailant's spear thrust and gutted the oncoming bandit with a hacking swing of his blade. He parried the next man's sword thrust with an effortless flick that sent the weapon's point wide and opened his attacker's body for the counter-thrust that tore his throat open. Stepping back into the combat stance, he shook the sword to flick away the blood coating its iron surface and then set himself to meet the next wave of men streaming towards him through the trees.

'If you stay to watch him die, then you will be next, once they realise he was buying us time. Don't make his sacrifice pointless.'

Victor reluctantly backed away at Scaurus's insistent grip on his arm, shaking his head in self-disgust.

'The moment will come for me to make the same sacrifice. And I will do so with equal contempt for a life no longer worth any value, beyond that of following his last request of me, and making amends.'

They turned and ran in the wake of Qadir's archers, disappearing into the trees with the shouts and screams of Sergius's last stand fading behind them.

'He died so that I might have the opportunity to atone for my error. I cannot allow that to go unrecognised. If it takes me the rest of my days to be worthy of that gift, I will earn it.'

Scaurus nodded at the praetorian's words as the detachment
and the men they had rescued made their way along the treeline
just inside the forest's edge, no longer in fear of the rebels' pursuit.
The shouts and calls of the men hunting for them had echoed
distantly through the trees as afternoon had turned to evening.
The hunters were ever-present but never quite close enough to
catch sight of the fleeing Tungrians, and as the light had started
to fail, they had faded to silence, as even the keenest of the rebels
had given up their apparently fruitless task. With a full moon to
light their way, the Hamians scouted ahead and behind them,
covering the party's front and rear, while Dubnus and his pioneers
provided an escort for the officers.

'Your colleague did his duty. He knew that one of us had to
die, and to die well enough to hold up those men hunting us, so
that we could break contact with them and make our escape.'

Victor stared into the forest's depths with eyes drained of any
emotion.

'He always was a man who could only ever see his way through
any given situation in terms of how best to do his duty. How I
envy him.'

Silence fell across the officers, but his fellow tribune broke the
praetorian's reverie in a matter-of-fact tone verging on the brutal.

'How you envy him? A good man gave his life to allow the rest
of us to escape from Maternus's plans for our slow and painful
deaths. He doesn't need your envy, colleague, nor even your
respect, although he's more than earned his place in Elysium as
far as I'm concerned. What his example demands of us is that
we ignore all thoughts of mourning him and start working out
what we have to do to prevent this minor setback from turning
into a full-blooded catastrophe.'

Victor turned and stared at him for a moment before shaking
his head at his own choler and shrugging, resuming his careful
progress through the trees and bushes.

'I cannot argue. And at least we know what it is that Maternus
intends, and have a chance to frustrate his design, thanks to his

urge to gloat over captives he believed would be dead before dawn. Which means that all we have to do is evade any further pursuit and make our way to Argentoratum.'

Marcus spoke up from ahead of the two tribunes.

'Is that the best course of action available to us, Tribune, to leave Maternus's men unchecked?'

The praetorian answered in the tone of a man unaccustomed to being challenged by his subordinates.

'And what alternatives do you believe offer themselves to us, *Centurion*?'

Scaurus spoke again, his voice pitched softly but the iron in his words unmistakable.

'I'd be careful throwing ranks around if I were you, Statilius Victor, or someone might remind you that you're the man whose indomitable will resulted in our current predicament. And for what it's worth, my first spear has served as a legion tribune, and has seen more good men die than you can imagine. So if he thinks something might be unwise, it would be *wise* of you to at least listen to him.'

Victor turned and stared back at him in stunned silence for a moment before resuming their march through the moonlit trees, his voice abashed when he spoke again.

'My apologies. A man can find himself struggling to deal with the consequences of his actions so badly that he forgets the basic manners expected of him.' He turned to look at Marcus with the faintest echo of a wry smile. 'So tell me, Valerius Aquila, why it is you feel that marching for Argentoratum is the wrong thing to do?'

'If we march away to the east, we're leaving a legion-sized army without leadership, without purpose and, worst of all, without either food or the gold to purchase it with. All of which I believe to be a reflection of Maternus's plan. He'll leave that mob to their own devices, counting on the chaos that must inevitably result to draw attention away from whatever it is that he's planning.'

'But surely our duty is to send word to Rome, and as quickly as possible? Every day that his intentions are unknown in the capital is another day wasted. Another day in which he will have access to wherever he chooses to take this revenge.'

Marcus shook his head.

'That amulet he took from you was useless to him the moment we escaped and turned his plan to ashes, as is the equipment he captured. He'll know that his plan to use the scorpion to gain access to the palace is in ruins, because with you free to send a message to Rome, there's no way that he'll get within a hundred paces of the emperor without being discovered and captured. And there's no way a man like Maternus would chance those sorts of odds. He'll have something else in mind, if he's as good as you say, a contingency plan to cover the possibility of his original scheme being thwarted. We can get a warning to Rome quickly enough, using the message network, and then relax in the expectation that it will only be a matter of time before he's taken. But our duty demands more of us than simply alerting the authorities to the potential of his plot to kill Commodus. Much more. Both here and in Rome.'

The rescue party found the new marching camp in the small hours of the next morning, guided to its location by the glow from the four cohorts' campfires reflected by the low clouds that had moved in to block the moon's light for much of their long march. Elated to have his comrades returned safely, Julius's enthusiasm was first tempered by the loss of Sergius, then completely crushed by the two tribunes' grim-faced verdict as to what they believed was necessary, given the circumstances.

'You want to go *back*?' Julius stared at Scaurus and Victor in amazement while they ate hungrily from the bowls of stew that he had ordered to be kept warm for their return. 'You want to take two cohorts of men and attack a legion-sized force in their own camp? We don't even have any cavalry to support us, not since their decurion decided to piss off back to his legion and give the legatus the good news. I sent Silus and his men after them to make sure the Legatus knows that we're in the shit and need reinforcement, not that my hopes are particularly high in that respect. So don't take this the wrong way, Tribune, but I have to ask . . . have you both lost your minds?'

'Not entirely, Prefect.' Scaurus shook his head wearily, rubbing his face in an attempt to dispel the fatigue. 'We have, after all, been inside that camp, and seen the state of Maternus's army. They were never that much of a threat, not unless they were able to take us unawares, which is why Maternus put so much time and thought into constructing a scenario where we would pursue him onto ground of his own choosing. Everything he did from the moment he threw the first spear at the Argentoratum wall seems to have been calculated with that single aim.'

Victor nodded at Scaurus's pronouncement, adding his own opinion with a degree of humility that was far from the bombast he had exhibited before his humbling at the hands of the rebel leader.

'A trap into which I put my head, despite everyone around me trying to warn me, only to have their opinions ignored and ridiculed. At the cost of hundreds of good men and the reduction of the survivors' fighting power to next to nothing. The honour of the imperial guard has been traduced, and at the heart of the matter is not Maternus's cunning, but rather my own stupidity. A failure on my part that I fully intend to make amends for.'

Julius looked back to Scaurus with undiminished incredulity.

'And you intend to allow this fantasy of vengeance to play out, Tribune? Even if it destroys our own cohorts? Aren't the losses we've already sustained enough?'

'This isn't about revenge, Julius.' Scaurus shook his head tiredly. 'I can see how it looks that way, and my colleague here truly does have a burning need to see every last one of those bandits dead, but the absolute imperative to go back in there and finish them off is actually is far more to do with expediency than revenge.'

The big man stared at him levelly, his tone one of disbelief.

'Expediency? It's *expedient* to throw our cohorts onto the same fire that destroyed the praetorians?'

'Yes. Because Maternus took us captive for two reasons. One was his simple need to humiliate the Guard, who he believes are as culpable for what happened in Germania as Commodus himself. The other reason was his clearly-declared intention of crucifying us last night, to provide a diversion for his already hopelessly-inebriated army. Our deaths were to be a distraction to provide cover for his quiet exit with those few men he has left from the century that deserted with him, with all the gold they can carry. He's abandoning his army in order to seek revenge on the emperor for making peace with the Germans, and he's probably already on the road for Rome. And without leadership and gold to purchase the supplies they need, his army won't remain intact for more than a few days before it turns it into a mob. Those men will turn on each other, and then all too soon on the immediate area, simply to feed themselves. They will splinter into a dozen or more bands, and each one will loot, burn, rape and murder its way across Gaul in an explosion of violence that will last for years before they can all be put down. Whereas now, at this moment, all of those men are lying insensate in their tents, stupefied by drink, providing us with an opportunity that will not be repeated.'

'That's now. It will take us hours to be in position to attack them.'

Scaurus laughed softly.

'You might have the constitution of an ox, Prefect, capable of sinking a bellyful of wine and rising the next morning with little more than a feeling of slight unease, but I'd give Morban good odds that most of those bandits have no such fortitude. We saw them at close quarters yesterday afternoon, and I can assure you that they were already very much the worse for wear. They'll be little better than what I've heard you describe as "hammered shit" when we attack them in the morning, and still coming to terms with the disappearance of their leader. I think they'll fall to pieces.'

Julius shrugged.

'It sounds to me like that would just speed up the process of disintegration that you said was the reason to attack them now. If they break, rather than just stamping us flat, what's to keep them from running? We'd have no chance of stopping most of them, not without the cavalry who, to my strongly expressed and completely ignored amazement, bolted back to their legion at the first opportunity. I expect that all we'll achieve is to bring about what you fear, only rather more quickly.'

'You don't have two cohorts, Prefect, you have *four*.'

The big man stared at Victor in silence for long enough that Scaurus opened his mouth to intervene, but the praetorian raised a hand to forestall him.

'I understand. Your view of my men's abilities is coloured by what you've seen of them. A battle you won in our absence because we can't run like your soldiers, and a battle we lost because of my stubborn refusal to accept the facts. You have hardly seen praetorians at their best, and to make matters worse, we've been disarmed. I have two cohorts of men armed with nothing much sharper than their resentment, and a good deal of that will be directed at me. But even men without weapons aren't men without honour. They'll fight.'

'For all the good they'll be, without armour, swords or shields.'

'I'll make you a bargain, Prefect,' Scaurus stepped closer to his deputy, going eye to eye with big man, 'even though I could simply order you to get the cohorts ready to march and let that be the end of it. But that's not the way we've worked together all these years and I don't intend to get my way at the expense of your alienation.'

Julius inclined his head in grudging recognition of the point.

'So what's your proposal?'

'If Victor can rouse his men to march with us without having to order them to do so, then we head west at first light and fall on that camp with the aim of killing every last one of them.'

'And if he can't?'

'Then we'll march east to Argentoratum and report to Legatus Niger, putting the problem in his lap where, to be blunt, it actually belongs. Is that fair?'

'Fair?' Julius smiled in genuine amusement. 'Hardly. Even if the praetorians are up for revenge, they might as well not be there once the fighting starts.'

Victor shook his head firmly.

'Not with what I've got in mind.'

The prefect shrugged.

'It's clear you two gentlemen will talk at me until I give in. Very well, shall we go and see how your guardsmen respond?'

They followed Victor into the heart of the praetorian half of the sleeping camp and waited while the startled sentries did as they were ordered and went to find the duty centurion, who, if equally surprised with the unexpected return of his tribune, had the presence of mind not to betray his discomfiture. He ordered the guards to rouse the sleeping officers of both cohorts and bid them to gather at the command tent, which had been pitched from long habit despite the absence of its occupants. When, at length, the praetorian centurions were gathered around him, he turned a slow circle, meeting every man's eye in turn and taking his measure.

'Centurions, I am the bearer of news that sickens me as much as it will sadden you. Sergius is dead. He sold his life to buy mine, and the lives of Tribune Scaurus and his first spear, as well as the men who had volunteered to rescue us from the rebel camp. I wish that it had been the other way round, and that he was standing here talking to you, not least because he would have been the better man for what I am about to order, but the facts are as they are. My comrade of the last twenty years is dead, largely as a result of decisions I made, so now it falls to me to take revenge for him, and to regain the honour that we lost at the hands of the rebel Maternus. We stand here bereft of our armour and weapons, so reduced in stature that the people of Rome will view us as a disgrace when news of this reaches them. We can be re-equipped with everything we have lost, except for one thing, the most important thing. Our pride has been shorn from us, gentlemen, and carried away by an outcast no longer fit to bear the title of praetorian. I have allowed myself to be deceived, and the consequence has been greater than any of us can bear. I take full responsibility for that consequence, and when the time is right, I will make amends, if I survive the day to come.'

The men around him tensed, small changes of posture betraying their reaction to the implications of their tribune's words.

'But today is not a day for mourning our lost honour, or for cursing my failure, for all that you have every right to do so. Today is a day for vengeance and for reclaiming what we have lost. Vengeance for Sergius, the best praetorian I ever served with. I'll see every one of those rebels dead before I proclaim him to have been avenged in full. And today is a day to prevent this rebellion from turning into a pestilence that will blight this province and those around it for years. We must join our Tungrian comrades to snuff it out before it can start a fire that will destroy everything within a hundred miles of here. Of course you're thinking to yourselves that I've completely taken leave of my senses, given our lack of any weapon larger than a dagger. And you're wondering how it is that I'm proposing to storm an encampment of men armed with the spoils of our defeat.'

He paused, and Marcus saw the disbelief on the faces of the men around him turn to astonishment as he pulled the dagger Sanga had given him from its scabbard and raised it, turning in another slow circle with the polished iron gleaming red in the firelight.

'I remember my training as if it was yesterday, as do you all. Our brutally fast relearning of the order of things at the hands of retired centurions whose only motivation seemed to be our pain and discomfort. And I remember gradually coming to understand what it was that those leathery old bastards expected of us. Demanded of us. They gave me the self-belief to be the best man I could be, to rise through the ranks and achieve this impossible dream of commanding a cohort of the finest men in the city. They did the same to all of us, brothers; they unlocked what we could be and demanded that we achieve it. And if they beat one lesson into us above any other it was that the Guard comes first. Not me. Not you. The *Guard*.'

Men were nodding around him, each remembering the hardships and privations they had endured at the hands of men they had viewed as sadists until the realities of their new life had sunk in and they came to see that their instructors wanted to achieve something more than their brutalisation.

'Well, comrades, today the Guard needs us to live up to what they taught us. Today we need to march alongside our Tungrian brothers in arms and take our revenge for Sergius. Our revenge for the honour of Rome. Our revenge for the Guard. That's what I'll be doing today, possibly at the cost of my life, but then my life has been forfeit since Maternus stripped away my right to it, and doubly so since Sergius showed me how a Guard officer should live and die. The only question left now is whether you're with me or not. Will you choose to sit here and allow these auxiliaries to fight our battle for us, or will you join them in overrunning that camp and killing every man in it?'

Victor's first spear stepped forward and saluted.

'What you say is right, Tribune, and we're with you.' He stared around at his brother officers, daring any one of them to argue. 'But what can we hope to achieve with just our daggers?'

'Just our daggers? I've not forgotten my training, and I doubt you have either, given I know we suffered under the same impossibly high standards. And I recall, as if it were yesterday, what that old bastard Lucius had to say on the ins and outs of winning a battle. Do you?'

The centurion smiled wanly.

'He said, "You fight with your spear until the shaft breaks. You fight with your sword until you're stupid enough to get it stuck between some poor bastard's ribs. And then you air this . . ."' He unsheathed his own dagger and held the foot-long blade up. '"And you compensate for its lack of length by getting in so close that you can smell the piss running down the next poor bastard's legs. Because when you're that close, there's no difference between this and a sword, other than the fear you just conquered."' He stared at Victor for a moment. 'I'm with you, Tribune, even if you're leading me straight to the gates of Hades. Which means that these men are with you, if they have any pride left in them. And if we're with you, our guardsmen will be too. What's the plan?'

Victor nodded at him, tapping the blade of his own dagger.

'The plan, First Spear, is a simple one. To get so close to the men we have to defeat that this becomes a sword.'

He turned back to the Tungrian officers with a questioning stare at Julius.

'We're committed, Prefect.'

The big man inclined his head in respect for the tribune's heartfelt appeal to his men's pride in their collective.

'And so are we, Tribune. There are two hours to dawn, so I suggest you get your men awake, fed and ready to march and we'll do the same. We need to be on the move at first light if we're going to catch them unawares.' He turned to Scaurus. 'I see no way that this can end without either our cohorts being destroyed or the rebels disintegrating into exactly the mob of brigands you fear, or both, but I will lead our men to their fate as you have requested. And may the Lightbringer look kindly on us all when the time comes.'

The camp came to life quickly once Julius started issuing orders. Marcus and Varus gathering their centurions for a briefing while each century's chosen men ordered tent parties of bleary-eyed, disbelieving soldiers to feed themselves and make the usual preparations to march at dawn.

'There'll be nothing fancy about what we're going to have to do, because there isn't the time.' The men gathered around the two officers were sober-faced, coming to terms with the enormity of the task their officers were planning even as Marcus outlined it to them. 'We'll make the approach march in silence, with no trumpets, no shouting, and no warnings of any kind. When Julius gives the signal, we'll deploy into line, four men deep and on a two-cohort frontage on the march, then go at them as fast as we can. We need to get over the wall before they have the chance to get themselves properly equipped, put them on the back foot and keep them on it. Julius wants us to be into them before they get a chance to organise any sort of defence or even to get their armour on, if we can.'

'What about them?'

Cotta jerked a dismissive thumb over his shoulder at the praetorian section of the camp.

'Tribune Victor will be leading his cohorts behind us on the march so that the rebels don't see them until the last minute.'

'But they're not armed with anything better than their knives. How much use are they going to be when the blood's flying?'

The Roman shrugged at his friend.

'In all truth? I have no idea, Centurion. We'll just have to wait and see, won't we?'

As the first trace of the impending dawn lightened the eastern sky, the cohorts formed into column of march, muttered curses and complaints punctuating their preparations as centurions and chosen men hissed warnings and pushed men into their places. Marcus walked slowly down the column of his cohort, as ever in the vanguard of the intended march, sharing a private moment with each of his officers in turn. When he reached the Fourth Century, Otho stepped out from the ranks and saluted, nodding his approval.

'You look the part, young Marcus, even if we've had to equip you in armour taken from the wounded and put my second-best crest on your helmet. And now you're going to lead us into our greatest victory yet.'

The Roman shook his head in amusement.

'Anyone would think you were looking forward to this fight against desperate odds, Centurion. You do know that most of your comrades think we're on a suicide mission?'

The big man's battered face split in a rueful grin.

'Any fight is a good fight, young 'un. And this one, as I understand it, is to make sure these rebel bastards don't rip up the rulebook and run amok. Which makes it doubly good.'

'The old bastard's probably got good odds on the outcome. Although I doubt it's likely to be a draw this time.'

Both men turned to find Dubnus beside them, and Otho shook his head in amusement at the jibe.

'Sounds like some men I know will need their teeth loosened when this is all done with.'

Dubnus shrugged.

'Morban told me your little secret over a large jug of wine. Seems that he *had* to be informed about the private wager you had those two idiots place on your behalf, just to get him to see sense and pay back all that stake money after the boxing final. He told me in confidence, and it's stayed that way.' The pioneer centurion shrugged. 'Relax, brother. Nobody thinks you had the money down for any other reason than you thought Plug was the best fighter in the cohort, and given that it was you that knocked him out, you could hardly be accused of favouring him, could you?'

The gap-toothed centurion grinned ruefully.

'If you put it like that . . . I'm still going to paste those two slack-mouthed idiots, though.'

Marcus turned away from the two men to continue his progress down the line of centuries, calling a final comment back over his shoulder.

'We have bigger matters to worry about today, I'd say. If your men are ready to march, to fight and, if necessary, to die, then nothing else matters.'

Dubnus followed him along the column, striding easily with his axe resting on one shoulder.

'Julius is right, you know. We could kill two-thirds of those animals and the remainder would still cause exactly the sort of mayhem that the tribune's trying to prevent. Without those craven donkey-wallopers, we've got no chance.'

The Roman exchanged salutes with Caelius, centurion of his Fifth Century, then allowed himself to be bear hugged by the man as his soldiers saluted, rubbed the good luck charms hanging from their belts and muttered the ritual 'Two Knives' that had formed a muted background to every such moment of mutual regard in the cold pre-dawn.

'Well now, Two Knives, this time might be the end of us.' The bristly-haired officer, still living up to his nickname 'Ditch Pig' for his resemblance to a hedgehog, slapped the younger man on the shoulder and stepped back with a lopsided smile. 'So I just want to tell you that I can't think of a better man to meet my end with.'

Marcus chuckled darkly.

'It seems every damned officer in this cohort is obsessed with our impending doom. I can only imagine the disappointment you'll all be feeling in a few hours when we're standing in a sea of rebel dead.'

'And if that comes to pass, nobody will be happier than me. Pays to be realistic, though, and say the things that need saying before it's too late. So here's to you, First Spear. Win or lose, it's been an honour.'

The Roman saluted wordlessly and carried on, Dubnus falling into step with him.

'The reason the tribune's asking us to do this isn't because he believes we can finish them, even if that isn't as remote a possibility as the rest of you might think. He's asking us to do it because to do anything different will leave our duty unfulfilled.'

The Briton shook his head in grim amusement.

'So someone needs to show the rest of the empire how it's done, this death-before-dishonour thing. And we're the ones fortunate enough to be the men on the spot.'

'Yes. Put simply.'

The big man shrugged.

'It's not as if we've not defied the odds before. But all the other times we've faced larger numbers and won, we've had the advantage of surprise, or better tactics, or even just some trick that the tribune's come up with out of the history books. It just feels as if this time we've got nothing on our side other than the fact we've got the biggest, hairiest balls in the empire.'

'I'll put that on the altar I dedicate to you if you fall today. "He thought he had the biggest, hairiest balls in the empire".'

Dubnus shook his head.

'Just have the stonecutter write that I died like a man, in the company of my brothers. That would be enough.'

With the column formed, the praetorians shivering in the absence of their heavy armour and padded arming jackets, Scaurus walked out from his command tent with Victor close behind, exchanging salutes with Julius in the pale dawn light.

'Prefect. Our men are ready from the look of things.'

'Yes, Tribune. All four cohorts are ready to march.'

The Roman nodded decisively.

'Thank you, Julius. I have offered prayers to Our Lord Mithras and entreated him to hear his servant's request for his strength in our sword arms this day. From this moment, the matter – as Homer wrote, if what my tutor told me on more than one occasion is to be believed – is in the lap of the gods. And I am hopeful that they will see fit to look kindly on our cause. Please start the approach march once you're ready to do so.'

The big man nodded, turned away to his first spears waiting behind him, and issued a terse command.

'Get them moving. Start at the slow march until we have the column formed, then at my command speed it up to the battle march. We need to get our spears over their walls and into them before they wake up to the fact that their leader's legged it with the gold they need if they're going to eat – because nothing wakes a man up faster than knowing he's been dropped right in the shit. Which, now I think about it, must be the reason I'm feeling so perky.'

Walking swiftly back to his leading century, Marcus issued the order for his men to start marching, watching critically as each successive century lurched into motion at the slow pace ordered, peering into the dawn mist to see the following cohorts start marching in their turn until the last of the praetorians were on the move.

'I always knew that my life was dispensable. It's just a bit harder to face up to it when it actually looks like I might have to live up to the oath's full terms.' Julius was at his shoulder, grimacing as the leading praetorians marched slowly past them. 'Mind you, if I think I've got it bad, I only have to look at those poor bastards. Tribune Victor must have balls of brass to have them contemplating the sort of massacre that'll result when they run up against the men who've borrowed their iron.' He shook his head, looking down the column's remaining length to where the cavalry would have been marching had they been present. 'And what I'd give for a few squadrons of cavalry right now. But, since we don't have what we don't have, I suppose we need to make the best of what we do. Shall we?'

He gestured to the column's head, and the two men strode up the snake of marching men to the leading century.

'Given that I'm too much of a gentleman to be shouting orders, perhaps you'd like to have the army switch to the battle march, First Spear?'

Marcus grinned and issued the order in a barked command loud enough to be heard down the column's length and by Varus at the head of the Second Cohort. With what sounded almost like sighs of relief from the closest men, they upped their pace to the battle march, moving so fast that the sound of their booted feet against the road's hard-packed mud was a constant drumming, like distant thunder.

'That's better. I've always preferred the idea of running towards my death, iron aired and teeth bared, to any thought of sidling up to it like a coward.'

Marcus nodded at Julius's musing.

'It has the feeling of doing something to take control of the situation. Even if that something ends up taking a man straight to the gates of Hades. But shouldn't you be back there with the tribune? I thought he'd forbidden you to join the action with the common soldiery?'

'Hah!' Julius shook his head with the look of a man well pleased with himself. 'I told him that if I was expected to throw away two perfectly good cohorts to satisfy his sense of duty and Victor's need for revenge, then we'd be also humouring my need to die with my men, rather than as part of whatever last stand he has in mind for when it all goes to rat shit. He had the good grace to take my point and not argue, so you're stuck with me here. Just like old times, except that I can't recall the old times ever involving anything quite as desperate as this.'

The two men marched in silence at the cohort's head while the sky in the east lightened from purple to a rosy pink, the rising sun's rays lancing down between the clouds. Julius looked at the mass of grey cloud in the western sky with a muttered curse.

'And as if it's not already bad enough, it's going to rain as well. Perhaps not straight away, but there's a good hard shower up there alright. And I don't see it holding off for long enough that we'll have a result either way before we get soaked.'

The Roman frowned at his superior's prediction, looking up at the clouds above their heads as they scudded along on a sharp west wind.

'How long do you think?'

Julius shrugged.

'No idea, but there's something in the air. Can't you feel that chill?'

'Now that you point it out, yes. And look at the clouds. When the rain falls, it'll conceal our attack and stop the rising sun from blinding us. The tribune's prayers weren't unheard, were they?'

Julius looked at him with a dawning realisation of what his subordinate was suggesting.

'You want to wait until it rains to attack?'

'Can you think of a better cover for our approach?'

'No . . . but . . .'

'But it's not the all-or-nothing balls-in-the-fire approach that Tribune Victor sold us. Dubnus said something to me earlier that's still ringing in my head like a bell sounding, that we've always beaten the odds in the past because of good fortune, or some plan that the tribune's come up with to level the odds against us. And here it is, literally out of the blue. Why wouldn't we take advantage of it?'

Julius pondered the question.

'What if it takes hours to rain? What if we wait all that time and it doesn't fall, leaving us with a far more alert enemy and nothing to show for it?'

'You said yourself, there's already rain in the air. Perhaps we need to back your judgement?'

The prefect thought for a moment and then nodded decisively.

'Very well. Keep marching, I'm going back to talk to the Tribune.'

'And if we reach the edge of the forest before you've persuaded him?'

'Then stop the column and wait for me.'

It took him less time than Marcus had expected to persuade the two tribunes as to the opportunity presenting itself, and he rejoined Marcus at the column's head with a half-mile left to march to the point where their attack would become evident to the encamped rebels.

'It's agreed. We're going to stop the column and get the troops into the edge of the woods. And you and I, First Spear, are going for a quiet look at the enemy.'

With the four cohorts halted and their bemused soldiers sent to huddle under the cover of the foliage at the forest's edge, the two officers moved slowly and carefully along the treeline, slipping into the trees and climbing the gentle hill until they reached a spot with a view of the rebel camp. Julius whistled softly at the scene laid out before them.

'Gods below, the entire place is asleep!'

A few lonely-looking sentries were standing guard on the camp's gates, men driven by either duty or fear to stay at their posts when the overwhelming majority of their comrades were clearly completely disinterested in anything approaching discipline. A trickle of dishevelled-looking men in tunic order was straggling to and from the latrine pits, some still staggering from the previous night's intake of alcohol. A few thin lines of smoke were rising into the air and being carried away by the stiffening breeze, evidence that cooking fires were being lit and food presumably prepared as the rebel soldiers began regaining consciousness from their long night of debauchery. As they watched, a pair of men walked out of the closest gate and headed with disgruntled purpose towards the forest edge two hundred paces distant, clearly sent to collect firewood.

'There's going to be more of them, and eventually someone's going to fall over us.'

Marcus nodded at his friend's morose comment, pointing at the range of hills to the camp's west.

'There is that risk. But look at the landscape over there and tell me what you see.'

Julius stared for a moment before replying.

'What can I see? Hills. All I can see is . . .' He fell silent as the most distant of the landscape features silhouetted against the western horizon vanished from view, fading from the dawn's roseate pink to grey invisibility. 'Rain!'

'Exactly. And those hills are what, five miles distant?'

'If that.'

'So that storm will be here soon enough, I'd say.'

Julius nodded.

'Come on then, we need to have them ready. I doubt a squall like that will last all that long!'

The two men hurried back to the waiting cohorts, Julius signalling for them to leave the forest's shelter and reform on the grazing land through which they had marched.

'Get them into battle line, and quickly! There's no way we'll be able to do it on the march if it's raining that heavily.'

Encouraged by their officers' hoarsely whispered commands,

pushes and occasional slaps, following standard bearers who were directed to their positions in the rapidly forming line by their officers, the centuries took their places in the order of battle as Marcus hurried from century to century telling his officers what was expected of them once the rain began to fall. The breeze was becoming colder as the storm front drove in towards them, the scudding grey clouds now covering the western half of the sky. Reaching the far end of his cohort's line, Marcus was about to issue the same orders to Dubnus when a single raindrop struck his friend's polished iron helmet with an audible *tok*. Both men looked at each other as they waited a moment before hearing another, the start of a swiftly-growing tattoo of impacts as the storm's tattered outriders streamed overhead, the wind gaining in strength enough that the Roman had to raise his voice to be heard over its moaning cry.

'You're at the far end of the line so you'll have to move fastest of all. So once Julius gives the signal, get your men mov—'

'First Spear!'

Marcus followed the soldier's raised hand to see Julius gesturing to him with his sword, raising the weapon over his head and then sweeping it down to point at their objective. Feeling the weight of his responsibilities lighten at the prospect of combat, he turned to the waiting pioneers, raising his own sword and seeing the big men tense at the sight of its unspoken challenge.

'We're moving. Follow me!'

Striding out in front of his men, the Roman realised that the rain was already falling in thick curtains, rivulets of cold water running down his neck to soak the tunic underneath his borrowed armour as he led the First Cohort's line forward. The formation was swinging through a quarter circle, the inside centuries practically marking time while Marcus and the pioneers behind him were almost running, and as their ragged line swept around the forest's corner, he saw that the enemy camp was already barely visible, its turf walls no more than a faint outline that vanished into the murk as he stared at them in gleeful disbelief.

'Their sentries will be sheltering from this!' Dubnus was at his shoulder, his eyes bright with the joy of impending action, raindrops falling from his beard as he shouted over the deluge. 'We're going to be over the wall and into them before they even know we're here!'

Storming across the open space into a grey wall of rain, Marcus could hear the grunts of exertion behind him as the pioneers strained their sinews to keep up with him. The turf wall materialised out of the rain's concealing curtain in the space of a half dozen strides, utterly undefended, without even a sentry to sound the alarm as the grim-faced Tungrians bore down on its illusory defence. Out of the depths of his memory, Marcus heard Cotta's voice from years before, in the early days of his military training, as the veteran centurion had emphasised the reasons why the legions were so fanatical about maintaining a watch on the walls of their marching camps.

'A wall without defenders, young Marcus, is like a sword with the end cut off. It's pointless!'

He leapt up onto the wall's flat surface, barely three feet above the ground, staring down into the rain-lashed camp with a predatory grin for a moment before jumping down and into the enemy. The rain-soaked tents closest to him were bulging with men, the rebels evidently having sought shelter from the abrupt downpour, steam rising from fires extinguished by the torrential rain. Looking back, he found the leading pioneers barely a stride behind him, gathering themselves to hurdle the flimsy turf barrier, and he stepped into the camp.

He selected a tent and severed its guy ropes away with a sweep of the long sword to collapse it, then drew the weapon's blade back before stabbing it through the soaked leather and into a man's body, wrenching a scream of amazed agony from his victim. To either side, the Tenth Century were over the wall and hacking their way into the encampment, their previous silence shattered by bellows and imprecations as each of them obeyed his training, roaring his lungs out with each stroke of his axe, two or three men gathering around each tent and erupting into a murderous frenzy of rising and falling blades. The horror they were inflicting on the occupants was largely concealed by the leather in which they were trapped, but the occupants' howls of agonised terror bespoke the horrific slaughter being done to them.

Men were starting to emerge from the tents deeper inside the camp, staring through the rain in disbelief at the vision of terror that was playing out before them as each century's soldiers leap-frogged each other by tent party, slashing and stabbing at each shelter in their path for long enough to wound or kill enough of the men inside to utterly break the remainder's resistance before moving on to find fresh victims. Some enemy tent parties died to the last man without ever realising what was happening, their senses dulled by the rain's drumming on the leather above their heads and the aftermath of the previous night's drinking. Others, alerted by the screams and shouts of mortal combat, got no further than managing to struggle out into the storm and onto their feet, before dying on the blades of their wraith-like assailants who materialised out of the rain with blood blasted across their armour and blades raised for the kill. Pausing for a moment, exhausted by the effort of murdering the broken rebels, Marcus turned to find the Second Cohort charging past him and into the fight, adding fresh impetus to the rampage that was threatening to overwhelm the enemy camp, and Varus stopped beside him momentarily with a look of concern.

'Are you hurt?'

'No! I just need a moment!'

He followed his friend into the heart of the slaughter, staying at his shoulder as the senator's son threw himself into the battle with utter disregard for his own safety, the two men fighting side by side as the rebel resistance started to stiffen. The men coming at them were wearing hastily-donned armour and carrying shields and spears snatched up from wherever they could be found, starting to form a line of sorts in obedience to the shouts of the strongest-minded among them.

'This is going to be close! There's still enough of them to—'

Varus gaped in astonishment as a wave of tunic-clad praetorians tore into the camp from the southern and northern sides, hurdling the turf walls with the eagerness of men unwilling to postpone the moment of their revenge for a moment longer, their onrush slamming into the partially-formed defensive line's end with all the ferocity that had been visited upon their own formation two days before. Heedless of their own lack of protection, they were among the rebels and fighting with the ferocity of wild animals, their daggers rising and falling as they fell on their tormentors with the frenzied fury of men who had already resigned themselves to death as the price for their revenge. Leading their charge, Victor threw himself headlong at an enemy officer, taking the armoured soldier at the knees and knocking him to the ground, his dagger flickering dully in the rain as he savaged the hapless centurion's throat with its foot-long blade to leave him coughing and choking out his lifeblood from the horrific wounds rent in his neck.

The rebels were wavering, unable to deal with the threat posed by the implacable Tungrians while a bestial horde of men they believed long since defeated tore into them from both sides of the camp with a terrifying disregard for their own lives. Abandoning their hastily-adopted line they ran in their hundreds from the avenging guardsmen, casting away their shields in their haste to escape. The men who chose the valour of standing against the odds stared at their doom as the Tungrians came at them again with bloodied swords and a renewed urge to utterly destroy them. Those that were not borne down by the enraged praetorians and unceremoniously hacked to death swiftly realised their error and turned to follow their fleeing comrades, casting away their shields and weapons as they ran. Marcus and Varus stood and watched, both men exhausted but unhurt, as the remainder of the rebel force took to their heels through what remained of their camp, the younger man shaking his head in disgust.

'A good half of them will get away. We beat them, but Julius was right, their remnants will still take a heavy price from the people of the Gallic provinces.'

Marcus shrugged, pointing out into the thinning rain to the

camp's south, the direction from which Victor's cohort had made their perfectly-timed intervention.

'Perhaps. And perhaps not.'

Horsemen were streaming past the camp, their spears lowered in readiness to start the grisly task at which they excelled.

'The legion cavalry!'

'It appears that Silus didn't ride back to Argentoratum in vain after all. And it appears we owe the legatus an apology for doubting his decisiveness.'

Legatus Niger himself was riding at the cavalry's head. He dismounted and strode into the destroyed camp's sea of corpses and blood-soaked litter, at the heart of a dozen jealous-eyed bodyguards, to congratulate Scaurus on his achievement.

'I wouldn't have believed it possible, Tribune! You have torn the guts out of this rebellion in a single fight. Am I to presume that their master is dead, if their lack of courage is any guide?' He grimaced at the news of Maternus's absconding, but swiftly redoubled his praise. 'But that's no matter! He'll either be captured on the road or taken in the city itself, now that we know his destination and intended target. He won't get within bow shot of the emperor, never mind close enough for the sort of revenge a man like that always wants, close enough to see the fear in his victim's eyes. But tell me, rain or not, how in Hades did you manage to break them so completely?'

The tribune extended an arm to indicate Victor, limping towards the knot of officers, and Niger turned to stare bemusedly at the blood-soaked apparition.

The praetorian came to a painful approximation of the brace and saluted with his left hand while the other hung limply at his side.

'Legatus, I'm happy to report my cohorts as ready for duty, pending the reclamation of certain items of our equipment from the battlefield.'

Niger shook his head in genuine admiration for a moment before finding his voice.

'You seem to have more than made amends for your defeat, Tribune Victor. How many of your men do you think you lost?'

The exhausted praetorian thought for a moment before answering, looking about himself at the corpses scattered across the wrecked camp, a good number clad in the white tunics and cloaks that were all Maternus had left his men to wear.

'It's hard to say, Legatus. Things are still a little confused, given that half my command pursued the rebels over their camp wall, but at a guess, I have two or three hundred dead or seriously wounded. Even cowards like the men Maternus recruited can do some damage when unarmoured men come at them armed with nothing more than daggers.'

Niger tipped his head in respect.

'Perhaps Tribune Scaurus can find a bandage carrier to put something on that leg wound, and later, my personal medicus will have a careful look at your arm.'

Victor nodded, looking down at the offending limb as if noticing the injury for the first time.

'It's broken, so I can only hope he's used to resetting bones. One of their centurions did it with his shield just before I cut his head off with my other hand.'

'Providing yet more evidence of your laudable commitment to the empire's service, Tribune. I had feared that your defeat by your former colleague might spell the end of your career with some degree of ignominy, but your actions today have convinced me that you and your men were simply unlucky on that day. Your unwavering dedication to the emperor proves that no such premature end to your service to Rome is required. Rest now, and I will direct my doctor to see to your injury.'

Victor saluted again.

'If you'll forgive me, Legatus, I must first make sure that my men reform into their cohorts, and that they find as much of the equipment that we lost as possible. And once this arm has been treated to whatever degree is possible, we will need to discuss my detachment from this task force and prompt return to Rome.

With Maternus at liberty, there's no time to be lost. We must search whatever he's left behind for any clues as to his intentions once he reaches Rome, and then a small party of officers must ride to the capital. As the only men to have laid eyes on him since the end of the German wars, we might be the only men who can stand between him and his revenge on the emperor.'

The command tent was a sad, trampled shadow of its former commanding presence, but once the ropes had been repaired and pulled tight again, the Tungrian officers were able to make their way inside to sift through the debris of Maternus's possessions.

'There's nothing here to provide us with any clues.' Scaurus looked about him at the debris of the rebel leader's life, shaking his head at the broken furniture and scattered scrolls. 'But we must at least try to discern his purpose in making his attempt on Commodus's life now.'

They picked through the books at random, finding them to be histories and geographical texts for the most part, but at length Marcus held up the parchment he was reading with a frown.

'He didn't strike me as a religious man, and yet here is a text which takes as its subject the empire's religions. I wonder what he . . .'

He fell silent, staring at the words before him with a look of dawning comprehension.

'At the bridge, when Maternus's comrade was wounded but not yet dying, he was trying to tell me something, spitting in my face that his master would have his revenge. He said something like "on the day that the bull bleeds for the great", and then a chance spear silenced him. It meant nothing at the time, but there is a section in this text on the subject of the Great Mother. There is a taurobolium every year in the Ides of March, a bull sacrifice where the priest places himself underneath the animal and receives its lifeblood to bless the emperor and the city for the coming year, and it takes place in the Circus Maximus. With the right access, an assassin disguised as a praetorian might well get close enough to Commodus to put a blade into him, as just one of the dozens of men around him for that critical moment. And you can bet that Maternus will save any grand statement of revenge until his blade is in the emperor's throat.'

Scaurus nodded slowly.

'Perhaps it was a second plan, a backup in case they failed to persuade my colleague Victor to deliver the amulet. But now that the scorpion has been rendered useless by our escape, they might well fall back upon it as a means of revenge.' He turned to Niger. 'With your permission, Legatus, I will take a party of my men south to deliver this news to Rome. As the only men to have seen Maternus, we might be crucial in foiling his plot.'

'Of course, Tribune. I'll have my medicus deal with Tribune Victor's arm and you can go south together.'

They walked out of the tent's gloomy interior into the morning's cold sunlight, the legatus pausing again to gaze across the camp's scene of devastation.

'This will take some time to clear away, I expect. I suggest that you gather the bodies for burial at one end of the camp and the tents for burning at the other. We'll leave the walls standing as a testament to—'

He turned at the sound of a scuffle to find Marcus helpless with a blade at his throat, the blood-soaked figure behind him unrecognisable.

'Step away, gentlemen, or the centurion gets his throat cut!'

The officers backed away from the two men, Scaurus shaking his head in bafflement at the events playing out before him.

'What in the name of—'

'Shut your mouth and do as I say! This man is a traitor, and I have been sent to deliver him to justice!'

The tribune frowned, recognising the other man's voice.

'Is that . . . Lupinus?'

'What in the name of all the gods is happening here?'

Scaurus replied to Niger's angry question without taking his eyes off the two men.

'The man holding a knife to my first spear's throat is a prae-torian centurion, Legatus, a man in the service of the chamberlain.'

'You're fucking right I am, so if you pricks have any of the sense you were born with, you'll back away and allow me to take this—'

Lupinus dropped to the ground behind Marcus as the man who had been stealthily approaching him from behind put his dagger into the praetorian's back, looking down at the stricken officer's writhing body without any obvious show of emotion.

'Well done, Flavius Titianus.' Scaurus walked forward to look down at the felled centurion in bafflement. 'Quite what this fool thought he could achieve other than his own death perplexes me, given his poor timing, but I suppose he saw his only opportunity to take the life he was sent for by Cleander and took a chance that he could use Marcus as a shield from our blades until he had a horse to escape on. We were fortunate that you were so close behind him, weren't we?'

Titianus bowed, sheathing his dagger and smiling winningly at the Tungrian officers.

'As I told you months ago, gentlemen, I never trusted the man, and I made it my role to stay close to him and wait for the moment when his treachery would reveal itself.'

'And you delivered an expert blow, I have to say, a killer's strike, or close to one.'

The young centurion gestured to the scene of chaos around them.

'A man learns quickly under these conditions. I've taken more lives today than I can remember, so perhaps my competence has been—'

His body contorted as a blade sank into the back of his thigh, the dagger long enough for the point to protrude from the front of his leg before the stricken man behind him tore it free. He fell to the ground with a scream of pain as Lupinus pulled himself forwards on his elbows, raising his dagger to strike again, spitting blood as he cursed the squirming Titianus.

'You fucker! I knew you weren't as wet behind the ears as you pre—'

Marcus stepped in and stabbed down at the back of his would-be assassin's neck with his borrowed gladius, dropping the stricken centurion face down into the camp's blood-flecked mud.

'Bandage carrier!' Scaurus called for assistance, squatting down by the wounded Titianus. 'We'll have that wound staunched. It doesn't look likely to be fatal, though, so I'd say you'll survive to face the wrath of Cleander when he finds out that you've prevented his assassin from killing at least one of us.'

The younger man looked up at him, white-faced with shock but still smiling through the pain.

'It seems I'm to join you in your uncertain status, doesn't it?'

'I wouldn't wish such a fate on any man, but it does seem as if your actions have put you on the wrong side of the table from the chamberlain, alongside us.' The tribune reached out and opened Titianus's belt purse before the praetorian could stop him, reaching in to scoop out the contents. 'But then perhaps that's just what you wanted?'

12

'Are you insane, Rutilius Scaurus? Has all rational thinking fled your mind, to be replaced by an urge to gamble with the emperor's *fucking* life?'

Cleander's incredulous stare lingered on Scaurus for a long moment before he switched his attention to Victor. The two tribunes had presented themselves, along with Marcus, in the chamberlain's outer office an hour before, their passage through the palace's outer environs smoothed by the praetorian's immaculate uniform and untroubled air of authority despite the circumstances. Ushered into the visibly irate chamberlain's inner sanctum they had stood, impervious to his increasingly angry denunciations until, with an insouciance he was far from enjoying, Scaurus had revealed what it was they had come to demand of the chamberlain.

'You want me to let you join the hunt for Maternus as my own representatives, and with my full authority? When it's your fault that he's here at all, and not buried in an unmarked grave somewhere in the wilds of Gaul? It's unthinkable! And how *you* have the nerve to show your face here is a mystery to me, Statilius Victor! I should order you to be dismissed from the Guard in disgrace!'

The praetorian nodded.

'Perhaps you should, Chamberlain. And perhaps you will. Although were I to find myself so sadly reduced, I might find it essential to bring certain facts to the ears of more than one highly-placed man in the city. After all, I've hardly ridden for the best part of a month with a broken arm for the pleasure of it. If you deny me my chance to deal with my former colleague in my own way, the disappointment I will feel might just prove too strong for me to master.'

Cleander's eyes narrowed.

'That sounds suspiciously like a threat, Tribune. You may just have achieved the feat of upgrading the punishment of dismissal to that of execution.'

'And that's understandable, Chamberlain. After all, a man in your position can hardly afford to be dictated to by such lowly individuals as ourselves . . .'

'But?'

'But what, Chamberlain?'

'I think we understand each other well enough, Tribune. I threatened you with death and you barely blinked. Which means that not only were you were expecting it, but you believe you have some means of avoiding that fate. So I suggest you share whatever it is with me, and I'll make a decision as to whether any of you should be allowed to live as long as the next dawn that rises over the city.'

Victor strolled forward to the edge of Cleander's desk, looking down at the chamberlain in a display of bravado that had the older man staring up at him in disbelief.

'Several officers were inserted into the cohorts that marched north under my command in the days before we left Rome, Chamberlain. Among them were two particularly worthy of note – one of them an especially evil-minded centurion who was until recently the emperor's playmate in his forays into the city under the disguise of a guardsman, the other a son of the aristocracy whose father contributed generously to Prefect Aebutianus's purse in order to buy his son's chance of glory. Except we both know that the purchase was unnecessary, don't we? Titus Flavius Titianus would have marched with us whether his father had bestowed his gold upon your praetorian prefect or not, because he was always your man and never really a praetorian. You recruited him into the Camp of the Strangers with us in mind, didn't you? You had him trained as a grain officer and gifted with all those skills the men who do your dirty work find essential. He's especially fond of diversion, in fact. Whoever taught him his skills in that area earned every last copper coin of whatever you paid them. Although all those slaves whose deaths were intended to make him the master of the art of killing with a single stroke of a dagger seem to have been wasted.'

Cleander stared back at him expressionlessly.

'I'm glad you approve of the choice. Evidently he failed, despite his skill with a lie?'

Scaurus laughed darkly.

'No, his skill in bending the truth was more than good enough to fool us. But he clearly didn't pay attention during his close combat training, because just at the moment when it looked as if he had achieved admittance to our trusted circle by stabbing Lupinus in the back, the man he had just betrayed somewhat spoiled the effect by putting his own blade through your man's leg. It seems that you'd failed to brief Lupinus about Titianus, presumably so that he wouldn't be ready when your young spy sank the blade into him from behind. But it seems you were equally unforthcoming with Titianus on the subject of Lupinus's robustness and tenacity. Which is probably the reason why your young grain officer was unwise enough to show him his own back for just a little too long. And Centurion Lupinus took full advantage of that lapse, before he died.' He waited for Cleander to absorb the news before resuming his story. 'It was somewhat remarkable that Titianus didn't die, given the force with which Lupinus put his blade through him, but it seems that in his advanced state of blood loss, the centurion's stroke went a little astray. He was doubtless aiming for the femoral artery, but only succeeded in putting a pair of quite decorative holes in the young man's thigh, scars that will easily be passed off as having been inflicted from the front, just as long as nobody spoils the illusion of that story by making the truth known. And thereby telling the story as to his real place in the order of things as a grain officer and your lackey.

'And how did we figure it out? Something Lupinus said as he was dying piqued my curiosity. He told Titianus that he'd not been fooled by his pretending to be wet behind the ears, and that resonated with me. After all, who's better placed to spot a killer than another killer? So I searched your boy's purse and found this.' He tossed a metal disc onto the desk before the chamberlain with a dull clunk of metal on wood. 'There are words engraved on it, small but readable, *frumentrius* on one side and *propinquos meos* on the other. "I am a frumentarius and you will obey me". It's as close as he would ever have needed to a badge of office when combined with all that self-assurance, isn't it? I wonder what his father would make of it all? It's not quite as bad as running away to sign up as a gladiator, but for a family of that class to have to admit that their firstborn is an imperial spy and murderer? That's not usually where the apple lands when it falls from that particular tree.

'You wouldn't dare.'

Scaurus smiled mirthlessly.

'Perhaps I would, and perhaps I wouldn't. Valerius Aquila here, on the other hand, feels that he has little to lose, given it was him that Lupinus attempted to kill on your orders.'

'Need I remind you both that Valerius Aquila's fucking son lives in the palace?'

Marcus stepped forward.

'No, you don't need to remind me of that fact, you can be assured that it's very much on my mind. Because one of the things you're going to do in the next hour is to order his release, along with Annia and the other two children. If you don't, then two things are going to happen. Firstly—'

'No, let me guess.' Cleander's voice was suddenly lacking its usual spirit. 'Firstly, you'll tell Senator Titianus that his son, far from being the hero of a desperate defensive action against overwhelming numbers in which he was grievously wounded, is in reality not much better than a common informer. Meaning that any time he declines to talk about his service to the throne, or how he came by that wound – which will of course be mistaken by one and all for the modesty of a true Roman hero – will suddenly come to light as what it is: avoidance of the rather sordid facts. Am I right?'

Marcus bowed his head in ironic respect.

'And the second threat you hold over me is equally obvious. The emperor will be the recipient of a message, perhaps left on his bed by a well-bribed member of his bodyguard, informing him as to the presence of an imperial bastard in the palace, brought here on my orders. He will of course be furious, and rightly so, because he will be correct in his assumption that I have done so in order to gain leverage on him in preparation for the day he turns against me. He would have me executed for treason, I'd imagine. However, you men, of course, would already be dead, as would your son, Valerius Aquila, and in the most bestial of ways.'

He raised an eyebrow at Scaurus, but it was Marcus who answered his attempted counter-threat.

'And I'm sure that will be a tremendous consolation for you while the imperial interrogators take you to pieces, tooth by tooth and bone by bone, to get the full truth from you. Presumably under the close and careful guidance of your successor. What better chance could a man have to prove his loyalty to the throne than the reluctant but commendably thorough torture of his predecessor?'

Cleander stared at him in silence for a moment before replying.

'I see your point, Centurion. And I suppose I should congratulate myself for having inculcated such ruthless calculation into your thinking. So what is it that you want from me, exactly? Presumably you're not expecting me to leave the emperor unguarded for this man Maternus to kill?'

Scaurus shook his head briskly.

'Of course not, Chamberlain. We only ask that Commodus keeps his official engagements, behind as many guardsmen as you like to have surround him. Search every rooftop and sewer that might afford an assassin the slightest chance to catch a glimpse of the emperor, and triple the number of men who would usually protect him from his loyal citizens, because we have no interest in his death. Far from it, we want him to live, because the alternative is too dreadful to consider. All we want is the chance to hunt this man Maternus down, and to put him in that unmarked grave for you.'

'And what about this one?' Cleander gestured to Marcus with an expression of disbelief. 'Are you really trying to tell me that the man whose wife was raped by the emperor wouldn't give everything he had for the slightest chance at revenge?'

The younger man stepped forward.

'I won't be anywhere near the emperor, Chamberlain, so it's hardly a question that we need to entertain, is it? But if it helps, I have sworn on an altar to Mithras, at my tribune's command, to renounce my vow of vengeance, and to focus my hatred on Maternus. Having sworn this oath, I am bound to do no harm to the emperor, and therefore to the empire he rules.'

Cleander stared up at him for a moment before replying.

'I see. Very well then, it shall be as you say. Every guardsman in Rome will be on the streets for the next week, every member of the Urban Cohorts and the Watch. And you, Tribune Victor, since I know you must be raging with the need for revenge on the man who stained your perfect career with the blood of your men, can take command of the operation to find the rebel. Just make sure you find him by the day of the bull sacrifice, eh? Because after that, Commodus won't be making any further appearances for a month, Rome can return to normal life, and your opportunity to regain your place in my favour will be at an end. I think you can imagine what that will mean, gentlemen? I'm not a man that takes to being blackmailed very well.'

★

'A message from Tribune Gracchus of the Urban Cohorts, Tribune!'

Victor took the tablet from the uniformed runner, turning back to the map of the city that had been placed on display in the office he and Scaurus had been allocated in the outer extremities of the Palatine complex.

'So what does this say . . . all streets in the fifth district have been searched, all households questioned, patrols doubled . . . and nothing to show for it. The Esquiline is declared clear, just like every other damned district that has reported since dawn. And yet I know he's out there, getting ready to carry out whatever plan he's had seven years to come up with. Where are you, Maternus? Where does a man like you hide himself until the time has come for your plot to take flight?' He turned to Scaurus with a frustrated expression. 'We've had every street in the city searched, thousands of citizens questioned – we've even tipped off the street gangs as to what they should be on the lookout for, with the promise of enough gold to swim in should they alert us to his presence – and yet we have nothing. The ceremony of the Great Mother's arrival in the city starts in less than three hours and yet we've had neither hide nor hair of him. How does a man like that just vanish into the city without trace?'

'If he's even here.' Scaurus, temporarily equipped in praetorian armour every bit as splendid as his colleague's, an essential if he were to carry a sword within the city wall, shrugged in the face of Victor's frustration. 'We don't know for certain that he crossed the mountains, do we? All those years of banditry must have left him sitting on a mountain of gold. There's nothing to have stopped him and his few remaining comrades vanishing into the depths of Hispania or even Britannia, somewhere they weren't known by anyone, if they decided to retire and enjoy the fruits of their brigandage. It must have been a tempting thought, when he realised that our escape would make his plan much harder to carry out.'

'No.' Victor shook his head with the look of a man who wasn't about to be diverted from his concerns. 'That's not the Maternus

I knew. He's here alright, hidden in some carefully chosen lair and waiting for his time to strike.'

'In which case he's doomed to disappointment. Cleander might have caved in to our demands, faced with the alternative, but he only did so once he was convinced that there was no way for your former colleague to get within a spear's throw of Commodus. There'll be a ring of iron around the emperor that could stop a charging bull, so, unless he can magic himself up out of the ground next to Commodus, his bid for immortality as the man who took revenge on a living god is doomed to fail. And whether we find them before the ceremony or after its conclusion makes little odds. Someone will betray him soon enough, given the amount of gold that we've lavished on the city in the last few days.'

The two men contemplated Scaurus's last point in silence for a moment. The leaders of all the city's major gangs had been gathered together two nights before, assembled on the promise of rich rewards if they obeyed the summons, and dire consequences if they failed to. They had been seated at a round table to prevent anyone claiming superiority, in places carefully chosen to separate immediate rivals, and each man had been shepherded by a pair of praetorians in a naked show of power that had left none of them under any illusions as to the seriousness of the matter they had been summoned to discuss. The most powerful of them, a man whose criminal enterprises controlled the Subura district's network of infamous societies, had sat in silence while the men around him grumbled at the pre-emptory nature of their summoning and bickered with each other as to their organisations' relative strengths. He nodded quietly as Cleander had walked into the room flanked by Victor and Scaurus.

'I presume you now intend to inform us what is expected of us, Cleander?'

The chamberlain had smiled back at him serenely, ignoring the perplexed expressions on the faces of most of the other criminal leaders.

'You presume correctly, Petrus. And my congratulations, most of your colleagues haven't the slightest clue who I am.'

'I make it my job to know the names and needs of every man with whom I might interact. A businessman in my position never knows when the smallest piece of information might be of vital importance.'

'Time spent scouting is rarely wasted?'

'Quite so. And apt, given the uniforms backing you up.' The gang lord's voice had been softer than the soldiers would have expected of a man who had risen to control a fifth of the city's crime, but it had an unmistakable edge of command that any military man would have recognised instinctively. 'Perhaps this is a military matter?'

'Perhaps you already know exactly what sort of matter this is. After all, a man like you must have sources in the most surprising places.'

'You wouldn't believe me if I told you, Chamberlain. But let's presume that even if I did have some hint of your need for our assistance, it would probably be fragmentary at best. Better if you tell us all how we are expected to help, I'd say. And what's in it for us.'

Encouraged by the promise of a quite-startling amount of gold for information leading to a successful capture of the bandit leader, the gangs had set to sniffing Maternus's hiding place out with enthusiasm verging on the frantic, offering rewards of their own whilst also leaning hard on the parasitic criminal societies that infested the city. But for all their frantic pursuit, no sighting had been reported that had played out as anything other than wishful thinking.

'I know, you think he'll fall victim to the greed of his fellow man, when he finally shows himself.' Victor shook his head. 'Whereas I think a man like Maternus doesn't put himself into harm's way unless he has a means of making his approach to his target unobserved. He won't care about having an exit route, because he'll know that there will be no escape once he's got close enough to Commodus to see the look on his target's face as he dies. We won't know what it is he's planning until it's in action, and by then it'll be too late for us to do anything other than react.'

A guardsman appeared in the room's doorway.

'A message for you, Tribune.' He ushered a skinny youth into view, one hand firmly grasping his dagger's handle. 'Speak.'

'I was sent by Petrus, sirs. He told me to tell you that he has the men you're hunting, and to meet him outside the barracks of the Urban Cohort in the sixth district.'

Scaurus smiled wryly.

It seems that the idea to have the gangs do some of the heavy lifting for us might have paid off.'

They took to the street, walking in an untroubled bubble of open space at the heart of a century of praetorians whose shouted warnings cleared the streets in front of them as they swept up the Via Triumphalis and past the Flavian Arena's gate of death. Scaurus glanced through the open gate into the arena and then shot a glance at Marcus, whose stare was locked rigidly to his front.

'It makes sense for them to hide in the Viminal, I suppose. Maternus knows the area around the praetorian fortress better than any other district of the city, I'd imagine. With any luck we can get this wrapped up and be back at the palace in time to watch the festivities.'

Victor gave Scaurus a sidelong glance.

'Each to their own, colleague. Personally I find the whole circus around the cult of the Great Mother repugnant in the extreme. That . . .' he pointed up approvingly at the towering one-hundred-foot-high bronze colossus of the sun looming over the arena, 'is a proper religion for Romans. Disciplined, and focused on renewal. Whereas the Great Mother's worshippers seem to be fixated on nothing more than blood. And it rankles me that we're expected to worship an Asian goddess on the grounds that she gifted us victory against Carthage; it's both an insult to our own gods and to the hundreds of thousands of men who died removing the threat Carthage posed to the city. And the priests, these *galli*, are just unspeakable. Just look at them . . .'

As if on cue, several of the cult's holy men came down the street towards them, surrounded by an entourage of their warrior acolytes, their triple-plumed helmets visible above the heads of the crowd which had thronged to see the exotic spectacle of the galli passing on their way to the goddess's temple high on the Palatine Hill overlooking the Circus Maximus. For a moment it seemed that the praetorians and the priests' escort might physically contest the right to pass, but at the last moment Victor shouted an order at his men in a weary tone that bespoke his disgust.

'Allow them to pass! I've no time to dispute the right of way with a collection of powdered eunuchs!'

The galli swept past half a dozen strong at the heart of their retinue, serene in their finery, each of them dressed and decorated in a subtly different way, but all wearing some variation of their traditional long, floating robes of silk. Their garments were secured with ornate leather belts, on which long, ceremonial knives almost the length of infantry swords were carried. Each of the priests wore extravagant jewellery at their necks and wrists, shiny black jet and gleaming polished bronze. Their hair was long, framing faces so heavily decorated with powder and cosmetics as to make them almost identical, their lips painted bright red and eyes set in veritable masks of kohl. Their gait was unmistakably feminine as they stalked past the staring praetorians, shooting cool stares at the guardsmen. Victor shook his head in disgust.

'It's not often you see so many of them together. Usually they take to the streets in ones and twos, on their way to butter up a client and secure the funds they need to live. I'd have them all thrown into the Tiber and washed out to sea like the deviants they so clearly are. Those perverted excuses for priests castrate themselves, or at least they're supposed to, and as you've seen, they parade around looking like nothing better than common transvestites. They probably take the women's role in sex too, and who knows what private rites they carry out for their patrons? They're nothing better than catamites.'

With the procession's noise and the crowd's excited uproar fading behind them, the guardsmen continued on their way up the Vicus Patricius, Scaurus casting a glance back at the priests as they went on their way with regal waves to the people who had turned out to witness their strangeness.

'Allow them their day in the sun, colleague. At least the fact that everyone in the city seems to be on their way to the ceremony will mean we have room to swing a sword, when we get to wherever it is this messenger is taking us.'

The street in front of the Urban Cohort's barracks was unusually quiet, and they had no trouble finding the gang leader who had summoned them. His demeanour was as calm as it had been two nights before, and when he spoke it was in the same soft tones that belied the ruthlessness for which he was famed.

'We have your men, gentlemen, on the top floor of an insula not far from here. They sent out for food, and the boy who carried it up to them saw their weapons and shields stacked in a corner of the room they're sharing. He made a report to the cohorts, but I was fortunate enough to have overheard him, and took the opportunity to alert you myself, in order to ensure no delay in your being informed, of course.'

Scaurus grinned at the bare-faced lie that the information had been innocently overheard.

'You *do* have good contacts, don't you, Petrus, to have heard the news so quickly? But no matter how the knowledge came, you're sure these men are . . . or were . . . praetorians?'

'They have shields in their room, the boy says, and those shields have scorpions painted on them, just like your men's.' The gang leader gave Scaurus and Victor a meaningful glance. 'They're praetorians, alright, but you have to ask yourself why they wouldn't be tucked up in your fortress less than half a mile up the hill, rather than slumming it in a shitty insula like that?'

'Why indeed?' Victor nodded, hard-faced. 'I suggest we go and find out for ourselves!'

The gang leader raised a hand in warning.

'The insula in question is just around the corner. I've had a few of my men stroll past, and it looks like they have a lookout posted, a man at the window looking out on the street. The moment any of you go round this corner, they'll know you're here, so I'd suggest that when you do go in, you do it fast and hard.'

'I've got a better idea.'

They turned to look at Marcus, who was regarding Petrus with an appraising expression.

'Two of us go in. Just you and me.'

The gang leader smiled slowly, recognising the challenge in the younger man's voice.

'You want to know if I still have what put me at the top of the pile, eh?'

Marcus shrugged.

'Some men reach the position of supremacy through the efforts of others. Some men are so hungry for blood and power that they do it themselves. Of course if you have a man you'd rather send in with me . . . ?'

The big man shook his head, his eyes still creased into an amused half-smile.

'No, that wouldn't be right. I accept the challenge. And in return, you guarantee me the reward that was promised for this find, no matter how I came by it. And you'd better get that armour off, hadn't you?'

Marcus stripped off his equipment, refastening his belt over the immaculate white tunic and wrapping his swords in a roll of cloth, discarding the scabbards.

'Ready?'

Petrus nodded, his dagger secreted in the long sleeves of his tunic in a clearly well-practised manner.

'As ready as I'll ever be. Let's go and see what we're both capable of, shall we?'

They strolled round the corner and into the street in question with their shoulders almost touching, two friends on their way somewhere and engrossed in conversation.

'How far up is the insula?'

The gang leader shot a quick glance up the hill.

'See the tavern with the red awning? Opposite that, more or less. Let's walk on the left so that the watcher has to lean out a bit to see us.'

'And so we don't obviously cross the road to get to them.'

'That too.' Petrus paused for a moment and then spoke again, his tone conspiratorial. 'Of course I'm not expecting to have to do much of the fighting once we get at them. I've seen you at work with a blade, and it was a wondrous sight. I didn't ever think I'd be walking alongside a gladiator of such fame as you, Corvus, but since you're here, I'm happy enough to guard your back while you do the real damage.'

Marcus shot him a swift glance without breaking stride.

'You mistake me for someone else.'

'No, I don't. When you live or die by your skill at judging people, you tend to become an acute observer. And I've seen you before, as we both know all too well. In the arena. You're the man that killed Mortiferum and then vanished from the fight game overnight. There were reports that you were seen in the royal box a few days later, watching the fight where dear old Flamma put Velox on his back and then killed himself, but you never fought again after killing his brother.'

'I—' Marcus groped for a convincing lie, then shook his head in amusement. 'You follow the games?'

Petrus patted his shoulder, chuckling at their mutual joke for the unseen watcher.

'Follow the games? I *am* the games, young man. Not in an obvious way, of course, but there's very little that happens in the Flavian that I don't make money from. The roasted meat that the punters chew on? Ten percent. The wine they guzzle? Ten percent. And the whores they fuck in the shadows of the walkways . . . ?'

'Ten percent?'

'Good guess. And since it's a sad fact that an unwatched pot usually vanishes from the kitchen, I tend to be very hands-on when it comes to the games.' He steered Marcus round a pair of men arguing in the street, continuing his speech as he did so. 'My oddsmakers were wondering what to make of you when you were put up against Mortiferum – and by that I mean how strongly to stack the book against you – but I saw you fight in that first bout, when you and the other two put down the blade fodder that was sent at you without breaking sweat, so I told them to make the odds on him generous enough to open the gamblers' wallets nice and wide, since they reckoned he couldn't lose. And I put fifty thousand on you, all in small bets, of course, and spread around to avoid spooking the market, but you made me half a million in a few minutes, and that was before my cut of the takings when Mortiferum's backers all walked away mourning their losses. And now I get to see how good you are at close quarters. That's going to be a singular honour that I could never have dreamed of before today. This man Maternus has done me a right favour.'

'You might want to be careful what you wish for. He and his men will fight like animals once the surprise wears off.'

'Hah!' The big man shook his head in amusement. 'I've had a good life, and men in my position have to know when the time has come to make their exit, before someone younger and hungrier comes to take their place and leave them face down in a puddle of their own blood. This might not be a bad day to make that exit, even if it's not the way I would have chosen. When you pointed the finger at me, believe it or not, my heart actually leapt at the chance to do something outrageous that will either kill me or make me a legend. And here we are.'

He pointed to the entrance of a tired-looking insula, peeling paint and crumbling mortar betraying the lack of love the building had endured over recent years, and Marcus shook his head at the building's decrepitude.

'Let's hope it doesn't fall down with us in it when matters get vigorous.'

Petrus grinned again.

'That's it, load on the misery.' He held up a hand. 'I'll lead until the knife work starts. This is what *I* grew up doing.'

Passing the wrinkled concierge in the building's hallway, he put a finger to his lips and held up a shining gold coin that made her eyes open wide and her lips compress so tightly that they were a white slash in the wrinkled seams of her face. Nodding to her and dropping the coin onto her outstretched hand, the gang leader gestured to the door with his thumb, speaking so quietly that Marcus could barely hear him.

'On your way, little mother. Bad men may come this way shortly, and they will not thank you for not challenging us.'

Pacing up the stairs behind him, Marcus realised that his own careful steps were generating more noise than the bigger man's swift ascent; Petrus seemed to move with the stealthy grace of a hunting cat. Floor by floor, they made their way up through the building's layers, each one a little smaller than the one below, until by the sixth the rooms were barely ten paces from stair to stair, and Petrus had slowed his pace to a slow, foot rolling stalk, his head tipped on one side to listen for any sound of alarm. The sounds of the street were audible only as a background murmur, and voices could be heard from the apartment they were advancing past with slow, cautious steps, shrill female dissatisfaction on one side, a man's voice replying with evident disgust to whatever the complaints were. Petrus stopped, bending close to Marcus's ear.

'Perfect. Their mutual hatred will be all the men above hear. Follow my lead, and when I clear the doorway for you, do what you do best.'

He led the younger man up the last flight of stairs, both of them holding their blades ready to fight. Lit by an unshuttered window open onto the street far below, the landing was quiet except for the sounds of discord from the apartment below. Padding silently to the top floor apartment's door, Petrus drew himself up, took three slow, deep breaths and turned to Marcus with a hard grin filled with the exhilaration of the fight to come, whispering so quietly that the younger man could barely hear the words.

'*Morituri te salutant,* Corvus. Show me your magic one last time.'

He turned back to the door, stepping over to the far side and raising a fist to pound on the wood.

'Landlord! Open up!'

Footsteps clattered across bare boards to the door, and a voice on the other side of the wood barked back a challenge.

'What the *fuck* do you want? We paid you fair and square!'

The gang leader grimaced, his response instantaneous and indignant.

'You've got weapons in there! Open up before I go and get the watch to break the door down!'

A voice close to the original speaker muttered two words that Marcus could nevertheless hear through the thin plaster.

'*Do him.*'

The door opened and a bearded and scar-faced man stepped through it with a short sword in his hand. But even as he registered Marcus waiting for him with swords in his hands and turned to face their threat, he found himself taken by the collar from behind and pulled off balance backwards. Petrus grunted with sudden effort, twisting like a discus thrower and hurling the hapless man at the open window with enough force to lift him off his feet. Smashing his head against the rough wooden frame, he staggered back towards the gang leader with a look of dazed astonishment, then screamed in terror as the big man lunged forward, planted a flat hand against his chest and heaved with all his strength, hurling him through the open window to fall to the street below.

Marcus went through the door crouched low, feeling the breath of air from a spear's flight as the missile buried itself in the plaster behind him. A burly man in a dirty tunic came at him from the left with a knife held high, his bladder and bowels emptying explosively as the Roman lunged forward with the twin blades aimed high and low to strike him in throat and groin. Ripping the swords free, he spun away rather than simply turning to face the room's other occupants who were frozen in momentary disbelief, one man's arm still extended from having thrown the spear that he had evaded a moment before. Crossing the sword blades before him in the low guard, he ignored the noisy sounds of impending death from the floor behind him and to his left, silently challenging the dying man's comrades.

'Have him!'

The words broke the spell, and with angry snarls they came at him with whatever they had in their hands, one pair armed with spears while their comrades snatched up short swords and pressed in behind them. A spear's long blade lanced out at him, the weapon's wielder staring stupidly at the shaft's stump as Marcus parried the weapon with one blade and hacked off its iron head with the other, then dropped the broken weapon as his would-be target dodged the other spear and stepped into sword-reach. He sliced off the fingers of the other spearman's right hand with a deft flick, ducked under a wild swing of the closest man's gladius and then rammed his left-hand blade up into the soft skin of its wielder's jaw with enough force to put the point through the top of his skull. Abandoning the sword, he turned to face the remaining three men with the sudden familiar sensation of time slowing, as his body responded to the danger of battle with its customary shock of other-worldly energy. And then, before he had time to attack, Petrus was through the door behind him, wrenching the spear from the plaster and turning it expertly in his hand before stamping forward to hurl it into the closest of them with such power that it transfixed his body and dropped him kicking to the wooden floor with blood pouring from the wounds in his front and back. Tossing his dagger from left hand to right, he stepped alongside Marcus and roared a challenge at the two surviving deserters, spittle flying across the room with the violence of his challenge, both of them flinching with the bestial fury in the new assailant's roared question.

'Who's *fucking* next?'

When Scaurus and Victor reached the scene, breathless from climbing seven flights of stairs at the run, they found the last two deserters under Petrus's watchful eye and unwavering spear, sullen but cowed, while Marcus examined the room's contents, the eagle-pommelled gladius already reclaimed and hanging in its customary place on his right hip. The urban watch centurion walked in a moment later and grimaced at the blood liberally sprayed across the walls and pooling around the corpses of the dead men and the keening, crouching man cradling his ruined hand.

'Gods below, it's a slaughterhouse.'

Scaurus raised a jaundiced eyebrow at him.

'It was never going to be anything else. I'd have thought the man lying broken in the street below having failed to fly would have given you some clue.'

'All the same . . .' The officer came to his senses. 'I'll take these prisoners.'

'You won't. Not yet, anyway.' Victor raised a hand to forestall the centurion's protest. 'There's no time. None of these men is Maternus, and these two may be the only men in the city who know where he is and what it is that he plans.'

'Leave this to me.' Petrus had propped the spear up against the wall and was flexing his big fists. 'I can do things to these two that you wouldn't even think of. After all, I want to make sure Cleander comes up with that gold he promised.'

Victor nodded, extending a hand to beckon him forward.

'As the only praetorian here, I'm the man who can authorise you to get the truth out of them. Do what's necessary.'

The gang leader paced forward, drawing the small knife from its place at his back.

'Which one of you girls wants to go first? You?'

The man in question shrugged, his face set hard.

'You can do what you want, I won't tell you anything. We're here to avenge hundreds of our brothers who died for nothing. That's a cause I wouldn't betray for all the gold in the city, so nothing you can do will get me to tell you what I know.'

'And there's no time.'

They turned to look at Marcus, who was looking into a sacking bag with an expression of sudden understanding. He reached into its depths and pulled out a small pot, pulling out the stopper and raising it to show them what had drawn his attention.

'Do you see?'

'See what?' The Watch centurion stared at the indisputable proof of Maternus's plot uncomprehendingly, but Scaurus made the connection after a moment's contemplation of its contents.

'Kohl? Ah . . . the bull sacrifice. Of *course* . . .'

As the party hurried back down the hill towards the city's centre, Victor raged at the ease with which their quarry had fooled them once again.

'He walked past us laughing. *Laughing!*'

'We can still spoil his scheme.'

The praetorian shook his head at Scaurus's panted opinion.

'There'll be half a million people in and around the Circus by now, all come to cheer the emperor while the galli perform their blessing and proclaim him to be under the protective benevolence of the Great Mother for another year! It would take an hour to get through that sort of crowd even with a dozen soldiers to push through the crush. Look . . .'

With the racetrack in sight, still half a mile distant, they could already see the back of the huge crowd that had gathered outside the arena to join the celebration of the sacrifice, standing patiently in their thousands under the watery spring sun and listening intently as one of a dozen commentators on the walls of the racetrack relayed a description of the scene to them. His voice reached them in snippets through the crowd's inevitable babel, occasional words enabling them to piece together some under-standing of what was happening inside.

'. . . *this magnificent bull dressed in . . . led by the* archigallus *around the . . . proclaim our emperor safe for another year . . .*'

The officers looked at the barrier they presented with dismay, Scaurus squaring his shoulders determinedly.

'They're parading the bull around the track, so there's still some time left. We *have* to try.'

'Yes. But we are bound to fail. If he's disguised as one of the galli, the emperor's life is already lost, unless some miracle prevents—'

'No. There is another way to protect him.'

They turned to look at Marcus, who pointed to the palace buildings rising to their right.

'The Palatine? What can you do from up there?'

'If I can see a thing, I can hit it. You press through the crowd; I'll take another path!'

Scaurus nodded, turning back to the Circus.

'Come on, Victor, let's see if a pair of Roman gentlemen in all this finery can't clear a path through the emperor's loyal subjects!'

They pushed forward into the press of worshippers, guardsmen to front and rear shouting for the crowd to make way for them. Marcus turned away and strode towards the nearest gate with his hand raised, Cotta at his heels.

'Let me in! I'm on an urgent mission for the imperial chamberlain! The watchword is blood!'

The men on duty on the gate's other side snapped to attention at the sight of a pair of centurions, opening the heavy iron framework at Marcus's command and staring after the two men as they ran up the steps that led to the emperor's private stadium.

'Do you actually know where you're going?'

Marcus nodded grimly in response to his friend's question, leading him into the walled garden that was the stadium's anteroom.

'I've been here before, remember?'

'But that was to the imperial nursery!'

'I was escorted in through that gate and brought through the palace via this stadium. And with a bit of luck . . .'

He led his friend across the immaculately-maintained grounds to the stadium's entrance, barking the watchword at the two guardsmen standing duty on the gateway.

'Take me to the place where the emperor's bow is stored! Quickly, his life may depend upon it!'

Leading them through the gate and into the stadium's austere environs, one of the sentries took them to a small outbuilding and pointed to the heavy wooden door.

'The bows are kept in there, Centurion. But it's kept locked at all times, emperor's orders. He says that if any other man touches his bow, he'll—'

'Who can unlock it?'

'The emperor's master archer, Centurion, but he's off duty.'

'We need to speak with him, immediately! It's literally a matter of the emperor's life! Is he in the palace?'

The guardsman nodded his head uncertainly.

He should be, Centurion, in his private quarters.'

'Take us to him, Guardsman, and quickly if you value your emperor's life! *Run!*'

'Well, Chamberlain, all seems set for the sacrifice?'

Cleander inclined his head in agreement with his master, grateful that Commodus seemed to have been taken by a sunny mood at the sight of a quarter of a million of the city's people flocked together to give thanks for his continued well-being.

'It does, Caesar.'

'So *everything* is ready?' The emperor's tone had become a little testier, and the chamberlain, well accustomed to spotting and avoiding imperial angst, recognised the early signs of a loss of his master's wafer-thin patience. 'It's already taken long enough that we could have sacrificed a dozen bulls and been back in the palace, has it not?'

The chamberlain had spent the previous hour closely supervising the arrival of the priests and their intended sacrifice, watching as the praetorians had performed a thorough search of all concerned, including the bull, to ensure that no weapon was secreted about them. He was all too aware of the time that had gone into ensuring that their unusually close proximity to the man who ruled the empire, at least in name, would pose him no threat. He had escorted them in person onto the platform that had been erected next to the statue of their goddess that was part of the divider's panoply of religious and imperial imagery, now so heavily garlanded with flowers that the graven image was almost invisible apart from her beneficent smile. The galli had been their usual inscrutable selves, their dull eyes bespeaking the narcotics with whose aid they were strongly reputed to perform their rites, and their archigallus had proceeded in a stately manner at the heart of his softly chanting followers. His ceremonial mask had glinted in the sunlight as he stalked haughtily up the ramp that had been built to access the temporary altar on which the sacrifice was to be carried out. He now stood ready at the centre of the gently swaying priests, clearly ready to begin the ceremony which, Cleander had been gratified to discover, they planned to keep as brief as possible in recognition of their emperor's well-known intolerance of overly-prolonged ritual. The archigallus himself had reassured Cleander that no protracted declamations were planned, his voice both knowing and reassuring from behind the mask cast in the likeness of the goddess's consort Attis.

'All that is required of us by the Great Mother is that we praise her name, before I take my place and we end this magnificent beast's life for her sake. I will bathe in the beast's blood for a short time before emerging into the daylight, cast the smallest portion of that blood onto the emperor's toga as a blessing, and then bid him to go with the good wishes of the Great Mother to watch over him for the coming year. Once he has left us, I will bid my followers to perform the more complex and time-consuming part of our ritual, doubtless to the great entertainment of the crowd.'

Recognising the unmistakable signs of imperial impatience, a state of mind that often resulted in unhappiness for those who became the unwitting subjects of their emperor's ire, the chamberlain sought to soothe his master's quixotic personality in ways he had, through trial and error, come to realise were the best means available, even if they always left him feeling as if he had just placated a bad-tempered child.

'The preparations are indeed complete, Caesar, and your esteemed colleagues of the senate are taking their places. Soon we will proceed with the ceremony, the entire city will give thanks to the Great Mother for extending her protection over you for another year and we can return to the palace for the afternoon's celebratory feast. After which you can withdraw to your private suite to take further refreshment, and to indulge a carefully-chosen audience with your presence. I took the liberty of selecting several new partners for you to consider, and of course your favourites will all be in attendance should you prefer to tread a familiar path.'

He gestured to the Circus's tribune, where a stream of toga-clad men was making their way down the stairs to their seats with the dignified grace expected of them, each one pausing to bow to their ruler in his place at the very heart of the Circus's perfectly sanded and brushed track on the central divider. Commodus turned and glared across the track at them, his anger becoming more evident by the moment.

'As usual, Chamberlain, my *colleagues* of the senate seek to prove themselves superior to me by making me wait while they endow themselves with as much pomp as they can scrape out of the occasion. I suggest that we proceed with the ceremony immediately, so as to demonstrate to them that their antics *have not gone unnoticed.*'

His last words were spat across the fifty-pace gap between altar and tribune loudly enough that the senators closest to the emperor were left in no doubt as to his state of mind. Cleander was unable to suppress a smile as word of the emperor's latest outburst rippled up their seated rows.

'Indeed so, Caesar, a wise and telling message to send to the senate.'

Commodus beamed back at him, clearly delighted to have his

bad temper validated, extending a hand and gesturing to the waiting bull in a regal wave. 'And yes, let us command the archigallus to proceed with his ritual which, he assures me, will be kept commendably brief.'

They found the master fletcher sitting at a table in his office, lovingly polishing a bow that was laid out before him on a pair of stands, working a waxed cloth in tiny circles with the obvious patience of a man in love with his profession and the object before him. He stood, bowing slightly.

'Well now, Centurion, how is that I can help you today, now that I have been torn from my contemplation of the greatest bow I have ever made?' Marcus stepped close to the master fletcher so swiftly that the older man stepped back an involuntary halfpace. 'I meant no disrespect, of course—'

'I need a bow. The best possible bow, with which to take the single most important shot of my life. Tell me, which of your bows is worthy of a shot to save the life of the emperor?'

The archer gestured to the weapon lying before him.

'This is my own personal bow, Centurion, better in every respect than the other weapons I have here. It is stronger and more powerful than any other bow in my possession, and made to such an exacting standard that I sometimes sit and stare at it for hours, in awe of its—'

'Has the emperor ever used it?'

'Commodus? No. I would, of course, have put it in his hands, were his skill to have demanded it, but the emperor is a different kind of archer to myself. I am an artist, a man to put an arrow into the eye of a bull at one hundred paces, whereas the emperor's needs are more prosaic. He loves nothing better than to kill with a well-placed arrow, just as his skills with sword and spear, as I hear it, are oriented to the dispensation of death and destruction. His arm is strong from unremitting practice, and he could loose the hundredth shaft with the same power as the first, but he lacks the finesse to wring the best from this beautiful device.'

Marcus nodded.

'And do you have arrows to match this perfection?'

The fletcher lifted a shaft from one of the baskets hanging from the rack in which the other bows were secured.

'But of course, the best bow in the world is of no use without arrows made with the same love and care, perfectly balanced to fly as straight and true as can ever be possible.'

He passed the arrow to Marcus and waited expectantly for the younger man to make some comment.

'It seems . . . unremarkable.'

'Perhaps, to a man who has not spent his entire life around such things. But were you to give this single arrow to a Parthian horse archer he would hide it away for that moment when he needed the very best. It is quite possibly one of the finest examples of the fletcher's art anywhere in the world.'

'Very well. I have need of your services.'

'But—'

The fletcher fell silent as Marcus turned back to him, quailing at the look on the younger man's face.

'Your emperor is under a mortal threat, and there is no man that can avert it other than me. Will you help me, or do you wish Commodus to die and it be known that you could have prevented that death?'

The other man was silent for a moment, evidently considering the short and brutish nature of his life, were there to be as much as a hint of his collusion in the death of an emperor.

'I must do as you wish, Centurion, I know my duty. But how will my bow help you?'

'You know this part of the palace as well as any man alive, I suspect.'

'I suppose I do. I've been the official court fletcher for half my life, it seems.'

Marcus nodded, bending to speak quietly into the older man's ear.

'Then suppose that you needed to put an arrow into the statue of the Great Mother that stands on the Circus Maximus lane divider. Where in this stadium would you choose to take the shot from?'

The fletcher frowned, thinking for a moment.

'It is a strange question, but the answer to it is obvious enough. The highest balcony overlooking the track has a good view of most of the track, indeed they say that Domitian himself used to—'

'How would you take the shot?'

The older man nodded, happy at having his professional opinion sought.

'It would be no more difficult than any other shot at a distance of one hundred and fifty paces and with a drop from the bow of . . .' He thought for a moment. 'Forty . . . no, fifty paces. As long as the archer is sufficiently careful not to allow his form to be influenced by the requirements of the shot, and if he knows what he is doing, then it should be straightforward enough. If he has the mind for it, of course, and has spent half his life practising shooting upwards and downwards at all distances and elevations. Have you lived such a life, Centurion, or are you simply competent with a bow?'

'Me?' Marcus smiled. 'I am better than competent with all weapons you can name, but I am no master of the bow. Whereas you clearly are. So take up your weapon, and select a spare string to use in case of a mishap. Then choose the five best arrows that you have. Your moment of destiny is upon you.'

The master bowman smiled sadly.

'My life might depend on such a shot, Tribune, but still I could not take it.' He raised a hand to gesture to his eyes. 'I lost the ability to see clearly enough to shoot at any distance beyond twenty paces five years ago and more. I was retained in my position because I have the ability to look at a man's stance with the bow and immediately correct what he is doing wrong. I can tell you how to make the shot you describe, but I could not make it myself if the empire depended on it.'

★

'These priests don't look very motivated.' Commodus sniffed as the archigallus descended into the foss beneath the heavy iron grating on which the bull was tethered, climbing down a set of wooden steps into a pit tall enough for him to stand in, his intricately carved staff of office held in one hand while the other gripped handholds set in the foss's wall. 'They're usually a good deal livelier than this, are they not?'

Cleander looked up at the skies above momentarily before turning back to the emperor.

'They perform under the influence of narcotics, Caesar, and the archigallus tells me that they will dance like wild men once the music starts.'

'Huh.' Commodus's grunts were another eloquent indication of his state of mind, and as grunts went, this one was solidly placed in the mental territory that his chamberlain considered best avoided. 'Let's hope they do, or it won't just be the bull that gets its throat cut.'

The chief priest's voice boomed out from his place in the foss beneath the bull, a veritable roar of command that was loud enough to be heard in the crowd that was packed into the Circus.

'I am ready! Begin the sacrifice!'

The most animated of the galli drew the long knife from his scabbard and began to caper, albeit with little of the abandonment that was usual on such occasions. Cleander's eyes narrowed as he pondered the lack of flair in the man's movements, but before he had any time to consider the disparity between expectation and reality, the priest was at the bull's side with the long blade poised, raising it to the sky with a sharp ululation, polished iron gleaming in the midday sun as the beast shuffled its tethered feet nervously. The boy whose job it was to soothe its nerves blew into its ear to distract it in the last moments of its existence, stroking its head as the beast lowed in protest and rolled its eyes fearfully. At the sight of the knife, the crowd which encircled the rostrum on all sides roared their approval, knowing from long experience what would come next.

'Now we get to it!' Commodus sat forward in his place of honour, close enough that he would see every detail of the animal's death and exsanguination, his eyes suddenly wide with the anticipation of the bloodletting that was close at hand. 'The Great Mother demands blood, and so does your emperor!'

'There. That is the shot I must take.'

The two men stared down from the highest balcony of Domitian's palace, Marcus pointing to the spot at the very heart of the seething mass of humanity that was gathered around the sacrificial altar.

'Do you see clearly enough to make out the tethered bull? It is standing above a pit that holds a high priest of the Great Mother's sect, who will bathe in its blood once his acolytes open its throat. And when he emerges from that pit I must kill him, or risk the empire being torn apart by civil war once again.'

The archer looked down into the Circus, shaking his head slowly.

'It is as I told you. I can barely make out the bull, and the men around it are nothing better than a blur. If one of us is to make this shot, it must be you. Give me the bow.'

Stringing the weapon, his hands moving expertly to secure the cord, he tugged it to ensure that it was securely fitted. He handed it to Marcus and took an arrow from the quiver he had carried up to the vantage point, feeling the length of its shaft between both hands. Shaking his head, he tossed it aside and took another, repeating the assessment and nodding in satisfaction.

'I made these arrows myself, for my own use, in the days before my sight failed, and I know each of them like a child. No other man has ever been allowed to use them, because each one is a labour of love. Perfectly fletched, perfectly straight in the shaft, and fitted with heads that are weighted and polished to perfection, to fly as true as it is possible for any arrow in the hands of an imperfect creature such as ourselves.' Marcus took the missile from him and nocked it to the bow's string, pulling it back experimentally to feel the power in the wooden frame. The master archer smiled at his expression. 'Beautiful, isn't it? The smoothest, most finely constructed bow you will ever have in your hands. Now, show me your stance.'

Below them in the Circus horns blared, the signal to the quarter of a million spectators gathered around the makeshift altar that the bull sacrifice was on the point of being carried out. Marcus shook his head.

'There's no time for a lesson on the finer points of archery. I must be ready to shoot at any moment.'

'Very well, prepare yourself. Begin to breathe deeply, and close your mind to any other thought than that of that most perfect of arrows flying straight and true to strike whatever target you select. I will try to help you.'

The younger man drew the arrow back again, pulling its fletched tail towards him until it was level with his cheek, settling himself into the shooting stance that Qadir had worked with him to perfect in their years of friendship.

'You have the makings of a master yourself, young man.' The archer walked around him in a slow appraisal, then leaned in to lift his right elbow fractionally. 'Raise your aim a little, Tribune. The tendency with men not practised at taking such a shot is to aim too low. Good. You are as ready as you will ever be without another hour of tuition. Hold your stance and await the moment to loose that shaft, and I will pray to the Great Mother herself that you find the mark.'

The priests at the bull's side performed the sacrifice with sufficient expertise that Cleander's momentary glimmer of concern as to their lack of animation was dismissed. Several of them held the animal still while another wielded the knife like an expert, opening the beast's throat and severing the arteries beneath its flesh to release a spurting flood of crimson blood that cascaded through the heavy wooden bars on which the tottering beast's hoofs clattered, as it staggered from side to side against the restraining priests, drenching the archigallus in his foss beneath the animal. Collapsing onto its knees, the bull let out one last, desperate, bubbling moan of distress and then fell onto its side; the platform's wooden joints creaked in protest but held firm, as its builders had assured Cleander it would, especially when it had been pointed out to them that any failure would result in their paying the most significant price possible.

'*Yes!*'

Commodus was on his feet, lurching forwards to stare down into the pit to see the archigallus. The priest stood with his arms spread wide beneath the diminishing flow of blood, drenched by the heavy flow, and after a moment the emperor turned to bark at the crowd and, it seemed, most specifically at the gathered senators seated in the tribune opposite. 'Blood for the Great Mother! Blood for your emperor!'

The flow of blood had subsided from its initial torrent; the spurting gouts of gore driven by the beast's mighty heart gave way to a gentle trickle that splashed the priest's upturned face as he stared through his bloody mask at the emperor above him. Commodus gestured for him to climb from the foss and complete his ritual, turning on his heel and walking to the appointed place within the circle of his bodyguards with a regal wave to the crowd, whose renewed roar of delight was enough to show their continued favour for an emperor who, for all the stories as to his idiosyncrasies, continued to put bread on their plates and provide them with the spectacles that every Roman considered theirs as of right. Turning to the senate, he raised both hands wide in an obvious gesture, part question, part command, and on cue they rose, as every man present knew they must, clapping their emperor in a more dignified form of adulation than that of the crowds surrounding them, but nevertheless clearly united in their respect for their supposed colleague and absolute master. His need for sensation temporarily sated, Commodus nodded satisfaction to his chamberlain with a gracious wave of his hand.

'Not bad, Cleander. Not bad at all!'

The chamberlain bowed deeply to his emperor, sighing inward relief that yet another opportunity for the man's inexhaustible anger to rise in its usual bloody fashion had been averted by the sacrifice's speed and savagery. He shot a glance at the foss, out of which the archigallus was climbing with deliberate steps up the wooden stairs, his staff held in his right hand, and then, as the realisation of what he was seeing imposed itself over what he was expecting to see, his jaw dropped in horrified amazement.

'Now . . .'

Far below the two men on the palace balcony, the emperor was walking away from the altar, raising his hands to the adulating masses as they bayed like animals at the sight of the bull staggering in its death throes. From the pit beneath the dead animal, the priest was climbing into the sunlight, the blood that liberally coated his head and garments a striking dark red under the sun's rays. As Marcus made the final tiny adjustments to his stance, he saw Cleander rise from his seat and point, even as a pair of figures in the armour of praetorian officers sprinted across the track beneath the senatorial tribune. Emptying his mind of everything but the shot, he loosed the arrow, aiming for a spot three feet ahead of the archigallus as the priest abandoned his stately stride and began to lunge forward. His right arm trailed as he drew the spear's glinting head back to his ear in readiness to sling the weapon across a gap so short that the missile would punch through the unarmoured emperor's back and leave him transfixed by the weapon's shaft. Time seemed to slow as the arrow whipped away and down into the arena below, its pristine white fletching a swift-moving dot against the backdrop of the massed spectators.

'*Guards!*'

Even as he roared the warning, Cleander knew that the guardsmen arrayed around Commodus would offer no protection, so unexpected and swift was the change in the priest's demeanour from stately ritual to violent assault. His mask tossed aside in the foss below their feet, his face was contorted in a snarl of hatred that told the chamberlain everything he needed to know as to the man's true identity. And then, at the very moment the would-be assassin lunged forward to cast his spear into the emperor's unprotected back, and take the life of the one man whose death would result in hundreds of thousands more, he fell, clutching at his leg, the weapon dropped and forgotten, an arrow buried deeply in the thickest part of his thigh.

'*What!*'

Commodus turned with the speed of a striking snake, snatching a spear from the closest of his guards and putting its blade to the fallen assassin's throat, as the guards obeyed Cleander's bellowed order and formed a circle of iron around their emperor, facing outwards with their spears ready to strike at any further attempt at his life. Allowing himself to be relieved of the spear, Commodus acquiesced as he was hustled away, leaving his chamberlain to approach Maternus as he was dragged to his feet.

'Get him out of sight . . . no, wait.' Cleander stared at the snarling rebel leader for a moment. 'Gag him. I have a better idea.'

Pinioned by two of the biggest men, and crippled by the arrow in his thigh, Maternus was unable to resist as he was shuffled forwards across the altar to face the senatorial tribune, displayed like a prisoner on trial as Cleander raised a hand to gesture to him in a show of confidence that he hoped would be convincing.

'Here is the deserter and bandit Maternus! He sought to take the throne by masquerading as a member of the galli and taking advantage of that camouflage to murder our beloved emperor!' The senators were staring back at him aghast, all too well aware that imperial assassination plots frequently rebounded on the ruling classes just as much as upon their perpetrators. 'But his plot was betrayed by his own men, and so he has been thwarted by the vigilance of the city's Praetorian Guard!'

He turned and shot a glance at Praetorian Prefect Aebutianus that told his subordinate that there would be a reckoning for his evident failure to secure the emperor's safety before turning back to crowd and senate.

'And now he will be imprisoned, made to talk and then, in the fullness of time, executed for his heinous attempt to rob the city and its empire of our dearest master! So will die an enemy of Rome! Give thanks to the Great Mother for her protection of the emperor!'

Aebutianus was on his feet, knowing what was expected of him, raising his voice to a parade ground roar.

'All praise the Great Mother!'

The crowd erupted into furious cheers, the sound of their acclaim deafening in the arena's centre, and Cleander raised his voice to be heard over the din, flicking a hand at the helpless prisoner's captors.

'Take him to the palace dungeons by way of the tunnels. Have him cleaned up and ready for interrogation, but leave the arrow where it is. He can take that to the grave, once we know all we need to know about what he's been doing for the last few years. Arrest all of these so-called priests as well, and we'll soon find out how this plot almost succeeded.

'You think he was assisted?'

The chamberlain turned to find Aebutianus at his side.

'What do you think, Prefect? That spear didn't come from nowhere, did it? Accomplices there doubtless were, and in the fullness of time I'm sure we'll know who they were. Won't we? With enough evidence I can make the lie that he was betrayed unchallengeable, and thereby avoid the truth. Which is that without whoever loosed that arrow, your term in office would have ended in the ignominy of your having overseen the death of an emperor.'

'It seems that you bear a charmed life, Tribune Scaurus.'

Tired, but nevertheless clearly content with the outcome of the day's events, Cleander was sitting back in his chair behind the wooden desk at which he usually conducted his business, a glass cup of wine in his hand, contemplating Scaurus and Marcus over its rim as he sipped at the contents.

'I'm not usually given to drink; I find it dulls the intellect and leaves me feeling less than myself the day after, and let's face it, a man in my position can rarely afford even one less than perfect day. On this occasion, however, I feel that a small celebration is called for. Will you join me, gentlemen?'

'Thank you, Chamberlain, but on this occasion . . .'

'You think not? Wise of you, Rutilius Scaurus. Who knows what an unprincipled man might have had smeared onto the cup you would receive, although I'm sure you realise that were I to desire your deaths, I wouldn't feel very much need to be that subtle. You're sure you won't join me? Very well, to business then, my last business of the day before I retire for what, frankly, will be a well-earned night's sleep. You kept your part of the bargain, by the very smallest of margins, and so I will keep mine. Tribune Victor is to be granted an honourable retirement, and will be received by the emperor as a signal of the throne's gratitude for the part he played in bringing Maternus's revolt to a timely close. His colleague Sergius will be publicly declared a hero of the empire, and his family will receive his retirement pay in recognition of his sacrifice in the face of overwhelming numbers of the enemy. And Maternus, who is already enjoying the attentions of one of the palace's more skilful interrogators, will by now be desperate to unburden himself of every last detail of his revolt, which will be recorded by a team of scribes, collated and filed for future reference.'

'Forgotten, you mean? Why not just execute him and have done with it?'

'That would be far too easy on the man. He has to stand trial before he dies, with the inconvenience of Centurion Aquila's arrow to deal with, a nice public trial to remind the senate that the reward for treason is an unpleasant and very public spectacle, followed by an execution of the same nature. And as for you two . . .' Cleander drank again, staring up at the impassive officers.

'Really? You're determined to show no sign of concern as to your fate?'

'Would it help us in some way?'

'No, Rutilius Scaurus, it probably wouldn't. Very well, as to you two and your assorted hangers-on.' He tossed a scroll across the desk. 'While I would dearly like to have someone carry out the job that Lupinus and Titianus both seem to have made a mess of, I'm very much aware that you may well still have friends in the Guard, and that your threat to expose my cultivation of Commodus's bastards remains alive. Which is not a risk I can afford to court, and so it seems that we have achieved an uneasy state of truce, neither of us able to threaten the other. I, however, am still the imperial chamberlain, and you still owe your continued existence to my willingness to tolerate the threat you present me, willingness which you will buy with your service to the empire and therefore, obviously, to me. So here are your orders. There is a minor issue in the province of Aegyptus that requires the attention of an independently-minded officer capable of commanding a body of troops sufficiently strong to afford him protection from the tribes who have been harrying our trade routes to the Indo-Scythian kingdoms that lie across the Erythraean Sea. I could send any one of a dozen of the keen young men who have served as thick-stripe legion tribunes and are champing at the bit for something to do before they take their next step on the path of honour, but the reports I'm receiving indicate that I need someone with a little more experience than that. And sending a full-blown legatus to that province in particular would be seen as a major breach of protocol, given the prefect in command is an equestrian. As are you, Rutilius Scaurus and indeed your colleague here, too.'

He waved a hand at Marcus.

'And my familia?'

'Your familia, Tribune, will be well looked after in your absence. Given that you'll be departing immediately, with your cohorts still weeks behind you, you will clearly be leaving the latest member

of the equestrian order behind you in Rome to look after them,
if that will make you happy. Doubtless his wife will be pleased to
have him to herself for a while. You and the men who rode south
in advance of them to save Rome from the deserter will doubtless
be perfectly capable of performing this small task for me without
him and his men.'

'So Julius is to be a hostage, too?'

Cleander smiled.

'Such an ugly word. Let's call him a further surety for your
return, once the job is done. I presume that you'll accept this new
mission without hesitation? I do so dislike any show of reluctance,
especially when I've had a very full day and want nothing more
than to go to bed.'

Scaurus shrugged, looking at Marcus who simply nodded.

'As ever, Chamberlain, we seem to have little choice in the
matter.'

'Excellent. As I said, your men are marching south via Masillia,
I am informed, and will be here in a matter of weeks, which is
commendable but too slow for my purposes. You are to proceed
to the naval base at Misenum at the earliest opportunity, where
a vessel of the praetorian fleet is waiting to carry you across the
sea to the province in question. So, if that's all, gentlemen?'

'I do have one more question, Chamberlain.'

'And what would that be, Centurion?'

'The master fletcher who guided my hand in making the shot
that felled Maternus . . .'

'Was received by the emperor not long ago, called to the inner
palace when Commodus discovered that it was he who had taken
the shot that saved his life. It was a miracle, it seems, a momentary abatement in the malady that has obscured his sight for most
of the last decade, allowing him to make the most marvellous
shot, which not only took down an assassin but left him alive to
be interrogated, a gift to them both from the Great Mother herself.
He was so astounded that it seems he could do nothing more
than kneel before the emperor in silence, and accept his master's

fulsome praise with a bowed head. Shortly after which his pride became so great that it seems to have burst his heart.'

'He's dead?'

Cleander nodded sadly.

'So it seems. Sad, and yet fitting for him to leave this life after performing the most perfectly miraculous act in saving his emperor's life.' He raised an eyebrow at Marcus's expression of disgust. 'What did you expect? I can't have it be known that an enemy of the state sworn to revenge on the emperor was able to put himself in a position from which he could have put an arrow into the master of the world, can I? The old man provided the only possible alternative, given the pair of you were found up on that balcony and that one of you must have been the one to send the fateful missile. Tell me, Centurion, were you aiming at the emperor, or at his would-be killer?'

'You know I swore a vow to Mithras to renounce my need to revenge myself on Commodus.'

The chamberlain smirked.

'Yes, so you did. Which proves that there are still men who obey the finer points of the Roman gentleman's code. How delightful. And now, I presume, with that last item of curiosity satisfied, you will both go about the business I have delegated to you? Or do you have any further means of trying my patience? No? Excellent.'

His secretary opened a door and beckoned the two men to leave. Cleander watched them with an expression which even the man who ran his office was unable to decipher.

'You seem perturbed, Chamberlain.'

'How very astute of you.' The man on whose shoulders the governance of a hundred million people rested sighed, drinking the rest of the wine in his cup. 'I'll take another. I doubt I'll sleep quickly after a day as full of incident as this has been, and besides, we need to write to the prefect of Aegyptus. I have some very specific instructions for him regarding those two men. Let us try to approach this problem from a different angle.'

In the cold air outside the palace, Marcus and Scaurus stood overlooking the Circus Maximus, just as they had done months previously before their march north in pursuit of the rebel leader now resident in one of the palace's darker corners.

'I can only commend you on that shot, Centurion. It seems you have a skill to match that of your colleague Qadir.'

The younger man grunted a laugh, shaking his head at the compliment.

'I watched the shot all the way from bow to target, and until the last moment it looked doomed to miss Maternus. I had aimed too low, just as the master fletcher warned me, but as the arrow crossed the Circus it seems that the hot air emitted by thousands of bodies lifted its trajectory just enough to put the point into the lower part of his body. It was luck that put that arrow where it struck, not me.'

Scaurus shook his head, staring out over the darkened city.

'When you master the teachings of the Lightbringer, you will understand better how Our Lord works in the most unexpected and mysterious of ways to achieve what he wishes to come to pass. You were his instrument, Marcus, and you fulfilled his plan even if it felt like luck. And I commend you on obeying your oath. The temptation to send that arrow at the man who caused your wife's death must have been close to overwhelming.'

Marcus nodded.

'It was. But I swore an oath.'

'And an arrow at that distance was a somewhat uncertain chance to take revenge?'

'That might have been some small part of my thinking.'

The tribune nodded.

'Kneel.' He waited until the younger man was on his knees, then put a hand on his head. 'In the name of Our Lord I absolve you from your oath, Marcus Valerius Aquila. You are freed from the constriction we jointly placed on your free will. When next you have the opportunity to take iron to the man who has so dishonoured your family, you will be free to do so.'

'Why?' Marcus looked up at him in puzzlement. 'You said yourself that Commodus's death can only result in a civil war the like of which has not been seen for over a century.'

'I did. And it will. But it will happen when the time is right, and not at the whim of a man whose honour was long since abandoned. And now, Centurion, I suggest you regain your feet and come with me to find the rest of the men we rode south with. I have the feeling that we will be needing every one of them if we are to master whatever trap lies hidden within this latest conundrum that our imperial master has laid out for us to resolve.'

The younger man got to his feet with a sigh.

'The oath made the whole thing easier. Being forbidden to kill the emperor by my god at least allowed me some rest from my dreams of vengeance.'

Scaurus nodded sympathetically.

'I know. And I do not lift its restriction on you lightly. But be in no doubt, when the time comes, you will be the Lightbringer's chosen means of expunging the shame that Commodus brings to Rome every day of his depraved existence.'

Marcus nodded, putting his hand to his forehead.

'And when the time comes, I will not hesitate. I owe too many people too much to shirk another chance for vengeance.'

The two men started down the long flights of steps that led to the palace gates and the dark streets below.

Historical Note

As always in this rewarding series (from the author's perspective, and hopefully yours too), this story has been based as much as possible on real history. There really was a bandit leader called Maternus, identified by the writer Herodian in the third century as having been a military deserter who assembled a band of fellow renegades, terrorised the western provinces of the empire and ultimately devised a plan to murder Commodus, the emperor of the day. Whilst there is nothing that has survived from Dio Cassius's more trustworthy *History* that mentions these events, the fact that Herodian seems to have used Dio as his major source makes it likely that he too recorded the bandit's exploits.

Maternus was not, it seems, a 'noble' bandit, an imperial challenger whose attempt to usurp the throne is the result of his 'princely values', but rather a common bandit, motivated by a simple desire to take the money of others. So it may be that I have taken a liberty in making him more than a soldier on the run and on the make (let's not introduce too big a spoiler if you've not read the book yet but have started with the historical note), but for this I make no apologies. It was just too good a chance to miss, and for all we know Maternus was indeed part of the empire's military elite. Let's examine what we do know.

Maternus, it seems, was a 'daring and spirited soldier' (I'm quoting from Thomas Grunewald's excellent *Bandits in the Roman Empire*) who deserted and took a number of his colleagues with him – although we have no idea how many. Nor do we know why he chose to take such a momentous step, punishable by death. Herodian makes a point of telling the reader that Maternus had already distinguished himself by his audacious courage, which makes 'why throw it all away?' the biggest question to be asked here.

After considering, and to some degree dismissing, the theory that the use of gladiators and slaves to fill the gaps torn in the legions' ranks by the plague from the east that had (at least) decimated the empire's population left the army ripe for dissension, Grunewald settles instead on the known state of the empire at the time. The Marcomannic Wars, he postulates, had placed the upper Rhine and upper Danube provinces under unusual pressure (attested by evidence of unrest in Dacia, Pannonia, Britannia and Gaul), placing Maternus's rebellion against the backdrop of social distress in the western empire. What I've suggested (purely as a literary device and not in any way to attempt to position the idea as actual history) is that the very nature of the war against the Marcomanni and the Quadi was sufficient to leave parts of the army traumatised and ripe for dissent.

Whether there's any grain of truth in that plotline or not, the stated facts are that once he had deserted, Maternus carried out incessant bandit raids, gaining wealth and strength, and escalating his ambitions from the sacking of farms and villages to entire towns in his later career. This may, of course – since it follows a well-trodden path in the description of Roman uprisings (consider Spartacus) – simply indicate the repetition of a stock literary theme to conceal a lack of any real information.

There is also some question as to whether Maternus really freed and armed slaves and prisoners to grow his army – as this might have been Herodian casting him as a thug rather than 'noble' – but it's clear that his movement reached a very considerable size. And it may well be fact, and not simply a literary device, that the time came when he was relabelled from 'brigand' to 'enemy of the state'. Certainly there is fairly firm archaeological evidence that he laid siege to *Legio VIII Augusta* at its base in Argentoratum (including an inscription in honour of C. Vesnius

Vindex, military tribune of that legion, during whose service it was rewarded with the titles 'faithful, constant, the emperor Commodus's own' after the relief of a 'recent siege').

Herodian tells us that Maternus's movement – whether in the form of a single army or a number of bands – overran large parts of Hispania and Gaul. And archaeological finds – coin hoards in the main, money buried in haste and never retrieved – indicate destruction events at the mouth of the Seine and to the south and north of the mouth of the Loire and in Germamia. It has therefore been theorised that the various indications of military activity, destruction layers, coin hoards and various inscriptions together provide a compelling case for there having been a *bellum desertum* – a deserters' war – in the form of Maternus's widespread revolt, centred on Germania Superior and Gaul. There is no hard evidence that *all* of the manifestations of trouble are specific to Maternus's activities, and it appears that there was a wider incidence of unrest and social disturbance than can perhaps be attributed to one bandit leader. (As Grunewald points out, one sign of a wider problem is the fact that Augusta Treverorum, a city founded two hundred years before in Gaul, built its first city wall at around the time of Commodus's succession to the throne in AD 180, having presumably not needed one before.) Maternus, perhaps, was just one symptom of a more deeply-rooted crisis in the empire, and our focus on his revolt in particular is the result of Dio and therefore Herodian's recording of his insurgency, and the resulting attempt to usurp the throne.

And what of that latter and more shocking crime – to the Romans at least? This is the conclusion of Herodian's telling of the story. Realising that he had no hope of defeating the forces being brought to bear on his army, Maternus, he tells us, ordered his men to infiltrate Italy in small groups. They were to attempt to kill Commodus on the festival of the Magna Mater, but their plan was betrayed his own followers, probably as the result, as Herodian puts it, of *phthonos* – envy – at the thought of him gaining imperial power. Maternus was arrested and executed. This is all likely to have been fictional, or such is the opinion of modern historians who tend to distrust Herodian, but of course in the context of my retelling and gentle embellishment of the history of the time, absolutely perfect.

My own depiction of Maternus's ruse to get close enough to Commodus to kill him is completely fictional and pretty much my own work, unless I've been subconsciously influenced by someone else (I did watch the *Rome* series and found the exsanguination of a bull by the acolytes of a priest of the Great Mother both disturbing and powerful, which might well have contributed). Herodian's bandit is recorded as having disguised himself as a praetorian to blend into the city's scenery and get close to his target, whereas mine . . .

Perhaps you just need to read the book, all you who like to devour the historical note beforehand? All I will say is that it took me no more than a few minutes of so reading about the cult of the Great Mother, and in particular the *galli*, the self-castrated priesthood who served her – a fascinating story in itself which I strongly commend – to see the perfect way for a would-be assassin to approach his imperial target undetected. And I hope you enjoyed – or shortly will enjoy – the means I used to put him a spear's throw from the throne.

The Roman Army
in AD 182

By the late second century, the point at which the *Empire* series begins, the Imperial Roman Army had long since evolved into a stable organisation with a stable *modus operandi*. Thirty or so legions (there's still some debate about the Ninth Legion's fate), each with an official strength of 5,500 legionaries, formed the army's 165,000-man heavy infantry backbone, while 360 or so auxiliary cohorts (each of them the rough equivalent of a 600-man infantry battalion) provided another 217,000 soldiers for the empire's defence.

Positioned mainly in the empire's border provinces, these forces performed two main tasks. Whilst ostensibly providing a strong means of defence against external attack, their role was just as much about maintaining Roman rule in the most challenging of the empire's subject territories. It was no coincidence that the troublesome provinces of Britannia and Dacia were deemed to require 60 and 44 auxiliary cohorts respectively, almost a quarter of the total available. It should be noted, however, that whilst their overall strategic task was the same, the terms under which the two halves of the army served were quite different.

The legions, the primary Roman military unit for conducting warfare at the operational or theatre level, had been in existence since early in the republic, hundreds of years before. They were composed mainly of close-order heavy infantry, well-drilled and highly motivated, recruited on a professional basis and, critically to an understanding of their place in Roman society, manned by soldiers who were Roman citizens. The jobless poor were thus provided with a route to a valuable trade, since service with the legions was as much about construction – fortresses, roads and

THE CHAIN OF COMMAND
LEGION

LEGATUS — LEGION CAVALRY (120 HORSEMEN)

BROAD STRIPE TRIBUNE

5 'MILITARY' NARROW STRIPE TRIBUNES

CAMP PREFECT

SENIOR CENTURION

10 COHORTS
(ONE OF 5 CENTURIES OF 160 MEN EACH)
(NINE OF 6 CENTURIES OF 80 MEN EACH)

CENTURION

CHOSEN MAN

WATCH OFFICER   STANDARD BEARER

10 TENT PARTIES OF
8 MEN APIECE

THE CHAIN OF COMMAND
AUXILIARY
INFANTRY COHORT

LEGATUS

PREFECT

(OR A TRIBUNE FOR A LARGER COHORT SUCH AS
THE FIRST TUNGRIAN)

SENIOR CENTURION

6-10 CENTURIES

CENTURION

CHOSEN MAN

WATCH OFFICER   STANDARD BEARER

10 TENT PARTIES OF
8 MEN APIECE

even major defensive works such as Hadrian's Wall – as destruction. Vitally for the maintenance of the empire's borders, this attractiveness of service made a large standing field army a possibility, and allowed for both the control and defence of the conquered territories.

By this point in Britannia's history three legions were positioned to control the restive peoples both beyond and behind the province's borders. These were the 2nd, based in South Wales, the 20th, watching North Wales, and the 6th, positioned to the east of the Pennine range and ready to respond to any trouble on the northern frontier. Each of these legions was commanded by a legatus, an experienced man of senatorial rank deemed worthy of the responsibility and appointed by the emperor. The command structure beneath the legatus was a delicate balance, combining the requirement for training and advancing Rome's young aristocrats for their future roles with the necessity for the legion to be led into battle by experienced and hardened officers.

Directly beneath the legatus were a half-dozen or so military tribunes, one of them a young man of the senatorial class called the broad stripe tribune after the broad senatorial stripe on his tunic. This relatively inexperienced man – it would have been his first official position – acted as the legion's second-in-command, despite being a relatively tender age when compared with the men around him. The remainder of the military tribunes were narrow stripes, men of the equestrian class who usually already had some command experience under their belts from leading an auxiliary cohort. Intriguingly, since the more experienced narrow-stripe tribunes effectively reported to the broad stripe, such a reversal of the usual military conventions around fitness for command must have made for some interesting man-management situations. The legion's third in command was the camp prefect, an older and more experienced soldier, usually a former centurion deemed worthy of one last role in the legion's service before retirement, usually for one year. He would by necessity have been a steady hand, operating as the voice of experience in advising the legion's senior officers as to the realities of warfare and the management of the legion's soldiers.

Reporting into this command structure were ten cohorts of soldiers, each one composed of a number of eighty-man centuries. Each century was a collection of ten tent parties – eight men who literally shared a tent when out in the field. Nine of the cohorts had six centuries, and an establishment strength of 480 men, whilst the prestigious first cohort, commanded by the legion's senior centurion, was composed of five double-strength centuries and therefore fielded 800 soldiers when fully manned. This organisation provided the legion with its cutting edge: 5,000 or so well-trained heavy infantrymen operating in regiment and company-sized units, and led by battle-hardened officers, the legion's centurions, men whose position was usually achieved by dint of their demonstrated leadership skills.

The rank of centurion was pretty much the peak of achievement for an ambitious soldier, commanding an eighty-man century and paid ten times as much as the men each officer commanded. Whilst the majority of centurions were promoted from the ranks, some were appointed from above as a result of patronage, or as a result of having completed their service in the Praetorian Guard, which had a shorter period of service than the legions. That these externally imposed centurions would have undergone their very own 'sink or swim' moment in dealing with their new colleagues is an unavoidable conclusion, for the role was one that by necessity led from the front, and as a result suffered disproportionate casualties. This makes it highly likely that any such appointee felt unlikely to make the grade in action would have received very short shrift from his brother officers.

A small but necessarily effective team reported to the centurion. The optio, literally 'best' or chosen man, was his second-in-command, and stood behind the century in action with a long brass-knobbed stick, literally pushing the soldiers into the fight should the need arise. This seems to have been a remarkably efficient way of managing a large body of men, given the centurion's place alongside rather than behind his soldiers, and the optio would have been a cool head, paid twice the usual soldier's wage and a candidate for promotion to centurion if he performed well. The century's third-in-command was the tesserarius or watch officer, ostensibly charged with ensuring that sentries were posted and that everyone know the watch word for the day, but also likely to have been responsible for the profusion of tasks such as checking the soldiers' weapons and equipment, ensuring the maintenance of discipline and so on, that have occupied the lives of junior non-commissioned officers throughout history in delivering a combat-effective unit to their officer. The last member of the centurion's team was the century's signifer, the standard bearer, who both provided a rallying point for the soldiers and helped the centurion by transmitting marching orders to them through movements of his standard. Interestingly, he also functioned as the century's banker, dealing with the soldiers' financial affairs. While a soldier caught in the horror of battle might have thought twice about defending his unit's standard, he might well also have felt a stronger attachment to the man who managed his money for him!

At the shop-floor level were the eight soldiers of the tent party who shared a leather tent and messed together, their tent and cooking gear carried on a mule when the legion was on the march. Each tent party would inevitably have established its own pecking order based upon the time-honoured factors of strength, aggression, intelligence – and the rough humour required to survive in such a harsh world. The men that came to dominate their tent parties would have been the century's unofficial backbone, candidates for promotion to watch officer. They would also have been vital to their tent mates' cohesion under battlefield conditions, when the relatively thin leadership team could not always exert sufficient presence to inspire the individual soldier to stand and fight amid the horrific chaos of combat.

The other element of the legion was a small 120-man detachment of cavalry, used for scouting and the carrying of messages between units. The regular army depended on auxiliary cavalry wings, drawn from those parts of the empire where horsemanship was a way of life, for their mounted combat arm. Which leads us to consider the other side of the army's two-tier system.

The auxiliary cohorts, unlike the legions alongside which they fought, were not Roman citizens, although the completion of a twenty-five-year term of service did grant both the soldier and his children citizenship. The original auxiliary cohorts had often served in their homelands, as a means of controlling the threat of large numbers of freshly conquered barbarian warriors, but this changed after the events of the first century AD. The Batavian revolt in particular – when the 5,000-strong Batavian cohorts rebelled and destroyed two Roman legions after suffering intolerable provocation during a recruiting campaign gone wrong – was the spur for the Flavian policy for these cohorts to be posted away from their home provinces. The last thing any Roman general wanted was to find his legions facing an army equipped and trained to fight in the same way. This is why the reader will find the auxiliary cohorts described in the *Empire* series, true to the historical record, representing a variety of other parts of the empire, including Tungria, which is now part of modern-day Belgium.

Auxiliary infantry was equipped and organised in so close a manner to the legions that the casual observer would have been hard put to spot the differences. Often their armour would be mail, rather than plate, sometimes weapons would have minor differences, but in most respects an auxiliary cohort would be the same proposition to an enemy as a legion cohort. Indeed there are hints from history that the auxiliaries may have presented a greater challenge on the battlefield. At the battle of Mons Graupius in Scotland, Tacitus records that four cohorts of Batavians and two of Tungrians were sent in ahead of the legions and managed to defeat the enemy without requiring any significant assistance. Auxiliary cohorts were also often used on the flanks of the battle line, where reliable and well drilled troops are essential to handle attempts to outflank the army. And while the legions contained soldiers who were as much tradesmen as fighting men, the auxiliary cohorts were primarily focused on their fighting skills. By the end of the second century there were significantly more auxiliary troops serving the empire than were available from the legions, and it is clear that Hadrian's Wall would have been invalid as a concept without the mass of infantry and mixed infantry/cavalry cohorts that were stationed along its length.

As for horsemen, the importance of the empire's 75,000 or so auxiliary cavalrymen, capable of much faster deployment and manoeuvre than the infantry, and essential for successful scouting, fast communications and the denial of reconnaissance information to the enemy, cannot be overstated. Rome simply did not produce anything like the strength in mounted troops needed to avoid being at a serious disadvantage against those nations which by their nature were cavalry-rich. As a result, as each such nation was conquered their mounted forces were swiftly incorporated into the army until, by the early first century BC, the decision was made to disband what native Roman cavalry as there was altogether, in favour of the auxiliary cavalry wings.

Named for their usual place on the battlefield, on the flanks or 'wings' of the line of battle, the cavalry cohorts were commanded by men of the equestrian class with prior experience as legion military tribunes, and were organised around the basic 32-man turma, or squadron. Each squadron was commanded by a decurion, a position analogous with that of the infantry centurion. This officer was assisted by a pair of junior officers: the duplicarius or double-pay, equivalent to the role of optio, and the sesquipilarius or pay-and-a-half, equal in stature to the infantry watch officer. As befitted the cavalry's more important military role, each of these ranks was paid about 40 per cent more than the infantry equivalent.

Taken together, the legions and their auxiliary support presented a standing army of over 400,000 men by the time of the events described in the *Empire* series. Whilst this was sufficient to both hold down and defend the empire's 6.5 million square kilometres for a long period of history, the strains of defending a 5,000-kilometre-long frontier, beset on all sides by hostile tribes, were also beginning to manifest themselves. The prompt move to raise three new legions undertaken by the new emperor Septimius Severus in AD 197, in readiness for over a decade spent shoring up the empire's crumbling borders, provides clear evidence that there were never enough legions and cohorts for such a monumental task. This is the backdrop for the *Empire* series, which will run from AD 192 well into the early third century, following both the empire's and Marcus Valerius Aquila's travails throughout this fascinatingly brutal period of history.